A SERPENT OF STONE AND SPITE

HADES X PERSEPHONE
BOOK TWO

LENA J. CASTLE

A Serpent of Stone and Spite

First Edition 2025

ISBN: 979-8-9916825-2-7 (Ebook)

ISBN: 979-8-9916825-3-4 (Paperback)

Cover Design by Jaylene Combs Design

Editing by Sparks Editorial & Lawrence Editing

For those who walk forward, even with old wounds.
This is for you.

AUTHOR'S NOTE

This book contains subject matter that may be difficult for some readers, including violence, murder, panic and distress, and depictions of past abuse (shown in flashbacks).

PERSEPHONE

*W*hat *could be worse than this?* Hades' gaze raked over me with the same desperate look he'd been giving me all week, like if he blinked, I'd be gone. I couldn't take it anymore. His hand tightened around the brush, knuckles whitening.

The bond between us stirred in my chest. Hades' love was steady, but laced with worry. It wrapped around my heart as if trying to hold me together from the inside. *I don't deserve it.*

We were in Hades' art studio, a room I hadn't known existed until today. Even after all the time I'd spent in the palace, I hadn't explored all of it.

Dust coated everything when we first entered, filling my nostrils and forcing my chest into a heave. The souls cleaned daily, but Hades had told me only he touched this space and his study. Gold recessed ceiling fixtures shrouded the room in dim lighting. The fireplace crackled, hissing as orange sparks spiraled into the air. White candlesticks burned lower along the lip of the windowpane, the aged wax dripping into a pool at its base. The twin moons outside cast silver slices of light through the crack between the window's heavy red velvet curtains, clashing with the honeyed glow of the fire.

I had suggested painting. To give Hades a momentary escape from his responsibilities—sentencing souls, holding the gates of Tartarus sealed, and managing the ceaseless demands of ruling the Underworld. Something had flashed in his eyes when he'd confided in me at the gala about how he used to love painting.

Peace.

It had felt like a good idea when I suggested it, but now I wasn't so sure. The seven feet between us might as well have been a chasm. Not because of anything he'd done, but because of what *I'd* done. "Do you really have to paint *me*?" I croaked, clearing my throat. "Couldn't you paint a bowl of fruit instead?"

"Why would I paint some measly fruit when my mate is the most beautiful subject?" Hades asked. A soft smile revealed his perfect teeth.

The word mate landed differently now. Back when we'd sealed the bond, it had just sounded like something magical and simple. Something I hadn't questioned. I'd leapt in without looking, drunk on the sweetness of something warm after so much cold. But now the word felt heavier. Real. Permanent.

Blood rushed to my cheeks, and I shifted on the marble dais, my silk dress sliding against the cool stone. He dipped his brush in paint, concentration on his face, like this was just another evening. My stomach twisted. How could he stand there so calmly when I'd fractured the ground beneath us? Nothing was normal.

The firelight carved shadows along the sharp panes of his face—cheekbones, strong stubble-covered jaw, straight nose. New lines from stress settled between his brows, at the corners of his mouth and eyes. Strands of short, messy black hair fell across his forehead, casting his gaze in shadow.

His fingers tapped against the tapered wooden brush handle. He flexed them once, twice. In the quiet, even the soft rustle of bristles against the canvas reached me. His shoulders slumped just enough for me to notice, the collar of his black button-up shifting with the movement.

Stop it, I told myself. I was doing it again. I thought I'd broken free of the habit, but now I scanned for cracks like I used to do with Demeter—reading every breath, every silence, trying to outpace her fury. Watching for the moment it would all go cold, for the love to leave.

I bit the inside of my already chewed-up lip.

I had thought the trials would ease his burdens… and my own. If I could earn my place on the court, unlock my full power, maybe I could take some of the weight off his shoulders. We'd have another vote on our side. I'd be free of Demeter.

His hand moved over the stretched canvas. He stood tall beside it, the size of him making it look small. *You don't have to do that*, I said through the bond.

He paused, one brow lifting. *Do what?*

Pretend things are normal.

"You're tense," Hades murmured, his voice low as he ignored my words in his mind. "Try to relax, little goddess."

The nickname tugged at something deep inside me. I remembered how much I had hated it when he first called me that. Now it grounded me in a reality I didn't want to face. I forced a small smile. "Easier said than done."

The brush clanked against the palette as he set it down, where small mounds of paint—red, yellow, blue, white, and a few others in shadow—sat waiting.

He crossed the room and kneeled beside me, his thumb

brushing over my collarbone and lower to the mating bond mark covering my chest. It pulsed beneath his touch, its white light reflecting in his steel-colored eyes. The slow, torturous glide of his finger sent my breathing into ragged bursts. I suppressed a shiver as I leaned into his touch.

"Stop punishing yourself," he whispered.

My lips parted, but no words escaped. Instead, I stared at him, hoping my eyes were saying everything I couldn't.

"You've been lost in those stories of yours again." His thumb caught a tear that slipped down my cheek. "Persephone?"

I nodded and shifted my focus to the fire. The flames swayed and the edges glowed white before softening to a dark gold and bronze. I couldn't look at him. "I can't—" I paused, searching for the right words. "It's the only place I can escape…" Another tear followed the first, and he brushed it away with the same care. "Escape the guilt."

Hades sighed. "We'll get through this. I promised you that. I don't break my promises."

I swallowed hard. "I just can't forgive myself."

Hades gathered me into his arms, repositioning me onto his lap as he sat on the dais.

"I thought you said I had to stay still," I said with a huff of laughter that didn't contain any humor.

"I have your image burned into my mind. I don't need a reference to paint you." He hugged me tighter.

Warmth flickered in my core for the first time since pledging myself. The surge of heat faded almost as quickly as it came. I hadn't been in the mood for intimacy.

Hades didn't push me, didn't ask for anything. He just held me, waited. Something sour twisted inside me.

I thought back to Basile. That wasn't love. It was utility. I still hadn't worked up the courage to ask Hades about him. Maybe I never would. What was the point in letting my mind wander back to him now? Basile had served his purpose—answers in the library, nothing more.

"I thought I was helping, but it was the wrong choice, and now we both have to face the consequences." Maybe I would've been able to live with myself if they only affected me.

Hades and I had gone through the same loop all week since the gala where I pledged myself to the trials, my doubt and his reassurance. He cupped my face, forcing me to meet his eyes that mirrored my own. "You did what you thought was right. We'll deal with it, no matter what."

Despite how many times he'd repeated himself, his promise still washed over me, never sinking in.

The trials were dangerous, and I still didn't know all of what they entailed. Hades' magic had broken through the court's blood bond just enough to warn me that I could die in them, but with his magic so strained, he couldn't do much more. He shouldn't have been able to break through that bond at all.

That itself was a troubling sign.

Was the magic of the court growing weaker? The court was all that held Demeter in line. Hades told me not to worry about it, assuring me that when a mate was in danger, magic could swell and grow stronger.

But still, I worried.

It seemed to be all I did these days, besides burying myself in mortal books or crafting stories in my head to drown out the grim reality of our situation.

"I don't know how to make this right," I whispered.

"You make it right by being the strong goddess I know you are." Confidence I wished I could possess filled his voice. My lips parted, ready to tell him I couldn't do that, but he continued. "It's okay to make mistakes. All that matters is how you deal with them."

I exhaled something that might've passed for a laugh. "Even catastrophic mistakes?"

"We all make mistakes."

I pursed my lips. "Even you?"

He smirked, his eyes brightening. "Hmm. Maybe not me, but everyone else, yes."

A reluctant grin broke through the heaviness settled on my face. "How arrogant."

"You love me anyway."

I chewed on my bottom lip. "I do."

His expression softened. "In all seriousness, I have made mistakes. But I dealt with them head-on."

I shook my head, letting out a shallow breath. "I don't know how."

He hooked a finger under my chin, and the intensity of his gaze pinned me in place. "We'll find a way. You're stronger than you think, Persephone. And I'm not going anywhere."

I wanted to believe him, but every time he called me strong, all I felt was the lie I was living. Like I was trying to wear someone else's skin.

Someone stronger.

Someone worth the effort.

He pressed a soft kiss to my lips like he was memorizing the shape of them all over again. My eyes fluttered closed. He pulled back, and the loss of him was immediate. Gently, he lifted me from his lap, setting me aside on the marble. When I opened my eyes, he was already walking back to the canvas.

We'll find a way. We'll find a way. We'll find a way.

He mixed golden yellow paint with a tiny amount of red and blue, merging them into a shade of ochre before applying it to the canvas. Hades' words swirled around my head.

Could we do this?

We didn't have a choice.

Hope was a fickle thing, prone to slipping through my fingers just when I thought I had a firm grasp on it. But I couldn't let it go, fragile as it was—for Hades, for the Underworld, for everything we were trying to protect. The consequences of failure were too great to consider.

Demeter gathering the Nexus Stone and spell pieces before us would be catastrophic. She'd have more power than any one Divine was meant to wield. Enough to defy the court. Enough to abandon her duties as Goddess of Harvest. If she chose to let mortals starve, they would. Entire realms would be at her mercy. The stone didn't just grant power; it corrupted those wielding it. And her grip on sanity was already slipping.

For now, I would hold onto his promise and pray to the Fates it would be enough. Hades set the paintbrush down and ran a hand through his hair.

I glanced around the room. "Is something wrong?"

Hades cleared his throat. "Hermes is here."

I smoothed the ivory silk of my dress and ran the fabric between my fingers. I had known this moment was coming.

Hades had warned me that Hermes would eventually arrive with more news about what lay ahead. Part of me hoped he wouldn't come, that I could stay trapped in my familiar guilt.

I pushed myself off the dais. Hades closed the distance between us, his hand moving to the small of my back. I turned, moving toward the painting. "I want to see," I murmured. Maybe I was stalling, but I did want to see his art.

"When it's complete."

I sighed. "But I've never seen your work."

His eyes softened. "You've seen it plenty."

"What?"

"Many of the paintings along the corridors," he explained,

guiding me to the door. "I painted them through the centuries."

My mind raced back to the countless hours I'd spent admiring the art, the intricate brushstrokes and the vivid scenes they triggered. "Why didn't you tell me?" I'd been so caught up in myself that I'd barely stopped to look at the things that mattered to him.

He shrugged. "You didn't ask. Not all of them are by me. I have known many famous artists in my time, and many of them still paint here in the Underworld." He brushed some stray hairs away from my face. "Let's go."

With the chaos I knew was coming, I wasn't sure when we'd get another chance for a painting session. Silence between us stretched as we walked through the corridors. My attention was glued to the paintings, searching the corners for signatures, but Hades' repeated tugs on my hand gave me no time to linger.

When we stepped into Hades' study, Hermes was already there, pacing the length of the room. It looked just as it had the last time I'd been here. The lit fireplace cast shifting light across the dark shelves that lined three of the four walls. Each was packed with leather-bound spines, framing the door, fire, and window overlooking the courtyard. Hades' massive desk was buried under documents and books.

I'd only ever seen the Messenger of the Divine polished. But tonight, his light blue button-down shirt was rumpled, painting exaggerated, creased lines along the fabric. His white pants clung to his legs, pulled taut in all the wrong places as if they had been tailored to someone else's body. Hermes' dark brown curls were pushed back in uneven waves, evidence of his restless fingers raking through them.

Hades stepped forward. "Hermes."

Hermes stopped his pacing, his hazel eyes cutting toward me, full of the warnings I had dismissed in my pursuit of what I thought was right. How could I forgive myself when there were reminders of my failure at every turn?

"You shouldn't have pledged yourself to the trials." Hermes pinched the bridge of his nose and turned his back to us, staring at the Underworld's desolate landscape. He pivoted on his heel, his leather shoes whispering against the floor.

My tongue pressed flat against the roof of my mouth. A surge of shame washed over me, hot and bitter. "I know. I don't need another reminder of that," I said. "I thought I was doing the right thing. I only had three days left before I thought I'd be sent back to her."

Hermes shook his head and gave me a smile that had not an ounce of happiness. "I told you it would only make things worse…" His voice trailed.

I focused on the curve of my thumbnail, dragging its sharp edge across a line in my palm. The skin burned, but I didn't stop. Hades moved beside me, the back of his hand brushing against mine. "What's done is done, Hermes."

Hermes' face fell. "I didn't mean—" He stepped closer. "I just hate to see this happen."

"On with it, Hermes," Hades said.

Hermes swallowed hard, his Adam's apple bobbing. He focused on me. "When someone wants to pledge themselves to the court, it's usually all planned out in advance—the pledging and ceremony to ignite the trials where Zeus tells you the rules. It all usually happens the same day." He paused. "You skipped the planning part. Your court appearance is scheduled for tomorrow."

Hades had explained the igniting ceremony to me the night after I pledged myself. I'd nodded. Might've even said I understood.

I hadn't. Not really. I'd tuned it out, counting the cracks

in the stone and pretending the words were meant for someone else. "Tomorrow is too soon." My voice tipped up.

"You don't have a choice, Persephone. You must face the court within eight days of pledging your blood. Tomorrow is that eighth day."

My eyes squeezed shut, but solace didn't come. I saw myself again, standing in that damn courtroom, blood still fresh and dripping from my palm as I made the pledge. For one breath, I imagined running, disappearing somewhere, letting this realm and the Olympus realm forget I existed.

But I had given my blood, and it was binding. I clenched my hands into fists and swallowed hard. "What happens if I don't go?"

Hades' fingers tightened around mine. "We'll be going, Persephone."

"Tell me. Do I get out of the trials?"

Hermes cringed. "You would die. You have pledged yourself to the court, and by going back on your contract, your life thread would be cut."

Not punished. Not exiled. *Die.*

Would it hurt when my life thread was cut? Would it be a sudden snap or slow? I clicked my molars together, the vibration a reminder that I was still here, still alive. My life thread was still whole, but tomorrow's court appearance hovered like scissors just a fraction of an inch away.

I was not ready to die.

I didn't know exactly what I wanted. But I wanted the choice to find out. For once, I wanted my story to be mine.

"You should know what you'll be stepping into," Hermes said.

I shifted my weight onto the balls of my feet. "What do you mean?"

"Olympus has blown up since you left," he replied. "Everyone is talking about it."

I cringed. While I was sure the truth was out, so were the lies the Divine had probably spread.

Hades scoffed. "We don't need to know the gossip. That's for the bored and petty."

"Do you want her to go unprepared?"

Hades hesitated, his lips pressed together. After a few charged seconds, he shook his head. "No."

Heat crawled up my neck. They were making decisions while I stood right here. My jaw tightened, but the fight fizzled before my words could form. My choices hadn't exactly been brilliant lately. Maybe it was better if they decided for me.

Hermes extended his hand like he had when he'd revealed Demeter's actions in the mortal realm. I hesitated before stepping forward, my fingers trembling as they met his cool skin.

A shiver ran up my spine as the world around me warped in a blur of colors and sensations. Hermes' magic gripped me. The floor vanished beneath my feet. It wasn't a sudden drop but a sickening pull. My stomach flipped as everything snapped into place with a clarity that made my breath catch.

The courtroom appeared around us—too real. We stood at the edge of the room, spectators of a memory that haunted me. Now I had to watch it happen all over again, completely aware and *powerless*.

There I was, my body crumpled on the cold, unforgiving stone floor. A broken scream rippled through the air. I flinched, my neck and shoulders tightening. The scream hadn't come from someone else.

It had come from me.

From *her*, my past self. The sound echoed through the chamber, sharp and desperate, like the cry of a wounded animal. It clawed at my ears. An icy thread drove through my veins. My toes curled in my ballet flats.

A crowd surrounded my fallen form. They moved around with frantic energy, shocked and curious. Hades cut through, scooping me up and pressing me to his chest before running through the heavy wooden doors.

But it was the disappointment in his eyes as he carried me away that somehow hurt more than anything Demeter had ever done to me.

The courtroom remained in a frenzy after we left. Demeter stood at the edge of the room, and my vision tunneled in on her. Just seeing her made my knees want to buckle, but I kept them locked. I could feel the grip of her fingers in my hair, the coldness of her voice in my ear. Though this was Hermes' magic, I refused to fall, refused to let her phantom claws sink into me again.

"This is what you left behind," Hermes said as my vision shifted to the present. "The Divine are demanding answers. They see your actions as a disruption of the natural order."

My voice cracked. "What do we do?" I hated how small I sounded.

Hades' arms encircled me and pulled me close. The warmth of his body, the scent of amber clinging to him steadied me. "We face them."

I buried my face in his chest, inhaling a long breath. Hermes' voice cut through the brief moment of solace. "There's no room for weakness anymore, Persephone."

Weakness.

Weakness.

Weakness.

I turned in Hades' arms, peeking over my shoulder at him. Hermes glanced outside, his jaw tight, before shifting his attention back to me. "When you show up, you need to be strong. Even if you don't feel like it."

The weight of his words settled over me like a sodden cloak. *This is the only way.* I nodded and forced my face into the widest grin I could muster, for practice. It was all a show. "I can be strong." My voice didn't shake, but beneath the surface, my pulse pounded a chaotic beat against my ribs. A muscle twitched under my right cheekbone, like a thread yanked too tight beneath the skin.

Even my body was rejecting the lie I was wearing.

Smile. Move. Pretend.

2

———

HADES

I sank deeper into the library's leather couch. The smell of books mingled with the lavender from Persephone's hair. I balanced a book in my left hand, using my right to turn the pages. Pausing often, I toyed with strands of her hair as she rested against my chest. I hadn't realized how much I needed that weight.

I tried to focus on the words on the beige paper, but they all blurred together in a swirling mess of aged black ink. The pages might as well have been blank. My grip tightened on the book, the worn edge cutting off circulation in my palm. I glared at the name on the page. I didn't give a damn what a long-dead philosopher had to say. I'd met the man who wrote this, and his life wasn't as impressive as he made it out to be. Nothing about him was wise. He'd begged me for mercy just like all the rest.

All I could think about was Persephone and what was coming. My magic pulsed beneath my skin, waiting, searching for something to strike. Something tangible that I could fix. But there was nothing, just her breaking beside me without a single way for me to save her. I loathed that I couldn't protect her from everything. If I could, I would stick her in a gilded cage, keeping her to myself and safe from the dangerous universe around us.

But that wasn't love.

That was fear.

Her fingers were steady as they curled around the edges of a thick paperback book. She kept it close, her thumb cradling the spine steady as if the words littering the pages could shield her from everything outside of them.

She'd been devouring them, one after the other. The small table beside us had become a shrine to her new obsession—paperbacks stacked in teetering towers. Some were marked with ribbons, some highlighted, and others covered with colored ink in the margins.

I'd sent a reluctant Minthe to the mortal realm for a store's worth of books. She had complained, but as irritating as Minthe could be, she did her job well. Persephone had asked for just a few mortal books, her voice shaking as if she thought it was too much.

There wasn't a thought more unbearable to me than her reaching for something new and not having it. I couldn't give her peace—not really. I couldn't take away what the trials would demand of her. But I could give her this.

Persephone still rested against me, but the warmth through the bond was distant, like she'd retreated somewhere within herself that I couldn't follow. I'd seen her like this throughout the past week, when she was hurting but didn't want to speak it out loud. When the silence felt safer than anything I could offer.

I hated the silence.

I shifted, careful not to disturb her peace, but she tensed. My fingers traced idle circles over the fine, nearly invisible hairs on her arm, goose bumps blooming beneath my touch. "How's the book?"

She angled it enough for me to catch a glimpse of the cover, a dramatic gold-foiled serif font with a couple locked in a kiss. "I like it."

"Good." I cleared my throat. "I want to show you something later."

She folded the corner of the page, the stiff paper rustling as she closed the novel and set it down. Persephone shifted on my lap, wrapping her arms around my neck and facing me head-on. Her eyes were puffy and tinted red. Her lips were swollen with subtle indentations from her teeth. Even now, I wanted to kiss her until she forgot how to worry.

I ran a palm from the top of her head, down to her cheek, and cupped her jaw, tugging her close into a light kiss. Persephone's skin was soft, her lips warm against mine.

It took every shred of willpower I had, but I pulled back. The soft sigh that slipped from her lips sent heat through me, and I suppressed a groan. My lips still tingled from the press of hers. I wanted nothing more than to bruise those parted lips, to show her just how much I wanted her. To worship her until she believed she was enough, *more* than enough. But I couldn't fix the way she saw herself with my hands or my body. I didn't want her to numb her feelings by chasing desire.

Persephone's throat bobbed. Her eyes bore into mine, begging for a distraction. "What do you want to show me?" Persephone's lips curved up into a smirk as she pressed closer, her center aligning with mine. Only a few layers of fabric separated us. It was a maddening temptation.

I clenched my jaw, forcing myself to release her and grip the leather couch. "Stop doing that."

Her eyes almost undid me. "Doing what?" she teased.

On instinct, I took hold of her hips and held her steady, but the little goddess shifted anyway. She let out a low laugh, and I relished it. "I want to show you something I do. It will help you feel better."

"Oh." Her smile faltered, the shadows creeping back into her expression.

I'd promised her no more secrets, and I intended to keep it. But some truths were heavier than others. Persephone needed to know the extent of my struggles, how I dealt with the darkness within me—the darkness that came with being the God of the Underworld. She needed to see the lengths I went to manage it, to prevent it from consuming me. Maybe she'd find her own way to navigate the shadows that chased her. She deserved to understand everything, especially when my shadows were leaking into her.

Tonight, I would take her to the mortal realm. I'd show her how I released that energy so she could ignite the trials with a clear head.

I couldn't lose her.

"Okay." Persephone shifted on my lap and picked up her book. The court and everything that loomed would still be there in the morning. For now, I could just hold her close.

The door to the library opened. Minthe walked in, Hermes trailing her. "My king, Hermes is here," she said. One corner of her mouth pulled down. "Again." She didn't wait for a response. Just turned and walked out, her steps clipped, back straight.

I eased Persephone off my lap and stood. "You're back."

Persephone's fingers brushed against mine as she rose beside me.

"I'm afraid I have some bad news." Hermes laced his fingers together, his knuckles popping in the silence.

"Well." I resisted the urge to scoff. "Are you going to tell us?" My voice came out sharper than I'd intended, but I didn't give a damn. I tapped my fingers against my thigh.

Persephone pointed a finger at me. "What he said."

I anchored her by the waist and pulled her close.

Hermes shifted on his heel. He sucked on the inside of his cheek, and his jaw tensed before he exhaled. "The court has moved up the timeline. Your igniting ceremony will begin at midnight."

Midnight. I assumed they'd moved up the timeline because of their vendetta against me. Zeus especially. He saw a threat where there wasn't one, twisting others to his side. It was irrational. I wanted nothing to do with leading the court. *Life would be easier for her if she had a different mate.*

"I'm sorry," he said.

Silence followed, stretching too long. He looked at me, not Persephone. Sadness hit, crashing through the bond, sinking under my ribs like it belonged to me too. I pushed back with warmth, with steadiness. Anything to hold her together. But all that came through was the word *midnight*, echoing like a tolling bell.

Persephone's breath hitched. "They can do that?"

I groaned. "Technically, it will be the eighth day. We're at their mercy."

Persephone pointed toward the large clock hanging above the library's double doors, her finger twitching halfway through the motion. Higher up, smaller, silent clocks marked the hours of other realms, stretching toward the ceiling. Her index finger moved as she tried to figure out which clock corresponded with the Olympus realm.

"It's three hours away," I said.

Her hand dropped. "That's hardly enough time," she whispered.

My touch slid up to her jaw, tilting her chin up to meet my gaze. "Everything will be okay."

Her eyes searched mine for answers I didn't have.

"I hate to break this up, but—" Hermes coughed, not moving a limb. "I'm sorry. I wish there were something I could do." His voice lacked its usual edge. There was no smirk, no joke to lighten the news he'd just dropped. "I'll see you there."

Hermes gave us a half-hearted wave, turned, and left the room without another word.

Persephone leaned into me. A tremor ran through her, mirroring the ache threading through our bond. I tightened my hold on her, but she didn't say anything.

I didn't ask her to speak. I just held her tightly, let her fall apart in my arms. I wasn't good at this, the feelings, the emotions. I'd spent centuries perfecting the art of holding everything in.

But I didn't want that for her.

I didn't want her to disappear into silence like I had.

I didn't try to fix it. I didn't feed her hope.

I just held her because sometimes when it felt like the world was slipping out from under you, the only thing that mattered was someone choosing to stay.

3

____

PERSEPHONE

y fingers traced the beaded patterns of the dress laid out over the bed. The deep emerald gown shimmered under the moonlight spilling in through the window. The beads caught the light like tiny stars, arranged so intricately they seemed to move. I blinked and leaned closer, but it was only my imagination. Sera's voice took me out of my daze. "Are you ready, Persephone?"

My eyes flitted between the two sisters, Sera and Evangeline. They stood before the vanity, translucent. Matching smiles curved into place, mirrored down to the smallest twitch. They looked even more similar today, with their curly hair pulled into the same tight hairstyle that gathered at the napes of their necks. Looking at them again now, I couldn't believe I hadn't realized they were sisters when we'd first met.

I took my seat at the vanity. Sera and Evangeline moved around me, working with deft, delicate hands to do my hair and makeup. I fought the urge to wipe all their hard work away.

I didn't want the dress or the makeup. But I had to face

what was coming, and this was part of the act. I sat rigid while Sera dabbed pink shimmer across my cheeks.

The sisters murmured to each other, and I tried not to pay attention. Their conversation likely had nothing to do with my situation, yet the little voice in my mind insisted that every low word was about me. Everyone had been like that for the past week, speaking in hushed tones as though they feared one wrong step would shatter me into a thousand tiny, sharp pieces.

The worst part? They might not have been wrong.

I thought back to the meeting where Hades had told the team I'd pledged myself to the trials. I hadn't even been able to say the words myself—too much of a coward. All of them had tried to be kind, but doubt and disappointment had been clear in their eyes.

I hadn't been to a single meeting since, even though there had been one every day. Orion and Gabriel had taken over the planning for our trip to Faerie to find the Nexus Stone piece.

Training was the same. I'd begged for a break, and they'd given it, too nervous to argue with someone on the brink of a mental breakdown. I huffed a laugh. Evangeline gave me a worried look in the mirror.

I told myself I needed the rest. That a little over a week of missed training days wouldn't undo all my recent sessions. But the truth of why I avoided it was simpler.

Training made it harder to escape reality.

I took a deep breath, trying to find some semblance of control amid the chaos swirling within me. The room slipped away before I could stop myself.

I no longer stared at the mirror. In my mind, a lush garden unfurled around me with colors so rich that they bled into one another, a painter's palette after the hues had been mixed. The sun cast a warm glow over everything, bathing the scene in a serene amber light.

I wandered among the flowers, a riot of reds, pinks, and yellows against the green. I kneeled on the soft, dewy grass to smell a narcissus flower—sweet, just like always. The delicate white petals brushed against my nose, the fragrance bringing a smile to my lips. It left behind a dusting of pollen, but I didn't bother brushing it away. I pushed myself up, the blades of grass tickling my skin, and continued walking through the garden.

Birds swooped down, weaving light melodies through the air. They danced around me, their songs a sweet accompaniment to my wandering thoughts.

In this sanctuary of my mind, no eyes followed me. There were no whispers, just the suns, scent, and sky. Here, no one expected anything from me.

Leaving the grass behind, my bare feet sank into the soft green-and-yellow moss, cool and springy beneath me. I reached a crystal-clear stream, its surface glimmering in the light. Kneeling, I dipped my fingers in. It was the perfect temperature, cool but not cold. The gentle current caressed and tickled my skin.

A comb tugging at my hair pulled me back to reality. The vision faded, replaced by the reflection staring back at me in the mirror. In the time I'd spent lost in my head, the souls around me had nearly finished their work. My hair, usually a cascade of dark waves, was now woven into an intricate, braided crown atop my head. White five-petaled flowers with thin golden veins were scattered through the braid. Small white diamonds ornamented the spaces between them.

Light makeup enhanced my features. A thin outline of black liner traced my eyes, making my gray irises stand out. Some blush brought warmth to my face and made me look less sad.

The goddess in the mirror looked strong, poised. But beneath the surface, my stomach churned, and my heart pounded with a relentless rhythm, like it was trying to warn me.

Run. Run. Run.

The woman staring back at me looked like she had answers. My fingers gripped the edge of the vanity.

"Are you all right?" Evangeline's soft voice pulled me from my thoughts.

I glanced at her, the concern obvious in her eyes. "Yes." I forced a smile. *Can they hear the lie in my voice?* "I'm fine."

Evangeline's brows twitched—not a frown but close. "Mm-hmm," she hummed, her gaze still fixed on me.

I chewed on the inside of my cheek. "Do I not seem all right?"

Sera placed a gentle hand on my shoulder. "I hope this isn't out of line, but you seem far from it."

I gulped. "Just nervous. That's all."

Evangeline and Sera exchanged a look, heavy with words they wouldn't say aloud. They didn't press, though, just lowered their eyes and busied themselves with the final touches—smoothing stray hairs, adjusting the little flowers threaded through my braid, and helping me put on my dress and heels.

I wondered if all sisters were like that—able to speak entire conversations without a single word.

When the pair finished, Sera squeezed my shoulder lightly, and Evangeline offered me a soft smile. "Good luck," they said, almost in unison before the pair left the room.

I sat back down and leaned closer to the mirror, placing my palms flat on the vanity counter and scrutinizing every detail of my face. It was designed to present an image far from what I felt. Soon, I would stand before the Olympian

Court, their unforgiving gazes picking at my carefully constructed armor.

"You look beautiful."

I lifted my eyes in the reflection, finding Hades leaning against the doorframe. Our eyes met in the glass. Hades' black hair was tousled like he'd run his hands through it a few times before coming here. He wore an impeccably tailored suit, the dark fabric hugging his broad shoulders. The light caught on his sharp, sculpted features as he stepped into the room, softening the hard lines of his face.

His words seeped into my skin, chasing the chill that had settled in my bones. My stomach fluttered in response. I forced another smile, the corners of my lips trembling. "I don't feel beautiful. I feel terrified." I cleared my throat. "You look handsome."

Hades moved closer, resting his hands on my shoulders. "I'm here with you. We'll face them together."

I tipped my head back, my hair brushing his torso as I met his gaze. *How did I get so lucky?* I pushed back from the vanity and rose to face him.

Hades smiled. *I should be asking that question.*

Thank you, Hades.

You never need to thank me.

Hades placed his hand under my jaw and pulled me into a kiss. For a few moments, I didn't have any worries. There was no Nexus Stone. No court, no trials—nothing but Hades and me.

I whimpered against him, my lips parting. Hades seized the opening, deepening the kiss. His hand cradled my chin, and I arched closer to him.

He pulled away, leaving a trail of fire down my spine. I sucked in a shaky inhale. I could still taste him. "Can I have a moment?" I asked, glancing toward the washroom.

"Take all the time you need," Hades said.

I hesitated, pressing my lips together. We both knew I couldn't afford to take long. Time was slipping through my fingers. Hades was just being polite.

I nodded and went into the washroom. The door clicked shut behind me, and I braced my hands on the cool, dark stone sink. I raised my head, staring at my reflection, willing myself to find the strength I needed.

"I can do this," I whispered. I repeated the mantra on a loop as memories flickered through my mind—surviving years of Demeter's abuse, escaping Olympus, enduring the theft of the Nexus Stone. Each memory stung, but it had forged me into who I was now.

With a steadying breath, I straightened and stepped back into the bedroom.

Hades' eyes locked onto mine. My pulse raced as I moved toward him. "I have something for you," he said, his voice a low, velvety whisper that sent a shiver down the exposed skin on my back. We stood near the window, the moonlight casting silver ribbons across the floor. He reached into the pocket of his jacket, pulling out a dagger and a bundle of leather.

The dagger was sleek and so, so beautiful. The blade mirrored the light of the twin moons, but the hilt stole my focus. It gleamed gold, etched with the same pattern that marked our chests.

"Come here," he murmured, extending a hand.

I drew closer. Hades' fingers brushed mine as he guided my hand to the dagger's hilt, wrapping my fingers around it. Heat from his skin seeped into me, lingering even after he let go. "Do you like it?"

"I—" The word faltered on my tongue as my fingertips traced the golden engravings. "It's perfect," I said, still unable to look up from it. "It's beautiful."

"I had it made for you." Hades' voice contained a softness I knew only I ever received from him.

"Thank you." Before I could say anything else, Hades dropped down onto a knee before me. The gesture stirred something deep in my chest. He smirked up at me.

He slipped his hand through the slit in my dress. I gasped at the sudden warmth of his palm. It raced through me, every inch of me alive for him.

He traced a deliberate path up the inside of my thigh. His touch was featherlight. He took the bundle of leather and wrapped it around my leg. He moved slowly.

So slowly.

"Give me the dagger." He opened his palm.

I handed it to him. He didn't look away as he guided the blade to rest in the sheath, the handle pressing against my skin. The brush of his fingers heightened every nerve ending. "Don't take it off." His voice dropped, turning to a near growl. "Not until you complete the trials."

"The trials." I mirrored his words. I appreciated that he said *when* I completed the trials and not *if* I completed them. His fingers traced lazy, affectionate circles on my skin, as if he could will the fear out of me with touch alone.

"You'll survive. I know you will." He stood with a quiet sigh and pressed a kiss to my forehead. "Are you ready?"

I didn't feel ready, but I didn't have a choice. "I am."

From his jacket pocket, Hades drew his leather gloves and slid them on before taking my hand. His magic unfurled and wrapped around us. The Underworld vanished as we whisked away.

4

PERSEPHONE

I hadn't expected to be back so soon. The marble steps of Divine Hall glistened beneath a wash of silver light. The white pillared structure loomed before us as if trying to touch the moon above. It shone brighter than I'd seen it in a long time, and I squinted. The wind rustled around us, goose bumps rising across my exposed skin.

Hades squeezed my hand. "Let's do this," he said.

There was no turning back.

With each step, my heels struck the stone like a countdown I couldn't stop. The massive doors to Divine Hall stood open, the siren song spilling toward us. It clung to the air, alluring but suffocating.

The moment my high-heeled feet crossed the threshold, the conversation and siren song died. The eyes of all the Divine, the Divine associated, the sirens and nymphs turned toward us. It wasn't because of who I'd arrived with. It wasn't the mark on my chest or the dress that clung to my body like a second skin.

They were here for me.

The foyer was opulent and overwhelming. Just like it had

been the night of the gala. Every surface screamed of excess. Marble floors gleamed beneath my feet, gold veining catching the chandelier's light. Pastel floral arrangements spilled from tall crystal vases surrounded by other gaudy decorations on small standing tables. The scent of a warm, musky incense hung in the air. Everything was exquisite, but it just made my stomach turn.

The crowd parted, creating a pathway for us to the center of the foyer. I wished so desperately that we could just slip into a corner like we had the last time. I knew that was something that couldn't—*wouldn't*—happen again. I was front and center, with nowhere to hide.

The sirens resumed their singing. Chatter returned, too. The crowd still stayed distant from us, but their glances clung to my skin.

Hecate approached us. She wore a gown of the deepest midnight blue. A large silver crescent moon necklace hung from her throat. Her smile was small.

Of course she was beautiful. Of course she glowed while I stood, unraveling.

I curled my fingers into fists at my sides, nails biting into my sweaty palms. Hades was my mate, not hers. The bond said it, logic said it, but insecurity didn't listen to reason.

"All I'm going to say is that you should pay attention." Her smooth voice lacked warmth. "You can't afford to lose your focus during the trials." Her smile widened. It reminded me of a wolf baring its teeth at me. "I remember when I undertook them."

I nodded, a strange, cold detachment flowing through me as I studied her. Perhaps it came from knowing she'd had a history with Hades. He claimed they were never intimate, but the thought still unsettled me. Maybe I was just jealous she'd known Hades at a different time of his life, a time before me.

She rambled about meditation and how it would help me. I just smiled and nodded. Sometimes, when I paid enough attention, I'd even add a few words. Hades was deep in conversation with Thanatos. Still, with just a glance, he sensed me and met my eyes. I shifted my focus back to Hecate. She'd continued on about how it had been too long since we'd all met for dinner.

"It has been too long," I agreed. I meant the length of the conversation, but I wouldn't be the first to end it. We needed all the support we could get, and icing her out would be a mistake. I was trying to avoid making those for a while.

She brushed a strand of her violet hair out of her face. "Well, I won't hold you any longer. I'm sure others wish to speak with you."

I shook my head. "You're not holding me up. It's a pleasure to see you." The lie slid out too easily, wrapped in a fake smile.

"You're kind, Persephone," she replied, her gaze unreadable.

For a moment, I felt bad, but then I thought back to Hades' name on her lips. She pulled me into a hug, and her gardenia scent surrounded me. It was… so good. I fought the urge to stop breathing in her arms. Her jewelry was cold against my chest. "Good luck," she whispered.

"Thank you." That I truly meant. I needed as much luck as the Fates could grant me.

She wandered off, and I didn't watch where. I was too overwhelmed by all the socializing. Poseidon approached me next, standing tall and looming over two heads above me. His white hair flowed around him, though the air was stagnant. His eyes, a deep oceanic blue, occasionally shifted to a lighter seafoam green. The golden trident in his hand gleamed under the light, its sharp edges producing a soft yellow and white glow.

Then Aphrodite. She was far more striking than her statue in Athens Square portrayed her. She wore a flowing gown, shimmering with rose-golden threads. Her flawless skin sparkled and reflected light off the chandelier above us. Her eyes mirrored her dress. Waves of black hair with thin braids woven throughout cascaded down her back. Even just talking to her, heat pooled low in my center. Hades had murmured through the bond, reassuring me that it was a typical reaction to the goddess and to shield my mind. Her lips curled into a knowing smile, though she said nothing. I wasn't attracted to the Goddess of Love and Beauty. Yes, she was otherworldly, but my thoughts were consumed with Hades. Every note of her melodic voice only stirred images of him.

I'd never talked to many of the Divine one-on-one. Hades spoke into my head, letting me know who sided with us, but I kept the conversations shallow.

It would take more than an empty smile and a hollow toast to earn my trust.

Hermes walked up to me with a broad grin. He pulled me into a hug and whispered, "Fix your face."

I went still. Hermes had been so different just hours ago. He must be good at pretending. I envied him for that.

"What do you mean?" I kept my lips still so no one could read them.

Hades chuckled beside me. "He's right. You look like you want to leave."

"Is that not the truth?" I asked, forcing a laugh.

"The truth won't help you here. Look around. This place thrives on pretty lies." Hermes took a sip of the ambrosia in his gold goblet. "Strength and power will, and you need to show that."

I plastered on a phony smile. Thanatos, standing nearby, chuckled. "I can't seem to do anything right," I muttered.

"Now that's too much," Hades said, rubbing his gloved palm along my arm. I softened it, feeling like a child encountering a mirror for the first time, discovering how their face could shift and move.

Hera approached me. Her lips pressed into a thin line, her piercing blue-eyed stare sweeping over me like I was something unpleasant. The lift of her chin and the cold flicker in her eyes told me how this interaction would go.

Her gown, a cascade of ivory silk covered with small reflective filigrees, rippled with each calculated step she took. Hades moved closer to me. Hera's gaze flickered between me and him, a smile full of sharp edges on her face. "Relax, Hades," she purred. Her voice was a honeyed drawl laced with venom. She sneered when her eyes returned to mine as if she'd forgotten she came over to me. "Zeus sent me to wish you luck."

"Is that what you're doing now?" Surprisingly, my voice held steady.

Her smile widened, revealing more of her perfect white teeth—a predator's smile. "That's exactly what I'm doing. Zeus doesn't wish to divide the court even further." It was as if my existence was an inconvenience. With Hera so firmly on Demeter's side, it wasn't hard to guess why she didn't like me. Her eyes lingered on the mate bond displayed on my chest. "You may think you're important"—her voice lowered —"but I can't wait until I never hear your name again." Before I could respond, she spun on her heel, fabric billowing around her.

Hades' hand found the small of my back, his gloved fingers on my exposed skin sending a smooth pulse through me. I looked up at him.

Hades leaned in, his voice a low murmur. "Ignore her. She wants to rattle you. Don't give her the satisfaction."

I nodded and straightened my spine.

A nymph approached, her slender form draped in gossamer fabric like all the others making their rounds. She carried a tray of goblets filled with ambrosia. "May I offer you some ambrosia, Lady Persephone, Lord Hades, Lord Thanatos?" The nymph lowered her gaze.

I took a goblet, but just as quickly as it was in my hands, Thanatos snatched it from me. The suddenness of the movement stilled me, my fingers tingling from where they had touched the cool metal.

"We don't need any," Hades said. The nymph's emerald eyes that matched her hair widened. She nodded and scurried away, the tray trembling in her hands, the goblets clinking together. I was surprised she hadn't spilled them. I could only imagine the punishment she would've received.

Thanatos had already downed my goblet of ambrosia. He pulled a piece of silk from his pocket and dabbed his mouth.

"Why would you do that?" I asked, trying to hide the bite in my voice.

His brows drew together, and he rolled the silk between his fingers. "You need to keep your wits about you."

"He's right," Hades added, his eyes not on me but scanning the room.

I swallowed hard, but the sting of his words lingered. Hades' hand tightened on my arm, his touch both grounding and tender. His eyes softened. "I know it's not easy. But we can't afford any risks."

I stared at the floor. The familiar voice inside me whispered that I didn't belong here. The walls I'd once built to shield my emotions had been gone for a while, leaving me exposed. "I know."

A deafening boom shattered the music, and the foyer trembled. The sound rippled through the floor, the walls, and rattled the chandelier over our heads, the crystals clinking together. The vibration slammed through my chest and ran through my bones.

"Time to go to the courtroom," Hades explained. He took my hand, and together we made our way through the corridors, along with the rest of the court. The last time I had been here, I had been so desperate, driven by a reckless need to assert my independence and free myself from Demeter. The memory twisted inside me. What had once felt like freedom then, now felt like weights chained to both ankles as I sank to the bottom of the roaring sea.

We stepped through the large double doors of the courtroom. It was the same as I'd remembered it, an elevated bench in an inverted U-shape filling the majority of the room.

The Divine flitted around the bench, making their way to their seats. "We're going to our seats," Hades said, looking over at Thanatos.

"You're leaving me?" I cursed at myself for the vulnerability in my voice. If I wanted to stand as an equal—if I wanted them to see me as more than Demeter's fragile, isolated daughter, I needed to act like it. I belonged here. My Divine blood proved it, but without Hades beside me, their gazes pressed in. They peeled me open, crawling through the fractures to the imposter trembling beneath.

Hades pulled me into a slow, soft kiss. "I'm not leaving you." His voice was low. He guided me to the stand facing the inverted U where the court members would sit in judgment. "We have to play our parts," he murmured as a wave of comfort pulsed through the bond. "But I'm still here, Persephone."

"I—" I swallowed. My throat tightened around the words. I needed to say something, but everything felt inadequate. "Okay."

"If you need me, you know how to reach me."

The bond.

Hades and Thanatos left, leaving me standing before the towering bench alone. I gripped the edge of the stand.

Her fragrance hit me first. Lilies. I'd tried to prepare myself for seeing her, but nothing could've readied me completely.

Demeter approached me. The tightness of her face, the lines of disapproval I'd grown so accustomed to, had softened. Her blonde hair was pulled into a severe updo with purple crystals embellishing it, not a strand out of place. She wore a pale pink gown that flowed around her like a living thing. It reminded me of a flower we had in the greenhouse.

I locked my knees.

I need to be strong.

"Don't get yourself killed, my lily." Her voice, though sharp, carried something I hadn't heard in years. Her lips pressed into a thin line before she turned and went to her seat. I remained rooted in place, catching only a flicker of something in her eyes and voice.

Concern.

A part of me wanted to cling to it, to reach for that fleeting connection, that piece of the mother I'd lost long ago. I longed to be that little girl again, the one who adored her mother, believed she could do no wrong, and trusted she would protect me from the universe. Every time I thought I was getting past the hurt she left in me, the anger and fear rose up and cracked me open all over again.

Why would she care now, after everything? Why would someone who broke me be concerned if I made it out alive? *Just another part of her game,* I told myself. But I agreed with her. I didn't want to get myself killed.

A familiar current flowed through me.

Hades.

His love swept through the bond like a tide, filling the

hollow places that Demeter had left behind. I closed my eyes, letting the sensation anchor me.

A sharp boom cracked through the courtroom as Zeus clasped his hands together. He stood at the apex of the U-shaped bench, positioned higher than everyone else. His blond hair caught the light like a crown, a natural spotlight in a room that already revolved around him. "We convene today to ignite Persephone's trials. While her path to the trials is not traditional, the outcome remains the same." Zeus glanced between Hades and me. "Persephone, by pledging yourself to the court, you are tying your blood and loyalty to us. Do you understand this?"

The weight of the Divine's stares pressed down on me, but Hades' I felt the most. I reached for him through the bond. *What happens if I say no?*

They only ask out of procedure. You will still have to complete the trials. It won't get you out of them, Hades spoke.

Okay.

I swallowed hard. "Yes." Somehow, my voice was strong. I met Zeus' gaze without flinching. The word echoed in the silent room.

Zeus continued, "The rules are these. You will receive no information from the court members on their experiences. They are bound by blood. You must complete each trial, and the consequence of failure is death."

Death.

The word hung in the air, chilling my exposed skin. No softening the blow. Though I'd known that part, the truth hit me harder than I'd expected. *I am really doing this.*

The Divine sat in silence, their faces masks of calm. I looked at each face, except Demeter's. I couldn't.

"Do you have any questions? You only get one," Zeus asked.

I hesitated but lifted my chin. "When do the trials begin?"

Across the courtroom, Hades' and Thanatos' faces gave nothing away.

Zeus smirked, a small curve of his lips that made my stomach tighten. "They could begin in minutes," he said, a dangerous glint in his eyes, "or in years. The trials are unpredictable, meant to test your loyalty and strength."

I wished I could be angry at Hades for not telling me, but I'd done enough of taking out my misplaced reactions on him. He was bound by blood. He couldn't have told me. He'd already strained himself enough by telling me I could die.

Hades' gray eyes met mine. *You can do this.*

After the moment of silence, I flinched at Zeus' loud voice. "Open your palm."

I uncurled my fingers, following his instruction. Resting in the center of my palm lay a single wooden match with a bright red tip.

"Strike it," Zeus barked.

On the gold, Hades said.

My eyes darted around, searching for the meaning behind his words. A massive golden chalice materialized before me, its surface gleaming like liquid sunlight. I paused, then placed the red tip against the shiny metal and struck it. The flame flared to life.

"Drop it in."

I stared into the tiny flame, warm in my hand.

I let it go.

When the match hit the clear liquid inside the chalice, fire exploded upward in a cyclone of red, orange, yellow, white, and black flame. Each color was distinct, yet bled into each other at the edges. A deep pulse settled in my ribs.

"Persephone Koralis, Goddess of Spring, has officially ignited the Divine Trials. May she prove her worth or die trying." Scattered applause followed his words, the hollow, uneven sound bouncing off the walls. Hades clapped, his gaze anchoring me in place. He believed in me so deeply. *What if I let him down*, I thought.

Don't worry, little goddess. That won't be your last name forever.

I managed a weak smile. *That's what you're thinking about right now?*

Hades chuckled, a sound that reverberated through the bond. His laughter was more than just a sound; it was a sensation, a caress that radiated through my chest, soothing the frayed edges of my nerves. *All I can think about is our future together*, he confessed. A cascade of vivid images surged through the bond.

The images transported me to a vision of a life yet to come. We stood side by side, not as King and Queen of the Underworld, but just as mates in a lush, verdant garden teeming with life. The sun filtered through a canopy of leaves, casting a dappled light that bathed everything in a gentle glow. My bare feet sank into the soft earth. A cool breeze rustled my hair.

Gentle touches.

Smiles.

Laughter.

We walked hand in hand through the Underworld.

I saw evenings spent by a crackling fire as we sat together, his arm around my shoulders, my head resting against his chest. In the quiet moments, we spoke of everything and nothing. We planned for a future filled with joy, free from the burdens of the past and the trials that now loomed.

Every moment of love I saw, the more spite the sharp edge of what it would mean to lose it pressed in.

The vision faded, leaving nothing but the echo of what I didn't have yet. I balled my hand, trying to hold onto it just a second longer. My eyes searched Hades', finding the same longing reflected there. *I didn't know you could do that*, I said.

Our connection is strengthening. We will continue to connect in every way.

Do you really think we can have that? I didn't want to snuff out the hope that flared in my chest before it had a chance to burn.

Yes. You will complete the trials, we'll find the Nexus Stone pieces, and we'll be bound.

I don't even know your last name. Last names weren't very important as a Divine. Mine had only been used maybe two or three times within my entire life, including today.

Our last name is Chthonis.

The way he said *our* sent a shiver through my body.

Drink from the chalice, he urged. *It's for good luck.*

I eyed the flames still dancing. *It's not going to burn me?*

Trust me.

I lifted the large, heavy chalice and found that the metal was somehow cool against my lips. I tilted it, the liquid sloshing against the sides and extinguishing the flame. The first sip was an explosion of flavor unlike anything I'd ever tasted—so, so sweet. I drank deeply, warmth spreading through my chest and curling low in my stomach. I'd chosen this path on my own. No one forced me. If I died, I'd have no one to blame but myself.

I lowered it. A single drop of the liquid trembled on my lip before I swept it away with the tip of my tongue.

The Divine approached me one by one, offering their well-wishes. Some were genuine, others less so.

Thanatos offered me a small, crooked smile. "I know you'll make it through."

I nodded, a knot tightening in my throat. His faith in me meant a great deal, especially knowing how little he'd trusted me when I first came to the Underworld.

Demeter approached me. I forced my spine straight.

"Be careful." The two words landed like a slap, containing

no hesitation. "You're not any good dead." She clicked her tongue and walked off before I could say anything. The train of her dress swept the floor behind her. A bittersweet ache twisted through me.

As her heels clicked away, a small, desperate—pathetic—part of me hoped she might return and say something. Anything to make me believe a part of her still loved me. If even my own mother could turn cold without warning... who was to say someone else I loved wouldn't?

Hades was the last. He'd waited until everyone else dispersed and left the room, surely back toward the music and food.

His hands found my waist, and he pulled me flush against him. And then his lips were on mine. It wasn't a gentle kiss. It was raw as if this could be the last one before I went into a trial.

And as much as I hated that, it was true.

Hades' thumb traced the curve of my jaw, then my cheek. He tucked one of the strands Evangeline had left out behind my ear. Hades squeezed the back of my neck, tilting my head, deepening the kiss.

When he pulled back, his forehead pressed against mine, our ragged breaths mingling in the thin space between us. *I don't want to lose this.*

5

———

HADES

*P*ersephone and I walked out of the courtroom, the heavy doors swinging shut behind us with a loud thud. My hand tightened around hers as we trailed after everyone else.

This ceremony was supposed to be about her. Instead, the court had clearly turned it into a celebration of themselves, all but a handful who were on our side and still remembered what mattered.

I glanced over at Persephone again. She looked radiant, her dress hugging her frame and her dark hair styled into a beautiful braid. Flowers I'd picked from the greenhouse were woven into it. No amount of beauty could hide the tension in her, though. It was in the set of her shoulders, the tightness of her grip in mine, and the anxiety I could feel flowing through the bond.

I kept staring at her. Part of me was just waiting for her to vanish. It would happen eventually.

The memory of my own trials crowded my mind. They'd been brutal, and I nearly hadn't survived. I wished I could tell her everything, prepare her for what she would face. But I

40

had broken through the blood bond as far as I could, and when I'd tried to go further, it refused to yield. And I believed for every member, the trials were different, playing on individual strengths and weaknesses. The best I could do was to train her, even if it didn't feel like enough. She'd asked for time off, and though I hated it, I'd abided by her wishes. For now.

Her heels tapped against the marble as we walked through the foyer, passing all the elaborate decorations. "How long do we have to stay?" She was holding herself together, but barely. Guilt over pledging herself to the trials pressed against me in waves.

I glanced down, forcing a small smile. "You have to do the customary dance."

Her brow furrowed. "By myself? What do you mean?"

"It's tradition. A partner dance." I squeezed her hand. "For everyone to see you, to celebrate you." My voice trailed off.

"Who did you dance with for yours?"

I suppressed a chuckle at the trickle of jealousy flowing through the mate bond. "I never made it to this part." The reminder that she could just disappear at any time made my jaw tighten. "My first trial started as I set down the chalice."

She swallowed hard, her gaze flicking to the entrance the rest of the court had already walked through. "How many people don't make it to this customary dance?"

"Most make it."

Her mouth twisted before she let out a sharp laugh. "Most." The realization must've set in because her laughter died. "It's strange to think about, isn't it? That it can just... happen. That I could disappear before the end of the night."

"You'll be okay," I said, both to her and myself.

She had to be.

We stepped through the glass doors and into the grand room. The moment we entered, the music burst to life, a traditional melody that seemed too quick and cheery for my mood. Persephone glanced around, taking it all in—the gold dripping on everything, the floral arrangements I'm sure she would've appreciated more had this event not been to ignite the trials. All eyes were on her.

"This is the music they chose?" she asked. "It's like they want me to trip and fall."

I chuckled, raising her hand to shoulder level. "Don't worry. I'll guide you."

Persephone's eyes narrowed.

I guided her into the center of the dance floor as the Divine circled it. Stepping closer, I rested my other hand against the small of her back. I ached that I couldn't feel her warm skin through my gloves. After I'd left a scar on another Divine with my death touch, I'd been ordered to wear them inside Divine Hall.

I hated being a puppet, having them tell me what to do.

The bond between us hummed, steady and low in my chest. I led her into the rhythm of the music, my steps confident. She moved, her posture too straight, too careful. "You're staring."

"Of course I am." I let my hand slide lower on her waist. "You're breathtaking."

She flushed, the scarlet hue on her cheeks turning to a deeper shade. "Are you trying to distract me from all the eyes on us?" Her smile faltered, her eyes staying distant. Like she was here and somewhere else in her mind at once—somewhere heavier.

My fingers traced small circles on her skin. "Is it working?"

"A little." Her lips twitched at the corners. "I just hope I'm not making a fool of myself."

I steered her into another turn. "You're not."

She cast a quick look at the crowd around us. Most of

them were occupied in their own conversations, but I understood why she was intimidated. They were beyond judgmental. "There's no way I'm letting that happen. Besides, I don't think you give yourself enough credit."

Persephone rolled her eyes. The gesture held no real annoyance, though. "You know dancing isn't my thing." We stayed in step for another thirty seconds. She cleared her throat. "You're still staring."

"I don't think there's anything you could say to make me stop." I leaned closer. "You should be used to my staring by now." I pulled her into a turn and then closer, my lips brushing the shell of her ear. "Is it a crime to admire what is mine?"

She arched a brow. "Do you practice these lines, or do they just come to you?"

"You think I'm trying to charm you?" I teased.

She didn't laugh. Didn't roll her eyes or shoot back a dry remark. She gave me a smile that climbed halfway up her cheeks before dying, never reaching her eyes. "Maybe you can't help yourself." Her voice cracked at the end. "Or maybe you're just saying all of this because you have to. We're fated mates, after all. It's practically in the fine print, isn't it?"

The bond carried it to me—the coil of dread, the shame, emotional echoes of memories that weren't mine.

My steps slowed, faltering. My smile wavered. I knew she didn't mean to cut me so deeply with the comment, that it wasn't just about me. It was about all the years someone had told her she wasn't enough, and the part of her that still believed it. I wanted to stay silent, unaffected by her words, but I couldn't help myself. "Do you think that's all this is?" I let out a long breath. "The bond?"

She hesitated. "I don't know. Maybe." Something in her tone frayed. "Isn't it?"

"No." The word came out sharper than I intended, and

Persephone cringed. "The bond ties us, yes. We're connected. But it doesn't *force* me to feel this way." My hand slid higher up her back, my thumb drawing slow circles on her spine. "It doesn't control what I feel. It just makes the connection between us louder. Falling in love with you… that's always been me." Persephone had doubted herself plenty throughout our time together. But doubting *us*?

She stared up at me, her lips parting as her brows knit together. Her wide eyes searched mine. "I don't understand," she murmured.

I pressed a soft kiss to her forehead. "Then let me make it simple. Just know that I'd choose you, with or without the bond."

The music shifted, and the Divine moved on to the dance floor. I held Persephone close, unwilling to let her go just yet.

"Can we talk somewhere?" Her voice was low, only for me.

I nodded, and without a word, we slipped out of the room, leaving the crowd that couldn't care less behind us. My hand remained wrapped around hers, her fingers tightening as we walked. She didn't look at me, her posture fixed straight ahead.

I guided her up the crimson-carpeted stairs, the same ones we'd taken last week at the gala, when I'd led her to do something far less innocent. Her blush deepened as we reached the highest floor.

"Let me show you something."

She gave me a side-eyed glance. "The last time you said that, you ended up taking me over the Divine."

My eyebrows rose. "That isn't a complaint, is it?"

She stayed quiet, trying to fight the smile taking over her face. "No," she finally said.

I smirked and kept us moving, leading her down a short corridor. I opened one of the curtain-veiled glass double doors and held it open. I motioned her forward, guiding her through the doorway and out onto the balcony. The view unfurled before us, Athens stretching out in a sea of glittering lights and winding cobblestone. I hated to admit it, but it was striking.

"This is…" She gazed out at Athens, her voice soft, almost reverent. "It's beautiful."

"It has its moments." This realm was vast, a variety of terrains and territories. But its beauty was only a mask. Underneath lay that same ugly hunger for power. It was a distant memory, the time when the court had first been established and this realm had been led by the common interest of the people. Now those people prayed to leaders that would not help them.

Persephone turned to me, leaning her back against the stone railing. Her fingers fidgeted, twisting and untwisting. I reached out and enclosed her hands in mine. "I didn't mean to hurt your feelings." The confession fell from her lips like thin, brittle leaves carried by a breeze.

The words I wanted to say hovered on the tip of my tongue, easy, reassuring lies like *I'm fine* or *It doesn't matter* that wouldn't sting her. But I swallowed them back and exhaled. "I never want you to think that what I feel for you isn't real. That it's just because of the bond."

Her shoulders sank as she looked down, her teeth catching the inside of her lip. "Sometimes it's easier for me to think of it that way." She looked up at the stars before meeting my eyes. "That you love me because the bond tells you to." Persephone stayed silent for a few moments. "Because if it's not the bond… and you change your mind because I did something foolish—" She swallowed. "I don't think I'd survive that. Demeter loved me. Until she didn't. I can't go through that again."

The words were a knife. I didn't speak right away. What

could I say to undo years of damage someone else had done? Persephone avoided my eyes, like she regretted speaking her fear aloud. Like she was already preparing herself for me to prove her right—to turn on her just like her mother had.

Slowly, I stepped closer, placing my hands on either side of her, gripping the stone railing. I didn't touch her yet.

"Don't say that," I said softly. "Don't even think it." How could I make her realize she was good enough? Persephone wasn't wrong to fear being discarded. She'd lived it. But I would never do that to her.

Her wide stare locked onto mine as she flinched.

"You are enough, Persephone." I ran my hands up her arms. "You're more than enough. The Fates might have chosen us, but I would choose you over and over. No matter the circumstances."

Her lips thinned, her eyes searching mine. "You make it sound so easy." Her whisper barely reached me. "This whole ceremony just made everything so... *real*. The trials are actually going to happen. And I can't stop wondering how someone could still love me, knowing how reckless I've been."

"Love doesn't vanish because someone makes mistakes. Love isn't conditional. Stop calling yourself reckless, Persephone. While I wish you hadn't felt like this was your only way forward." My voice was tight. *I had a plan—the Rite*, I reminded myself. But I swallowed it down. She didn't need another reason to feel more shame on top of everything else. "You were brave. You made a choice for yourself because you wanted to be free. Because you wanted something more than what was forced on you. With or without the bond, that's the kind of person I'd choose every time."

Her lips parted, but no sound came out. She tilted her head back to take in the night sky.

I cleared my throat and looked up as well, just in time to

catch a silver streak tearing across the dark, star-spotted canvas above. It burned for a few seconds before vanishing as if it had never been there at all. "A shooting star," she said.

"Must be a good omen." My voice was low.

"I hope so."

Her eyes returned to mine. "I meant what I said," I murmured. "The bond didn't make me love you. It just made it easier for me to see you. You're smart and kind and brave and infuriating and funny and loving and everything I didn't know I needed."

Tears glistened before she blinked them away. "I'm sorry—"

"Stop." I cut her off, cupping her jaw in my hand. "You don't have to explain. Don't try to make yourself smaller to be loved. You are not hard to love, Persephone. You never were."

Persephone nodded and gave me a small smile, but it broke apart quickly.

I leaned down, pressing my lips to hers with a kiss full of everything I couldn't put into words. She melted against me, her hands wrapping around my neck.

We pulled back. She turned in my arms, facing the city as I drew her closer. "This place looks like a dream from up here."

I let out something between a scoff and a chuckle. "And I still hate it."

"That's something we have in common."

We stared out at the city and the stars. Not in peace but together.

6

———

PERSEPHONE

I stood in the greenhouse, my fingers curled around the worn wooden handle of the metal trowel. The silver caught the moonlight filtering through the stained glass ceiling, scattering reds, blues, yellows, and greens across the room. I focused on the leafy plant before me, carefully loosening its roots as I prepared to move it into a larger pot. It needed more room to grow.

I huffed a laugh. It was ridiculous of me to be jealous of a plant. Yet I still was.

"Aithne, that's enough." Mother's voice drifted down the corridor.

I flinched at the sound. My shoulders tensed as footsteps echoed against the marble floors, growing closer. My limbs were heavy from the medication still dulling many of my senses, but I moved as quickly as I could. I shuffled toward the back of the greenhouse and pressed myself into the corner. If I stayed still, if I kept my breathing shallow, maybe they'd pass.

Maybe she'd leave me alone today.

The footsteps stopped at the door of the greenhouse. I imagined Mother's gaze sweeping over the plants, searching for me. My fingers tightened around the rim of a burnt orange pot. The tiny imperfections on its dry, sunbaked surface pressed into my skin.

"I can see you," she said, her tone sharp like broken glass.

My stomach turned. Don't vomit, I told myself. She'll punish you for that. I placed a hand over my mouth and sucked a lungful of air through my nostrils.

"Basile," Mother barked, her voice cracking like a whip. "You're late on her medication again." Rattling and footsteps pounded down the hall, moving closer to the greenhouse. I dared a peek from behind the broad, glossy leaf in front of my face.

Basile skidded to a stop in front of Mother. He shoved back the strands of brown hair on his forehead. She didn't look at me anymore. Instead, her expression twisted toward him. "Are you incompetent or just defiant?"

His mouth opened, but no words came out.

Mother stepped forward, pressing a single manicured finger to his chest. He jerked back as if she'd used excessive force to strike him, his spine slamming against the corridor wall with a loud thud. "It doesn't matter which it is. If it happens again, I will end you and find someone more useful."

Basile's throat bobbed. "Yes, Lady Demeter."

She exhaled sharply, looked back at me, and walked off, Aithne at her heels.

But Basile remained.

He stepped into the greenhouse. "Come here," he spat. "You got me in trouble again."

I pressed myself farther back into the plants.

He lowered his voice. "Come. Out."

My heart stammered. I glared at the metal trowel stuck in the soil beside me. I didn't reach for it—I'd made that mistake before.

Basile took another step closer. A tremble started in my hands, spreading through my limbs. My vision narrowed at the edges, and I squeezed my eyes shut. I was almost sure the Fates were granting me my wish. They would finally let me die.

But one second passed.
And then two.
And then three.
They hadn't killed me.
Unfortunately.

Slowly, I stood and stepped forward, shivering when the leaves brushed against my skin. Basile's lips curled into a snarl as he nudged one of my pots aside with his brown leather boot. It was just enough force to send it toppling onto its side, cracking the ceramic and letting soil spill like blood from a wound. Basile didn't flinch, didn't even look down. He just watched me.

"Finally," he said. The little bottle rattled as he clicked off the lid. He shook a single tiny white pill into his palm and thrust it toward me. "Take it."

I stared at it. I hate this. I hate him. I hate her. I hate myself, too. I hate all of this.

I took the pill from his hand and placed it on my tongue. The bitterness spread instantly, sending a hot wave through my middle, but I swallowed it down without a word.

"Open your mouth."

I followed his instructions, opening wide. I let a moment pass before I lifted my tongue, showing the empty space beneath. Basile narrowed his eyes as he studied the inside of my mouth, then exhaled. "Good."

The word made my skin crawl.

He turned and stalked away. The moment he disappeared from view, I moved back to the corner, my limbs folding beneath me. The plants leaned in, curling close like a shield. Even without magic, they still responded to the fear I carried.

Numbness set in almost immediately, rolling over me in thick waves. The rainbow of colors in the greenhouse blurred together. My vision swam. The shapes of the leaves twisted and bent together. My head sagged until it hit the cool glass.

~

HADES

"*Just ignore him," Thanatos said.*

I wished I could. I tapped my fingers against my thigh.

One.

Two.

Three.

Four.

Five.

It was a coping mechanism, one I'd picked up years ago. It didn't soothe me, but it kept me from unraveling. I couldn't in front of them. A long, narrow table stretched before us. Torchlight flickered across the surrounding walls.

Zeus laughed, Apollo and Ares joining in. Even the Divine that didn't directly participate in the ridicule stood by, watching with thin smirks or vacant expressions.

I clenched my jaw, my teeth aching. I forced my grip to stay on the table's edge instead of the throats in front of me. I hated that after everything, all the blood we'd been shedding during this Titan War and fighting alongside them, they still saw me as lesser.

For years, I kept my head down and stayed away. By myself and sometimes with Thanatos. When the Titan War began, their torment had lessened. Not because they grew kinder. Not because they saw me as an equal.

They needed me.

But now that we were on the edge of victory over the Titans, their old habits had returned. I stood. I needed to get away. A hand shoved my shoulder, hard enough to send me flying forward. My ribs collided with the table, stone biting into bone.

Probably just another broken rib.

I pushed myself up and back onto my feet.

"What's the matter, Hades?" Zeus stepped closer. His lips quirked up into a smile. "Still can't take a joke."

A joke. That's what they always called it. I dragged my tongue over the split in my lip, another gift from one of their earlier jokes. The metallic, stale taste flooded through my mouth. My fingers twitched at my sides. My power surged, urging me to act, but I forced myself to be still.

Thanatos shifted beside me. He hadn't moved to intervene. We both knew how that worked. If I fought them, it only made it worse.

Zeus' gaze bore into me. His eyes traced me from head to toe. He moved, and I broke my statue-like position. His grin widened as if he had won something. He stood before me for another minute, but I made no move to fight him. That was exactly what he wanted, and I'd be damned if I gave it to him. Zeus scoffed and turned.

"Coward," Ares muttered. "What a waste of power."

I said nothing. Inhale. Exhale. I tapped my fingers against my thigh.

One.

Two.

Three.

My eyes fluttered closed as their footsteps retreated into the distance. I would help them win this war. I would stand beside them and get the power they promised me. I would let them believe they had me under their thumbs. And when the time was right, I would take this 'waste' of smoldering magic inside me and burn them all to the ground.

I jolted awake, running a hand over my face. I glanced over at Persephone. She was having another nightmare. I'd just been trapped in one myself. I hadn't had a nightmare in years.

She'd had one every night since she'd pledged herself to the trials, and despite igniting them, tonight was no exception. I could feel the thread of fear tugging at her, pulling her deeper into the abyss of her own mind. It flowed through the bond, different from the familiar darkness I knew.

I pushed up onto one elbow, the sheet sliding from my shoulder. Persephone's brows knit together, her chest rising and falling in quick movements, her fingers twisting in the sheets. Incoherent words spilled from her lips.

I knew whatever terrible dream she was having had something to do with Demeter. I could've pulled on the second bond with her, the one created when she bound herself to me after I caught her in the Underworld. It had been a way to ensure she wasn't acting under Demeter's orders. Through it, I had the ability to slip into her mind and see what haunted her, but I wouldn't. I couldn't violate her privacy like that.

It took all that I had not to rip through Olympus and destroy anything Demeter cared about. I wanted to make her pay for every tear, every stolen moment of peace. I wanted to shatter the ground beneath her feet, to harm her in the most violent ways I could think of.

I wanted to break her.

But rage was a reckless thing—for now. I forced it back, letting the rational part of my mind surface just enough to keep me from losing control. Persephone's every choked breath, every single whimper, lacerated a permanent wound into my chest.

I knew who had put that fear in her eyes, who had forced my mate into running. My fingers clenched and unclenched. Finding the stone pieces was the best course of action, but it didn't lessen my desire to make Demeter suffer.

Persephone stirred again, a soft cry escaping her swollen lips. The sound cut through me, more painful than any weapon I'd ever encountered. Sweat glistened along her temple. I pulled her close, her body sprawled on top of mine. "I'm here, little goddess."

Her feverish skin pulsed beneath my fingers. I smoothed my hand down her arm, across the curve of her torso, until my fingertips brushed the dagger still strapped to her thigh. Her heart beat rapidly against my chest. My lips brushed against her hair while I murmured words of reassurance.

Little by little, the tension in her body melted away. Persephone's shoulders, once drawn rigid, loosened. Her clenched fingers unfurled onto my chest. The furrow in her brow smoothed out.

The trials could summon her at any moment. The magic had a mind of its own. I locked my arms around her, reminding myself that, for now, she was still here.

$\sim$

PERSEPHONE

The nightmare still clung to the edges of my mind as I studied the intricate patterns carved into the molding covering the ceiling. In the silver glow of the moons streaming through the windows, the details blurred and blended in the shifting play of light. I turned my head, watching the clouds drifting across the sky, momentarily veiling the moons' light and plunging the room into deeper shadow.

I shifted in Hades' arms. His hands moved along my waist, pulling me closer. "Can't sleep?" His words were unhurried, pitched low, a quiet yawn slipping past his lips.

I sighed, shutting my eyes. "I woke up a little while ago. A lot on my mind." In the darkness, I recalled the small flame dancing on the tip of the match before dropping it into the chalice at the igniting ceremony.

Hades hadn't spoken about the trials since we'd left Olympus just hours ago. Maybe he had wanted to give me one last night of *peace*, though I didn't think that was possible with the threat of them beginning at any moment.

His familiar scent—amber, leather, and musk—enveloped me. He pressed a kiss to my forehead, his lips lingering. I shifted again, leaning my weight onto one arm as I hovered above him, our faces only a few inches apart.

His lips found mine. Desperation threaded through the kiss, slow and hard. His hands in my hair pulled me closer, pressing me into him like any space between us was unacceptable. My heart ached. Need flowed through the bond and coiled in the pit of my stomach. I moaned into the kiss and ground my hips into his.

Hades growled, his grip closing around my wrists before he rolled us, pinning me beneath him in one smooth motion. He kissed—devoured—my mouth. I couldn't think of anything except *more*. I needed more. Hades pulled back. Our chests rose and fell in sync. His gaze lingered on my lips before drifting to my eyes. I arched into him, hungry for contact.

"We can stay here, or I can show you something."

My curiosity flared. "What do you mean?"

He hesitated. "I wanted to take you before igniting the trials, but plans shifted. Since we're both already up, I want to take you to the mortal realm."

My brows knit together, and a mixture of a dry laugh and a yawn slipped from my lips. *You really know how to kill a moment, don't you?* I spoke through the bond.

Hades' lips tilted up into a smile. *It's my specialty.*

"Why would we go to the mortal realm?" I'd never been, though recently, I'd spent a lot of time reading stories of mortals—romance and their imagined worlds. It was interesting to entertain their delusions of what they thought was fantasy. If only they knew.

Hades' eyes darkened. "I go there often. I cut threads myself."

It took a few charged moments before my tired mind understood the weight of what he'd said. "You kill people?" My voice came out sharper than I'd intended.

His expression was unreadable. "If that's how you'd like to put it, yes."

"How else would you say it?"

"I remove the scum from the mortal realm, the ones who don't deserve to live."

He said it like it was nothing. There was no weight or shame. Just fact.

"Oh," I said as he released my wrists and pushed himself upright. I scooted back, shoving the pillow out of the way until I sat with my spine pressed to the headboard.

He ran a hand through his tousled black hair, still rumpled from sleep. "When I was first tied to the Underworld, I didn't know how to control the darkness within me. It's a part of me. I spent much of my time in Faerie, taking my mind off it." He paused. "Now, with my magic stretched thin keeping the gates of Tartarus sealed, it's been harder to contain the darkness. It leaks out, and I fear it's been affecting you." Hades shifted so he sat up against the headboard too. His eyes searched mine.

I frowned. "What do you mean?"

"I know things have been chaotic, but you've been more emotional... impulsive." His voice was gentle as he said the last few words. "You snap easier."

My fingers traced a deep crease in the crumpled sheet. Hades tapped the top of the duvet. "For people like us, we need to release that darkness somehow, or it will consume us."

People like us.

I wanted to deny the words, but their truth settled

uncomfortably within me. I swallowed hard, but the lump in my throat didn't disappear.

Emotional.

Impulsive.

I stayed silent for a few moments. "What happens if it consumes us?"

"You lose control." Hades stared straight ahead, a muscle in his jaw twitching. He didn't elaborate. Had he ever lost control before? The thought sent an unexpected chill through me.

My pulse hammered. Each beat reinforced a single fact—I couldn't *lose control* during a trial. "So what do we do?"

Hades squeezed my hand. "Get dressed. I'll show you."

I slid out of bed, the cold floor biting against my bare feet. I threw on black silk pants and a matching long-sleeved top. The dagger strapped to my thigh shifted under the loose fabric—not the most convenient, but it would do. I'd be with Hades. I doubted I'd need it.

I reached for my sandals but hesitated. "I'll wear my boots," I muttered to myself, tucking the ends of my pants into them.

"Ready?" Hades held his hand out.

I still didn't know how to whisk—intentionally—it was something I'd need to work on another time. "Yes." I took his hand and we whisked out of the Underworld.

A ripple of magic washed over me as we materialized in the mortal realm. My eyes adjusted to the low lighting, and I took in the room around us.

The furniture was sparse—a couch, a small table, and two lamps with wooden bases, their shades yellowed with age. The large gray couch dominated the space. Its cushions sagged, their flattened fabric suggesting its plushness had been gone for years. Faint stains covered the linen fabric on the arms. Scratches and white rings scarred the low wooden table in front of the couch. Knickknacks covered shelves skewed from their weight. Whatever colors they once had were dulled beneath layers of dust.

"Where are we?" I asked.

Hades pressed a finger to his lips, and his attention cut to the door across the room. It creaked open. Hades pulled me back so that we stood in the shadow of a large cabinet. Heavy footsteps crossed the hardwood. Hades wasn't wearing his gloves. He placed a hand on the small of my back, and his warmth seeped through the fabric of my shirt.

From where we stood, we could see just past the cabinet. A man stepped into our view, tall and broad-shouldered, his movements unhurried. In the lighting, it was impossible to tell if his cropped dark hair was black or brown. His posture was relaxed, clearly at home. Hades leaned close to me, his lips brushing against my ear. I struggled to focus on the man when my mate was so close. *He's a serial killer*, Hades spoke through the bond. *Just this month, he's killed three more.*

I went still, blinking. *Serial killer?* I noted the shadows under his eyes, the tightness he tried and failed to roll out of his shoulders.

As I've told you before, I get a soul's secrets when they come to our realm. I see their lives.

I placed a hand over my lips as the man shrugged off his jacket. *You kill these people for justice.* I glanced at Hades.

He nodded, his focus not leaving his target. *I am committed to serving those in my realm. I will get their justice and stop any more from suffering at his hands. It's the only way I can channel the darkness in a way that does something good with it.*

That's very noble. Do you only do this in the mortal realm?

Hades' jaw flexed. *Don't mistake me for that.* The killer pulled a few trinkets from his pocket and pushed other things aside to make space for them on the shelf. These were brightly colored, their vibrancy jarring against the room's muted hues. Hades' eyes tracked the movement. *That's not what this is.* He paused. *I only do this in the mortal realm.*

Before I could respond, he continued. *This is the neutral realm. If I were to go uninvited to the other realms and cut threads early, there would be recourse.*

I frowned, not letting him brush away my words so easily. He had a similar reaction when I'd called him a good man after he surprised me with the greenhouse. *But you're helping people. You're stopping killers, avenging the dead. How is that not admirable?*

I don't want you to think of me like I'm some kind of hero. I'm not. Hades' hand settled on my shoulder, giving it a light squeeze. The gesture was a loud contradiction to his harsh words.

I studied Hades as he did the man in the room. *But, Hades—*

No.

You don't even know what I'm going to say.

He shook his head. *Yes, I do. Surely you know that it's not good to tell lies, little goddess. Don't you?*

I'm not lying.

You think there's good inside me. Any of that is from you, not from me. His eyes met mine. His warm palm framed my face, the knuckle of his other hand brushing over my cheek before gliding down my arm, shifting the silk to find my wrist.

My eyes fluttered shut under his touch. *You protect people.*

I protect you. His grip on my face tightened, and my eyes snapped open. *Don't get this twisted. I would let realms collapse, so long as you're safe in my arms.*

His thumb traced over my bottom lip, the pad grazing over the curve before pressing lightly. He traced the shape as if memorizing it. It was a slow, claiming stroke. *I don't care about being good.*

A shiver raced through my body.

He leaned in close, his lips just inches away from mine. *The only thing I care about is you. The darkness inside me is a tool.* He leaned back, leaving me breathless. Without warning, he grabbed my hand, whisking us across the room.

Within seconds, we stood behind the stranger. The battered couch and skewed shelves were now at our backs. My heart roared in my ears at the sudden shift.

Dark bands of Hades' magic unfurled from his fingertips, snaking around the killer, restraining him and forcing him to face us. His brown eyes widened, flickering with the reflection of the streetlights, their glow filtering through the narrow gap in the curtains. They were open just enough for me to catch the view outside, but not enough for anyone to see in. Panic bled into his features, every movement stifled and useless against the force of Hades' power.

Even in a weakened state, Hades was so powerful. The mortal was nothing compared to him. A scream tore from his throat, and I cringed. Hades' magic made its way to his mouth, choking off any more sound.

I barely recognized the god beside me. Gone were the playful charm and teasing smirks I'd grown used to. In their place was something colder, sharper.

He didn't flinch. His gray eyes turned a darker shade as he watched the condemned man struggle, like he was savoring every moment of it.

This wasn't the version of him who whispered reassurances in my ear. *Could Hades ever be like this with me?* The thought made my chest constrict, my anxiety creeping back in, curling cold fingers around my ribs. I shook my head.

When Hades finally looked at me, he gave a lazy wave of his hand, urging me forward as if this was nothing more than a simple exchange.

"What do you want me to do?"

"Whatever you want. Whatever you feel comfortable

with." His tone was casual, detached. He leaned back, his chin tilting up.

The man's face turned mottled shades of purple as Hades' magic bound him, squeezing with unrelenting force. I stiffened. The idea of taking a life, even one as tainted as his, felt wrong. "You want me to kill him?"

Hades' dark gray eyes lightened to their normal shade. "I'm not going to force you to do anything." His voice remained calm, disturbingly soft.

Nothing about this put me at ease. I was in an unfamiliar realm, in some random killer's home, about to take his life. Hades' eyes searched mine. Was I truly okay with this? The question ricocheted through my mind. I'd taken a life before —Basile—and I had enjoyed it. That had been survival. This was a choice, a judgment.

"You feel bad for him," Hades said.

I nodded, looking down at my hands. "I don't know what's wrong with me."

"There's nothing wrong with you." Hades caught my hand, his fingers wrapping firmly around mine. The world narrowed to the feel of his touch on my skin, the bond humming between us. The man, still suffocating in Hades' magic, faded to the edges of my awareness. "You have so much life in you. It's hard to take life away."

"I didn't feel this way with my guard Basile," I whispered. I'd told Hades only the bare bones of what happened between us, and that was enough.

"That was different." He let go of my hand. "You felt first-hand what Basile did to you."

I glanced up at him. If I wanted to survive the trials, I needed to be strong. I needed to be able to make hard decisions. "Show me what he's done."

He nodded. Images flooded my mind, brutal and violent. I saw everything through the eyes of the victims. Their terror and pain were my own. Their suffering was my own. Their last desperate pleas for mercy were my own.

Heat surged in my veins, my hands trembling at my sides. I stared at the killer bound by Hades' magic, seeing the monster he was—but also seeing the one I'd been too powerless to stop.

Demeter's smile flashed in my mind. She'd stolen my power, stripped me of everything that made me feel whole, and called it love. My mouth went dry. I could walk away. I could let this man face justice without my hand in it.

But the longer I stood there, the heavier the weight in my chest grew.

I was tired.

Tired of fear, of helplessness. Of watching people like him —like *her*—take and take and take.

Power thrummed beneath my skin. Dark, twisted vines unfurled from my palms, snaking the distance between us and wrapping around the man's ankles, then up his body to snare his wrists. He struggled, his eyes wide as realization settled in—I would not be his savior. I would be his reckoning. Hades' magic faded, leaving only mine to hold him.

The killer's eyes locked onto mine, and for a moment, I recognized a flicker of hope. But my vines pulled him to the ground. I saw the lives he'd ruined without mercy. I would get justice for their souls.

My vines constricted tighter and tighter, and then a sickening crack filled the air. The mortal went limp.

Hades placed a hand on my arm. "You can stop now," he said softly. "He's already dead. He's been dead for the last five minutes, Persephone."

I blinked a few times, and the world slowly bled back into focus. My vines were still knotted around the dead man before me. Life had clearly left him, but I hadn't stopped.

My stomach turned, bile rising in the back of my throat.

My fingers trembled as I pulled my magic back. I couldn't look away from him. His head lolled to the side, eyes dull, lips parted. Beneath him, a dark puddle spread across the floor, seeping outward in uneven rivulets. The acrid stench of urine rose from it, lodging itself in my throat. Every breath tasted of it.

But the nausea passed.

In its place came something heavier, hotter. Slow warmth spread through my chest, filling me from head to toe. Relief. Satisfaction… *Power*.

I did it.

I'd expected to feel horrified, sickened by what I'd done, but instead, I felt lighter. The tension that had been gnawing at my muscles for weeks unwound, replaced by a strange calm.

I took inventory of my senses. I hated how good it felt. I had done it. I had killed him. No one held me down. No one silenced me. I wasn't helpless.

Hades watched. "How do you feel?"

I turned to him, bracing myself. His eyes weren't full of judgment or concern. He looked at me with *love*.

How did I feel? Safe? Was that what this was? I wasn't even sure what safety meant to me anymore. "I feel… good." My voice came out low and rough. I hadn't realized how heavy the darkness I was carrying was. It was as if I had been operating with a veil over my mind.

A small smile played at the corners of Hades' lips. He pulled me into a crushing embrace. "You did well. I should've brought you here sooner," he murmured, his voice a warm rumble against my ear. Heat welled through the bond. "Let's go home."

I shifted in his hold, leaning back just enough to point to the dead man on the floor. "Do we just leave him here?"

He nodded. "I'll see his soul in the Underworld."

7

PERSEPHONE

We whisked back into our room. I didn't get even a moment before Hades' lips crashed onto mine. I poured everything into the kiss—heat, guilt, everything I hadn't let myself say. I moaned into his mouth.

He pulled back. His stubble dragged over my cheek, a delicious scrape that sent a shiver through me. Hades' eyes were so dark. He pressed his body flush with mine, his rigid length straining through the barrier of his pants and nudging my belly. Hades kissed me again, hunger and desperation twining until nothing existed but the taste of him.

It was exactly what I needed. My fingers curled into the fabric of his shirt. His heat surged against me, chest rising and falling in a chaotic rhythm.

A whisper in my mind pierced the heat: *You're not immortal anymore.* Would he look at me the same if I failed the trials? If I stood before him as a soul? My hands, so sure just a second ago, twitched against his chest. I didn't want to think. I shoved the thought away and held on to the one thing that felt real.

Him.

He cradled the nape of my neck, his fingers flexing against my skin. "You don't know how hot it was to see you do that." His voice rasped against my lips, low and thick, like he couldn't hold himself back.

Hades' mouth grazed mine, his teeth catching my lower lip in a tease that sent heat curling through me. He lingered there, lips skimming over mine as if he enjoyed watching me come undone in the wait. One hand tangled in my hair, tugging just enough to make me arch into him. He pulled back. "How do you feel?"

Like I was buzzing. My magic thrummed in sync with the rapid beat of my heart. "Like I can focus." My words came out between ragged gasps.

The corner of his mouth quirked up into a dangerous smirk, one that had the power to unravel me. "That's my goddess." His voice was molten with pride.

Hades' fingers slid from my neck, tracing the line of my shoulders and down my arms until he found my hands. He laced our fingers together with a grounding squeeze, and then let go.

His hands slipped under the hem of my shirt, palms gliding up the plane of my stomach in a slow sweep. I leaned into him without thinking.

Hades pulled the fabric higher, baring inch after inch of my skin to the cool air. With a final tug, the shirt slipped over my head. He tossed it onto the floor somewhere. His fingers found the clasp of my bra, and with practiced fingers, it came undone. The straps slid down my arms, the fabric following.

His thumbs barely brushed over my nipples, and my back arched, a soft gasp escaping my lips. "So fucking responsive."

I reached for his belt, fumbling to undo it, desperation making my fingers clumsy.

"Fuck this," he murmured like he was seconds away from losing every shred of control. "I need you now." His magic whirled around us, leaving us bare. I shivered, wearing nothing but the dagger strapped to my thigh.

My hands moved to remove it, but Hades caught my wrist. "Leave"—he pressed a kiss to my cheek—"it on."

I swallowed hard and nodded. I wrapped my arms around his neck, and with an effortless haul, he lifted me, his hands gripping my ass as he carried me to the bed. The pressure bordered on bruising, but it wasn't painful.

He threw me. The world lurched sideways for half a second before my back hit the plush surface. Air whooshed from my lungs.

He stood at the edge of the bed, towering over me, his sculpted body haloed in shadow and silver light. His dark gaze pinned me in place, mapping every inch exposed to him.

He wrapped a hand around his length, stroking himself with slow, deliberate pulls. The mark of our bond pulsed bright white against the shadows coating his skin, illuminating the sharp lines of his face. "Fuck, you're so beautiful." He pumped harder, his eyes never once leaving mine. "Look at what you do to me."

My whole body burned under his attention. I couldn't look away.

"Come here."

I crawled to the edge of the bed, my hand reaching out to stroke him. I needed to touch him.

He stopped me. "I want your mouth, little goddess." His voice was a low growl. "I want you to remember, with every stroke of your tongue, exactly how much I want you."

I swallowed and lowered my head, his cock just inches away from my face. My tongue flicked out, teasing his velvet-smooth tip with slow circles. He shuddered beneath me and groaned. "Fuck."

I took my time working his shaft. I glanced up through my lashes, catching the heavy-lidded look in Hades' eyes. Wetness pooled between my legs.

"This is how you use your mouth, Persephone. Not for doubts or lies, but for truth. For devotion." He ran his fingers through my hair, tugging lightly. He thrust his hips forward. "I want you to memorize how I feel on your tongue, so even if your mind forgets, your body won't."

I moaned around him, the sound sending a violent shudder through his body.

"Are you going to remember how much I want you?"

I nodded, hollowing my cheeks, unable to say anything more than a broken, "Mm-hmm."

Hades placed a hand against the side of my face and drew me back a fraction, just enough to watch his length moving between my lips.

He pushed me in a swift, controlled press, guiding me until my spine hit the mattress. I tried to lean up, desperate to reach him, but the air between us shifted. Power poured from him in an invisible wave before it took shape, dark tendrils unfurling through the air. They slid over my wrists and waist, thick like velvet ropes, pinning me with unyielding strength.

My heart stuttered as he dropped to his knees beside the bed, yanking my hips toward him. The sheets bunched and shifted beneath me as I slid forward. His magic disappeared.

His face hovered inches from my center, his breath ghosting over my slick skin. I bit my lip hard enough to hurt. He hummed, a dark, satisfied sound, and then he placed a soft kiss against my clit. "My mate wants me to devour her?"

I nodded far too quickly.

Hades chuckled before sucking my clit. My back arched off the bed, a strangled cry ripping from my lips.

"Say it out loud, Persephone. No need to be ashamed." His voice vibrated against me.

I knew my cheeks were red, but I bit my tongue.

"I can feel it," he murmured. "All those filthy things running wild in that beautiful head of yours." He sucked harder, adding a flick of his tongue that forced a full-body tremor out of me.

"Fine." I gasped, air slicing into my lungs as he slipped a finger inside me, curling upward in a way that made my vision blur.

"I'm waiting."

Each pump of his finger made it harder to hold on. My stomach flipped as my walls clenched. "I want you to devour me."

"How?" he asked, his voice low, coaxing.

"You're really going to make me do that?"

He sucked, and put pressure on my clit. "You know what they say… something about practice making perfect. Say the words." Hades pumped his finger. "Practice."

My head tipped back as a moan slipped through my lips.

"You don't need to be ashamed, little goddess. I want all of it. Every word that's been locked up behind your tongue."

Another moan broke free. My hips jerked against his mouth, chasing the vibrating friction. Pressure coiled hot in my core. I was close—so close. "Fuck, I love your mouth." The words were out before I could stop them.

He glanced up at me with a grin steeped in wicked intent. "Say that again."

"I-I didn't mean to—"

"You did." The two words were too gentle for how dangerous his eyes looked. He brushed a kiss over my trembling inner thigh. "Say it again."

My throat worked as I swallowed. "I love your mouth." Each word teetered on the tip of my tongue.

He rewarded me immediately, sealing his mouth over my clit with a slow, deliberate worship.

My moans poured out like confessions. "Don't stop. Please don't stop."

"So fucking sweet," he murmured against me. "The sounds you make? Those are mine. No one else gets to hear you like this."

"I'm so close," I whispered, my hands buried in his hair. "Keep doing that."

Hades pulled back.

My head snapped up. "Why did you stop?"

He sat back on his heels. "Because I'm not going to let you come yet."

I sucked in a shaky breath, and Hades chuckled, his tongue dragging slowly across his bottom lip. "I'm not going to let you come until you let yourself go. Break down that wall in your head."

Before I could complain, Hades' mouth was back on me. My spine snapped off the bed again, one hand still tangled in his hair and the other gripping the twisted sheets. He glanced up at me, lips curved into an all-knowing smile as he sucked harder, daring me to completely fall apart. I let out a soft moan.

He kept going. I tried to bite down the sounds, tried to keep control—

Hades placed a hand on my abdomen. "Don't you dare hold back on me," he growled.

My chest rose and fell in frantic bursts, but I still tried to suppress my moans... to hide just how close I was. I didn't want him to stop.

His tongue circled my clit in slow, devastating swipes,

fingers moving just right and hitting the spot that made the edges of my vision blur. My orgasm crested.

He pulled back. He dragged his fingers out slowly. I whimpered at the loss. "Sneaky."

"How"—my chest heaved—"did you know?"

He smirked. "How did I know you were about to come all over my face?"

I nodded, air caught in my throat.

"You thought if you stayed quiet, I wouldn't notice."

I glared at him, heat flooding through my chest and up into my face.

"I can feel the way your body is telling me without words. The way your pussy hugs my fingers. The way your breathing changes. The way your legs shake. I know you."

I sat up on unsteady arms.

"You don't have to say a thing." Hades climbed onto the bed slowly, his body hovering over mine. "You're my mate." His hand cupped the back of my neck, and he pulled me into a kiss. When his tongue swept into my mouth, I gasped— because I could taste it.

Me.

On him.

Taste how sweet you are, he said.

Hades pinned me onto the bed, a hand on my sternum as he kissed me. He shifted, pressing the head of his cock against my entrance. My hips bucked up. He pulled back from the kiss and I chased the air he stole.

"Tell. Me. What. You. Want."

"I want you." Before he could demand more, I was already giving it to him. "I want your cock." I huffed, chewing on my lip. "Please."

He smiled. "And what do you want me to do with my cock?"

I rolled my eyes. "Hades," I bit out. "I want you to fuck me. Hard. Devour me. Make me forget everything but you."

"See?" He thrust into me, inch by inch. "Ask me, and I'll give you whatever you want."

"Hades." My hands clutched his shoulders as he fully thrust into me. I let out a loud moan. I tugged at the mating bond, love and need tangling so tightly that I couldn't tell where one ended and the other began.

His lips dragged down the column of my neck, teeth grazing over my skin before he sucked hard. "Hades," I repeated, like his name was the only prayer I knew.

His hands were everywhere, sliding down my sides, gripping my hips. "You drive me fucking insane," he whispered against my collarbone, lips trailing higher. "You're mine, mate," he said against my ear. "Mine to love." Hades pressed a kiss to my jaw. "To protect." A kiss to my neck. "To ruin." Teeth scraped over my skin. "You were made for me."

He growled low in his throat, pulling back, looking down, watching his length thrust into me. "Just like that," he rasped. "You take me so well."

I wound my arms around his neck, circling my hips, needing him deeper. "More."

His movements grew frantic as I raked my fingers down his back. He growled as he thrust, a smile sharp on his lips. "Gods, that feels so good," I whispered.

"No, not gods. Just me." His lips brushed against the shell of my ear. "The other gods don't touch you like I do. They don't make you scream their names like I do."

Pleasure thrummed through me, the bond a live wire under my skin.

"The other gods don't make you come like I do either." His thumb reached down to stroke my clit in tight, brutal circles that made my whole body seize. "Isn't that right, little goddess? Whose cock do you come on?"

I moaned a string of incoherent words.

Hades pulled out, just the tip of his cock still in my core.

I let out a gasp.

"Which god makes you come?" he asked.

"You, Hades."

He thrust back into me, stroking my G-spot, his thumb still brushing my swollen clit.

"Hades," I moaned.

"I love when you say my name while my cock is buried in that little pussy," he groaned.

"You're mine, Hades."

His mouth curved—not into a smile, but something sharper.

"Say it." My voice shook. "Say you belong to me too."

"I'm yours," he said, his words carrying weight.

My legs tensed, my thighs quivering, the orgasm building faster than I could stop it. "I want to come." I gasped. "I need to."

"Good goddess. I want you to scream my name as you come on my cock."

Pressure detonated inside me, tearing his name from my throat. I convulsed around him, my world narrowing to the god who held me, claimed me.

"Fuck," Hades muttered as his thrusts sped up. "Fuck," he repeated as his warmth spilled into me.

Hades pulled me close, his arms locking around me. He buried his face in the curve of my neck, his ragged breathing hot against my throat. He didn't speak at first. He just held me.

My throat tightened, but I didn't look at him. "If I lose everything… I want to remember this." My voice cracked. "Don't let me go."

He pulled back just enough to meet my eyes, his jaw tight, brows drawn together like the words physically hurt him. "I won't." He pressed a kiss to my forehead. "You'll survive the trials," he said against my skin.

"But—"

"You will," he cut me off.

I didn't answer.

We stayed like that, wrapped up in each other, hearts still pounding. For once, nothing else was falling apart.

Not yet, at least.

8

___

HADES

oom. Boom. Boom. Boom.

Wailed moans broke through the rhythmic war drums in my skull. They were hollow, stretched thin like something leaking from the cracks between realms.

I blinked my eyes open. Twin suns high in the gray sky glared down on me. I sat up too fast. The air churned, lifting fine grains of golden dust into a slow, spiraling accent around me.

The wind shifted. Sand caught in my eyelashes, tangled in my hair, and scattered a fine grit across my skin. It lodged itself deep in my mouth. I wiped at my face, but it clung stubbornly.

People moved around me... translucent people, drifting in every direction.

A sour churn twisted in my gut.

I stood. Blood rushed to my head, dizzying me. My throat clenched around nothing as I tried to swallow. There was no spit, no relief, only dust. Where am I?

I took a small step forward. I reached instinctively for a weapon at my side. There was nothing there. How did I get here? *My hands twitched and clutched at the empty air. My spine locked.*

Pressure built in my throat. I turned my head from left to right. I sucked in a breath of air that didn't feel fresh.

A tendril of shadow flowed in through my parted lips. It wormed past my teeth and pressed against my tongue, then shoved itself deeper, forcing my jaw open. I choked, but it didn't care. It wanted inside. I gagged at the ancient, bitter taste.

My lungs seized. I stumbled, my arms flailing as more shadows snaked around my face and plunged deeper down my throat. My limbs convulsed, but I stayed standing. Stop, stop, stop, *I tried to yell.*

They didn't stop.

Everything inside me froze. My eyes widened, but I couldn't move. Don't panic, *I told myself. I counted, imagining I was playing darts with Thanatos.*

One.

Two.

Three.

Four.

Five.

Six.

Seven.

The shadows stopped and I staggered back, dropping to my knees. My neck strained as a weight settled on my head. I couldn't raise my hands.

Burning took root in my chest. It wasn't pain exactly, but something worse, like a brand on my soul. Heat snaked through my veins, humming as it moved, curling and dancing like it belonged there.

I collapsed onto my back. The dull, gray sky above pulsed a blinding white, then black.

The ground trembled beneath me, a deep groan of the land itself.

Then—

Thousands of voices screamed all at once, carried like wind around me. "Welcome, King Hades."

9

PERSEPHONE

Soft sheets lay in loose tangles around my legs as I sat up, stretching, savoring the pleasant pull of muscles that were well-rested for once. I rubbed my eyes. The space beside me was empty. The only sign of Hades was a small white folded card. His scent lingered around me, so he must've woken up recently. I unfolded the note.

Look in the closet. Surprise. Meet us in the sparring room. -Hades

Today I was training with Orion and Gabriel. Hades had told me last night, his voice low against my hair before we fell asleep. I'd been away from training for a while, trying to sort through the weight of my own choice to pledge myself to the trials. But ready or not, it was time to move forward.

I stepped into the closet. A new section caught my eye, one that hadn't been there last night—an array of garments and shoes perfectly positioned on the wooden racks and shelves. The soft overhead light accentuated the rich, earthy colors of the fabrics. I ran my hand over wool, leather, cotton, fur, and silk. Each piece looked designed to protect me without hindering my flexibility. Seven different pairs of shoes lined the shelves, ranging from heavy knee-high boots to lighter shoes.

The longer I stood there, the tighter the knot grew in my stomach. This wasn't just a gift. It was preparation for the trials.

After choosing a black cotton long-sleeve, I paired it with fitted brown leather pants. I adjusted the sheath on my thigh over the leather, my fingers tracing the engravings on the gold handle. I lunged. The leather surprisingly allowed for a lot of movement, the seams in just the right places.

I put on one of the lighter pairs of shoes, considering we would be inside. I laced them up, mentally running through all the training I'd done with Hades and Gabriel in the past. I pulled my hair back into a tight ponytail.

Quick steps carried me through the corridors, the walls lined with the paintings I'd studied for hours. I didn't pay them much mind now, not with my thoughts racing about training.

Still, something tugged at the corner of my eye. This time, it was a figure I hadn't seen before. Tucked in the shadows of the battlefield scene, almost hidden by the gold frame, stood a woman draped in a black cloak. Her silver hair spilled in tangles over her shoulders, and her eyes—a solid white—stared forward. I could've sworn that hadn't been there before.

I shook my head and kept moving.

When I entered the sparring room, Hades, Gabriel, and Orion were already waiting. Weapons covered the white walls, gleaming under the lights. Orion walked to the center of the room. His smile stretched wide and his face shifted like he was barely holding back a laugh.

Orion wore a red sleeveless shirt and brown leather pants similar to mine, but with a more relaxed fit. His worn black leather boots reached his mid-calf. He had the build of a person crafted for war.

"Ready to get started?" Orion asked. His deep brown hair looked almost black as it clung to the sweat on his forehead. It was clear he'd already started training.

I nodded, pushing away the flutter of nerves in the pit of my stomach. He moved faster than I'd thought he would. My pulse stuttered. I didn't have any time to react before I was on the ground, a cold dagger pressed against my throat. Where had he even hidden that? The metal bit into my skin, not enough to cut, but enough to make my breathing ragged.

"I could kill you," he hissed, his red eyes locked with mine. "But I won't." He pushed off me and rose, then extended a hand. I eyed it but took it. Hades watched off to the side. His expression was neutral, no emotion in his eyes. But through the bond, his worry pulsed.

Orion raised a brow. "Why didn't you draw your dagger?"

Heat rushed to my cheeks. "I… forgot it was there," I admitted. "It all happened so fast."

He nodded, pursing his lips. "Do you know why you're wearing it?"

I crossed my arms. "Because Hades gave it to me." My words came out more defensive than I'd intended. "He told me to keep it on."

"Hades and the other Divine can't tell you about the trials, but I've been around long enough to know a few things."

The reminder of Orion's age struck me. I remembered just how little I knew about him, and about the rest of the team: Cassius, Gabriel, Aurelia, and Thanatos. I had been so consumed by our current battles, so wrapped up in my own struggles and fears, that I had never taken the time to learn much about them. How old was he? And the rest of them?

Orion continued, "I know that whatever you carry into the trials, you keep. You need to be prepared at all times."

"So I should always be armed?"

"Ideally, yes. But let's be practical. You won't sleep or shower in full battle gear. Just keep the dagger on you."

Orion's attacks were relentless and his movements precise, exploiting every hesitation, every flaw in my stance. He fought dirty, using tactics I'd never seen to keep me off balance. My muscles burned, and my breaths came in sharp gasps. Though the floor of the sparring room was padded, each impact still rattled my bones. Sweat dripped down my back, soaking my shirt and making it cling to my skin. The leather pants had seemed like a good choice before, but now they felt like a personal prison. I tried to adjust the material, but they didn't budge. *Great.* I was marinating in them. I shifted my focus back to Orion and not the sensory nightmare on my legs.

He shifted, and I readied myself for a strike, ducking and moving. Just as a smile spread on my lips, Orion took me down again.

I lay sprawled on the ground, copper flooding through my mouth. I ran my tongue over the tender spot on my lip; it was split. Shame burned hotter than the pain. He'd taken me down so easily, *again.*

I glared at the smirk on Orion's face. "You're cheating," I said, wiping the blood on my face away with the back of my hand.

He raised a brow. "And you think anyone trying to kill you will play fair?" He offered me a hand. "This isn't about fairness. It's about survival. The sooner you accept that, the better."

He was right, but I couldn't fight the anger bubbling within me. I pushed myself up, and he shrugged. "We'll keep going until you get it. You need to be prepared."

The training continued, each round a brutal reminder of my own mortality. If this had been real, I'd already be dead. Orion was merciless, but I supposed that was what I needed. I gritted my teeth and pushed through.

Finally, after what must have been hours, Orion stepped back with a satisfied look on his face. "That's enough for today," he said. "You're getting there."

It didn't feel like I was getting anywhere. I had learned one lesson today, though: survival had no rules.

I was glad we were done for the day. My shoulders sagged. Thank the Fates.

"My turn," Gabriel announced, his voice light with enthusiasm, green eyes bright in a way that was difficult to comprehend in my state of exhaustion. "Time to practice some magic."

My stomach plummeted. I blinked at him, praying he wasn't serious. I stared at Gabriel, but it didn't look like he was joking. I bit back a groan. My body was screaming for rest, but I nodded. This was my life now, a steady march toward an uncertain future. I wanted to prove myself to Hades, to the team, the entire pantheon, but most of all, to me.

I glanced at Hades. He gave me a small nod before leaving the room. The door clicked shut behind him, and I straightened. "Where should we start?" I said to Gabriel, and a ball of magic hurtled toward me.

10

HADES

I left Orion, Gabriel, and Persephone in the sparring room, sensing Hermes' presence. Though my power was strained, I'd grown attuned to the signature of his magic over the years. I walked next door to my study, expecting that he'd arrive any minute. I crossed to my desk and straightened one of the piles of books.

Sure enough, a soft knock rapped on the door. "Come in," I said.

Minthe entered, followed by Hermes. I barely spared her a glance, offering nothing more than a clipped nod before shifting my focus to Hermes. His shoulders were rigid, his jaw tight. It was the same look he'd worn when he came to deliver the news about Persephone's igniting ceremony.

Hermes, usually quick with a wink or smirk, stood stiffly, expression set. There was no laughter or any flirty remarks thrown Minthe's way.

"Hermes," I said. "Minthe, you're dismissed."

"Yes, my king." She nodded before scurrying away.

Hermes gave me a soft smile, his fingers twitching at his sides.

I placed my hand flat on my desk. "How can I help you?"

His smile widened, but it wasn't full of happiness or charm. The corners of his mouth quivered. "I have someone who wants to meet with you."

I narrowed my eyes. "Who? Can you have them send a parchment? I'm busy."

He shifted on his feet. "I think it's best if—"

I tapped my fingers on my desk in a rhythm. Index, middle, ring, pinky, then repeat. "Just tell me who it is and what this is about." My tone sharpened. "Now."

He let out a long exhale. "Demeter. She wants to meet with you."

Had I heard him right? "Demeter?" I parroted. "Why would she ever want to meet with me?"

Hermes shrugged and rolled his shoulders. A slow breath slipped from his lips. "I don't know. She wouldn't give me details."

"Where?"

"She's invited you to her estate."

"Of course she has." Where else but her sanctuary of marble and gold? "Fine."

～

After a few hours spent sentencing souls, I whisked to the Olympus realm, to Demeter's estate in Athens.

"Let's get this over with," I muttered to myself.

The sun lowered in the sky, casting a molten gold light and long, slanting shadows on the structure and the sprawling grounds. The estate loomed in a flawless white rectangle, every edge and angle in symmetry. Hedges were trimmed within an inch of their lives. Not a single leaf dared to fall out of place.

I pictured Persephone growing up here, a child in a home

full of breakable things. Small hands hovering over polished surfaces, porcelain one movement away from shattering.

I pushed open the iron gate. It didn't creak, though I knew it was old. It was well cared for, like everything else here. Except Persephone. My boots tapped against the stone path leading to the front door. Someone was watching. I could feel their eyes. I glanced around, but I saw no one.

Sheer curtains veiled every window on the front of the estate. They allowed just enough opacity to provide privacy. Long, thin candlesticks were set on the windowsill, neatly framed between the curtains and the glass. Their flames were perfectly centered, no wax dripping down their sides. They flickered and glowed, reflections dancing on the windows.

I lifted my chin and stretched my magic outward. The candles snuffed out, one by one, the smoke drifting up from them in lazy curls that shifted between silver, white, and a deeper gray. I'd expected the place to have serious wards on it. A dark part of me itched to set it ablaze and watch it crumble to ash.

The candles would have to be enough for now. I raised my fist, but a blond guard yanked the door open before I could knock.

He stood there with his shoulders slouched, shifting his weight from one foot to the other. Incompetent, from the looks of him. No wonder my mate had managed to break out of this place. No wrinkles marred the guard's buttoned shirt, but his belt was too high on one side. He lowered his head, his expression blank. He didn't say a word, only held the door wide.

I would have thought she'd have better guards, but I supposed she was using her resources elsewhere.

She had to be.

She had multiple stone pieces. If they were here, she'd have this place warded.

"Lady Demeter is waiting for you," the guard said stiffly.

I didn't acknowledge him as I walked past. The foyer hall stretched ahead. The walls were bare, except for one plain painting, a flat, lifeless landscape. It had no movement or depth, just brushstrokes made to fill space. There were no photographs, nothing to hint that this was anything more than a museum.

The floors gleamed, so polished that my reflection stared back at me. I continued until the corridor opened up to the living room. Demeter sat on one of the couches, tea in hand, her eyes locked on the roaring fireplace across the room. Her back was to me, her blonde hair styled into a tight bun.

I extended my magic just enough to snuff out the fire. It died without resistance. My jaw tensed. No wards outside her home and none inside either. This was either arrogance or something worse. Had she disabled them for my arrival?

Demeter turned her head to the right, just enough to look at me in her peripheral vision. Her fingers stilled on the armrest. "You came." She gestured, her hand sweeping through the air. "Sit."

My footsteps died as they touched the rug covering the floor. I lowered myself onto the couch across from her. The cushions didn't yield as I sat on the pristine fabric. Another item in this estate meant to be seen, not used.

She pointed to the bright gold teapot sitting on the glass table and a matching empty cup. "Tea?"

"No." My tone was flat. "What do you want?"

She let out a soft laugh, then crossed her legs, the teacup clinking as she set it down on the table. "Persephone has ignited the trials."

I locked any emotion behind my practiced mask. "Yes." I swallowed, hating the reminder. "And?"

She crossed her arms, her chin rising. "You're not actually

going to let her go through with that, are you?" Her voice rose. "The trials will destroy her."

My jaw tightened. "There's no going back now." Inhale in. Exhale out. I kept them controlled. I knew Demeter was hyper-analyzing me now. She'd invited me here under the guise of concern, but it was rooted in control, not care.

"It seems to me that you don't even care about her, then." Her sharp sigh surprised me. She ran a palm across her forehead. For the first time since I'd sat down, she looked less like the monster I knew she was and more like a mother unraveling.

I bit back a snarl. Her performance was good, but I wouldn't let myself fall for it. "Of course I care about her. She's my mate."

She scoffed. "I'm her mother."

Mother. "You abused her for years. You drugged her. You stole the stone piece that held Tartarus closed, endangering her. Shall I continue?"

Her hand rose. "I did those things for Persephone's own good. You wouldn't understand. You're not a mother."

I leaned forward. "No, I'm not, but it doesn't take being a mother to be a decent being."

Her lips thinned. She picked up her teacup and looked back at the smoke curling from the glowing fireplace logs. Her chin dipped ever so slightly as she folded her arms across her chest again, resting the cup against herself. "That isn't why I called you here. Do you have any plans to help her, or will you let her prance off to her death?"

"Why would I tell you?" I stood. "You've forfeited the right to consider yourself any kind of protector."

"She's my daughter." The last word was almost a plea.

I wouldn't be so easily bent. "Stop using that word," I snapped.

Her nose twitched. "There has to be something that can be done to stop this."

I stared at her, trying to see anything motherly in her expression. Why now? Why did she suddenly care what happened to Persephone after years of tearing her down? This was the woman who had taught Persephone that love was conditional, something that needed to be earned and could be revoked. She'd stolen the stone piece that kept Tartarus sealed, risking releasing the Titans and beings imprisoned. Was the threat of the Titans being released merely a potential consequence of getting the stone piece? Or worse—was trying to unleash them part of her plan? I waved a hand. "Want to use the stone pieces you've collected to dismantle the court?"

She sneered. "I don't know what you're talking about."

I let out a throaty laugh. "I don't know what game you're playing, but stay out of the trials. She's stronger than you think." The last thing Persephone needed was her *mother* meddling with the magic she'd already invoked. I walked away, glancing over my shoulder as Demeter downed the rest of her tea.

"You're a fool," she called after me. "She's not strong, and the little strength she has is only because I made her that way."

I pivoted to face her completely. "Strong because of you?" My voice drew taut. "The woman I know is stronger *in spite* of you, not because of you." I spat the words.

She stood, slamming the teacup down on the table. "You don't scare me. Remember you've always been a pathetic recluse. That's why they banished you to the Underworld, to get rid of you."

I chuckled, the sound rumbling low enough to blur into a growl. As if she could throw my past at me. "I don't have to scare you. You're busy scaring yourself. You're watching that little girl you tried to control, realizing that she's grown into a woman you can't manipulate anymore."

I took a few steps closer to her, leaning down to account for the height difference. "Mess with my mate, and I'll remind you what real fear feels like. I will reduce you to nothing." I bared my teeth in a humorless smile and straightened.

Her lips parted as if she was going to respond, but she stopped herself. I walked out of the prison she called a *home* and whisked back to the Underworld. I steadied, bracing myself on the corridor wall for a minute before going into the sparring room.

It was empty.

I walked through the halls, following the mating bond to our room. The door was ajar. I pushed it open, revealing Persephone sprawled on top of the duvet, wearing a red silk nightgown edged in black lace trim. Her sheathed blade peeked from beneath. I sank onto the bed, the mattress dipping under my weight. Persephone let out a muffled sound of protest.

"Hey." I leaned close to her, running a hand over her damp hair that curled at the ends. "Rough training?" I *knew* it had been rough. I'd watched before Hermes arrived. But that's why I was confident with Orion and Gabriel training her. They would push her.

Her eyelids cracked open just enough to see the gray I loved. "Understatement. Pain. My body." She closed her eyes again.

A low chuckle rumbled in my chest. She groaned as I shifted her so that she lay on her stomach. I repositioned myself and placed my hands on her shoulder blades, my thumbs pressing into the tight knots beneath her skin. Her head tipped forward, giving me more access. I worked in slow, deliberate circles.

She made a low sound, half a groan and half a sigh. "Wow," she murmured.

I kept my fingers moving, coaxing her muscles to relax. "You told me not to keep secrets from you."

She stilled under my touch.

"I saw Demeter today." My words were low as I continued to massage her soft skin.

"I don't want to hear about it now. Was it bad?"

"It was nothing important."

She blew a breath. "Then I don't want to hear about it at all. I have too many other things to focus on."

I pressed a kiss to her back and continued massaging her in silence. My mind wandered. I imagined her as a child and then a teenager. I understood all too well what it was like not to have the childhood others did. Persephone and I had grown up the same way—never safe.

Her breath deepened. After a few minutes, she emitted soft snores. I lifted and tucked her under the duvet, lingering to stroke the back of my knuckles along her cheek. "Rest, little goddess," I whispered, pressing a kiss to her forehead.

I turned off the lights and remained for a few beats, watching as the moonlight traced the soft rise and fall of her breathing. I'd join her soon. I had more souls to sentence first.

I paused in the doorway, my hand resting on the frame. I couldn't bring myself to leave her. Every instinct I had was anchored to Persephone. She could be pulled into the trials at any moment. I crossed back to the bed sank down beside her, settling above the duvet, my back pressed against the headboard. I could work from here.

I closed my eyes and took a deep breath as I turned inward.

Time to sentence souls.

In my mind's eye, the world shifted. The quiet bedroom

fell away, replaced by the familiar chill of the throne against my back. A faint smile tugged at the corners of my mouth as I remembered the first time I showed Persephone the Underworld's magic. The way her eyes widened when she understood the truth: that sentencing souls all existed within my mind.

My fingers curled around the throne's jagged edges. Torches lined the walls leading up to the dais, where my seat of judgment loomed, their flames flickering in restless patterns. The light caught the black gemstones dangling from the wrought iron chandelier above.

The line of souls stretched before me, and off to the side, I could feel him.

Basile.

My jaw clenched, a bitter taste coating my tongue at the thought of his name.

I kept him seated on the floor, apart from the others. I hadn't sentenced him.

Not yet.

He had served as one of Persephone's guards. He had stood by, watching the abuse she endured. He had first appeared in the queue a few days ago. Time was not straight between death and sentencing. Some souls arrived in the Underworld quickly, others wandered before the magic of this realm eventually dragged them here. In the past weeks, Thanatos and I had been trying to keep up with the line, but with all the current stressors, we were falling behind.

When I'd reached into Basile's mind, I had seen her. His memories had slammed into me. I'd heard her scream, her voice raw as she'd pleaded for help. He'd given none. I'd had to stop, pull back before I did something irreversible. I wasn't ready.

I couldn't be reckless. Not now.

So I had left him there.

I shifted my gaze to the next soul in line, an older man with a stubborn patch of black hair clinging to his scalp. His sunken eyes lowered to the floor. He bowed, his hands trembling in front of him. "Your name?" I asked.

"Jeffrey."

"Anything you wish to tell me?"

He swallowed, lacing his fingers together. "I-I lived a long life. I have regrets, of course, but I ask you to bring me to my wife, Margaret." He toyed with the gold band around his left ring finger. "I don't know how this afterlife works, but—"

I held up a hand, silencing him. I pressed into his mind. Regret bloomed first, memories of men he'd killed on a battlefield. Fire. Smoke. Screams.

Then memories of his wife washed over. Anniversaries. His fingers in her hair. Late nights together. The first cry of their child. The warmth of his lover in his arms. Their wrinkled hands laced together as she whispered goodbye.

Something tightened in my chest. This mortal had exactly what I wanted with my mate. He did not beg for a light sentence. He didn't choose to weep and lie. He thought of her.

I nodded. "All right." With a thought, he vanished, the magic of the Underworld pulling him to his sentence. He'd face his wrongs. But once he did, Margaret would be waiting for him.

I forced myself to focus and move on to the next soul.

But Basile's presence lingered at the edge of my vision. I turned my head. "Do you think I've forgotten about you?" My voice boomed around the throne room. He could've stopped her pain. He should've.

He said nothing back because he couldn't. He was bound by my magic. I'd leave him there to rot until I was ready to sentence him—or let Persephone do it.

11

PERSEPHONE

I sat on the stone bench in the heart of the courtyard. The breeze wove around me, carrying the scent of blooming flowers. Petals unfolded in every color, some veined with contrasting hues. Sunlight washed over my skin. It filtered through the lush foliage, casting patterns on the ground that reminded me of lace and beading on a dress. Wisps and iridescent butterflies fluttered nearby. Birds chirped melodies. The space was a living painting, every inch brimming with life.

A gust whipped past, lifting strands to tickle my face. I didn't brush them away. I couldn't break the moment. "You're the drama of Olympus," a voice broke through my peace.

Minthe.

My eyes snapped open and the lush setting disappeared, replaced by reality—the dusty courtyard. Minthe stood before me, her presence cold as always. Her lips were curled into a smirk, the very image I imagined when I read of villains. I met her gaze, forcing a wide smile. "Minthe. How surprising to see you."

A red-painted nail tucked a strand of her blonde, shoulder-length hair behind her ear. The glossy polish caught the light of the twin suns. "It seems you can't help but be the center of everyone's attention. Always the drama."

I had neither the energy nor the inclination to engage with Minthe. I had to focus on training for the trials. I closed my eyes, drifting back to the peace I had before. "I'm rather tired today," I said. "I'd prefer not to feed into this."

She let out a maniacal laugh, the sound so sharp that it sliced through the air. "You really think you have what it takes to be on the court?"

"Mm-hmm," I hummed, the sound vibrating my mouth. The question stirred my anxiety, but I'd never reveal that truth to Minthe. I bit the inside of my cheek and gave her an unfriendly smile.

Minthe opened and closed her mouth, a perfect impression of a startled fish. "Well, you don't." Her perfectly kept light eyebrows knit together as her voice escalated.

I wouldn't give her the reaction she clearly wanted. "Thank you."

"Seriously?"

"If you're looking for a reaction, you're not going to get one." At times like this, I wondered why Hades kept her around. No one could ever be good enough at a job to justify an attitude like this. He'd offered to get rid of her for me before. I should have let him.

Minthe huffed, her nostrils flaring. "You think you're better than everyone."

My pulse thundered in my ears. I wanted to react, but I wouldn't. If I let one very irritating nymph bother me, how could I ever trust myself to stay focused when I was pulled into a trial? This wasn't about her. She was nothing but noise. "I think you're projecting."

"You—"

Part of me wanted to ask her why she didn't like me, but I held the words back. "Just stop," I said.

Silence. She stormed into the palace. I sank back into the stillness behind my eyelids. This encounter would've bothered me weeks ago, but now I had bigger issues to worry about. I needed to have a clear mind, and I wouldn't let anyone distract me from what I needed to do.

Survive.

12

HADES

My chest heaved, the remnants of the dream clawing at me. I sat up too quickly, my head going light. I closed my eyes and braced my hands on my thighs. My breathing slowed after a few deliberate inhales and exhales, but my frantic heart refused to follow suit.

I glanced over at Persephone. The moonlight draped her body with a soft, silvery glow. Her dark hair spread across the pillow, creating a shape that reminded me of twisted trees. I picked the duvet up, glancing at her body. She wore a navy blue silk nightgown that had shifted as she moved in her sleep. It was irrelevant compared to what needed to be strapped to her thigh. My gaze slid down her legs.

There. The dagger was still in its sheath.

I let out a breath and pulled myself out of bed. My footsteps were soft as I moved to the washroom. I flicked the switch on with a single finger, closing the door behind me. Brightness flooded the room. My fingers splayed on the countertop. The chill was sharp. My eyes fixed on the dark stone sink, the gold drain reflecting the light fixture above.

I welcomed the cold. I welcomed anything but the memories. I rolled my neck up slowly, a faint pop running through my vertebrae. My muscles groaned, constantly tight from stress. I brought one of my hands to my cheek, tugging slightly under my eye and staring at the reflection in the mirror. I looked terrible. The dark circles were worse than yesterday, and I knew they'd deepen tomorrow.

We needed the stone piece to keep Tartarus shut. Keeping it sealed drained my energy. I clenched my teeth and let my eyelids fall closed. Fuck the memories that haunted my dreams. I'd spent so long trying to forget them, trying to replace them, only for them to dredge up at the worst possible moment. There was no time for me to try to catalog my feelings.

They didn't matter.

I summoned Cerberus.

The dog spent his days roaming the Underworld. We shared a bond that allowed me to call him with just a thought. Cerberus had been part of this realm long before I had been assigned to it. Heavy footsteps padded across the bedroom floor. I pulled open the washroom door, careful to keep quiet. I didn't want to wake Persephone.

I walked over to Cerberus and gave the loyal dog a long pat, running my hand over the sleek, jet-black fur. I'd never named any of the heads. They'd always just been one to me.

I slipped into the closet and threw on some clothes. I'd need my magic to whisk, so I wouldn't waste it on simple tasks. I went back into the bedroom. "Watch her." I pointed a finger at my mate, still sleeping soundly in our bed.

I hated leaving her, especially now. But if I stayed, I'd rot from the inside out, the darkness taking over. "Please."

Cerberus let out a soft yip. I stared at Persephone for a few more moments. The thought of her vanishing into the trials while I was gone sent cold dread spreading through my chest. But she needed me steady, ready for whatever came next. I tapped my fingers on my thigh.

One.

Two.

Three.

I will be quick.

I whisked to the mortal realm. I took a deep inhale, letting the cigarette smoke fill my lungs. I never did understand why mortals liked these things.

The lighting was low, ceiling fixtures casting a bronze glow over everything. Cinnamon-colored leather booths wrapped the walls in supple curves. In the seats the patrons favored, the material had faded to a lighter, worn shade. A stage stood at the side of the room, just one step off the ground. The single light above it illuminated its scarred wooden surface, serving as some semblance of a spotlight.

The club was closed. Three men sat at one of the booths. They nursed whiskey and cigarettes—one with a cigar—counting their money and murmuring to each other, oblivious to my presence. I was here for Jack Gondice, but since Mark Elether and Dan Reponso were here, I would take them too.

Jack leaned back, lacing his hands together and cracking them. His salt-and-pepper hair was slicked back, but a few stubborn strands stuck up. A thick scar curved along his jawline, a relic of a fight I had witnessed from a soul's memory.

Mark was the youngest of the trio. His mouth barely moved as he spoke, his dark eyes searching the other two men for approval. He licked his thumb and counted the money.

Wrinkles creased Dan's face like the worn leather underneath them. His silver hair was cropped close, glimmering even in the dim lighting. He raised the short glass to his lips, sipping slowly.

A loud, wet hack, surely full of phlegm, cut my careful observation of the room. I stepped closer. Jack's gaze flicked to me. "We're closed. Outta here." His thick, shaky finger pointed to the stairs off to the right.

Mark groaned, looking up from the money he was counting. "We always have these fucking stragglers. I thought you said Joey cleared the place out."

"He did," Dan said with a grimace.

I stayed silent. Tendrils of my dark magic slithered outward, curling and twisting through the air toward the men.

"What the fuck are you doing?" Dan yelled, clenching his fingers around the glass.

I smirked as shock spread across their faces. I loved this part. They made an awkward attempt to stand, the alcohol and table working against them. My power was faster than they could ever be, wrapping around their ankles and snaking up their legs and torsos until it coiled around their throats. Their screams turned into grunts, which turned into strangled gasps as I cut their air off.

I stood a few feet away, my hands tapping on my thigh. My eyes half-closed, dimming the cheap lighting until only the men remained in focus. A shudder rolled through me. The tension that had coiled tight in my muscles melted away, and my shoulders sank. I basked in their suffering, the way agony contorted their expressions. I willed my magic to constrict, then eased it back so they could draw in a breath.

And just as they'd thank whatever deity they prayed to for air, my magic would cut it off again.

I stood for maybe five minutes, letting my darkness terrorize them. In moments like these, I was able to chase my own pain away.

Numb it.

Force it into something useful.

Persephone deserved better than a mate full of darkness, especially when it was seeping into her. Something knotted in my chest, and I pressed a knuckle there.

My mate's face flashed in my mind. My fingers curled into fists at the thought of her being tainted by me. A growl tore from my throat. I pushed harder, the energy I could spare surging from me like a roaring flood.

The men stiffened, spasming once before going limp. I pulled my magic back. Their bodies slumped forward onto the table, tipping glasses and scattering cash. The still-lit cigarettes and cigar smoldered, tiny burns eating at the bills. I took a step closer. "See you in the Underworld."

I whisked back to my realm. Persephone was still asleep.

"Thank you," I said to Cerberus. "You're dismissed." I gave each head a little scratch before he disappeared.

I tugged the collar of my shirt over my head, then swept my hair out of my face. My pants followed, landing in a small pile on the floor. As I climbed into bed, Persephone stirred beside me. I let my eyelids fall shut.

"Hades?"

My eyes snapped open and I turned, facing her. "Yes?"

"Are you all right?"

I tugged her close, letting her form rest on mine. Warmth seeped into my skin, her breathing soft against my chest. I hesitated. "I'm here."

Persephone yawned as she shifted. "You would tell me if you weren't all right, right?"

Quiet stretched between us. I wanted to say yes. I wanted to tell her the darkness was getting louder, that memories I'd worked hard to push to the recesses of my mind were now bleeding into my nights. But what good would that do? She had enough burdens. I wouldn't make her carry mine too.

A small snore escaped her. I swallowed hard and let my gaze drag up to the ceiling. Sleep had spared me the shame.

13

PERSEPHONE

took a deep breath. "I'm honored," I said.

Minthe scoffed. "I don't care if you're honored."

I glanced up at her and away from the invitation Sera and Evangeline had sent. Minthe leaned against the doorway to Hades' and my bedroom. My lips curled into a sneer before I could catch myself. Right. Minthe. I needed to remember who I was talking to. She was not worth the energy.

I pressed my lips together to keep from smiling. Sera and Evangeline were inviting me to spend time with them, outside of the services they performed for me. I'd never been invited to just... hang out.

"So are you going or not?" Minthe asked, her voice cutting like a whip.

"Gods," I muttered under my breath, but I nodded.

Minthe turned on her heel, and I followed. We slipped through the palace corridors and out into the open air. I kept close, moving through one of the small communities of souls.

The vibrancy in this realm had long since vanished—no plants, no bright colors. The houses stood stripped down to their bare necessities, a reminder of what was lost.

We needed the stone piece.

The souls moved about, dipping their heads when they saw me. I pressed my nails into my palms. If they knew the truth—that I was the one who had let Demeter into this realm by completing the mating bond with Hades—would they still think I was worthy of respect?

I blinked hard, willing the sting of tears away. I wouldn't cry. I'd done enough of that.

"This is it," Minthe said as we stopped in front of a small gray house. It reminded me of the one I'd slept in when I first came to the Underworld. Before I could say anything, she'd already turned away.

I knocked on the door.

"Come in," Sera called from inside, stretching the words in a playful lilt.

I took a steadying breath, gripped the knob, pushed the door open, and stepped inside. The house was dark, aside from the slivers of light filtering through the gap in the drawn curtains. I shut the door behind me, blinking as the room flooded with brightness.

"Surprise!"

My shoulders snapped back, my heart slamming against my ribs. My chest tightened, working to pull in a breath. A group of souls stood before me, their faces alight with excitement. Sera and Evangeline stepped forward. Beside Evangeline stood a man with short, curly hair, his fingers laced with hers. This must have been her husband—her soulmate, as she called him.

White-painted walls made the small room feel a little larger despite the low ceiling. A couch and coffee table were pushed off to the side to make room.

"We know you've been stressed, so we wanted to throw you a little party," Sera said.

My throat prickled as I glanced at the souls. My mouth opened, but no words came out. "W-wow," I finally stammered. "I've never had anyone throw me a party before."

"Well, now you have." Sera pulled me into a hug.

One of the souls stepped forward when Sera released me, an older man with a large black beard. "Lady Persephone, it's an honor to meet you."

"Just Persephone is fine. There is no need for formalities."

Evangeline wiggled her eyebrows. "One day, it will be *Queen* Persephone."

Sera clasped her hands together. "Time for the music."

A few souls lifted violins, the soft gleam of polished wood catching the ceiling light. They raised the bows above the strings and unleashed an upbeat melody that filled the space. I stood there drinking it in, my cheeks aching from my smile. The room burst into life as the souls whirled and danced to the music.

Evangeline grabbed my hand, pulling me closer. "I hope this cheers you up, even just a little."

"I—" I swallowed. "I really appreciate this."

She squeezed my fingers. "It's the least we could do."

I shook my head. "None of this was necessary. This is all just—" I paused. "Thank you."

"Well, we wanted to." She smiled. "I apologize. We don't have any food."

Right. Souls didn't eat. "Oh, no, that's okay. I'm not even hungry."

Evangeline tugged my hand and spun me. She twirled me around, and a breathy laugh bubbled up my throat before I could stop it. "Dance, Persephone. This party is for you."

~

 I sat in the greenhouse Hades had built for me, the only place in the Underworld where lush foliage still existed. Everything in here was perfect. I should've found this comforting, but as I looked around, I felt hollow. I shifted on the blanket beneath me. My fingers curled into the fabric of my dress. The warm, damp air clung to my exposed skin.

The landscape of the souls' home had been taken away, and here I was in this small oasis. I chewed on my lip, my gaze flitting to the soft glow of the floating lights hovering between the clusters of hanging orchids. I had too much, while they had so little left.

"What's wrong?" Hades asked, breaking through the mess of my thoughts.

"Nothing," I whispered.

Hades' lips pressed into a thin line, the corners of his eyes crinkling. For a moment, I thought he might say something, but he only exhaled. Thank gods he didn't press. He sat beside me, one hand tucked behind him. "I brought you here for a reason. I don't know if you're aware, but... happy birthday."

He pulled out a white plate he had hidden. A small pastry coated in pink, glossy frosting rested on it, a lit candle at its center.

"I know you like the mortal books," Hades said as he watched me. "This is something they do. They make a wish and blow out the candle." His expression shifted into a smile. "Happy twenty-fourth birthday, Persephone."

Twenty-four.

I hadn't even realized it was November fifteenth.

Time had blurred since I came to the Underworld. I had stopped counting the days, the weeks, the months. I used to count them all, tracking as many seconds as I was alert enough to, waiting for the day I would finally be free.

Birthdays had been small milestones that might've brought me closer to freedom—or death, which for most of my life had felt like the same thing.

I swallowed. I'd never had a pastry with a candle before. Most of my birthdays, I had spent huddled up in my room, living the same day as the rest of them. "Come on," Hades said. "Blow it out."

My fingers trembled as I leaned forward. "I have to think of what I want to wish for."

Hades placed a hand on my back. "I'm sure there's something you want."

I squeezed my eyes shut, my hands clenched into fists in my lap. *Fates, help us find the piece of the Nexus Stone in Faerie for Tartarus. Please. Restore the balance in the Underworld.* I blew.

The thin pink and white candle flickered out, a spiral of smoke rising into the air. Hades said nothing as he pulled me into a hug, careful to keep the plate steady with one hand. His chin rested on top of my head. I let my eyes close, sinking into the comfort.

When he pulled back, he offered me the plate. I plucked the candle from the pastry, setting it aside. Lifting the dessert to my mouth, I took a bite.

It was soft and sweet on my tongue. "It's really good," I said between a few mouthfuls. I blinked. "Did you tell the souls it's my birthday?"

His brows pulled together. "No."

I swallowed another bite. "They threw me a party."

Something flickered in his eyes, but it quickly disappeared. "A birthday party?"

"A party to cheer me up." I licked frosting from my

fingers as Hades watched me. A heavy knot tightened in my chest as a pale, iridescent butterfly settled on my knee, its wings opening and closing in a slow rhythm—as if the world outside this glass structure didn't exist. *How unfair it is that I sit here in a beautiful greenhouse, while the rest of the Underworld suffers?*

14

PERSEPHONE

The next morning was quiet, save for the clink of cutlery against the plates. Despite the facade of calm that Hades, Gabriel, and Orion wore, I knew they were nervous. It had settled over the four of us yesterday when Orion and Gabriel told us everything was ready—that we'd be leaving today—just after Hades and I had returned to the palace from the greenhouse.

The two fae had been planning the trip for a while, but I hadn't expected it to come so soon or with so little warning.

This might've been the last peaceful meal we'd have for at least a week. The plate before me sat untouched, the meat, bread, fruit, and jam still perfectly arranged. The colors blurred as visions of what might await us in Faerie stole my focus.

"You're not eating," Hades said from beside me, his voice cutting through my thoughts.

I glanced at my plate, then back at him. His steady gaze saw through the walls I'd once thought impenetrable. Part of me loved that. The other part loathed it. I supposed it was part of having a mate. I shrugged, but the movement felt forced. "I'm just thinking."

"I know." He placed a hand on my shoulder, his touch grounding. *Eat*, he said through the bond. *You'll need your energy.*

Across the table, Gabriel ate quietly, his light brown hair gleaming in the morning light streaming through the glass ceiling. He cut his meat with mechanical movements, not looking up once. Orion lounged next to him, but even his lazy sprawl couldn't hide the tension in his hands, clenching and releasing around his fork.

"We should leave soon." Gabriel's words were clipped as he set his utensil down.

I nodded, forcing myself to pile food into my mouth. My nerves had stolen any sense of an appetite, but I knew that Hades was right. I needed to eat. Eventually, the hunger would catch up to me, and it would only slow us down if I didn't fuel my body now. I'd be even more of a burden.

Around the table, the others did the same. No one spoke.

Thanatos strolled into the dining room, his heavy black boots echoing against the floor. His dark eyes swept over us.

Orion stood up with a crooked grin, and Thanatos pulled him into a rough hug, clapping him hard on the back. Orion chuckled, though the tightness around his eyes didn't fully ease. Thanatos moved to Gabriel next, pulling him into a firm, brief embrace.

When he turned to me, I hesitated before pushing to my feet. His arms wrapped around me, and my muscles tensed as I thought back to the resentful glances Thanatos used to give me.

Thanatos released me, stepping away and moving closer to Hades. He gripped his shoulders and yanked him close. They came together with a thud as Thanatos clapped Hades' back. It was a firm, quick hug, one I imagined brothers would give each other.

"Be careful. Bring yourselves back alive," Thanatos said, his gaze flickering between each of us. "And bring back that stone piece." His mouth quirked up into a grin.

~

We stood in the Realm Gateway. "One last thing. The glamour." Gabriel waved his hand, and magic bloomed at his fingertips. I closed my eyes and braced myself, the familiar weight of his magic enchanting us.

Hades and I couldn't risk being recognized. Divine didn't exactly blend easily in Faerie, where Hades had told me our kind rarely went. If word of our travels reached Demeter, I was sure she'd waste no time trying to find the stone piece before us. Aurelia and Cassius had given us the stone's location at the cost of many of their own, a sacrifice that would mean nothing if she reached it first.

I smiled at Hades despite how strange it was seeing him this way again. His blond hair gleamed under the dim light, a stark contrast to the black it had been moments ago. His gray eyes had deepened to violet.

I glanced down. My simple garments were gone, replaced by a dark green long-sleeve with small flowers embroidered at the cuffs, chocolate brown leather pants, and mahogany riding boots. I twisted a strand of my now-golden hair around my finger. The texture was the same, but the color wasn't. I pushed it behind my tapered ears.

"Don't forget. No magic for the two of you," Gabriel said, pointing a finger between Hades and me.

I nodded. Using our magic would alert the Faerie Courts to our Divine presence.

"Let's do this." Orion grinned and rubbed his hands together, shaking out his legs and arms. Gabriel stepped through the shimmer. Orion followed.

Hades took my hand in his and squeezed. I nodded, not needing him to ask if I was ready. I didn't have a choice. We stepped through together.

The world shifted violently around us, and for a moment, I was weightless. The ground tilted dizzyingly, and I reached out, gripping Hades' arm to steady myself. He held me firmly. The last time I'd crossed into Faerie, the disorientation had been overwhelming. Now it was gentler, though the air shifted and rippled around me in ways my body couldn't keep up with.

I stilled and took in the Spring Court. The vibrant green trees stretched high into the endless sky, leaves shimmering with veins of gold. Everything was radiant, flowers in vivid shades I didn't have names for. Magic hummed under my skin, but I pushed it away. I pressed a hand to my stomach, surprised to find it settled, unlike the last time I was here.

"Are you all right?" Hades studied my face.

I managed a smile. "I'm fine." I'd grown used to saying that, but this time it was true. "More than fine. Faerie feels different this time. Better."

Hades' lips twitched into a big smile. "You're adjusting to Faerie's magic."

The rustling leaves, the gurgle of a nearby stream, and the songs of the birds drowned out my low laughter. "It's definitely better than vomiting everywhere."

He laughed. His hand still gripped mine, and we followed Gabriel and Orion down the winding path. The fae looked more luminous in this realm. Everything about them was just *more*. Stones crunched and skittered to the sides, some patches covered with moss. "We're here," Hades said.

Just as the last word left his mouth, the stone cottage

came into view, nestled between two towering oaks. I hadn't had the chance to see it during the day last time.

A break in the trees let harsh sunlight pour toward me. I squinted into the glare ahead raising a hand to shield my eyes. Shapes moved among the trees and in front of the sun, casting a shadow that eased the brightness and allowed me to drop my arm.

"Hades—" I whispered. My body locked rigid, every beat of my heart battering my ribs as I took in the massive, serpentine shapes ahead. They were enormous.

Dragons.

The ground trembled as one of them moved. All of their scales—crimson, chestnut, and obsidian—shimmered under the sunlight like liquid metal. "You didn't mention *dragons*."

"Must have slipped my mind." Hades' tone was playful, far too calm in the presence of the beasts before us. He looked at them as if they were nothing more than a flock of birds. Hades tugged on my hand, dragging me closer to the beasts behind the cottage. My feet dug into the ground, my toes curling inside my boats as if I could anchor myself to the earth. "Come," he said.

As we drew closer, one of the dragons let out a low growl that vibrated through the air and my bones. The hairs on my arms rose underneath my long sleeves. It made me feel small and insignificant. The obsidian dragon lowered its massive head toward me. I pulled away, using Hades as a shield. Waves of heat rolled from its nostrils, and sweat trickled down my back. My pulse kicked up. Its gaze locked on me, pinning me into place.

"They won't hurt you," Hades said softly as he stepped forward, patting the dragon's snout, his leather-gloved hand gliding over its scales. The creature's eyes shut, and its growl turned to a purr as it leaned into Hades' touch. "They're bonded to me, Orion, and Gabriel."

"Friends, in their own way," Gabriel added as he approached the one with scales so rich they reminded me of blood. The dragon's massive, taloned foot stepped forward and sank into the moss-covered ground as it lowered itself. He reached out, resting a hand on its snout like Hades had.

"Friends?" The word came out more like a squeak than I'd intended.

Gabriel let out a breath of laughter. "They are fae just as much as Orion and me."

It was difficult to think of these things as fae.

Give them a chance, Hades spoke into my mind.

"We'll be riding them," Orion said as he walked over to the chestnut one.

My mouth hung open. "Ride?" My voice broke. "Ride the dragons."

"Yes, little goddess. This will be a much faster way to travel since we can't whisk, not without using magic. The Spirit Court is far." Hades paused. "There are only two Realm Gateways in all of Faerie—one in the Spring Court, and the other in the Winter Court. The latter will be closest to us once we have the stone piece, but that one is guarded. We'd never get in *and* out with the stone before someone noticed. We can only risk using it as our escape."

He stepped away from the black dragon that was still eyeing me—hopefully not like a snack. Hades' body brushed against mine. "Trust me."

Those two words held more weight than he knew. I met his gaze. "Fine."

"We're all packed up," Gabriel sasid. I'd been so shocked by the creatures that I hadn't even noticed the band around each dragon's midsection, with bags attached to them and a saddle on top. Gabriel shot me a knowing look. "Enchanted saddles." He grinned. "Fire-resistant and durable. They were expensive but so worth it."

Orion wandered over to Gabriel, speaking something too low for me to hear.

Gabriel's brows furrowed. "You didn't buy goggles? I already got rid of our old ones."

Orion shrugged. "You're the one who wrote the supply list. You didn't put goggles on it." He emphasized each word.

Gabriel opened his mouth, then promptly shut it. "We'll have to fly without goggles for now," he muttered.

Hades pulled me toward the black dragon. "This is Faladonax."

Hello, goddess. You may call me Falon, a low voice said in my mind. *Do not be scared. I will not let you fall.*

The dragon was speaking to me. I froze and gave it a weak smile. *Comforting. Thanks.*

The dragon huffed, dipping its massive head as low as it could. Hades helped me onto Falon's back. I gripped his arm, the dragon's scales smooth beneath my fingers as we climbed. Hades swung up behind me, the saddle creaking under his weight as he pulled me back against his chest. I tightened my grip on the handle as if that could save me from the idea of flying on this large beast. Hades secured the straps around me.

I'm a beast?

My eyes widened. *You heard me think that?*

You're bonded to my rider. When you're screaming your thoughts, I hear it.

Screaming?

Loudest I've heard in a long time. You are very bad at protecting your thoughts. You'll have to work on that before we get near the Spirit Court. Spirit Faeries are dangerous. They can tap into your mind.

Oh.

Falon laughed. *Yes, maybe learning how to whisper is in order.*

Uh, all right.

So, beast?

I cringed. *Is that offensive?*

Of course not. I am a beast. I am vicious and strong.

Stop, Hades said.

Falon huffed. *I enjoy when pretty goddesses call me a beast.*

Hades patted Falon. *Hey.*

You used to be more fun, Hades.

Hades let out a long, low chuckle, the sound vibrating against the skin at the back of my neck. He ran his hands up and down my arms before landing on my shoulders and squeezing.

I studied Gabriel and Orion on their dragons. They looked small on the beasts beneath them. The saddles were little more than scraps of leather over the muscle and scales. Hades must've noticed my gaze because he added, "Gabriel's dragon is named Rysshe. Orion's dragon is Sepheronx. I wish we had more time for introductions. Are you ready?"

I glanced back at Hades. "Truthfully, no. But I suppose I don't have a choice, do I?"

Hades' grip on me tightened. "You'll love it."

I swallowed hard. Gabriel's and Orion's dragons shot into the sky, their massive wings beating, shaking the ground beneath us. The air whipped against my face and hair. Orion let out a long yell that was swallowed by the rush of wind. His dragon surged forward, Gabriel's trailing close behind.

Falon's muscles rippled under our legs. He let out a low growl, the vibration traveling through my body, working its way up to my teeth and ears.

We lifted off the ground. Air tore past us as Falon drove higher. My stomach dropped. I screamed. "Oh, gods!"

Remember, inside voice, little goddess.

If I hadn't been so scared, I would've rolled my eyes. Panic flared in my chest, each breath coming short and uneven. The ground fell away beneath us, and the sky stretched in every direction. I gripped the saddle with one hand and Hades' arms around me with the other. Hammering filled my ears—my pulse. My fingers trembled. Stray strands of hair lashed around my face as the dragon soared higher, cutting through the clouds. I should've tied it back, but I hadn't thought of it.

The land below us was a blur of colors and shapes, and for the first time I understood what that little bird perched outside my window experienced.

Untethered—free.

I remembered clearly how the bird had darted into the sky, its delicate yellow wings catching the sunlight. How I had envied that tiny creature, wishing I could follow it and break free from the life I lived. Looking back, I couldn't help but cringe at how foolish and simple the planning of my escape had been. It could've ended very badly.

Maybe the Fates had helped me, or maybe I'd just been lucky. Either way, it was irrelevant now. A bad plan only mattered if it failed, and mine hadn't.

I was free.

And sitting on a dragon, slicing through the sky, with my mate's arms around me.

Movement caught my eye, a dark shape sweeping through the clouds far ahead. It was another dragon, its rider a blur against the sky. "Wow," I whispered.

Tension still lingered in my body, but I couldn't help the smile that spread across my face. I turned just enough to catch a glimpse of Hades' expression. He was watching me, his eyes filled with something raw. "You're smiling," he said against my ear.

I'm flying, I spoke through the bond. I didn't want to compete with the wind or the laugh bubbling up from deep within me.

His arms tightened around me. *We're going to the Viento*

Field. Before I could ask what that was, he continued. *It's a dragon field. Dragons who are looking for a rider wait there. Should one of them think you are worthy, they will pick you.*

They will pick me? Not the other way around?

Absolutely not. Dragons don't like to be owned, picked, or do anything they don't want to.

I was tired of going into so many situations unprepared, so I asked. *How did it go when you went?*

Obviously, I was successful, but I remember it being exciting and stressful. I needed a dragon so that Gabriel and Orion could show me more around Faerie. It's really the most efficient way to travel.

What happens if no dragon picks me?

Hades smirked at me. *Then we'll have to share this saddle.*

I shrugged. *That doesn't sound like the worst thing in the world.*

I love being close to you, but these saddles get a little uncomfortable over time. In truth, I don't think you'll have any issues having a dragon pick you. You're arriving with dragons, which will keep you safe, you're strong, and I'm sure that any of them would enjoy having you as a rider.

A dozen worst-case scenarios looped in my head, each more irrational than the last, but none of them felt impossible. *Safe from what? Do people die at this field? I'm nervous.*

No one who comes with dragons at their side is harmed. It's an unspoken rule among their kind. Just keep your eyes low. You don't want a dragon to think you're challenging it. Stand in the ditch and wait.

That's it?

Yes, you'll see. We're here.

15

PERSEPHONE

"Oh gods." My stomach twisted as Falon lowered, his wings beating in rhythmic, powerful strokes. The field stretched before us, a sea of scales and wings. Dragons of every size and color filled the space, most of their forms glinting under the sun. Others stayed in the shadows of the mountains with jagged peaks that loomed high, their hulking forms little more than ominous outlines.

From above, I'd thought the line carved into the earth was just a scar of the land. But as we dipped lower, I realized it was the ditch Hades had mentioned, a narrow channel that stretched across the entire field.

Faeries stood along it, scattered at wide intervals, motionless, their heads bowed.

A few dragons turned toward us, their heads tilting to watch our arrival. Falon landed with a loud thud. Orion's and Gabriel's dragons touched down beside us. I couldn't believe the sheer number of scaled giants gathered here.

Hades gave my shoulders a squeeze, the gesture sending comfort flooding through me. He swung out of the saddle and slid down Falon's side. "Come down." Hades waved a hand.

I glanced at him and tried to replicate his movement. I rushed toward the ground. I yelped as my boots scrambled uselessly for traction, my body tipping sideways. My stomach swooped, and my face twisted into a grimace. I braced for impact, my limbs flailing—

But I never hit the ground.

Strong arms caught me. Hades' arms. "You didn't think I'd let you get hurt, did you?"

I stared up at him, a shiver running through me from the rush of it all. I couldn't speak, too overwhelmed.

Something unreadable flashed in his eyes. His hand slid to the back of my neck, and he leaned in, his lips brushing my forehead. Warmth skimmed over my skin before he pressed a light kiss. "You're my mate. Of course I would catch you."

My cheeks prickled with a flush I couldn't stop, and a flutter bloomed in my chest. Hades pulled away. "Let's do this," he said.

Gabriel and Orion stood nearby. They gave me small smiles. "Eyes down. Let's get you a dragon," Hades said as he steered me only a few feet away, guiding me into the ditch. Dry earth crumbled beneath my boots, fine dirt swirling up in little clouds around my feet. The ridge of the ditch barely shielded me from view, but it felt safer than just standing out in the open with all the dragons.

"Stand here." Hades pressed a quick kiss to my lips, the heat of him fading before I could savor it. "You've got this. Don't be scared."

"I've got this," I replied, though the words wobbled on my tongue.

"We'll be waiting right up there." He pointed up to Orion, Gabriel, and the dragons.

I nodded. He turned and climbed out. I lowered my eyes to the cracked soil. I trusted that Hades was where he'd said he would be.

Within a few minutes, the dragons moved closer. Their steps shook the ground beneath me. I could feel the heat of their attention. Maybe they were looking at me with curiosity, maybe like a snack. I hoped it wasn't the latter. I chewed on my lip to stop my fingers from fidgeting at my sides. *I've got this*, I repeated the mantra.

A high-pitched scream tore across the field, sharp enough to make my ears ring, followed by a deafening roar. I flinched, instinct yanking my head toward the sound. *Don't look over there*, Hades said.

Wind swept toward me, and with it came the stench of thick, acrid smoke.

It reminded me of rotten, roasted meat left too long over flame. And underneath that… something else. Like the time I'd singed my hair on a candle as a child, only stronger, heavier.

The realization sank in. *Oh gods*. I held my breath, but I gagged anyway, bile creeping up my throat.

I froze and squeezed my eyes shut. Someone had clearly failed.

A long, warm gust slapped me, lifting strands of my hair and tossing them across my face. Every survival urge in my body screamed to curl into a ball, but I forced myself not to flinch. I had no intention of being a meal today.

Don't worry about that. Goddesses don't taste very good, Falon said.

I clamped my eyes shut. *You've eaten one?*

If I told you, I'd have to kill you.

Great, I yelled.

I disagree with him, Hades said with a chuckle that reverberated through the bond. *I think goddesses taste fantastic.*

Of course you do. My hands fisted at my sides, nails digging into my palms. I wasn't in the mood for jokes.

I stood for twenty-five minutes. I counted each second from one to sixty, repeatedly. I could've been off by a minute or two, but it was still far longer than I thought this would take. How much longer would Gabriel, Orion, and Hades wait on me before they regretted bringing me at all? *I'm not worth the trouble.* Dragons still moved around me, snorting, exhaling, judging. The ditch offered no real protection, only the illusion of it.

Is it supposed to take this long? I finally asked Hades.

He hesitated for thirty-four seconds. *Usually, it doesn't.*

Wonderful.

Time dragged. Another fifty-three minutes, give or take. We didn't have time to waste, and I was holding everyone up. Again. A shadow swallowed the sun over the ditch, and the air grew colder. I kept my eyes down.

A few drops of rain splattered against my skin. After two minutes, the drizzle turned into a heavy downpour. Rain trickled down from my hairline, sliding down my forehead and over the tip of my nose. I had to be careful not to inhale it. It traced a path across my lips, then dripped from my chin and fell onto the ground.

Water collected at my feet. It must've been a while since it last rained. The ground was so parched that it had trouble absorbing all the water at once. I knew that feeling well—starved and cracked, unable to take in anything good when it finally came.

My sodden clothes chilled me to the bone. I trembled but stayed upright. My knees ached from standing in one position for so long, and my thigh muscles clenched and unclenched, trying to hold steady.

Anxious thoughts circled in my mind like bloodthirsty sharks, their teeth flashing silver, sharp as scythes. They whispered the same things they always did. *You don't belong here. You never did. They'll see it sooner or later.* I wanted to retreat into that peaceful place inside me where none of this mattered, where I could be anyone, anywhere I wanted. But I couldn't. Not now. I needed to focus.

I stood for another thirteen minutes. The rain eased, softening into a gentle drizzle before stopping. Thank the Fates. It was a reprieve, though a damp bite still lingered in the air. A strange warmth stirred behind my ribs, like the quiet click of a lock.

Hello, goddess, a silky, feminine voice slithered into my mind.

I didn't have a chance to question the voice or to respond before a rough shove sent me sprawling into the shallow pool of water and mud. The wet ground squelched beneath me, clinging to my hands and clothes. My face twisted.

I lifted my head. There, a massive snout hovered just inches from my face, its exhale ruffling my soaked hair. Steam emerged from the dragon's nostrils, and its lips pulled back into what I could only describe as a smile. Its scales were a rich purple so dark they bordered on obsidian. The dragon's blazing pools of liquid gold locked onto mine.

"I'm not supposed to look," I whispered to myself as I tore my gaze away, my head snapping down.

You may look.

I lifted my eyes.

My name is Hessthoneetis. I would love to join you on your journey.

"Hessthoneetis," I repeated slowly, trying to say it correctly. "H-hello."

Stand up. Her voice was stern, but amusement curled around her words. *You look pathetic just lying there. If you stop embarrassing me, you may call me Hess.*

You were the one who pushed me. The words slipped out

before I could stop them. Who was I to argue with a creature that could eat me with one bite?

I scrambled upright, my boots sliding on the wet ground. My balance wavered. I pitched forward, my face inches from a humiliating dive into the sludge. I managed to steady myself. Mud clung to my palms in thick layers that I wiped against my shirt, leaving long streaks of brown.

Careful, Hess said. *With all that mud, you're going to get me dirty.* She tilted her head, her eyes glinting under the sun that had come out, and her tail flicked behind her.

I narrowed my eyes. *I don't enjoy being covered in grime either.* I brushed a clump of it off my sleeve.

Her chest rumbled with something that felt like laughter. The sound filled my head, rich and warm.

Hades offered me a hand and helped me out of the ditch. Gabriel stepped forward, his head dipping and his eyes lowering. "May I place the saddle?"

Of course, handsome, Hess said.

Gabriel chuckled and patted her.

I groaned before I could stop myself. A deep peal of amusement flooded my mind like a storm.

Great. My dragon liked to flirt. I rubbed my face, realizing too late that I'd smeared mud across my cheek.

What? He is handsome.

"You can hear her too?" I asked.

Gabriel nodded, busy checking the straps on the saddle. "Dragons choose who they speak to. They don't speak with everyone."

That's right, goddess. Some gratitude is in order, Hess purred, her tone so smug that it practically hummed inside my skull.

I fought the urge to roll my eyes and focused on Gabriel's hands as he finished attaching the saddle with ease.

For the record, Hess added, *your mate is just as pretty. Maybe prettier. He can't hear that.* Hess winked at me with one large, golden eye, the scales around it rippling.

That's enough.

As you wish, goddess. The tail flicking behind her made it clear she was enjoying this.

This is going to be a long journey.

You should be grateful, her voice purred in my mind, dropping so low that it sent a chill racing up my spine.

I'd crossed the line. Why did I have to ruin things so quickly? Why couldn't I just stay silent? My pulse thundered in my ears. *I'm sorry—*

Her laughter rang out. *I'm joking. Cheer up.*

I gulped.

"Hello," Hades said, placing a palm on Hess' scales. She purred, her tail lashing. "Let's get you in the saddle." Hades climbed up easily, his grip firm as he helped me up. Hess was huge.

How is this so difficult for you? Hess' voice slid into my mind.

You're so big.

Thank you. I am the largest female in my family. My parents were disappointed I wasn't a male, until I proved how strong I am. She snorted, her tail sending a spray of mud across the ground.

I wished I could be like her—unbothered. I was entirely *too* bothered.

Dirt was smeared on Hades' leather gloves and arms where they touched my clothes, but he didn't seem to care. He settled me into the saddle, securing the straps and adjusting the fit.

"How long did it take you to learn to mount a dragon?"

"About a week." He double-checked the fastenings. "There."

The saddle felt strange beneath me, the leather slick

against my legs. I gripped it, unsure if it was the residual mud or my nerves making me feel like I might slide off at any moment.

I do love a handsome man crawling on me, she purred.

I'm not even going to respond to that.

Hades cupped my face, and his lips pressed against mine with a heat that drowned out everything—the cool air, the semi-damp clothes clinging to my skin. His fingers threaded through my hair, holding me steady as he deepened it. When he pulled back, his forehead rested lightly on mine.

Movement flickered at the edge of my vision, a piece of fabric arcing through the air. "Catch," Gabriel called.

Hades caught it fluidly, the weight and texture revealing what it was. He unfolded the heavy cloak, then tugged it over my head and adjusted the fabric around my shoulders. "This way, you'll stay warm," he said, his voice low. "Your clothes are already drying, but I don't want you to catch a chill."

"How are you all dry?"

"The dragons provided us cover," Hades said, sliding off Hess' back and landing on the ground. He mounted Falon's saddle.

Let me know if you need anything, including any washroom breaks... though I can't guarantee there will actually be one.

I nodded.

Hess wasted no time. She launched into the sky with a powerful thrust of her wings. The world lurched, and my stomach found residence in my throat as the ground dropped beneath us. I clung to the saddle. *I will die today.* A cry ripped free from my throat, leaving a trail of fire in its wake. The wind howled around me, drowning out the sound entirely.

What's wrong, goddess? Afraid of heights?

Do you even know where we're going?

North. I already connected to Falon, Rys, and Seph.

I took a slow breath, my heart still thundering. I took in the wild, untamed landscape below. Mountains met the sky in a jagged line. I glanced behind me. Hades, Orion, and Gabriel followed.

Wait. I never told you I'm a goddess.

Hess huffed. *Every dragon in that field knew you're a goddess. That's why no one wanted to claim you.*

You did. Why? And what took you so long? I thought back to all that time I'd spent standing.

I wanted to see if you'd squirm. My anxious thoughts must've been loud because Hess continued. *Don't worry, no one will say anything. But most dragons don't want to be associated with you, either. I don't even know all the information, and I'll make you tell me, but I know two Divine glamoured as Faeries are bad news.*

Yet you are helping me. Can you see through the glamour?

No. But I can feel it, Hess said. *Your magic is different. You better be grateful. You're lucky that sometimes I make questionable decisions. Don't make me regret this one.*

I won't, I promised. It was a promise I hoped I could keep. *How are you sure the other dragons won't say anything?*

Dragons at the field don't have riders. If your little secret is revealed, it won't be from one of them. Most dragons don't bow to the Faerie Courts. The fae think they control us, but we allow them to believe that. Should they try to tighten a leash around our necks, it will only chafe their own wrists. Her words were heavy. *You're lucky I picked you.*

You keep reminding me of that.

You should celebrate. You didn't die at the field. That already puts you ahead of over half the faeries who've stood in that ditch.

That many people die? Hades told me I was safe at the field.

You were, she said. *The others? Not so much. Most of them show up without dragons. Do you think those males you arrived with would put you in intentional danger?*

I shook my head. My fingers traced the stitching along the saddle. *I'll celebrate if I survive this.*

Oh, you'll be fine, she said.

Easy for her to say. She didn't know I was talking about surviving the trials, not just the flight.

The clock was ticking.

16

PERSEPHONE

Wind whipped against my face, dragging me back to consciousness. My eyes fluttered open, stinging against the rush of air. My vision sharpened. The crescent moon, the clouds, and the twinkling stars broke up the endless stretch of black above us. My gut clenched and I shifted upright. How had I managed to fall asleep on… a dragon? *How long was I out?*

Every muscle protested as I shifted. My back, neck, and limbs were stiff from the awkward position I'd slept in, held in by the strap around me. I dug my nails into the handle, pressing so hard that I was sure I'd leave marks in the brand-new leather.

A forest stretched out below us, the trees dark silhouettes speckled with patches of silver where moonlight found its way through the clouds. Hess banked. *Finally, you're up.* She chuckled, vibrating under me. *You were out for hours. I let you rest. While you're on me, you're safe,* Hess said. Her voice held no hesitation. *Once we land, you'll need your strength to protect yourself.*

I swallowed hard, my mouth dry from the ceaseless gusts

and lack of water. Gabriel rode to my left, Hades to my right, with Orion behind me. The wingbeats of the four dragons filled the air around us.

The buffeting gusts made it difficult for me to raise my arms. I settled for tilting my head to the left, then the right, releasing a crack and pop that echoed in my ears. I'd have to wait until we landed to truly stretch.

Hess' wings tilted into a descent. The other dragons mirrored her. My insides lurched as the ground raced up to meet us. "Where are we?" The wind howled in my ears, stealing nearly all my words. I gripped the handle harder.

On the edge of the Spring Court, near the forest that divides it from the Summer Court. We're going to find a spot to set up camp.

Each movement of my eyelids scraped like sandpaper. Tears blurred my vision, but they didn't relieve the dryness. I blinked hard, and it only made things worse.

Hess landed first, the other dragons following with a loud rumble. The impact rattled my body, leaving my stomach in my throat. *Don't puke on me,* Hess growled.

Fortunately for her, there was barely enough food in me to do more than retch up bile. *I won't. I guess.*

You guess?

I glanced over Hess' side. The moon illuminated the surroundings enough to see, but the ground was shrouded in the shadow of her large form. Could I make it down on my own? I wanted to stop being a burden to everyone. I undid the strap and tried to gauge how far the forest floor was. It was a patchwork of dark shapes and shifting shadows. I pushed myself off.

"Persephone, give me a moment. I'll help you down," Hades yelled as he slid off Falon.

It was too late, though.

I slid down Hess' side, far faster than I had when

dismounting Falon earlier. I landed with a loud thud, my ankle twisting hard. "Oh gods," I moaned.

The sharp sting in my ankle, knees, and palms quickly deepened into a throbbing ache. Surely my ankle was already swelling. It had its own heartbeat.

Goddess, I didn't choose you because you were stupid, but you're doing an excellent job proving me wrong.

"Sorry," I muttered. *I'm trying to be independent.*

And failing, she growled. *At least ask me next time before you go flinging yourself off my side like that.*

I stayed quiet. She was right. I was failing, like I always was.

You'll get stronger. I'll make sure of it. Her tone had softened. I wasn't sure if that made me feel better or worse.

I glanced up. Hades stood at my side. "I told you I would help you down." He slipped his arms around me and lifted gently, supporting most of my weight as I trembled.

"I'm fine." My voice shook as I tried not to scream.

"Don't lie to me," he said, his voice edged with warning. Even through the darkness, I caught the hard narrowing of his eyes.

I gave him a weak smile. "Okay, I only *slightly* injured my ankle."

With a frustrated sigh, he scooped me up and set me down on a log. My sore backside protested at the hard, rough surface. So many hours of riding made sitting like its own kind of trial.

"Stay here. We're going to build the fire, then I'll take a look at your ankle."

"I put up the ward," Gabriel said.

Orion grumbled about being hungry, his voice muffled by the sounds of the night, hooting birds and humming insects. He joined Gabriel and Hades in gathering wood. They worked quickly, collecting fallen branches and tossing them into a growing pile. Gabriel walked past me with full arms. "Normally, we'd be out of luck. This wood is too wet to burn well"—he smiled—"but we have dragons."

I nodded, taking in the seamless way they moved—efficient, almost instinctive. Hades stopped beside me, his attention locked on Gabriel. One look passed between them, Hades giving the slightest tilt of his head. The exchange was so subtle that if I hadn't been watching, I would've missed it. It was amazing how a single glance was enough for them to communicate.

"All right," Gabriel said, kicking a few branches aside. "We've got enough now. Let's get this fire started." He pushed his hair away from his forehead with the back of his hand. "Rys, light it up." Gabriel stepped back, motioning his dragon forward.

I live for an excuse to set things on fire, Rys said, his rough voice slamming into my mind. The crimson creature lumbered closer, his massive frame looking even bigger between the trees and brush. Rys let out a deep rumble from his chest, the sound vibrating my own. He drew in a sharp breath, then unleashed a long jet of fire. Flames engulfed the pile of branches, crackling and hissing as they battled the damp.

Within a few seconds, the fire roared, the flames casting an orangey-golden glow over everything. *I'm starting the next fire,* Seph said. His voice was lighter and quicker than Rys' and Falon's.

Seph, no, Falon immediately added. *You like fire too much, and you have too little control. Last thing we need is another forest fire.*

Seph huffed. *It was one time.*

Rys chuckled as he moved toward the clearing, joining the other dragons.

The fire's heat rushed over me, licking my skin and prickling before sinking into my bones. The warmth didn't quite erase the throbbing in my leg. I shifted, wincing at the movement.

Hades pointed a finger at my ankle. "Let me go get some supplies and I'll take care of you right away."

I nodded, watching as the flames flickered orange and yellow. Embers glowed, and the sparks floated up until they turned to nothingness. The scent of burning wood hung heavy in the air, so thick it coated my tongue. I ran my fingers over the rough surface of the log beneath me, then lifted my hands toward the fire.

Hades jogged through the clearing over to Falon and dug through the large leather pack attached to him. Rys, Hess, and Seph were settled nearby.

Gabriel and Orion were busy putting up the tents, snapping together the long poles, draping and tying all the canvas over them. The damp fabric glistened, catching the fire's glow as they spread it over the framework.

I watched them work. "Since you two can use magic in this realm, can't you just put the tents up with it?"

Gabriel shook his head. "Fae magic doesn't necessarily work like you're thinking. These tents are designed to resist magic. I'll still put up a ward at each of our campsites, but extra protection never hurts."

Nearby, a long stick caught my attention. It was smooth and looked strong enough to serve as a makeshift crutch. I reached for it, one hand on the log to steady my weight. My fingers burned as I hyperextended them.

Almost there.

My hand curled around the wood, and I dragged it close, then used it to push myself upright. I barely made it to my feet before my boots skidded on a patch of wet leaves, sending me wobbling.

Hades was back. "I told you to stay here." His hand closed

around my arm, steadying me as he guided me back onto the log, though I could've managed on my own.

"I heard. I just didn't really want to listen."

"Stubborn," he murmured, affectionate. "So stubborn." Hades kneeled at my feet.

I huffed, leaning back and shifting my leg. He reached for my boot, his fingers brushing against the leather. The worst of the mud had been swept away by the wind during the flight, though faint traces still clung to the seams. I tensed, heat rising in my chest.

Hades glanced up at me. "Relax." He unbuckled the strap, one hand steadying my leg while the other worked to free the boot, careful not to jostle my injury. I dug my nails into the rough surface beneath me, feeling bark scrape under them. I welcomed the ache in my hands, distracting me from the pain radiating up from my ankle.

He slid the boot off, setting it aside, and sharp fire exploded up my leg. I bit down on my lip, but a cry still slipped free. "Gods," I said through gritted teeth. "It hurts."

Hades paused, his eyes lifted to meet mine before he continued. He peeled off the thick sock covering my foot. Cool air brushed against the throbbing heat of my swollen joint. Even in the low light, I could see the angry crimson swelling and the dark bruise already forming.

"It's worse than I thought." Hades pulled out a small jar from his pocket and twisted it open. "This balm will help. Your Divine healing should do most of the work, though." He dipped two fingers into the yellow mixture, then slowly applied it.

His touch was featherlight, as if he was afraid to hurt me further. A cooling sensation spread across my skin, soothing some of the fire in my injury.

"Deep breaths," he murmured. The tenderness in his movements made my heart ache in ways I wasn't prepared for. When he finished applying the balm, he pulled out a bandage wrap. "This may hurt a little."

"Okay. Do it."

He moved quickly and carefully, wrapping the fabric around my ankle, each pull tightening it, the pressure sharp. I shut my eyes, focusing on the rhythm of my heart instead.

He stopped.

Warm fingers brushed my chin, positioning my face toward his. His lips pressed against mine, and I melted into the kiss. One hand moved to cradle my face, thumb grazing small circles. My ankle's pain and the aches from the saddle all faded away.

He pulled back, his breath mingling with mine as a soft smirk tugged at his lips. "How's that? Better?"

"Much," I whispered.

"Good." Hades placed a hand on his knee and pushed himself up. He threw a couple more thick branches into the fire.

Gabriel sat beside me. "How are you feeling?" He handed me a silver-foiled bundle.

"Hurting, but I'm okay." I took it from him. "What's this?"

"Dinner," Orion said, dropping onto a nearby log.

Hades joined us, settling in next to me and opening his own foil. "It's not much, but it'll keep you going."

The males and I are going hunting. I'm hungry, Hess said.

Okay. Enjoy?

Oh, I will. I can't wait to have a fresh meal.

I winced. No matter how normal it was for dragons, the idea of *fresh* meat turned my stomach.

I followed Hades' lead, peeling back the thin silver wrap. The smell was inviting—warm bread, roasted meat, and vegetables charred dark with grill marks. I took a small bite. The bread had crunch, not because it was stale but from being toasted. It wasn't bad, but it wasn't the best thing I'd ever tasted. "Interesting," I said, examining the foil. "How is this still warm?"

Gabriel was already halfway through his sandwich. "I had these enchanted to stay fresh for days. We should have plenty for our entire trip. If we need more, though, we can get some at Orion's home."

"You'll meet my parents," Orion said between a bite of food. "And all my brothers and sisters."

I gave him a soft smile. "Speaking of that, can anyone inform me of what the plan is for this trip?" I took another bite as the men looked at each other. "I've been waiting for someone to clue me in."

Orion snorted. "Maybe if you'd shown up to the planning meetings"—he waved his hands, gesturing around us—"you wouldn't be in the dark. We did have one *every* day."

I stopped chewing, the bite heavy in my mouth. My gaze dropped to my hands.

He's teasing, Hades' voice slipped into my mind.

I managed to offer Orion a small smile as I flicked a few crumbs off my fingers.

Gabriel nodded. "Fair enough. We're almost to the Summer Court. If we make enough progress tomorrow, we can stop at an inn I've been to before. It will take us another day and a half-ish before we make it to the Autumn Court, where we will stay with Orion's family. We can get goggles while we're there."

Orion chuckled, rubbing at his eye with the heel of his hand. "My eyes are so dry."

"Mine too," Hades said, tipping his head back and squinting at the sky.

"Then we'll go through the Winter Court, which will take longer because of the weather." Gabriel took another bite of his sandwich. "So almost six days if we are quick, but likely seven days before we're near the stone. This is all subject to change, though."

"We'll take it one step at a time." Hades crinkled his foil into a ball, finished with his meal, and he wrapped an arm around my shoulder. "For now, focus on healing."

Orion let out a throaty laugh. "Nothing says a great trip like an injury on the first day."

I glared at him.

He held up a hand. "Joking. I'm joking."

I folded my foil into a little square and set it into my lap. When I leaned into Hades, the contrast between us hit me— he smelled so good, while I was covered in dirt and nervous sweat. I shrank in on myself. I was gross. "Is there any chance I can bathe?" I yawned. "I'm not sure I can handle another day like this without at least washing off some of the grime."

Orion snorted. "It hasn't even been one full day, Persephone."

I rolled my eyes.

Hades ignored him and looked down at me, his brows pulling together. "You're injured."

"I'm also filthy."

Hades shifted me into his arms and stood. "I'll heat some water," Gabriel said. "You can bathe in the tent while seated."

"Thank you," I said. "Truly." I nuzzled myself into Hades as he carried me to the tent. The scent of leather and smoke clung to him. How did he still smell good? The tent flaps brushed past us.

Inside, a lantern hung from the pitched ceiling, and a thick, brown woven rug covered the ground. On one side, a bedroll lay spread out with a pile of blankets stacked beside it. Across from it, two leather bags sat open, revealing neatly packed clothes and what looked like other supplies.

Hades set me down on the bedroll, the soft fabric sinking

under my weight. He straightened, the tent tall enough to accommodate his full height. "Let me go get the water."

I couldn't even respond before he disappeared, the entry rustling behind him. He returned a few minutes later with a metal bucket filled with steaming water, the wisps of heat spiraling into the air. The surface rippled as Hades set it down beside me, lowering himself into a crouch.

I peeled off my layers of clothes, stopping as I reached the waistband of my pants.

"Let me help you," Hades muttered, slipping off the boot from my uninjured foot before gently sliding the sheathed dagger from my leg. Then he eased the pants down, careful not to hurt my ankle further. Once they were off, he secured the weapon back in place.

I bit my lip as he dipped a tan-colored cloth in the bucket, turning it to a darker shade. "I can bathe myself," I whispered. "I'm not completely helpless."

"It's not about being helpless. Let me take care of you."

My heart gave a small, disloyal flutter. I hesitated, my gaze catching on the lantern's reflection across the water. My fingers curled tighter into the single blanket draped across the bedroll. Hades dipped the cloth again, wrung it out, and pressed it to my skin. I let out a sharp exhale. "Too hot?" he asked.

"No. It's perfect."

He worked in silence. Glamoured or not, he still felt like him. A different hair color, a different shade to his eyes—none of it changed the way he moved, the way he touched me. His hands were careful as he wiped away the grime from my arms, shoulders, and neck, the cloth gliding slowly over my skin. Silence stretched between us, aside from the occasional splash of water. He gathered my tangled hair and pulled it aside, a few strands sticking to the back of my neck.

Goose bumps prickled along my arms and legs under the

weight of his gaze. Part of me wanted to lean into his touch, but another screamed that it wasn't safe, that if I let myself believe in this too much, it could all be taken away. The bond between us hummed, and I knew he could feel what I was trying to hide. "You don't have to do this."

"I know." He chuckled, his knuckles running across my cheek. "I want to take care of my mate." His words carried a softer edge.

He leaned closer. I let out a slow breath as he worked around my shoulders. "Relax," he murmured. "I'm not going to hurt you."

"I know that."

He stilled. "Do you?" His gaze flicked up to meet mine. "I've felt you pulling away from me through the bond since you pledged yourself to the trials." His words didn't contain anger, but they still hit me like a blow.

I swallowed hard. "I—" The words sank in my throat. I dropped my gaze, ashamed of the thoughts, the fears that had been lingering in my mind.

His Adam's apple bobbed as he swallowed. "You don't have to explain."

A dull pressure built in my sternum. "I do." My voice cracked.

Hades' hand stilled. "You're still bracing for me to leave."

"I'm not doing it on purpose," I whispered. How could he love me for *me* when he'd watched what I'd recklessly done?

"I know. Things have progressed quickly between us." He cleared his throat. "I just thought we'd found a rhythm. But maybe I missed how much you are still carrying from your past."

A tear prickled at the corner of my eye. His jaw tightened, but he didn't look at me. I reached up and cupped his face. "This is all just new and different for me."

"Me too." His voice was so soft. It broke me.

The single tear spilled from my eye. I had never once stopped to consider how he might feel. I really was as selfish as Mothe—as Demeter said I was. I had been so consumed with myself that I hadn't realized how much he was navigating too.

"I know it's a lot. Your life has changed immensely."

I nodded, the lump in my throat too thick to say anything. Changed didn't even begin to cover it. Months ago, I had still been a sheltered girl. And now? Now I was here, in the Faerie realm, tangled in fate and freedom and feelings I didn't know what to do with. Hades continued working, avoiding my ankle and leaving the wrap on. Maybe it was my mind playing tricks on me, but I hyperfocused on each micro-movement he made. Was he cleaning me faster because he wanted to get away?

My mouth opened and closed a few times before I worked up the courage to speak. "It's just… it's like there's this voice in my head that keeps telling me I'll never be enough. That this isn't real. That you'll stop loving me and leave me because I did something foolish."

"I'm not your mother."

I flinched as the last word hit me. I hated that he could see so much of me. I was sure if he kept looking, he'd leave me. It wasn't just my voice in my head—it was hers too, every word she'd spoken to me after she'd changed. She had gone from loving me to hating me so quickly. How could I be sure that wouldn't happen with Hades?

"I'm not going to leave you because things get hard. I'm not going to stop loving you because you're struggling."

"You say that now, but what if—"

"No. There's no *what if*. I chose you. I will keep choosing you every day, no matter what voice is whispering in your head. You're not your past. I'm not her. I'll just never walk away from you."

I wanted to believe him.

But the thing about being left was that it never came with a warning.

Finished, he tossed the cloth aside and leaned back. "Let's get you dressed again."

"I can dress myself," I said quietly.

"I know." Carefully, Hades eased a light brown knit sweater over my head, guiding my arms through the sleeves. He helped me slip on my underwear. We skipped the pants, deciding not to jostle my ankle.

"All done." He placed a kiss on my forehead and stood, taking the bucket of water and the cloth with him. He lingered for a moment, his gaze sweeping over me. "Get some rest. I'll be back to join you in a while."

I nodded, unable to find the words to keep him here. He hesitated again, his hand brushing the edge of the tent flap, and then he was gone, leaving me alone with my thoughts and the lingering heat of his touch.

17

HADES

I pushed through the canvas flaps, casting one last glance at Persephone. I needed space. Air. Anything.

Gabriel and Orion sat perched on a log by the fire, their voices low, deep in conversation. I caught fragments of words, but they were meaningless to me right now. My boots crunched against the earth as I turned away, the glow of the fire fading behind me with every step.

Branches clawed and caught on my sleeves, the damp undergrowth slowing my steps. I clenched my teeth, my jaw aching. The faint murmur of Gabriel's and Orion's voices disappeared, leaving only the sounds of the night and the rhythm of my feet on the forest floor.

Once, this realm had been a refuge after getting my touch of death.

Tonight, it felt like a prison.

I pressed a hand to my chest. *Physically, I'm fine. So why does it feel like I'm coming apart?* The trees loomed too close to me, their gnarled branches creating a cage. I stopped and stared up at the sky through the tangle overhead.

I'd lived for centuries without surrendering to anything. I'd gone to war. I'd controlled the fates of souls with a mere thought. *I am a God.*

I never asked the Fates for a mate. I'd never wanted one. But they had delivered her to me, my perfect half on a silver fucking platter.

It wasn't her fault. It was my own. I had completed the mating bond too soon. I wanted her before she was ready. I should've seen it—how much she was still carrying from a life that had taught her love came with conditions. She shouldn't have had to carry it alone. And pledging herself to the Divine Trials ripped open wounds she'd only just started to let heal.

I pushed through the forest. A winding river came into view. I kneeled at its bank, running my fingertips over the small, cold, jagged stones covering the water's edge. I picked one up and tossed it in, watching as it hit the surface, distorting the moon's reflection before sinking to the bottom.

I grabbed a handful and flung them one by one.

One.

Two.

Three.

Four.

"Hades."

"Gabriel." His name came out harsher than I intended, but right now, I didn't care. I kept my eyes on the water.

"I can see you're troubled." He stepped forward, his gaze burning into me.

"Persephone." My mate's name left my lips like a curse. I squeezed my last stone, and its sharp edge cut a small slit into my palm. A sting flared, but I didn't loosen my grip. I focused on it, on the way it pulled me from my feelings. Blood slicked my fingers until my Divine healing spread through the wound, sealing it shut. I stayed silent. Gabriel didn't push. "She's pushing me away. She's afraid."

He hummed, urging me to continue, but not irritating me with words.

I glanced over at the fae. I thought I'd wished to be alone, but now I just wanted an answer, some sort of wisdom from Gabriel that would fix this. "I don't know what to do." I stared at the water. "I've never felt like this before—" The words died on my tongue before I could finish them.

I am a god. I made things happen. I forced them into existence. But this…

He placed a hand on my shoulder, and tension coiled through my body. I didn't turn, keeping my eyes fixed on the dark trees and the shadows the moon cast on them. I didn't dare look at his face and see the pity that was surely dripping off it.

He had still said nothing, but I continued, "Maybe I ruined it. Rushed things. Maybe I didn't give her space to feel safe in it first."

"Ruined what? Your bond?"

I nodded.

Gabriel chuckled, and my fists curled at my sides. This was not the time for laughter. "Now why would you think that?" he said.

I shook my head. "Maybe I pushed too fast. I didn't give her enough time."

"You didn't ruin it." Gabriel said the words too casually. "Love is strange."

I picked up another handful of rocks and hurled one in, the familiar plunk sending rings across the surface.

"You have to be patient with her. With yourself."

Patience.

"Her whole life has changed, and she's still processing it. Let her."

I nodded, knowing he was right. That didn't make it any easier to carry. It only made me angrier at myself. I had rushed it. I wanted her too much.

"It hurts." The words scraped out of me. I'd never said them before. Pain was something I was meant to carry in silence. "Feels like rejection." She had every right to be scared—I knew that. Demeter had left shadows in her eyes. But knowing didn't make it easier to stand there, ready to give her everything, and feel her inch away. I wanted to tear down whatever walls were left between us, even if it meant breaking them by force.

But she'd never forgive me if I did that. She'd see me as no different from the one who'd caged her before. So I threw another rock, the passing breeze making the ripples dance across the water in a faster rhythm.

"Persephone's not rejecting you. She is just getting used to her new life," Gabriel said.

Words jammed in my throat.

"You cannot ruin anything that is meant for you. And you and Persephone are meant to be."

PERSEPHONE

I lay on my side with Hades' arms wrapped around me. He'd come into the tent a while after he'd left last night. I'd pretended to be asleep, and his fingers had tensed against my side for half a second before softening again. Still, he said nothing.

I stared at the canvas wall across from us and focused on the chirps of the birds, letting their mingling melodies flow into my ears. The fabric wasn't thick enough to muffle them.

Hades shifted behind me, his low yawn sending goose bumps down my spine. The tip of his nose brushed the nape of my neck, pausing—like he was thinking twice—before moving up and pressing a kiss to my skin. His arms wrapped around me tighter, the warmth of him seeping into me.

"Good morning." Sleep tainted Hades' low voice.

I turned in his arms to face him, hesitating as I searched for the right words. "Morning." My mouth opened, then closed again. I shifted under the blanket, grasping for a better response than *morning*.

I came up with nothing.

Hades leaned in, his forehead pressing against mine. The

feeling of his skin sent sparks racing through my body. *Just relax*, I yelled at myself. But I couldn't. My spine only stiffened. Again, I was overthinking. The length of his exhale, the sharp silence between us—every moment played through my mind, a relentless reel of words I wished I could unsay.

His scent wrapped around me. I relished its comfort. I stilled as his hardness pressed into my belly. His eyes snapped open, and he leaned back. "Sorry." He sat up, his jaw clenching.

"You don't have to apologize."

He rubbed the back of his neck, his movements clumsy and so unlike him. He didn't meet my eyes but gave me a weak smile.

My chest pinched. Was the awkwardness because of what I said last night? Maybe it wasn't what I said—maybe it was just *me*.

Hades cleared his throat. "We should get dressed. I believe Orion wanted to train with you this morning if your ankle is up for it."

"Are we not traveling today? I thought—"

Hades cut me off. "We are. You'll only train while Gabriel and I pack everything up. Then we'll eat something and head off."

"Oh, all right."

He pushed the blanket off and stood, crossing the tent to rummage through a leather bag. Fresh clothes and a bundle of toiletries emerged in his hands. The muscles in his back flexed as he moved, shadows tracing each line of him in the morning light leaking between the tent flaps. I watched as he dressed, clutching the blanket in my hands.

"Get dressed. I hear Orion and Gabriel moving." He ducked out of the tent, leaving the fabric entrance to sway behind him.

"Okay," I whispered to myself.

I lay on the bedroll for a minute or two after Hades left, sucking in deep breaths, my mind spiraling. Tears formed at the corners of my eyes. Why was I ruining everything? Why was I like this? I focused on my racing heartbeat, attempting to calm myself down. Hot tears slid down my cheeks, but I shooed them away with the backs of my hands. *Stop. Coming. Out. Of. My. Eyes. Damn it.*

I stood, testing and flexing my ankle, putting some weight on it. Better than yesterday. I reached for the leather bag, pulled out a fresh set of clothes, and got dressed without much thought—they'd be soaked with sweat soon enough.

Facing the back of the tent, I took in deep inhales and exhales. I couldn't step outside like this. Everyone already walked on eggshells around me. The last thing I wanted was to give them another reason to tiptoe. I needed to look normal. In control. I pressed a hand to my chest, willing its erratic rise and fall to slow. My breaths came in stuttering gasps, no matter how hard I tried.

Breath by breath, the trembling slowed. I grabbed my toothbrush and water, needing another minute. I brushed my teeth slowly, focusing on the small movements: back and forth.

When I finally stepped out of the tent, a shaft of sunlight broke through the trees and hit my face. I squinted, spat the foamy mixture into the foliage, and wiped my mouth with the back of my hand.

Orion had a big smile on his face, but the moment his eyes met mine, it faded, concern etching along his features. His lips parted, maybe at the sight of my eyes, which I could only assume were red and puffy. I didn't want to talk about it. "Don't ask, please. Can we just train?"

He swallowed and nodded, waving a hand for me to follow him. He didn't speak or ask any questions as I trailed him through the forest. "This looks like a good spot." He looked over at me for reassurance that I was comfortable here.

I shrugged. "Sure."

He eyed me but got into a fighting position, giving a clipped nod in my direction. I braced myself, shifting my weight off my weaker ankle.

He struck me, but I didn't go down. The impact should've sent me into the dirt, but my feet stayed planted. I stopped thinking. I just acted.

Orion's next strike came faster, but I didn't absorb it. I sidestepped, shooting my fist out and pummeling it into his side. "Good one," he grunted.

We continued to fight. With every strike he made, I moved faster. The pain had become power. I didn't feel the strain of my muscles, the throb of my ankle, the bruises I was sure were forming from Orion's successful strikes. Everything was secondary to the sadness that hurt more. I wasn't fighting Orion anymore. I was fighting the ache in my chest, the shame, the fear.

I launched another hit at him, colliding with his ribs. He let out a huff of air, but I didn't stop. I kept striking until he lay on the ground under me and my fists. "Enough," he said.

I didn't stop.

"Enough!" He grabbed my wrists and twisted, using my own momentum against me. My balance wavered, and the world tilted.

My back hit the ground, his weight crashing down and pinning me in place. A wicked grin spread across his face, his perfectly white teeth streaked with crimson. Slowly, he ran his tongue over them. "Good job. You're learning how to actually fight."

My chest heaved. Orion stood up and offered me a hand. I took it but said nothing.

"We're done for now."

I nodded, following him. By the time we reached camp, the tents were already gone. Hades and Gabriel had worked quickly. I wouldn't be able to change, but I didn't complain.

The dragons had returned sometime during the night. I'd felt the thud of their landing through the ground. Now they stood in the clearing, already packed and waiting, their massive bodies towering among the trees.

Hades handed me a foil pack. I sat on one of the logs in front of the pile of ash and stones, the ghost of last night's fire. Peeling back the silver, I found the same sandwich from yesterday. I didn't care. My stomach twisted with hunger, and a warm meal was better than nothing. Hades sat at my side, silent, eating his too, close enough that our arms could've touched, but far enough that they didn't. Once everyone had finished, we headed for the dragons.

Before I could protest, Hades scooped me up and helped me get on Hess. *Your eyes are red and you look terrible*, she said, her voice a low rumble in my mind.

Thanks. I shifted in the saddle.

Hades pressed a quick kiss to my forehead, so gentle I wouldn't have noticed if I wasn't paying attention. Before I could react, he was already sliding down Hess' side. Gone—onto Falon's back.

Hess launched into the air, following Rys, and wind whipped around me. My heart raced with each beat of her wings. Her violet scales glistened in the sun. I still wasn't used to the feeling of her enormous body beneath me or the way she cut through the air as I hung on for dear life. Below us, the forest sprawled out endlessly in every direction, trees and more trees stretching far.

19

PERSEPHONE

ours passed, and the sun slid toward the horizon. It bathed everything, the clouds, the treetops, and even Hess in a warm sheen. The wind shifted as Hess' wings beat slower, angling us into a descent. Below, the forest thinned, patches of open land breaking through the trees.

Hades tugged at the bond. *I want to show you something.*

I looked over at him, riding beside me on Falon. The sun carved golden edges into his sharp features. *What?*

It's something you'll like, a surprise.

He wasn't going to tell me more. I patted Hess, her sun-soaked scales heating my palm. My other hand drifted to the saddle, fingers absently picking at the leather stitching. *Where are we going?* I asked Hess.

You'll see, she said with a hum. *Even I think it's beautiful, and that's saying a lot. How romantic of your mate to think to stop here.* She snickered, wings shifting as we dipped lower. As Hess banked into a turn, the ground below bloomed with colors.

"Oh gods," I breathed. The sea of vivid shades sharpened as we drew closer. A field of flowers stretched as far as I could see—lavenders, deep blues, yellows, reds, oranges, greens, pinks.

The ground rumbled beneath the dragons as they touched down. It was a smoother landing than yesterday. That one was rough.

I heard that. You broadcasted that thought, Hess said.

I patted her scales and smirked. *It wasn't a complaint, just a statement.*

Sure.

Hades slid off Falon and rushed to Hess' side before I could collect any other injuries. "Here," he said, climbing up to offer me a hand.

I hesitated, then let his fingers curl around mine as he helped ease me down. My boots hit the ground with a soft thud. "Thanks."

He nodded once but didn't say anything.

I stepped forward slowly. I blinked, trying to take in the flowers laid out in neat lines. Faeries drifted between the rows, baskets on their arms, clippers in hand. "This is magnificent," I whispered.

"Hades insisted that we stop here for you," Gabriel said from behind me.

I turned toward Hades. "Thank you," I said.

"Of course." His voice was careful, low. He gave me a half-smile. "Maybe we can make something like this happen in the Underworld, once we have Tartarus sealed?"

The reminder was sobering, but I smiled. "I would love that."

"We can spend about half an hour here," Gabriel said, glancing at the small watch strapped to his wrist. "We need to make good progress toward the Autumn Court."

I nodded, though my eyes stayed on the field. "That's fine. I appreciate stopping." I crouched low, my fingers hovering above a flower I'd never seen before. Its petals were a striking twilight blue with a deep black center. Thick white veins threaded through the leaves that clung to its long stem. "Wow," I whispered.

I wandered deeper into the field, letting the soft, velvety petals brush my fingertips. The air was thick with the scent of their sweetness. I kneeled, studying a star-shaped flower with red iridescent petals and an emerald green stem. Beside it, a black blossom slowly flexed its petals, arching in and out to bare a pulsing yellow center like its own miniature sun.

"These only bloom for one day," a voice said.

A faerie with dark blue hair watched me closely, her lips tipping up. She wore a simple linen dress, the color matching a morning sky. "This one?" I pointed to the flower.

She nodded.

"That's beautiful," I said, then quieter, "and kind of sad."

She shrugged and pointed toward the lowering sun. "When light is gone, the flower will die. Nothing is meant to last forever. If they did, they wouldn't be special anymore." She turned and moved down the row, her brown woven basket swinging at her hip.

"We should go," Gabriel called from somewhere behind me.

I didn't move. Just stayed, unwilling to break the spell, lingering to take in the beauty a little more. Hades had suggested this because he knew I'd love it. Because he *knew* me.

I didn't deserve this kind of care.

Turning back to the dragons, I let the field around me sear itself into my memory.

Hess snickered through the bond. *Wow. If I had known*

taking you to a field of flowers would make you stop complaining, I would've suggested this myself.

I exhaled and gave her a flat look. But I didn't argue. My mind was too busy drifting, wondering why it hurt to be seen this clearly.

2 0

PERSEPHONE

he night air wrapped around us like a cloak drenched in hot water. My thin shirt clung to my back, each movement making my skin crawl. Sweat traced slow paths down my arms, dripping from my fingertips onto the floorboards of the wraparound porch beneath my feet. This kind of heat made time drag, stretching little moments into years. Overhead, the dragons had slipped into the sky, off to hunt, but they'd promised to stay close in case our plans went sour.

Orion stood to my right, the lantern's uneven light catching in his dark brown hair. His gaze swept over the deserted market square, shadows pooling between rows of shuttered stalls, a dirt road cutting through the heart of it. Lamps on tall wooden poles flanked the road, casting buttery pools across the ground.

Though night had fallen, the silence was unnatural. Only a few tentative insect chirps broke the stillness. To my left, Hades leaned against the porch beam as though he wasn't melting like I was. His arms were crossed, his attention focused on our surroundings. He hadn't said much since the flower field.

I glanced at the inn behind us. Its timber frame twisted like the wood had grown into its shape. It couldn't have held more than a handful of rooms. Red planters overflowed with clusters of small white flowers, each bloom no bigger than my fingernail. The sign above the door creaked in the breeze that was heavy with heat. I tried to peek through the window, but a white curtain blocked my view. We'd been waiting outside the inn for about ten minutes. Gabriel was inside, trying to book us rooms.

I cracked my clammy fingers. "This place gives me the creeps."

"Some Faerie villages are very—" Hades paused.

"Cautious," Orion finished.

I picked at my nail, thumb brushing over a small catch in the skin.

Hades nodded. "After the Faerie War, a lot of these villages only survived by keeping their circles small. Their parents were cautious. They are cautious. And their children will likely be cautious, too."

I nodded, recalling the words Gabriel had said before the gala about the war—that once, the courts had turned on each other in a bloody fight for dominance. It was clear it had left lasting damage.

Dampness dripped down the nape of my neck. I wiped it away and rubbed my hands on my pants, my lip curling. *Gross.* I was so excited to bathe and sleep in a real bed. The bedroll was fine for travel, but it wasn't a true mattress. Even in Olympus, I'd had a great one—a luxury Demeter afforded me, when I behaved.

"All right," Gabriel said from behind us. I turned back to see him grinning. He held his right hand up, two metal loops with bright red tags hooked on his index finger. The keys dangled, clinking together and producing a sharp sound in the quiet night. "Two rooms, and dinner, too."

"Perfect." The word came out breathier than I'd intended.

"Let me guess." Orion chuckled. "The innkeeper is thrilled to have us here."

"Something like that." Gabriel adjusted his grip on the keys. "Gold and cash are very persuasive." He motioned for us to follow and turned on his heel. Hades and Orion collected our leather bags resting on the steps. I'd offered to help earlier, but they had waved me off, muttering something about having it under control.

The stiffness in my limbs and the ache radiating from my crotch and up my back had silenced any arguments. I was too tired to push back, even if being dismissed left a sour taste in my mouth. I trailed after Gabriel, Hades and Orion close behind. Another sluggish breeze stirred the heavy air. I frowned. "Is it always this hot here?"

Gabriel glanced over his shoulder at me. "Usually."

I scoffed. How did all these men look so comfortable? I was dying.

My jaw went slack as my foot crossed the threshold. The interior was stunning, all in cherry wood. The walls, the floors, the counter, the stairs to its side all gleamed under the lantern lights, amplifying the wood's natural warmth.

Behind the counter stood a man with silver, wire-rimmed circular glasses perched on the bridge of his nose. A sparse sweep of his white hair was combed carefully to the left. The man didn't glance up as we entered, only tapped the small silver bell on the counter with one sun-spotted hand as the other scrawled in a notebook. This must have been the innkeeper.

A scrawny fellow with wild red hair rushed out.

"You have to be quicker, Nathaniel. We've gone over this." The innkeeper shook his head but still hadn't looked up.

"Sorry, Dad." Nathaniel stood in front of us for a few beats, hands at his sides, simply staring. He scratched the side of his head. "Your bags?"

"Right." Orion handed his over.

"I can help you carry these," Hades said, holding up three stacked bags.

Nathaniel rolled his eyes. "I think I can manage. Hand them over. You're going to make me look bad." He whispered the last part and cocked his head, gesturing to his father, who still had his eyes glued to the paper he was writing on.

"If you say so." Hades placed the stack on top of Orion's.

Nathaniel's eyes widened as he went tumbling backward, the boy and the bags sprawling all over the cherry wood floor. "I got it," he muttered, scrambling to get up.

"Damn it, Nathaniel." His father looked up from his papers, moving from behind the counter. The older man crossed his arms. Orion and Hades reached for the bags. "No," the father snapped, his glasses falling to the tip of his nose. "I said Nathaniel will take care of it."

"It's no problem. We can help carry them to our rooms," Gabriel said.

"I don't need help," Nathaniel said through gritted teeth.

"Nathaniel can do it, since he thinks he's ready to take over the inn and all. No nepotism allowed here. I had to work hard for my father, who worked hard for his father to get this place. You do all the jobs and make sure you're good at them before I hand over the business."

Nathaniel pushed himself to his feet. A muscle in his jaw tightened and his hands curled into fists. His lips pressed into a thin line, no doubt sealing in words his father surely wouldn't approve of. He took the bags one by one and placed them in a neat pile at the bottom of the steps. "I will take them up on separate trips."

"See, that's how you use your brain, boy."

He can't use his magic? I asked Hades. I was still unclear on the different types of magic faeries had. I'd seen Gabriel's but not much of Orion's.

Maybe he can. Every faerie has different magic, but most won't waste energy on ordinary tasks. Too draining. Summer Faeries are usually very traditional. They think magic should be used sparingly. It is not just magic to them. It's a gift from the land.

I must've made a face because Hades shrugged. *People have different beliefs. They're allowed to.*

I supposed I shouldn't judge, especially since I hadn't fully figured out my own magic.

We followed Orion through a narrow doorway that opened to a larger room full of empty tables. He chose one tucked into the corner. Hades took a seat beside me.

An older woman who distantly resembled Nathaniel approached us. They had the same nose and bright red hair, but that was where the similarities stopped. Her green eyes swept over us. She pulled silverware from her black apron pocket, placing a set before each person, then drew out a little notebook and pen. "Evening." She pursed her lips and didn't bother to introduce herself. "We're out of everything except the honeyed quail and lavender lemon tonic."

Orion flattened his palm on the table. "I guess it's settled then. We'd love four of those."

I tugged at a loose thread on my shirt, winding it around my finger until it went numb.

Her lips curved up, her cheeks crinkling, but the expression didn't reach her eyes. With a slight tilt of her head, the nameless woman turned away, walking through the swinging double doors into the kitchen.

Gabriel lifted his arms above his head, his fingers splaying wide as his spine arched off the chair's spindled backrest. It creaked beneath him. He exhaled and let his arms drop. "One day in and we're already going to have beds and a proper dinner. We're spoiled."

"And tomorrow?" I asked.

"Tomorrow we're setting up camp again. Soon we'll be staying with my family," Orion answered.

"Are you excited?" I asked, forcing a smile. I wasn't sure what else to say. I didn't want to let my twisted family dynamic cast a shadow over his obvious happiness.

His family was likely normal. They probably argued about who would get the last pastry and laughed about old memories. I could picture it clearly—smiles, hugs, laughter. I fiddled with my silverware and cleared the image from my head.

"So excited." Orion grinned. "I haven't seen my family in far too long. I've been spending too much time with that one"—he pointed at Gabriel—"in the Spring Court. And in the Underworld." Orion whispered the last word and looked at Hades. "No offense."

Hades raised a hand and made a face that said *none taken*.

"How long since you'd last seen them? Six months?" Gabriel asked.

"Eight. You're going to love my mother, Per—Prim." Orion glanced up at the woman as she set our food and drinks down and disappeared again without a word. "She has a massive garden overflowing with fruits and vegetables, and she's a fabulous cook."

"I can't wait to meet her," I said. The truth was that my stomach churned with more anxiety than excitement.

"She's truly wonderful," Gabriel said, and Hades nodded.

Hades hadn't said anything since we'd sat. I reached under the table and took his gloved hand, offering a small smile. He gave mine a gentle squeeze.

I grabbed my fork, stabbing a bite of food and bringing it to my mouth. It was okay. I swallowed hard and chased it with a sip of the lavender lemon tonic. The floral-citrus taste hit me with an unexpected pang, reminding me of the drinks Demeter used to make when I was a child, back when she still loved me. The memories curled through my chest, tight and unwelcome. I set the glass down a little too quickly. "Do you think Demeter is looking for the stone piece in this realm?" I asked.

Around the table, every fork stilled against its plate. Hades cleared his throat, and my gaze flicked toward him. His expression stayed carefully neutral, but his brows lifted, a small, almost imperceptible tilt of his head following.

I took another bite and slowly turned my head in the direction he'd indicated.

The swinging doors of the kitchen were still. I studied them until I caught not one but two sets of eyes peering through a slat. I recognized them—the woman who had taken our order and the man behind the desk.

I quickly looked away. A pulse of silence stretched between all of us. "Oh," I murmured. *Why are they watching us?* I asked Hades through the bond.

Hades took a sip of his drink. *They're not used to outsiders.*

Their eyes were still on us. *But...* I swallowed hard. *This is an inn. Shouldn't they be used to travelers?*

Gabriel, Orion, and Hades continued to eat, seeming unfazed by the four eyes watching our every move. *They should be,* Hades said. *But they aren't.*

Maybe we should go?

No. We'll be okay here. They're just curious.

I nodded, but the prickle of their stares clung to my skin.

~

*C*andlelight flickered from the wall mounts as we climbed the stairs, spilling a wavering orange haze along the narrow corridor. We stopped in front of a pair of doors set close together.

Gabriel handed me a small key, the metal warmed. "See you guys in the morning," he said, moving toward one and slipping the key in the knob. Orion and Gabriel went into their room, leaving me and Hades in silence.

I fumbled with the key, fitting it into the gold lock. I twisted the knob, feeling the subtle resistance give way as it clicked open.

Click.

I shivered at the sound. It was too much like the cabinet back in Olympus. I hated that such small things could remind me of my old life. I swallowed hard and pushed the door open, its hinges groaning.

A single bed dominated the small room, a red patchwork quilt embroidered with strawberries draped across it. Above the bed, a small painting hung on the wall—a field of rolling green hills beneath a bright sun. Matching lanterns glowed on the low nightstands beside the bed.

My boots clacked against the wooden floor as I stepped inside. The sound softened to a muffled thud when I reached the circular woven rug sticking out from under the bed. Hades followed, shutting the door behind him. He peeled off his sweaty brown shirt and gestured to the door at the end of the room. "You can shower first."

I chewed on the inside of my lip. Maybe I was imagining all of this. Maybe his distant gaze was nothing. My mind ran in circles anyway. "Hades."

He turned.

"Are you angry with me?"

"What do you mean?" he asked, unbuckling the strap and loosening the laces on his boots.

"You haven't said much since our conversation in the tent."

He sighed, kicking them off. "No, of course I'm not angry with you."

"Then what is it?" My voice cracked.

He ran a hand through his hair, gaze distant. He stood silent, like he was debating whether to speak at all. Hades reached for me, his fingers curling around my arm. His touch was comforting, gentle.

As silence stretched, his grip tightened. I barely noticed at first—just the faint pressure, the growing tension in his hand. But then it turned sharp, the painful sensation threading up into my shoulder. My muscles locked, every instinct screaming to make myself small, to keep still until it passed. For a heartbeat, the time between the estate in Athens and now collapsed as my body braced for this pain to become something worse. "Hades... you're hurting me."

Hades' eyes snapped to mine, and the realization hit. He released me, stumbling back. "I'm sorry." His voice cracked. "I didn't mean to hurt you." His hands flexed uselessly at his sides, as if he didn't trust them near me. "I would never—" He stopped, looking away before meeting my stare again.

"I'm okay." I blinked through the sting behind my eyes, forcing my face into a neutral expression. I didn't want him retreating from me any further.

Hades looked *ashamed*. Afraid of himself. "I'm giving you space. Room to breathe."

I shook my head. "You keep acting like I don't know what I want."

"Because you don't." His voice dropped, turning to a growl.

I flinched at his words.

His features tightened, then broke. He placed a hand on my shoulder. "You're all I think about." His voice softened as his attention landed where he touched me. "How much I want you. How much I need you. I'm a very selfish man, but right now, I don't want to take from you, not until you're ready to give. You have the trials to focus on."

"I do love you," I whispered.

The corners of Hades' mouth lifted into a faint smile. "I know you do, and I love you too. But you don't believe I'll stay. You don't trust us or yourself, not the way I do."

My mouth opened and then closed. My chest tightened. I hated that he was right. And I hated myself for bracing for the worst, expecting that at any moment, everything would change and I'd be left alone.

Again.

Even now, my arm still held the ghost of his grip. It wasn't painful anymore, but present enough to remind me how easily closeness could turn sharp. I looked down. How could I explain that I would just ruin things? And then he'd leave.

"I'm not going anywhere," he said. "But I won't force you to believe that. You have to choose to." I drew in a breath to speak, but Hades cut me off. "You can shower first, Persephone," he repeated.

I nodded, hugging my arms around myself as I walked toward the washroom. Stepping inside, I tried to push the conversation out of my head. Right now, all I wanted to do was rinse away the grime of the day.

The washroom was simple, equipped with everything I needed: a shower, a toilet, a sink with a small mirror above it. I avoided looking in that mirror. I already knew that I looked like a wreck. I didn't need another thing to hyperfixate on.

I peeled off my still-sticky clothes, raised my arm, and sniffed. "Ugh. So, so gross," I muttered. It was both humiliating and somewhat comforting to know I did smell awful. At least I had one problem I could easily fix. I huffed a laugh and reached up to my braid—messy and tight, strands glued together with sweat and gods knew what else. I worked quickly to loosen it, and the whole thing unraveled into a snarl of hair that fell past my shoulders. I finger-combed it, wincing at each snag.

I stepped into the shower and turned the water-stained dial until hot spray blasted against my back and neck. Steam curled around me. I grabbed the tiny complimentary pink bar of soap and lathered it between my palms until it foamed, the fruity scent filling the space quickly. My tension melted away under the steady stream. Despite it being so warm in the Summer Court, the heat soothed my sore muscles.

Stepping out of the shower, I wrapped myself in the red towel hanging from the long, golden rack. Droplets clung to my skin, leaving a momentary cooling sensation. With a sigh, I opened the door and stepped back into the bedroom.

Hades walked right into the washroom. On the bed, I spotted some neatly folded nightclothes and a metal water bottle. I managed a sad smile as I slipped into the smooth fabric. Taking a long sip, I let the coolness slide down my throat.

The bed creaked as I climbed in and pulled the light-weight quilt over me. The shower ran behind the washroom door. I shoved the cover off me; it was stifling.

My damp hair stuck to my skin, a single strand brushing beneath my eye, tickling with every blink. Moisture seeped into the pillow, soaking through in a slow bleed. Each small shift against the sheets sent thin rivulets trailing down my neck in ticklish lines and a *squelch* into my ear from the wet clump pressed against it. I closed my eyes. Eventually, the water shut off, and moments later, the bed dipped under Hades' weight.

He turned out the lanterns, the last traces of light fading behind my closed eyelids. My breathing stayed deliberately slow, though my heart was thudding a quick rhythm. The warmth from his body radiated to mine as he settled behind me.

Hades' lips brushed against the exposed curve of my neck. He pressed his lips to my skin and placed a slow, soft kiss.

I wanted to turn and face him, but something held me still. Maybe I was just a coward. His large hand settled on my shoulder and glided down to my hip, the heat of his touch sinking through my clothes. "I don't blame you for being unsure." His voice was low and raw. He let out a quiet laugh. "Seems to be a recurring theme in my life."

He shifted, the fabric of the quilt and pillow rustling as he settled into a comfortable position, his palm still resting on my hip.

Silence settled in, broken only by the occasional creak of wood. This room—this bed—felt too small. He lay so still, so quiet, I was sure he'd fallen asleep. I didn't probe the bond to confirm. He was shielding me.

Maybe he was resting, but I knew I wouldn't—not tonight.

I replayed the words in my mind, dissecting them. *I don't blame you for being unsure. Seems to be a recurring theme in my life.*

And I hadn't responded.

PERSEPHONE

The dining room had been quiet this morning. Only a few guests sat at the scattered tables, but the clinking of the cutlery slowed and the conversations thinned to murmurs when our group walked in. Their gazes had stuck to me like burr seed pods. Now the only sound was wind rushing past my ears.

The sun's rays had shone down on us all day. I ran a hand over Hess' dark scales and quickly pulled it back. They were still hot, like touching an open flame, even with the light fading.

I was looking forward to the Autumn Court. It was difficult for me to tolerate the heat. Hess' wings stretched wide, all of her movements precise, confident. I blinked slowly, my eyelids weighted. I pinched the inside of my wrist, hoping the sharp sting would clear the fog from my head. The slick skin shifted under my fingers, then settled. I hadn't slept well.

Why do you gnaw at your mind so much? Hess' voice slipped into my thoughts.

I'm not, I protested. *Gnawing.* I hunched forward in the

saddle. I was itchy in all the wrong places from the constant sweat and riding.

You are.

I glanced over at Hades, his glamoured violet eyes fixed on the horizon. We'd be landing soon, with one more night in the heat of this court.

I'm just thinking.

Overthinking, she corrected.

I would give her that one.

I don't share a mate bond like you do with the god, her snout pointed in Hades' direction, *but I am tethered enough to know. You let fear keep you from speaking. Why do you do that?*

I didn't respond, only gazed ahead.

What has that god done to earn your silence?

I had no accusation I could throw at him, no shield to hide behind. *It's not like that—*

She cut me off. *He is devoted to you.*

I know that.

And yet you doubt him. Why? If I had a mate, I definitely wouldn't be complaining.

I'm not complaining.

You're not happy.

I'm not unhappy.

Can't you feel what he feels for you?

Well, right now, I couldn't. He'd blocked me off, sheltering me from his emotions.

I'm not going to stop bothering you until you tell me. I can't take any more of this tension.

I'm scared he'll leave, that he will realize I'm not enough. The words flowed through our tether, so quiet I almost didn't trust I'd spoken them. Hess never coddled me, never wrapped me in false comfort. She treated me like I was still whole, and that made it far too easy to be honest.

Her wings faltered, and her chest rumbled with laughter.

Shame burned through me. *This isn't funny. I should've never told you.*

Hess scoffed. *You are a goddess. You have a devoted mate. You have three men willing to do whatever they need to in order to help you. You have four dragons that would die for you. And you're still here, aren't you? The Fates have decided you are worthy enough to keep living on your thread. If that is not proof of your worth, what will it take to convince you?*

You would die for me? I didn't understand how anyone could say that so easily.

She huffed. *Out of all that, that's the part you're asking me about?*

I stayed silent. I was ungrateful. She believed in me—without hesitation, without asking for anything in return—and I couldn't even see myself as someone worth saving. Hess deserved better.

Stop. You're doing it again. Yes, Persephone. Dragons do not pick riders lightly. We understand we are taking a risk, and that's one I'm willing to face if it means helping you. She vibrated as she chuckled. *I am also sure that if I died, the future Queen of the Underworld would take care of me? Right?*

Yes. A small smile crested on my lips before I pursed them. I knew all creatures, all souls went to the Underworld. But it made me want to learn more about the realm I now called home. Everyone seemed to know more about it than I did. *Thank you.*

Okay, now answer my question. What will it take?

I don't know. The admission threaded its slow poison through my chest.

That's the problem. Don't you see it?

I am painfully aware, I said.

At least you recognize it. Her wings beat through a cloud. *If you keep needing others to prove your worth to you, nothing they say or do will ever be enough.*

Well, how do I stop doing that?

It's different for everyone.

I let the silence stretch. *Helpful.*

I'm trying to help you.

I know, and I appreciate it. I shook my head, the words falling softer now. *The situation is just not that simple.* Hess didn't know. She hadn't spent years holding her breath. Demeter hadn't always hurt me. She'd loved me until that one cursed night. She had trained me to expect pain after softness.

It could be. Hess didn't speak again for a few moments. *We're going to land soon.*

Not five minutes passed before Hess lowered, her massive violet wings angling. Air churned around us in powerful rivulets, and the ground rushed closer. She flared her wings wide, slowing us before we hit the ground, then folded them with a smooth ripple of muscle.

Falon, Rys, and Seph followed suit. Hades slid off Falon and quickly moved toward me, probably scared that I'd try to get down on my own again. My ankle was mostly better, except for a dull throb when I moved it the wrong way. Surely that would be gone by tomorrow.

Hades stood below. "I'll catch you."

I nodded and slid down, my boots skidding against Hess' side before Hades caught me. I sagged in his arms.

Talk to him, Hess growled.

I'll try.

She made a *hmph* noise and headed for the other dragons. *We're going to hunt.*

Have fun. I waved.

Hades, Gabriel, and Orion set up the tents, moving with practiced ease that made it clear they didn't need me. Still, I stepped in. "Wow, look at that," Orion said as I crouched down and straightened one of the poles. "Someone is participating today."

"Shush," I muttered.

I handed the pole to Gabriel.

"Leave her alone," he said.

"Make me," Orion said with a chuckle.

"I hope something drags you into the forest tonight. You give me a headache," Gabriel grumbled.

"I hope so." Orion snorted and raked a hand through his hair. "It'll be so nice to be wanted for once."

We all laughed—real, full laughter that cracked the heavy tension that had been lingering over us. "All right, all right," Gabriel said through a ghost of a smile. "Let me set up the ward before something does actually drag Orion away. I'm not in the mood to have to rescue him."

He closed his eyes, and a soft light stirred in the air. A dome quickly formed over our campsite, glowing white before fading into invisibility.

～

We ate our dinner by the fire. The heat was suffocating. "I need to wash off. A bath would be nice."

"All right," Orion said, rummaging through a leather bag sitting next to him. "Catch." An oval-shaped white bar of soap flew through the air. Just as I was ready to brace for impact, Hades caught the bar just two inches away from my face.

"Don't ever throw anything at my mate again," Hades growled.

Orion shrugged. "I knew someone would catch it. It's fun to see you go all alpha male."

Hades glared at Orion, scoffed, and handed me the soap. I

took it slowly, trying to ignore the way my stomach fluttered. I cleared my throat. "Thanks," I said.

He nodded. "I'll come with you."

"I'm sure I'll be able to find water." I waved a hand. "You know, just walk until I hear it."

"I'm not worried about you finding it or bathing yourself. I'm worried about whatever could be waiting there. Many creatures of Faerie would love to catch you alone, and you can't use your magic to defend yourself."

I tensed, my heart stuttering. "Oh, okay."

"Let's go." Hades offered me a hand and pulled me off the log I sat on. We walked through the ward, the ripple of magic washing over us.

Hades walked ahead of me, pushing aside branches and brush so I wouldn't have to. I reminded him I could handle myself, but he insisted. We continued on for about ten minutes until we reached a thin river.

I swallowed hard, pretending not to notice the heat of Hades' gaze burning through my skin. It wasn't just a look—it was possession and hunger rolled into one. I turned my back to him as if that would help.

Slipping off the dagger sheath, I hooked it over my shoulder. I couldn't take it off completely, not with the threat of the trials hanging over me.

I started with my boots and then moved to my pants, peeling off the brown leather, the material fused to my skin. I hooked my thumbs in the waistband, but it barely budged, rolling down just an inch before catching. They clung to me like it had a vendetta against me.

With a mix of wiggles and a low string of curses, I shimmied them down, taking my underwear with them. "Stop fighting back." They finally bunched at my ankles. "Almost done," I said to myself. I kept my back to Hades, not wanting to look him in the eye while I did this humiliating dance of hopping, squatting, and yanking.

What a striptease, Hades said through the bond.

I don't want to hear it.

With one last hop, I yanked the pants off my feet and kicked them away. They landed in a heap nearby. I glared at them, glancing up to find Hades leaning against a tree with a look that made it very clear he had enjoyed the show. He clapped slowly, mockingly, the sound echoing through the trees.

My eye twitched. *Would you like me to drown you?* I fastened the dagger back on my thigh.

His grin widened. *Careful, goddess. Don't tempt me like that. My safe word is ferrule.*

I shook my head in disbelief. *And that's... what exactly?* I asked.

The metal piece that attaches the bristles to a paintbrush, Hades said into my mind. His tone made it sound like that was common knowledge.

Interesting. I turned away before he could see the smile I was trying to suppress. I pulled my shirt over my head, unclasped my bra, and threw them on top of the pants.

The cool water covered my feet as I stepped in. I walked until it covered my calves, my knees, and then my thighs. The smooth rocks shifted under my weight as I waded in deeper. I glanced back at Hades, half-expecting him to have moved.

He hadn't.

Hades still leaned against the tree, but his smile was gone. His expression had softened into one that made me feel like the center of the universe.

It was ridiculous. The bond we shared wasn't new, but it was so... *new* in countless ways. I focused on the water, sighing as I lathered the soap.

"Mind if I join you?" he asked.

"No," I said, trying to concentrate on the slick lather between my hands, willing myself to ignore the swirl in my belly. But my attention drifted to Hades, pulled like a thread.

The way he looked at me made my skin feel too tight and my chest too full. It made me want to hide and lean in all at once.

Hades' fingers found the hem of his shirt. He pulled it over his head, the fabric dragging over taut muscle and broad shoulders, mussing his glamoured blond hair. The moonlight traced along every ridge of his torso.

He undid his belt. The muscles in his legs flexed as he kicked off the pants, having a much easier time than I had. Hades moved into the water. His gaze never left mine as he closed the distance between us. "This water feels nice."

I swallowed. "It does."

Hades' hand rested on my arm, just below my elbow. It was as if he was waiting for me to pull back. His thumb brushed my skin, sending my racing pulse into overdrive. "Persephone," he whispered. "You're beautiful."

Heat climbed up my neck and flooded my cheeks. He stepped closer, the heat of his body warming mine. His hand moved from my arm to my jaw, cupping my face. I closed my eyes as he traced my skin with his fingertip. "Tell me what you're thinking about."

I appreciated that he hadn't probed either of the bonds. I closed my eyes. "Does it even matter?"

"Of course it does," he murmured. "Everything about you matters to me."

I shook my head.

His grip on my arm tightened. "Doubt all you want, but it won't change the truth."

I wanted to scoff, to let his words roll off me, but I couldn't. I took the lathered soap and ran it over my arms.

"I'm scared," I said finally, my voice low. Part of me prayed he didn't hear.

"It's normal to be scared. The trials are unpredictable, but you will be okay."

I squeezed my eyes shut and continued to wash myself. "Not the trials. W-well, yes, the trials, but that's not what I'm thinking about right now."

"I'm not a mind reader, you know."

I scoffed and folded my arms, clutching the bar of soap, slick and threatening to slip free. "It feels like you can always see right through me."

"That's because I can. I can't read every thought in that pretty head of yours, but I know you." His voice dipped lower. "I'm giving you some privacy, but if you ever think you'll be able to hide from me, you're wrong." He pulled me close, my naked body flush against his.

Hess' words from earlier fluttered through my mind. *Talk to him,* she had said. I swallowed my pride—at least some of it. "I don't know how to do this. How to trust. How to be… enough."

"All you have to do is be yourself."

"You make it sound so easy." I chuckled. I wished I could buy a book on how to let myself be loved, or how to love myself. That would truly make life easier.

"I'm not going to leave you. I'll wait."

"I don't want you to." The words came out softer than I'd meant them.

His mouth parted slightly, as if he wasn't sure he'd heard me right. "You don't want me to wait?"

"I don't want you to leave." I wasn't ready to lose what I hadn't even fully let myself have.

He leaned in, his lips brushing the shell of my ear. "Leave you?" His voice was rough as if the very idea had offended him. "I don't think you understand, little goddess. There is no leaving."

I tried to pull away from him, but he held me still.

"Not for me. Not for you. You're mine and you have been since the moment I laid eyes on you. Nothing will change that."

Goose bumps prickled across my skin.

"Not time. Not your doubt. Not distance. Nothing."

"I—"

"You can run. What will not change is this: I belong to you and you belong to me." His lips pressed to mine, soft then more forceful. For the first time in a while, emotions surged through the mating bond. His feelings flooded through me. Love. So, so much love. It was deep, raw in a way that sent a shiver down my spine.

I couldn't breathe. Couldn't think. I could only feel him —every single piece, all at once. I pulled back, gasping for air.

Hades' fingers slid into my hair, threading through my strands. "That"—he pressed a quick kiss to my lips—"is how I feel about you. Remember it."

I couldn't respond. I couldn't form a coherent thought. He pressed his lips back to mine, his tongue slipping between them. His grip tightened in my hair just enough to put tension on it, pulling my neck back again. "You're not getting away from me."

I licked my lips, a tremor catching in my chest.

"I don't care how many walls you build. I'll break through every single one." His cock jutted, pressing against my stomach.

I glanced down.

He raised a brow as if he was daring me to do something about it. I made the smallest movement, but before I could reach down, Hades turned me in his arms, pressing my back against his chest. "Am I"—I heaved a breath—"not allowed to touch you?"

His teeth grazed the shell of my ear. "Oh, little goddess, I want you to touch me, but right now, I just want to take care of you. I want to slip my fingers inside that little cunt of yours until you come around them."

His voice wrapped around me. My body betrayed me before my mind could catch up. My thighs pressed together, warmth sparking deep in my core. "And your cock?" was all I could say.

He growled. "Soon."

"Tonight?"

"When you're ready."

I yelped as Hades' fingers found my puckered nipple and squeezed.

"I want you to accept my love. I want you to feel worthy. I want you to feel every ounce of love I have for you as I fuck you. I want you to beg."

His fingers found my other nipple as his other hand drifted down my stomach and into the water. His touch circled my clit.

"How are you so sure I'll beg?"

"Because your body is begging me now. Your mouth just hasn't caught up."

My head fell back onto his chest as he pressed a kiss to my temple, and I moaned. His finger slipped into my center. My back arched, but Hades' hands held me in place.

"I love how your pussy is squeezing my fingers." Hades continued to finger me and rub my clit. "Fuck, you're so beautiful."

I writhed in his arms. The only thing keeping me on my feet was his hold. "More of that," I panted. "Please."

"You like when I play with your clit like that?"

I nodded violently against him. A rumble vibrated

through his chest. "I want you to come for me, Persephone. Come all over my fingers."

My body obeyed his words. I moaned, my eyes fluttering closed as my release crashed over me. Hades pressed a few kisses to my temple as I shivered in his arms. "Fuck," he muttered, picking me up bridal style. Water ran in slender lines down my skin. I wrapped my arms around his neck.

He held me for a minute or two as I recovered from my orgasm. I yawned, and he set me on my shaky legs. "Let's get dressed and head back. I'm tired too," he said.

"We should've brought fresh clothes."

Hades scratched his head and laughed. "That would've been a good idea."

I glared at the leather pants that had been so much work to put on. I picked them up and wiggled a foot in, the fabric bunching and refusing to cooperate. I yanked, inching them up my calves. The water dripping off me made everything worse.

It took a lot of work, but I got them on. "That was quite a show," Hades said with a light chuckle. He had been able to dress easily.

I gave a sharp huff as I took my shirt and pulled it over my head.

We walked back to camp, the ward washing over us as we stepped through it. "By the way, I dropped the soap. I'm sorry."

Hades chuckled and placed a hand on the small of my back. "I'll give you a pass this time. You were a little distracted."

"More than a little," I whispered.

2 2

PERSEPHONE

I dashed barefoot across the cold marble. The chill bit at my skin, but I didn't care. I clutched my little pot to my chest.

"Slow down, my lily," Mother called, her voice lilting. She lounged on the couch, her golden teacup poised between her fingers, and smiled at me. "I don't want you getting hurt."

"It bloomed," I said, holding out the plant like a treasure. The white petals on the green stem swayed from the movement.

I sat up, gasping. Hades lay beside me, his breath slow and even. I scrubbed my hand down my face. That dream—that memory—was a cruel joke, a vision of her softness before everything had turned to bruises and silence.

I hated the part of me that still craved the mother who smelled like lilies and not the one who locked the door when I cried.

I hated it.

I hated me.

I should've been grateful for the nightmares. The good memories were far worse.

~

*M*y eyes fluttered open, and I turned to my right. Hades wasn't there. No indentation marked the bedroll, suggesting he'd gotten up a while ago. In his place was a flower. A soft smile tugged at my lips as I picked it up, running my fingers over its curled pink petals, revealing a darker magenta center. I twirled the stem between my index finger and thumb. "Pretty," I whispered, taking a sniff. The flower had a fresh, honeyed scent.

I sat up with a groan. At the foot of the bedroll, the open leather bag waited. I rummaged through it for fresh clothes. After dressing, I brushed my teeth and took a swig of water, swishing it around.

Pushing through the tent flaps, I winced as the canvas snagged my hair. That would need to be braided before we left. I'd learned quickly not to leave it down. The sting from untangling the mats wasn't worth it. I turned my head and spat the foamy mint mixture, making sure it landed away from the tent.

Sunlight speckled the ground through the canopy of leaves above us. I was glad we were away from the center of the Summer Court. It was still warm here but not as unbearable.

Orion sat on a log beside the dead fire, its ring of stones holding nothing but ash and splintered black wood. He crossed one arm over his chest, raising the other and tossing something. A foiled bundle curved through the air toward me. Surprisingly, I caught it.

"Eat," he said.

I sat on the log across from him and unwrapped the foil. Another sandwich, the same as the others. "Where's Hades?" I glanced around. "And Gabriel?"

"They've started packing the dragons." Orion's head

tipped to the right, gesturing to the clearing in the distance. I could make out the bodies of the dragons, but though my vision was enhanced as a Divine, I couldn't see Hades or Gabriel.

My sandwich was gone in a few bites. I crumpled the foil into a tight ball, toying with it as Orion quietly ate. A loose splinter protruded from the log, and I flicked it to the ground. He cleared his throat. "You're training with Gabriel today. It's his turn."

I gave a short nod, remembering when they'd mentioned it yesterday. "I'll try not to embarrass myself."

His face scrunched. "You won't."

My laugh came out harsher than I'd meant it. "I'm barely getting by." I tugged at the dagger strapped to my thigh.

"You're getting better."

I glanced up at Orion, expecting to see a big smile on his face, but his expression was calm, steady. "Oh, you're serious?"

Orion nodded.

Boots crunched through the underbrush, pulling my attention away. Gabriel and Hades walked toward us. The fae stopped a few feet off. "You ready?"

I brushed crumbs from my thighs. "Ready as I'll ever be."

Orion lifted a brow. "She just ate. Give her a minute to digest? I don't want to see her vomit."

Gabriel crossed his arms and shook his head. "If she was pulled into a trial right now, she'd have to fight with a full stomach. No point in babying her."

"Ugh." Orion's nose crinkled. "Don't puke, Persephone. That's all I ask."

I made a show of dry-heaving, one hand pressed dramatically to my stomach.

Orion groaned and covered his eyes.

A shadow fell over me. I glanced up.

Hades. He said nothing, just rested a gloved palm on my shoulder and kissed the top of my head. Hades stretched out a hand, and I dropped the crumpled foil into it. He pocketed the ball and then squeezed my shoulders. "Try not to miss me too much."

I glanced back at him. "Bold of you to assume I'd miss you at all."

Hades placed a playful hand over his heart. *You don't mean that*, he spoke through the bond.

I do.

You would've had a very different answer last night when you were coming on my fingers.

Heat rose to my cheeks, but I raised my chin. *I don't remember last night.*

Would you like a refresher? The wall in our bond cracked, and a vision of last night slipped past—through his eyes. I nearly choked on my own saliva.

Enough. The vision disappeared. I blinked hard, trying to ground myself.

Hades grinned and reached for me. I took his hand, letting him pull me to my feet. It was nice—the shift between us. The heaviness wasn't gone, only lighter, my anxious thoughts still present, but quieter. I flexed my ankle back and forth. The pain was gone.

"Follow me." Gabriel led me through the trees. Soft earth yielded under my boots as I trailed after him. The forest thinned, giving way to the clearing where dew-speckled green blades shimmered under the sunlight. The dragons sat in the distance. "This will do," Gabriel said.

I turned toward him, and he lunged at me.

I twisted to dodge his strike. His fist clipped my shoulder with enough force to send me sprawling backward. The wet ground pressed into my back, soaking through my shirt. I pushed myself up.

A sharp sting bloomed in my shoulder and arm. Surely I'd bruise soon. Complaining would do nothing for me, though. Gabriel would only remind me that I always had to be ready.

And he was right.

I narrowly avoided slipping as I pushed myself into an attack. I didn't wait. My hand aimed for his midsection, but he was already in position, his weight shifting smoothly as he pivoted to avoid me.

We both took a few steps back, circling each other. The grass squelched beneath our boots. His movements were practiced, but mine dragged, clumsy and heavy. I kept my eyes locked on him and darted forward. He shifted at the last second, and my hand grazed the empty air. "Predictable," he said, his voice low.

I launched myself at him again.

"Better." His lips quirked into a grin. "But not enough," he said, and he pushed me back.

I hummed, looking for an opportunity to strike him.

"You know, you remind me of my sister."

I shifted on the slick ground, and my toes curled in my boots as I tried not to slip. My mouth parted slightly. "Your sister?"

He rolled his shoulders and put his hands back into position. "She was a lot like you. Stubborn. Reckless."

I might've bristled at being called both reckless and stubborn without hesitation, but the way he said them, it almost sounded like a compliment. "Did you teach her how to fight?"

He nodded. "I did. You have the same fire as her."

Fire. If he was referring to the mess of emotions simmering in my chest, that was appropriate. His weight shifted to his left, and I saw an opening. "How so?" I asked as I studied him.

"She felt everything deeply." His voice lowered. "She carried the weight of the world on her back."

I let out a breath. "Sounds very exhausting."

His eyes narrowed. He was studying me as well. "It's not a bad thing to feel."

"I prefer not to."

"Do you?"

I froze, a strange ache tightening in my chest.

"You feel plenty, Persephone. It's obvious."

My fingers curled, nails pressing crescent moons into my skin. "What happened to her?"

Gabriel's expression tightened. "She died."

That I knew, but I didn't press. Hades had told me the first time we'd come to Faerie, before the gala.

"She died during the Faerie War," he continued quietly. "I told her not to fight, begged her to stay home, but she wouldn't hear it. She said she'd stay with me. I couldn't protect her." His jaw clenched. "She died on the battlefield, in my arms. As a prize of honor in the Faerie War, I was rewarded with immortality."

My mind blanked. *How do I respond to that?* "I'm sorry, Gabriel." I knew the words would do nothing. Pity never did. I knew that well enough.

"It's life."

I rubbed the edge of my shirt between my fingers. "Have you visited her in the Underworld?"

"No."

"Why not?"

Gabriel wiped away the sweat on his forehead. "The dead deserve peace. They've earned it. I'll see her if I die. Faerie immortality is different from that of the Divine."

"I don't disagree. But it sounds like your pride is getting in the way."

His lips twitched into a humorless smile. "Maybe."

"You miss her." It wasn't a question.

"I do."

I swallowed my physical ache and charged, pouring my strength into a strike. My shoulder slammed into his chest, and Gabriel stumbled, his boots skidding.

Unfortunately, I went down with him, the impact sending a hard jolt through my body as we hit the ground. Gabriel let out a loud grunt. I half-expected him to be angry at me for striking him when he'd been vulnerable. Instead, a slow grin spread across his face. "Now you're getting it."

He pushed himself up, brushing crushed grass and natural debris off his clothes. "We're done for today." He gestured toward the trees, where Hades and Orion stood in their shade.

Orion grinned, holding out his palm. "Good job."

I slapped it with a tired laugh. Hades wrapped an arm around my shoulder. "I didn't know you guys were watching," I said.

"We didn't catch all of it, but we definitely saw you take down Gabriel." Orion chuckled.

~

The wind stung my cheeks—we'd been flying for hours. We were planning on crossing into the Autumn Court tonight, and I was glad about that. I was not made for the heat. Every hour on Hess tested me. My muscles ached from gripping her sides. The saddle had left my groin sore, and my arms and hands were tired from holding on to the leather grip.

I glanced down at the trees passing below us. I still wasn't used to the flight or the dragons, the constant movement. I wanted to go home to the Underworld. I missed it. It was something Demeter's estate never was; a choice, not a cage.

Can I ask you something? I questioned Hades through our bond.

Anything.

Earlier, Gabriel told me he was gifted immortality. What about Orion?

Faeries have long lives compared to mortal standards, but there are a few ways faeries can be immortal. One: If you are royal, you are born or granted with immortality. Two: If you do something extraordinary, you may be gifted immortality. Three: If you compete in the games.

Games? I asked.

Yes, every twenty years, each court holds games. It's a fight to the death, essentially. If you are the last man or woman standing, you win immortality. Orion won the Autumn Court's games a few years after I was assigned to rule the Underworld, as did his father many years before him. His mother won them too, but she's originally from the Spring Court.

So a family of winners?

Yes. But keep in mind, fae immortality isn't the same as that of the Divines'. Immortal fae don't age, but they can still be killed. For Divine, we can only die through breaking a contract with the Fates. And since Olympian Court members are bound by blood to the court, no one dares disobey it. Yet.

We continued to fly, my mind slipping in and out of focus.

Persephone, hold on tight, Hess said.

My grip tightened around the handle, my fingers cramping. I glanced over at Hades. His face was sharp with focus, scanning the sky around us. *Is something wrong?* I asked through our bond. My heart raced.

Yes, listen to Hess, Hades said.

Hess jerked, stretching her wings out to steady us. *Pirates,* she said.

What do they want from us? I asked, the question ripping out of me.

Riches. Valuables. Anything they can sell.

My stomach flipped. Pirates. I'd thought pirates sailed the seas.

Pirates on dragons? I blinked, struggling to catch up.

Yes.

The clouds thickened around us, swirling into a stone gray. Damp air kissed my skin, and the horizon vanished into nothing. A dark shape moved ahead. "Get ready!" Gabriel yelled, his voice distant and muffled.

The fog thickened, turning nearly black. Hess growled, and the sound vibrated through my legs and into my spine. *What's happening?* I asked her.

I can smell them, she snarled. *I know these dragons. Shield your mind. I sense one Spirit Faerie among them.*

I didn't ask her how she knew the pirates. The rage in her voice said enough. My heart hammered. Falon made a deep, thunderous noise.

My eyes darted around us. Through the fog, I could barely make out their silhouettes, but we still held our earlier formation. Hades rode to my right, Orion rode behind me, and Gabriel was at my left.

Wings beat hard, a roar shattering the sound.

I will protect you, Hess vowed, her voice a rumble in my mind.

I nodded, though I knew she couldn't feel it. I braced myself.

A shadow barreled through the fog.

Too fast.

A massive emerald green dragon moved toward us with precision that made it clear it wasn't its first time doing this. A rider crouched low on its back, body draped in dark cloth, face hidden behind a hood and mask.

Gleaming white fangs snapped inches from my head. The heat of the dragon's breath scorched my skin. I flinched, flattening myself on Hess' back, the saddle's handle poking my abdomen.

The force of its wingbeats shook the air, nearly knocking me out of my seat. Thank the Fates for the strap holding me in it. "Shit," I muttered, heart lurching into my throat.

The green dragon streaked forward after its failed strike, vanishing into the mist.

Hess surged after it, twisting through the air. A long stream of fire burst from her mouth, cutting through the fog. Somewhere in the haze, her target shrieked.

Another roar split the air, deeper than the emerald dragon's. I dared a glance behind me. Orion and Seph clashed with a golden dragon, their forms tangled. I tore my eyes away, too focused on a huge blue shape slicing through the air toward Hess and me.

Duck, Hess yelled at me.

I ducked as its claws swiped where my chest had been, talons missing me by inches.

Hess spun, her wings flapping hard as she climbed, but the blue dragon followed. I glanced back—too close. The rider wore a mask like the last one. The creature snarled, baring rows of sharp teeth.

Hess dropped, veering into a dive, and the world tilted forward. My insides heaved as the movement pulled me. The ground swelled, filling my sight. This was it. This is how I was going to die. *Watch this*, Hess said and roared.

We leveled out hard. Her wings caught the wind and she barreled through a full rotation. My neck craned back. *They're still following us.*

I know.

A shadow lunged from the fog beside us.

Hades.

Falon's black body slammed into the blue dragon with a sickening crack. It screeched, its body writhing midair as it was knocked off-course. Out of the corner of my eye, bursts of magic flared—Gabriel and Orion trading blows with the faerie pirates.

Hess moved fast to avoid the falling beast. One by one, the pirates peeled off, disappearing into the fog like ghosts.

Seph, Rys, and Falon swooped behind us, circling wide.

We flew in silence for a few minutes. "Let's land," Gabriel yelled.

I glanced over at Hades, flying to my right. His posture sagged, his grip unsteady on the handle, his jaw clenched. He shifted and a sharp wince flickered across his face. *Hades*, I said through the bond.

He didn't respond, only groaned as Falon glided down to land. Hess' landing was rough, but it didn't matter. I slipped out of the saddle and slid down her side. My boots hit the ground with a jolt and I staggered forward. I'd dismounted by myself for the first time—without injury. But all my concern was on Hades. "Hades," I yelled.

Falon landed a second later, his massive body shaking the earth. Slumped in the seat, Hades didn't move. Gabriel and Orion rushed to his side, helping him down. Hades was barely conscious, his face pale and his eyes unfocused.

I'd never seen him like this.

My legs wobbled, threatening to buckle, but I refused to stop. My pulse was a drumbeat in my ears, and I pushed forward.

They eased him down from Falon, then laid him on his front. My breath hitched mid-inhale as I froze. The world around me blurred, everything narrowing to the sight before me.

A deep lash tore across his back—jagged skin, soaked

with blood. "Oh my gods," I said. My fingers trembled. Tightness seized my ribs.

I kneeled next to Hades. His brows knitted together. He exhaled a sharp hiss through his teeth, eyes squeezing shut before flickering open. I slid my fingers through his glamoured blond hair, needing to touch him. Pain coursed through the bond, even though he tried to block me.

"I'll be fine," he whispered.

My hands shook as my eyes locked on the wound. "Gabriel." It was bad.

Gabriel leaned in close. "It's not poisoned."

"Thank the Fates," I whispered.

"But it's definitely painful—"

Hades cut him off with a strained laugh. "You think so?"

"We need to clean it," Gabriel finished.

"I'll pitch the tent quickly," Orion said, working to unpack the poles.

Gabriel nodded, gathering supplies. He handed me gauze, tape, random vials, and other essentials, rummaging through an aid kit.

I clutched the items tight to keep from dropping them. I couldn't be weak right now. "You're going to be okay," I whispered.

Hades huffed a quiet laugh, wincing as he shifted. "You're acting like I'm dying."

I shot him a glare, but he only smirked and said, "Damn. Seeing you all riled up over me is… intoxicating."

"You're bleeding out. Not the time, Hades."

"You screaming my name does things to me." His voice was hoarse but still laced with heat. "Do I need to remind you I'm immortal, little goddess?"

I shook my head, fighting a smile. "Unbelievable. Just stop moving before you make things worse. The blood is supposed to stay *inside* you."

"Fierce and bossy is a good look on you," he murmured, the last few words dropping to a whisper as his eyes shut.

I pressed one palm to his temple, and my other hand gripped his shoulder as I leaned in. "Hades."

No response.

Gabriel came up next to me. "It's just the blood loss. He'll be okay. He's been through much worse."

That didn't make me feel better.

Gabriel moved to help Orion put up the tent. They worked quickly, their movements practiced, but my impatience made every motion feel drawn out.

I tried to hold the things Gabriel had given me steady. Hades' breathing was shallow, a soft, constant rasp. "Just hold still," I whispered. I could barely hear my voice over the sound of my heart pounding in my ears.

Orion clasped his hands together. "All right, let's get him in the tent so he can rest without being moved again."

I nodded. The two men picked Hades up. I had to stop the sob threatening to claw its way from my throat at the sound Hades made as he came back to consciousness. They moved slowly, carrying him into the tent and laying him face down on the bedroll. Gabriel turned to me. "Do you want me to help him, or can you?"

I chewed on my lip. "I've never cleaned a wound."

"You can touch him. It'll be easier for you," Gabriel said.

I clutched the supplies in my shaking hands. "Okay. I'll do it."

"Do you want us to stay, or would you like privacy?"

"Privacy," Hades grunted.

Gabriel nodded.

"I can"—I swallowed—"I can do this," I said, more to myself than him. "Just tell me what needs to be done."

Gabriel pointed to one of the vials I held, filled with a deep chartreuse liquid. "Pour this over the wound. It'll sting like hell, but it will clean it out." Gabriel moved closer to me. "If he passes out, don't worry. That's normal."

My eyes widened.

He pointed to another vial that held a thick crimson liquid. "Then use this one. It'll slow the bleeding." He pointed to a turquoise one. "Have him drink this afterward. This will help with the healing. Make sure he drinks it slowly so that he doesn't throw up." He pointed to the gauze and tape. "Then cover the wound with this. If you have any questions, yell."

I pushed a few stray strands of hair away from my face with my forearm. "Can they find us?"

"The pirates?" Gabriel asked.

I nodded, and he shook his head. "They'd rather spend their time finding easier targets, and I put a ward around us as soon as we landed."

Orion and Gabriel left the tent.

I kneeled beside Hades, my hands trembling as I touched his blood-soaked clothes. "This might hurt," I said.

"I can take it," he told me, but the pain in his voice was impossible to disguise.

I grabbed a pair of steel scissors from the pile of supplies and cut through what was left of his torn shirt, trying to work quickly but carefully. I picked up the first vial of liquid and poured it over the wound. Hades' muscles tightened beneath my fingers. "Sorry," I whispered.

Hades let out a long string of curses.

I flinched. "You're doing great."

"I love spending quality time with my mate," he hissed.

"Oh, shut up."

"Your bedside manner could use some improvement," he gritted out through his clenched teeth.

I ignored him and rested one of my hands on his head, trying to soothe him as best I could. "Almost done." I tried not to make things worse, but it wasn't easy. His skin was hot beneath my touch. His fingers reached out and tightened on my thigh as I worked.

I poured the next vial on the wound, and Hades let out another moan. My fingers fumbled with the roll of gauze and tape, but I managed to place them both. Hades recoiled underneath me, his body trembling. "Sorry." I continued working. "I'm sorry."

Hades' head moved, his eyes flickering open. "Persephone," he rasped. "You should rest."

Why was he worried about me when he was the one with an open gash? "I'm fine." I kept working until I finished. The worst of the wound was covered. "It's done."

His shoulders dropped. "Thank you."

"Actually, one last thing."

He groaned.

I uncapped the last little vial and lowered it to his lips. He angled his head back as far as he could while he lay on his stomach. I threaded my fingers into his sweaty hair. His breath trembled and ghosted the skin on my wrist. I tapped the glass on his lips twice and tilted it. "Drink."

His throat bobbed as he swallowed. His glamoured violet eyes locked onto mine as he drank. A shiver passed between us. I wasn't sure who it started with. But I didn't pull away until the last drop was gone.

His head fell down onto the bedroll as he exhaled. I stayed there, running my fingers through his hair until sleep took him. I pulled back, my knees drawn to my chest, studying the rise and fall of his back.

∼

I sat in the tent for hours, watching him. I couldn't stop thinking about Hades. He slept, but his brow twitched often. Even now, pain wouldn't leave him alone.

My stomach rumbled, pulling me from my thoughts. I hadn't eaten since morning. Too long, probably. I pushed myself up and stepped outside. The moon hung high, pale and watchful. Its light sifted through the branches in silver threads, snagging on the edges of leaves. Gabriel and Orion sat by a fire they must've made while I was in the tent. Gabriel's eyes lifted to mine as I stepped closer, his green irises catching the firelight. "Sandwich?"

I nodded, taking the familiar foil pack.

"How's he doing?" Orion asked.

I took a seat. "He's sleeping. I did the best I could with the wound."

"He just needs rest," Gabriel said, his eyes narrowing on the tent.

I took a slow bite of the sandwich.

"I know it's easier said than done, but try to relax. Hades will be okay. He is strong, even with his magic strained."

I nodded and kept eating. "How long do you think it will take him to heal?"

"He'll probably be a little better tomorrow. Still in pain, but his skin will stitch itself together."

I finished my food and stood abruptly. I needed to move. I needed to do something, anything. "I'd like to bathe."

Gabriel raised a brow and nodded. "There's a river nearby, about a five-minute walk that way." He pointed off into the trees. "It's shallow, but the water's fresh." He stood and rifled through a bag. "Here's some soap." He handed me a bar.

"Thanks," I murmured.

I crossed the ward, the invisible magic rippling over me,

underbrush crunching under my feet as I made my way forward. It was quiet—the kind where I could hear my own heartbeat.

I reached the water quickly. It moved over the smooth stones, producing a soft flowing noise. I crouched and dipped my fingers in, the cool current lapping at my skin. A single leaf swirled past before slipping from sight.

Something rustled behind me. I tensed. A prickle crawled up my nape. My hand went to the dagger sheathed at my thigh. I turned, my muscles coiled tight.

A pale creature about my height standing on its hind legs with thick horns leaped from the shadows. The skin along its ribs stretched tight over bone, its pink, glassy eyes small and sunken. Claws sliced the air in front of me. The motion tore a strand of my hair free; it whipped across my mouth, tasting of sweat. The creature lunged for my throat—I struck first, dagger slashing its side, cutting through flesh with a sickening, wet sound. It shrieked, but I was already on top of it.

It clawed my skin, but the adrenaline masked the pain. I didn't hesitate. My chest heaved as I plunged the dagger deep. It was it or me.

And I wanted to live.

The creature's breath turned ragged, its movements frantic to get away from me. I wanted to scream.

I didn't.

I thrust the blade deeper, cutting through its throat until bone crunched. It went limp, and quiet returned to the forest.

I stood, my chest heaving, the blood of the creature covering my hands and my clothes. I didn't have any disgust or fear. *What is wrong with me?*

Stepping away from the carcass, I peeled off my blood-soaked clothes and kneeled by the water to wash my hands clean. I worked in silence, rinsing myself and scrubbing the pieces of fabric one by one. The stains faded, but the metallic scent lingered.

I hadn't brought a change of clothes, so once I'd wrung out the fabric and it was no longer dripping, I pulled the damp garments back on, shivering as they clung to my skin.

I stood, looking at the fallen creature one last time. I guessed I wasn't as weak as I thought.

But why didn't I feel strong?

I'd thought change would feel sharper. Obvious. Like something inside me would *click*. It came like a slow tide, touching everything but moving nothing. And all I felt was tired.

The walk back to the camp was a blur, my thoughts spinning.

I didn't feel clean. I set the bar of soap on the log to dry next to the pack of supplies, keeping my face turned toward the shadows.

Gabriel and Orion looked up as I passed, but neither of them said anything.

"Good night," I murmured.

"Sleep well," they said.

I headed for the tent. The ground was uneven beneath my boots, or maybe I was just too tired keep a straight line. The tent flaps brushed over me as I slipped inside, then fell behind me with a soft *thump*.

Hades still lay asleep. I moved to his side, kneeled, and pressed a soft kiss to his skin.

Holding my breath, I tipped a few drops left from the chartreuse vial onto the cut on my cheek. The sting bit deep, and I clenched my teeth against it before easing down beside Hades, careful not to wake him.

23

HADES

"*What do you want to rule over?*" *Zeus' voice echoed around the large, high-vaulted courtroom.*

The other Divine stared at me, lining the perimeter of the bench. Waiting, watching, judging. Thanatos stood at my side, still and silent. The two of us hadn't decided yet.

I cleared my throat, swallowed, and clenched my damp palms at my sides before forcing the words out evenly. "I want to be the God of the Arts."

Silence.

A moment passed. Then another.

Zeus tipped his head back, letting out a loud, throaty laugh. The sound cracked around the room, echoing off the marble and gold. "Why would you waste your power on something so meaningless?"

Heat crept up the back of my neck, but I didn't flinch. I squared my shoulders and straightened my spine. "It's not meaningless."

A murmur rippled among the Divine. The other gods and goddesses shifted, eyes flicking between each other as if they were sharing a secret without words. Like they always were.

"He has a voice now," Ares finally said, a smirk curling on his

lips. He crossed his arms over his chest like he was watching a comedic show.

"You're better suited for the Underworld." Zeus' voice was flat.

"Nobody wants the Underworld," I said.

Zeus clasped his hands together as he leaned back into his chair, one hand draped over the leather armrest. "Exactly. That's why you should have it."

My jaw clenched. "You promised me that if I helped you, you'd let me pick what I ruled over. I don't want any realms or territories. I want to be the God of the Arts."

"I promised you power." Zeus' voice hardened. "I never said you could choose."

My fingers twitched. I tapped them against my thigh.

One.

Two.

Three.

Four.

Five.

Zeus swept a hand through the air. "We've all decided."

"Except me," I said through gritted teeth.

Zeus leaned forward and lifted his chin. "The Underworld is a mess because no one rules over it. It's a wasteland of wandering souls. It needs order. You can bring that."

Tension bound my ribs. Thanatos took half a step forward. "I'll go to the Underworld with Hades," he said.

"What are you doing?" I whispered.

"We're at his mercy." Thanatos' voice was low, his lips barely moving so only I could hear him. "They're not going to give you a choice. It's better this way."

I wanted to lash out, to make them hear me. Thanatos was logical, but the tightness in my chest refused to loosen. My jaw locked and I turned back toward Zeus. "I don't want the Underworld."

Zeus arched a brow, shooting me a thin smile. "Too bad. We've all decided."

"I'm not accepting the Underworld."

Zeus waved a hand. "You can bring structure to that realm."

"I don't want to." But it was clear the Divine filling this room didn't care what I wanted.

Zeus' expression darkened, eyes narrowing into slits with lightning flickering through them. "It's not about what you want. You will thank me one day."

"You're so selfish, Hades," someone added, but my focus on Zeus prevented me from telling who.

I looked at Thanatos.

"We can do it, Hades," he said.

Zeus rose from his chair. "You bound yourself to this court, and I rule it." Lightning split through the air, bathing the courtroom in a flash of yellow, blue, and white. "Congratulations to Hades, the God of the Underworld. And to Thanatos, the God of Death."

This wasn't a gift of power. It was an exile.

"Hades."

The sound of my name dragged me from the dream. My body jerked, a gasp tearing from my throat as pain lanced through my back. Pressure built in my chest.

"Hades." Persephone's voice was softer this time, like she was afraid to scare me away.

The blankets rustled as she sat up. I blinked away the grit of sleep coating my eyes and forced my breathing to slow. I groaned as I turned onto my side. Every muscle screamed in protest, but I welcomed the pain. It was real. It was *now*.

She reached out, a hesitant, slow movement, her fingers settling on my arm.

Grounding.

Warm.

"Are you okay?" she asked quietly.

"I'm fine." The words came out sharper than I'd intended. Even through the darkness, her eyes found mine. They were wide, her brows pulled together, her lips parted like she had something to say but didn't know how. I closed my eyes and focused on her touch.

"You're not fine." She sighed and reached for the leather bag filled with supplies, tugging out fresh gauze and tape.

"I don't need—"

She lit the lantern and held it up, narrowing her eyes as she adjusted to the sudden warm glow. "You're bleeding again."

I focused on the soft contours of her face and the angry gash marring her skin. It sliced from her cheekbone to the corner of her jaw, the edges uneven. "What is that?" I reached for her.

She lowered the lantern, moving it away from her face. Her fingers traced the cut, running lightly along its length. A small twitch pulled at her lips, but she lowered her hand. "It's nothing."

Nothing? I sat up, biting back the groan the movement caused. I caught her wrist before she could pull herself farther away from me. Her skin was warm beneath my fingers, but a faint tremor stirred something primal deep in my chest. "Don't say that," I growled. "Who hurt you?"

She tugged at my grip, but I didn't let go. "It's just a scratch, Hades. Let me re-dress the wound."

"A scratch that shouldn't be there."

Her lips pressed into a thin line, and she glared at me. "I'm not a glass flower." Persephone tucked a piece of hair behind her ear, careful not to brush the gash. "I can handle a few cuts."

More pain clawed at me, but I barely registered it. "Don't do that."

Her brows drew together.

"Don't dismiss it."

Persephone yanked her wrist from my hold. It wasn't

violent, but it was final. The absence of her touch was instant. "I've had worse."

Her response hit like a punch to the gut. *Worse.* I knew what she was talking about—Demeter. The idea twisted something deep inside me. I opened my mouth to protest, but she cut me off.

"You don't have to fight every battle for me, Hades. I can take care of myself."

I met her gaze as she worked the gauze. She didn't flinch. Even though she was glamoured, I could see my goddess fully. Not as the woman learning how to navigate the bond between us, or the daughter stuck in the shadow of her mother, or the woman who'd pledged herself to the trials. She was a woman who endured, who fought, and would keep fighting. "You're stronger than you think," I murmured.

Her teeth grazed her bottom lip, brows lifting. "I don't want you to see me as someone who constantly needs saving."

"I don't." The words were raw. "But that doesn't mean I'll stop wanting to protect you."

Her lips parted, but she didn't respond right away. "I don't need protection," she finally said. *But I don't mind having you at my side,* she continued through the bond. She flashed me a faint smile. She didn't look at me, but her hands stilled before she continued working.

Persephone placed a hand on my shoulder, urging me to lie back on my stomach. I lowered myself slowly, careful of the pain radiating through my back. The moment I settled, her fingers brushed the edges of the covering, and even with her featherlight contact, it was difficult to stop myself from flinching.

"Luckily Gabriel gave me a few extra vials," she murmured, hesitating for a moment before grabbing one. After uncorking it with a soft pop, an astringent scent filled the still air in the tent. Then burning came as she poured some on the wound. "Sorry." With a firm hand, she placed the gauze. Pain flared, but I held myself still. I grunted as she pressed into a sensitive spot, securing it down with tape.

"You're doing good. Just hold still a little longer." Her touch against my skin made the muscles along my back tense, not from the pain, but from her closeness.

"Done," she said. The word was a relief, even though my heart hadn't quite settled. She moved back, sitting on her heels. Her eyes locked on the dressing over my wound as if it was the most important thing in the world.

I couldn't look away from her.

The silence in the tent deepened. I swallowed hard, my throat dry. Before I could think about what I was doing, I moved.

I pushed myself up slowly, feeling the familiar sting in my back, but I ignored it. I didn't care. The pain was distant, a buzzing hum at the back of my mind, outshone by the need to close the space between us.

Persephone's gaze locked with mine. She didn't blink, didn't breathe. Her hand curled into the fabric of her shirt. "Your back," she whispered.

I didn't answer. Instead, I leaned forward, my hands finding her shoulders. "Fuck my back." I pressed my mouth to hers.

The kiss started slow, then deepened with hunger. My pulse fell into rhythm with hers.

Her lips were soft. She lifted her fingers, threading them through my hair, and pulled me closer. The warmth of her body seeped into mine. I couldn't stop myself from reacting, pressing against her. I ignored the way my wound protested. She kissed me back with a fierceness I hadn't expected.

Her lips parted. I slipped my tongue in between them. My hands traced down her arms, running over the delicate lines of her body that I had long memorized. I loved the way she responded to me—willing, hungry.

I pulled back, my breathing heavy. "Persephone," I rasped. Her name fell from my lips like a prayer. Fingers still tangled in my hair, she drew me close again, breath coming fast and uneven. Eyes half-lidded, mouth slightly open—fuck. The way she looked right now, open, unguarded. I hadn't seen her like this in what felt like forever.

"Hades." She said my name gently, a tremble in it.

I didn't answer. I just kissed her again—slowly, deeply, savoring the taste of her, the feel of her body against mine. I pulled back. I ran a knuckle across the skin on her cheek, avoiding the gash. I wouldn't press her on it any more. Not tonight.

"Let's sleep. We have a busy day tomorrow."

She nodded and leaned back. I eased onto my stomach, clenching my teeth. Persephone moved in close, the curve of her body molding to mine like it belonged there.

Because it did.

I turned my head on the pillow. "Thank you for taking care of me today."

Persephone nodded against my shoulder, hair brushing my skin. "Usually, it's the other way around. It was the least I could do." She chuckled, her hand slipping into mine beneath the blanket.

PERSEPHONE

Sunlight slipped through the crack between the tent flaps, slicing through the shadows and landing on my face. I'd forgotten to tie them shut last night. I groaned as I stretched beneath the blankets. My every muscle protested the idea of moving. The night had been restless, plagued by my wandering mind. I longed to ask for a few more hours of sleep, but I knew those luxuries were for after getting the stone piece and heading back to the Underworld.

I raised a hand to my cheek. The skin was smooth again, the sting of the cut just a memory now. Thank gods. I was glad I wouldn't have to explain it to Gabriel or Orion. If it had been any deeper, it would've taken longer to heal and they'd ask questions. I could already imagine the interrogation, feel the invisible leashes tightening around me. They would never let me go off on my own again.

Hades knowing was bad enough.

My tired eyes shifted to him. The steady rise and fall of his breathing drew me in. His lips were slightly parted, the pillow dented beneath the curve of his jaw. I sat up and leaned over him, peeling away the covering across his back, careful not to rouse him. Even if I couldn't get more sleep, I would grant him a few more minutes.

His skin had knit itself back together, unbroken where it had been torn and bleeding. No fresh blood, no hint of infection—only angry pink lines left behind. His magic and the potions had done some work, but I could still feel pain flowing through the bond.

He stirred as I fussed with the used gauze and tape, rolling them into a ball and setting it aside. They weren't needed anymore. His violet eyes cracked open. "I'll never get used to waking up next to the most stunning goddess in the universe."

"Stop," I said, the heat rising to my cheeks.

"Never." He turned onto his side.

"I was just checking on you." I bit my already swollen lip. "Your wounds look much better, but—" I probed the bond.

"I'm fine." His words were steady, but the wince as he sat upright told a different story. The low murmur of Gabriel and Orion packing up the camp bled through the canvas. I pushed myself up and put on some fresh clothes. My fingers threaded through my hair, catching on stubborn knots. I gathered it, styling the strands into a mostly neat single braid that fell down my back.

Hades got up, dressing too. We stepped out of the tent and helped break down the camp. Tension was clear in Hades' shoulders.

"You don't have to do everything."

He didn't look at me right away, busy packing. "I'm fine," he repeated

"But you should rest," I said.

He turned to face me. His expression held no annoyance, just amusement, somehow. "Let's not make this a debate."

I chewed on my lip and swallowed down my argument. I

wouldn't waste my breath. I huffed a sigh and continued working.

Breakfast was over in a few quick bites—another sandwich. The tight ache in my stomach eased. I'd been hungrier than I thought. Hades raised a brow but didn't press me. "We'll skip training for now. It would be nice to reach home before nightfall," Orion said.

With the camp packed up, we made our way to the dragons. Hess watched me with sharp eyes as I approached her. Her violet scales glinted under the sunlight, her tail swishing behind her and pushing aside some fallen leaves.

Hades stood at my side. "Do you need a hand?" he asked as his gaze flickered between me and the saddle.

Of all the things he could've said, that was what he asked me? He was the one who was hurt. "No. I can do this," I said out loud—mostly to reassure myself, but it didn't do much.

He didn't argue, just lingered with his arms crossed, watching. Hess lowered herself as much as she could. *Oh, Miss Goddess is feeling independent today,* her voice lilted.

"Quiet," I muttered, pulling myself up her side.

My first attempt wasn't graceful. My foot slipped on one of her scales and I nearly fell to the ground. A low chuckle rumbled behind me. I glared over my shoulder at Hades. "Not a word." I would've pointed a finger, but I was already uncoordinated enough. He lifted his hands in surrender, lips pressed into a firm line, though the crinkle at the corners of his eyes gave him away.

Oh, please. Hades, just help her up. This is painful to watch, Rys said.

She's going to get hurt, Seph added.

Seph and Rys laughed, the sound echoing around my skull. Falon snarled at them.

Mock her one more time, and I'll clip all your wings while you're sleeping, Hess' voice thrummed like thunder.

We were joking, Rys said.

Mostly, Seph added.

Sure you were, Hess said. *Test me.*

"You don't have to do that," I said.

I don't protect you for just your sake. I can't let these males think they can act this way.

I continued climbing up Hess' large body. I swung my leg over and settled into the saddle. Hess purred underneath me. *Not bad. For you.*

"Such a wonderful vote of confidence," I said.

Only I am allowed to mock you, Hess growled.

Hades moved to Falon, mounting with ease, though slower than usual because of his injury. "You're getting better," he said.

I smiled. With everyone ready, Gabriel waved a hand, gesturing to take off. Rys launched skyward first, followed by Seph. Hades nodded at Hess, and she lifted off the ground, her wings slicing through the air. Falon followed.

Hours later, the forest stretched out in a patchwork of autumnal colors, rich golds, deep reds, and even patches of green. Rivers, mountain ranges, and villages marked the land. It was beautiful. Peaceful. Maybe that was enough for now.

My legs ached from staying in the same position. The wind bit at my cheeks, and my eyes drooped. I drifted in and out of awareness, lulled by the rhythmic beat of Hess' wings.

We're almost there, Hess said. I straightened, blinking away the haze of half-sleep. Orion insisted we make a stop to pick up supplies for his mother, which she'd told him to bring the next time he came home. Apparently, she rarely ever made the journey herself to the Autumn Court Capital Market. It was too far, and she stayed busy dealing with the family.

We landed in a clearing, Hess' wings spreading wide before folding neatly at her sides. I slid off her back with more control than I'd ever managed, landing on my feet without incident.

Better this time, she said. I grinned at Hess and patted her neck. Her scales rippled under my touch with a vibration. I glanced over at Hades. He dismounted carefully, his movements slow but steady. I closed the distance between us. "How are you feeling?" I asked.

"Not bad," he said with a faint smile. "But I can also say I've been better."

Orion stepped up with a grin and squeezed Hades' shoulder. Hades flinched, barely, but I saw it. The smile on his face remained, but his lips thinned.

"You'll heal soon," Orion said.

Leaves crunched beside us. "And Orion's father will probably have a potion to fix you up further." Gabriel moved closer. "He's a potion master. He made the potion that healed you when you first arrived in Faerie before the gala," Gabriel explained to me.

My lip curled, the remembered taste sour on my tongue.

Orion stretched his arms wide. "Now, this… this is the Autumn Court."

"It's beautiful." I turned in a slow circle, taking in the ancient trees, their branches heavy with foliage.

Orion chuckled. "Wait until you see where I'm from. This is nothing compared to that."

I raised a brow. "I can't imagine anything more beautiful."

I can. She's right in front of me, Hades spoke through the bond.

"Smooth," I muttered as I tried to bite back a laugh, but halfway through it turned into a cough. Gabriel and Orion looked between us before shrugging and turning, waving a hand for us to follow them. We left the dragons in the clearing and walked along a path through the trees, single file. It was bordered with ferns, moss, and fallen leaves. Music and distant chatter grew louder with each step.

"Stick close to me," Hades said as he moved in behind me. "Some merchants here can be"—he paused—"persistent."

I hummed in acknowledgment. Just before I could ask how much longer it would take to get there, the path opened up. "Wow," I whispered.

Orion glanced over at me. "It's cool, isn't it?"

I nodded and kept my gaze on the market. It was unlike anything I'd ever seen. Hundreds of wooden booths sprawled before us. Above, an intricate orange canopy wove through the gnarled branches of the towering trees, casting the space in shadow. But it wasn't dark. No, thousands of tiny twinkling lights hung from the fabric, swaying in the breeze. If it was this beautiful during the day, I couldn't imagine how breathtaking it must be at night.

Spices, baked goods, and florals thickened the air, twined with a smoky note I couldn't place.

"Come on," Orion said, waving a hand.

His enthusiasm drew a laugh from Hades. "We need to keep him on track, or he'll get too distracted."

Gabriel chuckled. "Nah. He won't. Can't keep his family waiting for too long."

"Fair point."

Orion moved ahead of us, pulling a crumpled note from his pocket. "All right, here's the list," he said as he smoothed it out. "A few things my mother asked for the next time I came home—spices, fabric, and some rare ingredients. Some things I can only get here. Oh, and I want to pick a few things out for my siblings. They'll never let me hear the end of it if I come back empty-handed."

"You're a good brother," I said. It came out softer than I meant it to, almost drowned out by the bustling market around us. I didn't know what that kind of love felt like, but it looked nice on him.

He smiled. "I try."

"Let's meet back here," Gabriel said.

We all moved into the bustle of the market. Vibrant banners hung above the stalls, merchants calling out their goods as if competing for who could be the loudest.

I paused, admiring a stall filled with intricately carved wooden dolls, and Hades stopped beside me.

A man stepped forward. "Necklace! Miss?" He stretched out his arm, the beaded necklaces clinking together. Tiny glass and polished stone beads caught the lights above in flashes of red, green, and gold, their colors shifting as they swayed.

Hades placed a hand on my back, urging me forward. "No, thank you."

"But, Miss! It would look lovely on you." The man took a step closer to me.

"No," Hades said, moving us out of the way.

The merchant didn't follow. The interactions didn't stop there. Vendors approached us from every angle, their eager voices trying to tempt us with fabrics, trinkets, and perfumes.

We passed the worst of them, getting to the quieter section of the market where the merchants simply sat behind their tables and let their items do the speaking. A beautiful display of jewels caught my eye, glimmering under the twinkling lights. I moved closer. Each piece was unique. "These are stunning." I reached out, drawn to a necklace whose gold chain held a large pendant set with a faceted violet stone, shimmering like Hess' scales.

"Do you want it?" Hades asked, his eyes moving between my face and the necklace.

I flipped the tag hanging from it. Five thousand dollars.

My stomach sank. I wasn't quite sure what the conversion rate from Olympian dollars was, but that sounded like a lot. "That's too expensive," I whispered, trying not to let the couple sitting behind the table hear me.

"It's nothing for us." Hades turned to the couple and pointed to the necklace. "We'll take this one." He pointed to a matching bracelet. "That too."

Heat rose to my cheeks as the woman smiled at me. "This is too much," I said.

"It's never too much for you." He leaned in closer. "You're worth it."

"You keep that much cash in your pocket?" I asked, keeping my voice low. "What if you were robbed?"

He shrugged, smirking. "Are you worried about my safety?"

"I'm worried about your poor financial decisions." My fingers curled around the edge of the table. I kept my eyes fixated on the necklace, my throat tight. I wished a script existed for this, on how to accept being *chosen*.

"Beautiful jewelry for a beautiful woman," the merchant said. I looked up to find a warm smile framed by walnut-brown hair, her sparkling amber eyes catching the lights. "Would you like to put it on now, or should I wrap it up for you?"

"I'll put it on now," I said, feeling a little flustered.

"Good choice. A bag costs an extra—" She held up two fingers, her nails covered in a metallic orange polish. "Eco-friendly laws and such."

I scrunched my nose. Two dollars for a bag? Hades reached into his pocket and handed her a wad of money. She counted it as Hades picked the necklace off the stand, ripped off the tag, and stepped behind me. His gloved fingers brushed the back of my neck as he clasped the chain in place, sending a shiver down my spine. He moved to my side and slipped the matching bracelet onto my wrist.

He stepped back. "Beautiful."

"This is… I don't know what to say. Thank you." Chandeliers, velvet, and gold were nothing new to me. I had walked among them for most of my life. But it wasn't *my* wealth. I had always been limited to the handful of things Demeter would provide for me.

"You don't have to say anything."

We continued through the market. I kept having to stop him from buying me more. Every time my eyes lingered on something for more than a few seconds, he insisted that I needed it. "We don't have enough space on the dragons," I reminded him.

"The dragons are a convenient excuse," he teased.

I laughed as we made our way back to the entrance. Gabriel was already waiting for us. He shook his head and told us about goggles he'd spotted—overpriced, so he'd put them back. "We can suffer without them a little longer," he said.

Orion was still somewhere in the bustle of the market. I trailed behind Hades and Gabriel as we waited, looking over some of the stalls nearby. The crowd pressed in, shifting between us. I moved in on a booth that had wooden figurines of animals.

Thin fingers clamped around my wrist. I twisted away, but the grip tightened.

Run, run, run, I thought.

The words repeated on a loop. The sounds around me blurred into a low hum. An old woman with a tangle of silver hair stared at me with hawklike eyes. They rolled back, turning milky white. Her black embroidered cloak hung around her. Beneath it, dark, layered fabrics clung to her thin frame. Her lips formed a grin that was too wide as her head jerked once, twice, then stilled.

"You," she hissed.

My skin tingled under her touch.

"Spring tangled in shadow," she breathed, though her lips never moved. "A crown will splinter, its bond unmade, and the heart it held will fall silent. Beasts will stir beneath the roots, and chains older than memory will break. The moon will swallow the sun's light, and silence will fall upon the dead. Seek the dragon—its gaze will bare what the darkness holds. Blood yet unseen will mirror, and the vessel that should never be found will call to you."

I yanked my hand back, bumping into a solid chest. Hades had moved in without me noticing. My heart pounded as her words echoed in my ears.

"Are you all right?" he asked. His brows furrowed as his eyes scanned my face and body like he was searching for damage. Hades' hand hovered around the wrist she had grabbed, not touching, like he didn't want to spook me.

"I-I think so," I stammered, glancing back at the woman. She had already turned, disappearing into the crowd. Something about her was familiar. "What was that?"

"A seer." His tone was grim. "They speak in riddles. Don't let her words linger in your mind. They cannot change your fate."

Easy for him to say. My skin was still crawling where she'd touched me.

Gabriel stepped closer to us. "What did she tell you?"

I recited the words I could recall. Gabriel and Hades glanced at each other.

"Seek the dragon…" Gabriel murmured and scratched his head. "Try not to let it bother you. Any seer that hangs out at this market is likely not reputable. Good ones are booked out for weeks."

I nodded, but I couldn't shake the sound of her voice, or the way her eyes had rolled back.

We waited another twenty minutes for Orion. I stayed closer to Hades this time and focused on a musician playing a harp with strings that lit up, but the seer's words floated through my head. Orion finally appeared, his arms laden with purchases. I cringed at how much he must've spent on just the bags.

"I did some damage," he announced.

"I'd say." Gabriel laughed. "Your mother is going to think you bought the entire market."

"She'll love it." Orion shrugged.

We headed back to the clearing where we'd left the dragons. I approached Hess and placed a hand on her scales. I climbed up her side and settled into the saddle, this time without slipping. "I did it."

You're getting less weak.

How sweet.

Hades mounted his dragon, and Gabriel and Orion followed suit. Orion's dragon took off first, then Gabriel's, sending gusts of wind through the clearing. We went next, with Hades behind us.

Orion's home was the next stop. I'd just faced pirates, a dangerous faerie creature, and a creepy seer, but the idea of being around a real family, of seeing what I'd never had, rattled me the most.

PERSEPHONE

I dozed in and out on the flight to Orion's home, occasionally toying with my new necklace and bracelet. For the parts I was awake, it was beautiful. The seer's words fluttered in my mind, refusing to settle.

After hours of travel, Orion called out, his voice competing with the wind, "There it is."

I leaned forward, gripping the handle as Hess banked, one of my fingers tapping a rhythm on the leather. Ahead, nestled on the side of a steep, tree-covered mountainside, was a sprawling house that looked like it grew from the land.

Wooden beams framed the structure, their rich honey tones drawing the eye. Moss blanketed the roof, green, light brown, and yellow. It didn't match the fiery orange and red of the trees, but the contrast blended effortlessly. Smoke curled from several chimneys in lazy rivulets. The front of the house gleamed with reflective windows, broken up only by a pair of brick-red double doors. The setting sun covered it all in a golden glow.

"Beautiful," I said, but our descent stole my words.

The dragons landed in a wide clearing just before the

house, their wings stirring up a flurry of leaves, spinning in the air like sparks before slowly drifting back down. I dismounted, bracing myself. My boots hit the ground harder than I'd meant, but I didn't stumble too badly.

I'm impressed, Hess purred.

I cut my eyes sideways at her and walked toward Hades, Gabriel, and Orion. Gabriel and Hades took our bags off the dragons.

See you soon, Hess said.

Be safe hunting.

Always am, she said in a sing-song tone.

Together, we crossed the open space. We were nearly there when Orion broke into a jog.

Just before he reached the red double doors, they burst open. A small woman stepped out, her arms outstretched and her dark brown hair whipping in the wind. "Orion!" She pulled him into a tight hug, her head barely reaching his chest. "You're home."

Orion chuckled and swept her into a quick spin before setting her down again. "Hello, Mom."

Behind her, a tall, broad-shouldered man stepped out. His red eyes caught the light, black hair woven into tight, parallel rows that gathered at the nape of his neck.

"Dad," Orion said as he hugged the man.

Neither of Orion's parents looked old enough to have a son who was centuries old, let alone an entire family pouring out behind them. Immortality wore well on them.

"Welcome home," his father said.

Children of varying ages and backgrounds followed one after another. Orion had mentioned that since being gifted with immortality, his parents had kept busy and used their blessings to bless others.

His mother tugged his arm. Her gaze swept over him,

brows knitting together. "You've lost weight. Are you eating enough?"

Orion groaned, though it held no annoyance. "Mom, I'm fine."

She rose onto her tiptoes to reach his face, cupping his cheeks, thumbs brushing his skin. "You'll let me feed you properly while you're here."

Orion ran a hand through his hair, a flush climbing his neck. But he didn't pull away. Orion leaned into her touch.

His father pulled Gabriel and Hades into quick, familiar hugs. "Nice to see you guys again." He stepped back. "I'm Dorian." He clasped my hand in his, warm and steady.

I froze for half a second. "Hello," I whispered.

"And I'm Avene," Orion's mother added as she hugged Hades, Gabriel, and then me. I found myself caught in her cinnamon-scented embrace. My arms stayed close to my sides, unsure whether I should lift them or wait. It reminded me of Demeter—before she'd changed. Back when her touch was still gentle, when I still looked at her with affection and the word *mother* rolled off my tongue easily. "It's a pleasure to meet you," Avene said, pulling back just enough to look me in the eyes.

"I'm Persephone, by the way," I said too quickly. I tucked a loose strand of hair from my braid behind my ear.

"Persephone," she repeated. "Very pretty name."

I smiled.

"It's an honor to have you all here. You are welcome in our home for as long as you need."

"Thank you," Hades said.

Avene chuckled. "It's strange seeing you glamoured, Hades."

"Tell me about it," Gabriel added as he waved a finger between Hades and me. "I have to look at them every day."

"All right, line up, crew. Introduce yourselves to Persephone," Dorian said.

The kids lined themselves up. A scrawny teenager with unruly blond curls spoke first. "I'm Norren."

Twin girls were next, maybe twelve or thirteen by the looks of them. They wore the same hairstyle, parted cleanly down the center and woven into dark, intricate braids.

"I'm Mika." Mika elbowed her sister.

"I'm Marlowe."

The next boy stumbled forward, looking a year or two older than the twins. He nodded, his shoulder-length, curly black hair swaying in the breeze. "Olive."

A boy was next, maybe nine or ten, with glasses too big for his small face.

"That's Rhys," Avene said for him. The boy waved.

And the youngest of the bunch, a small girl, maybe three or four years old said, "June." She barreled into Orion, wrapping herself around his legs. Her springy red curls bounced as she looked up at him with wide brown eyes. "I missed you," she yelled.

Orion slid his hands under her arms and scooped her off the ground. June squealed as he spun, curls flying around her face before he settled her on his hip. "I missed you too."

"Did you bring us anything?" Mika asked, bouncing on the balls of her feet. Her eyes went wide with exaggerated innocence.

"That's not polite, Mika. We've gone over this," Dorian said and shook his head.

Mika grinned. Her lower lip jutted out as she clasped her hands behind her back.

"Of course," Orion said as June played with a lock of his hair. "Did you think I'd come empty-handed?"

Mika elbowed Marlowe. "Told you."

Avene shook her head at the twins but smiled. "Let's go

inside. We were just about to sit for dinner. We have plenty for a few extra plates," she added with a wink. "I like having leftovers around, but I'm happy there won't be any tonight."

"Less work for me," Olive muttered. "Putting away leftovers after meals is my chore this month."

The warmth in the house was almost overwhelming. The scent of cinnamon and baked apples wafted through the air. Avene ushered us toward the dining area, where a long, weathered table was covered with food, surrounded by matching wooden chairs. Bowls overflowed with different vegetables, a large pot of stew sent curls of steam up, and baskets lined with white cloth were filled with fresh bread. Different colored mugs littered the spaces between.

A woven runner ran down the center of the table, embroidered with details I couldn't make out with the food covering so much of it. The empty plates around the perimeter didn't match, but it all felt curated in a chaotic, comforting way.

"We only need a few seconds to set up," Avene said.

"Don't rush. If you'd like, we can bring in our bags first? That would give you a few minutes," Gabriel offered. "Thank you for taking us in. I know it's a bit of a surprise."

Avene scoffed. "Don't be silly, Gabe. I love when you all drop by. You should eat before you settle in. Food first, always."

Dorian was quick to move, grabbing some mismatched chairs from against the wall and sliding them into open spots at the table. Avene moved just as fast, ducking into the kitchen and returning with extra plates in hand.

I sat next to Hades, the wooden chair creaking beneath me. I reached for a piece of bread, tore off a small chunk, and brought it to my lips. It was perfect—crispy at the edges and soft in the center.

I closed my eyes, letting myself savor it. When I opened

them, Avene set a steaming mug before me. "This is spiced cider."

"Thank you," I said.

She nodded and smiled.

I took a small sip. The cider carried just enough spice to tingle the back of my throat and enough warmth to chase away the autumn chill.

Avene moved with ease, piling food onto our plates—mine, Hades', Gabriel's, and Orion's first. Then she turned to the kids, giving each a generous helping.

Orion dug into his meal. "This is fantastic, Mom."

I picked up my shining silver fork, its surface catching a warped reflection of my face. Without pause, I shoveled food into my mouth. I tried to slow down, to appreciate it, but it was difficult. The flavors were rich, comforting. It had been a while since I'd had food this good.

Around me, chaos ensued between all the siblings—fighting over forks, jabbing elbows, reaching over one another without the concept of personal space, and the occasional shriek of "*Hey!*"

I didn't say anything. I just watched.

From across the table, Avene's hands busied themselves with her fork and knife, but her gaze softened as she looked at me. "You okay?" she mouthed.

I dipped my head and smiled.

Hades must've noticed because he leaned over and said, "It's a lot, right?"

I gave a small shrug. "I'm just not used to it," I explained. "All of this."

He nudged my knee under the table with his own. "It's loud. You'll get used to it."

"Will I?" I'd never seen anything like this. The laughter, the overlapping voices, the easy affection.

A family.

One that laughed and bickered and loved all in the same breath. My chest tightened. This was what I'd missed out on —while I had clung to the stories in my head and sat alone. The nights I'd wished for someone to come and tell me everything would be okay. The nights I prayed to the Fates not to let me wake up.

I swallowed another bite of my food.

"So, Persephone," Dorian said as he leaned forward. "What's your story?"

I set my fork down and smoothed the napkin beside me just to give my hands something to do.

"Dad," Orion said, drawing the word out.

"I'm curious. How did you end up with these guys?" He pointed his finger between Orion, Gabriel, and Hades.

The table quieted and eyes turned toward me. An invisible spotlight beamed down, heating the back of my neck. What was my story? Should I blurt out that I had run from my mother's abuse? Or was that inappropriate at a dinner table with children? I glanced at the young eyes on me— wide, curious, trusting.

Definitely inappropriate.

"I'm still figuring out my story," I managed to say as I picked a scab off my knuckle under the table.

Avene traced the rim of her mug with one fingertip. "Aren't we all? Besides, you must be extraordinary if you've kept up with these three."

"She holds her own," Hades said, and his hand found my thigh under the table. His touch was warm and possessive.

I shot him a look, but his smirk only widened as his fingers tightened. I didn't say anything. Just sat a little straighter and tried to believe the words too.

"What's it like where you're from?" Marlowe asked.

I blinked at the question. "I'm from Olympus." I looked over at Hades. "I live in the Underworld now, though."

"Is the Underworld scary? Hades told us no last time he was here. Years ago," Mika said. Her focus on me didn't waver.

"It's not scary. It's actually very beautiful." I kept the bareness of the Underworld to myself and spoke only of the lush foliage.

"And Olympus?" Marlowe asked.

"That one is scary."

The conversation shifted away from me. Thank gods. I learned about Mika's pranks on her siblings—glitter in places it didn't belong, swapping sugar for salt, hiding bugs in shoes. By the time the plates were cleared, my stomach was full and my cheeks hurt from so much smiling.

"Nothing better than a family dinner after traveling," Orion said.

Gabriel placed a hand on his stomach. "Definitely."

We all pitched in to stack the dirty dishes that the children ferried into the kitchen. Hades disappeared for a few minutes with Dorian before returning.

After a few more laughs, Hades took my hand and led me upstairs to our room. Floor-to-ceiling windows framed the star-spotted night sky and tree-covered mountains. The moonlight poured in, casting shadows on the wooden floor and the bed in the center of the room.

Hades didn't give me much time to admire the scenery. He closed the door and crossed the distance between us. Before I could take another step, he swept me up with a low growl and tossed me onto the bed. The mattress bounced beneath my weight, a laugh escaping as I propped myself up on my elbows.

He caged me with his arms and leaned down. His lips claimed mine in a hungry kiss, like he'd been waiting all day for the moment and couldn't wait a second longer.

He pulled back, our lips barely apart. "I wanted to kiss you," he explained.

I laughed. "I think I got it. No complaints from me."

"How about now?" He pressed another kiss to my lips.

I smiled against his mouth, then drew back a breath away. "Nope."

Hades' lips trailed down my neck, each kiss slow and torturous. All the thoughts in my head disappeared. The knot in my chest unraveled, replaced by calm. All I could feel was *him*. The way his hands moved, the way his mouth made my skin burn in the best way. "When you do that, my anxious thoughts are gone," I whispered.

Hades' eyes locked onto mine. "So I should do it more?"

I lowered my chin as heat crept up my neck. A low growl rumbled in his chest. My fingers fisted in his shirt as my head tilted back. His teeth grazed just below my jaw. I inhaled sharply.

"You may have your anxious thoughts, but remember that not everything you think is real."

I nodded, wordless, as his mouth found mine again. A loud knock shattered the moment. "We're doing match-style sparring," Orion yelled through the door. "Come out if you want."

Hades let out a frustrated groan, his forehead dropping to my neck. "Perfect timing," he muttered.

"You guys sparring or what?" Orion shouted.

Hades pushed himself up. "We'll be out shortly," he called back.

Footsteps retreated down the hall. "That's our cue," I said.

His eyes locked on mine, his lips curving into a slow grin. "We're not done."

"I would hope not," I whispered.

He pressed a final kiss on my lips. I sighed, pulling away. "Let's go."

I pulled a knit sweater over my head, the material catching at my shoulders before sliding down. Hades already stood at the door.

We made our way through the house again, slower this time. I couldn't help but gawk at everything. Everywhere I looked, something new caught my eye. A painting. A family photo. Framed maps on the walls. This place was lived-in and loved, nothing like the estate in the Olympus realm.

It was layered in memories.

Stepping outside, the chill struck me harder than I'd expected. My sweater took the edge off, but the mountain air still curled around me, laced with woodsmoke.

Ahead, everyone had already gathered in the clearing, a ring of torches burning around them. The breeze tugged at the flames, making them dance and flicker.

The family and Gabriel lined the circle's edge. June squirmed on Avene's hip, fussing with the collar of her sweater. Orion stood at the center. "About time," he yelled. "I was starting to think you two had backed out."

"Not a chance," Hades said, his gloved hand finding the small of my back as we approached the firelit ring.

"The rules are simple," Orion said. I assumed everyone had heard this spiel many times because his gaze locked on me.

"No weapons. No magic. Nothing lethal. Anything else is fair game." He clasped his hands together. "Norren and Marlowe, round one."

They both stepped up. Norren cracked his knuckles as Marlowe bounced on the balls of her feet. "Begin," Orion announced, retreating a few paces.

What followed was far from a casual fight. I'd expected something playful. Norren was taller and visibly stronger, but Marlowe made up for it with her speed.

He lunged.

She ducked low, sweeping his legs out from under him. Before he could even gasp, Marlowe had him pinned to the ground.

I let out a breath.

Norren flipped them, but it didn't last—Marlowe slipped free, landed back on top, and drove her fist into his face.

I hadn't expected Marlowe to be so strong for a young girl. I'd initially thought this had been an unfair pairing, but she wasn't just holding her own. She dominated. The fight moved fast and brutally. They exchanged a flurry of blows, neither pulling back until Marlowe avoided one of his punches and drove a final, precise hit to his jaw.

Norren groaned and spat to the side, wiping the back of his hand across his mouth as he sat up with a scowl.

My eyes widened.

"Winner: Marlowe!" Orion said.

Norren said some words I couldn't make out as he rubbed his jaw.

"Ha-ha, loser," Mika yelled at Norren.

"Easy," Dorian said.

Orion clasped his hands together again. "Next up, Gabriel and Dad."

They both moved into place. Gabriel rolled his shoulders. Dorian just stretched his neck from left to right and front to back. "Begin," Orion called out.

They circled each other, slow and measured.

Gabriel struck first, a quick movement aimed for Dorian's side. But Dorian shifted out of range with the kind of fluid ease that only came from years of training. Gabriel pivoted fast, adapting instantly, but Dorian was already there, hand locking around his arm.

What happened next was fast, too fast for my eyes to follow.

Dorian spun him around with surprising precision, using

Gabriel's own momentum against him. Gabriel pushed back hard, muscles tense, but Dorian's forearm pinned him at the throat. A choked sound escaped him as his airway compressed. His elbow slammed back into Dorian's ribs, but he barely flinched.

Gabriel wrenched to the side, trying to peel himself free. Veins stood out along his neck. He didn't stop. He kept fighting.

But the oxygen wasn't coming. His movements grew weaker. Only when his skin flushed with a faint blue did he finally tap twice, hard, against Dorian's forearm.

Dorian released him and Gabriel coughed as he drew in air. "I may be *old*, but that means I have had lots of time to practice," Dorian said as he gave Gabriel a handshake and walked over to Avene, then placed a kiss on her lips.

"Next: Hades and Persephone."

I sent a panicked glance at Hades. "Your back—"

He cut me off. "Is healed enough to spar with you. Are you scared?"

"Me? Scared of you?" I narrowed my eyes and stepped closer.

"Can't wait to have you pinned underneath me again," Hades whispered, only loud enough for me to hear.

I was glad for the darkness and the orange-colored light on my face because heat rose to my cheeks. "Are you sure?" My voice went higher than I'd intended it to.

Hades raised a brow. "Of course I am. I had a potion from Dorian after dinner." His gaze fell briefly to my mouth. "I feel *great*."

"Begin," Orion said.

Hades moved fast, faster than I expected. I barely dodged his first strike, ducking low as his hand shot out toward my shoulder. "You're quick," he said as he circled me.

I launched my fist toward him and clipped his side. "Quicker than you."

He shifted back but not far enough. I sent a low kick aimed at his legs. He stumbled but regained his footing. A grin spread across his face. "You're going to make me work for it, aren't you?"

"Someone has to," I said as I launched into another series of strikes. He deflected each one. His movements were almost lazy. To think, just earlier he had been in so much pain…

"You're good," he said.

"I'd say the same about you." I landed a blow to his shoulder. "But that would be a lie."

"Careful, little goddess," he purred. "You might hurt my feelings."

Before I could respond, he struck me again, faster, and more aggressive. I moved quickly and landed an elbow to his ribs. He grunted. I used the advantage to get a punch in. For a moment, I thought I had him.

But he caught my wrists and twisted me. I was pinned against his chest, one of his arms locked around my waist and the other holding my wrists above my head. "Yield," he whispered, his mouth close enough that I could feel the heat of his words.

"No." I hissed between my gritted teeth.

"Come on, Persephone," Avene cheered from the side.

"So stubborn," he whispered.

I shifted my weight and used his confidence against him. I ignored the stinging in my wrists as I broke free of his hold and spun to face him. I took inspiration from Marlowe, dropped low, and swept his feet from under him.

Hades hit the ground with a loud thud. I moved fast, swinging one leg over his form to straddle his waist. I slid one hand into his hair, tugging just hard enough for a good grip. With my other, I pushed his head to the side, pressing his cheek against the dirt. "Yield," I said between clenched teeth. Mika and Marlowe cheered something about girl power, but I was too focused on Hades to register it.

He stilled beneath me before laughing. "I yield."

"Winner: Persephone." Orion's family cheered. "Mom and Mika next."

Avene handed June to Dorian and stepped into the circle. They fought, but my attention was on Hades.

His hair was still tousled from my hand. The firelight cast shadows across his cheekbones. His eyes stayed on mine, full of something dark and possessive.

"You did well," he said.

I *hmphed* and pulled his hand into mine. "You did okay, for someone who was just pinned."

His grin deepened, and he leaned in close. *Trust me, little goddess. I enjoyed it,* he said through the bond.

Shut up.

The sparring continued for nearly an hour, match after match. But I barely noticed who won what. All I could feel was the phantom press of Hades' body beneath mine, and it didn't help that I was standing right beside him. Close enough that his heat radiated onto me. Close enough that every time his arm brushed mine, a spark zipped up my spine.

26

PERSEPHONE

The air was thick with the scent of biscuits and spiced tea. I savored every bite of breakfast, not ready to let the comfort go just yet. I watched Orion's family as they laughed and teased each other. There was *so* much love here.

I chewed slower. It would do me no good to let the misery seep in. I couldn't change the past, as much as I wished I could.

Chairs scraped against the wooden floor as everyone stood up, clearing the table with the kind of ease that only came with years of routine. I grabbed a few plates to help, trailing after Avene into the kitchen.

Avene turned, facing me. "Oh, you didn't have to do that."

"I wanted to."

She pressed her lips into a kind smile. "You all stay safe, please?"

"We'll try." I truly meant that.

"I don't know all the details of what you're doing," she said, taking the stack of plates from my hands. "And I'm not sure I want to, but based on the few things Orion has told me..." she trailed off, setting the dishes into the sink before turning back to me. "Just be careful, please."

Before I could respond, she pulled me into a hug. It was sudden but not unwelcome. I didn't pull away. Instead, I leaned in and closed my eyes. Her cinnamon scent enveloped me. My nose twitched as my face brushed against her hair, but I didn't dare pull away. Gods, Orion was lucky.

"And you and Hades," she said as she pulled back, keeping her hands on my shoulders with a light squeeze. "You're good together. I hope to see you both again soon."

I gave her a weak smile.

"You remind me of Dorian and me when we were younger. So passionate." Her gaze turned distant. "And you remind me of myself—always questioning, always over-thinking."

"Did Orion talk to you?" I tried not to let my voice pitch up at the end.

She shook her head, her dark brown hair falling over her shoulders. "No. I've been around long enough to recognize it." She pursed her lips and clasped her hands together. "And it happens to be one of my gifts."

My brows lifted. "Your gifts?"

She smiled again. "Not quite reading minds, but once I touch someone, I can sense their emotions. A lot of them."

I froze. She... knew my emotions? "So yesterday, when you hugged me for the first time—"

"I felt it," she confirmed. "You love him, but you're anxious." She shook her head, huffing out a breath. "About everything, not just him."

I opened my mouth, then shut it again, words catching on the edge of my tongue. It should've felt intrusive. Maybe it was. But something about her warm presence made it hard to feel anything but seen. "I don't know why I do this. My mind just"—I paused—"gets in the way. I overthink everything, and it's so frustrating. I know it hurts him, and gods, does it hurt me too, but I can't stop. It's like—"

She raised a hand, cutting me off. "I know." She smiled. "Don't lock him out."

"I'm not trying to—"

"He feels it, that hesitation. It bothers him more than he lets on." She ran a hand under her chin.

"I just… I don't know." I couldn't silence the voice in my head that always spiraled.

She placed a hand on my shoulder. "He's been rejected a lot in his life. I don't know how much he's told you."

I swallowed hard, guilt pooling in my gut. My chest tightened. Maybe it was my fault for not asking more questions. Hades was careful, always steering conversations away from the past. I'd been so focused on my own scars that I hadn't stopped to consider his. Demeter's accusations echoed in my head—selfish, always selfish.

"Stop beating yourself up," Avene said.

I offered her a weak smile. "I'll try." Clearing my throat, I changed the subject. "And I'm excited to come back." I didn't want to talk about feelings anymore.

"Again, be careful." She guided me into the living room. Orion's siblings sat on the floor, eagerly tearing into the small gifts he'd bought for them.

Hades stood near the window, the pale morning light framing his silhouette. He'd already been awake when I got up.

Avene's words flowed through my mind.

"All right," Dorian said as he patted Mika's head. "Let's say our goodbyes."

"It's not fair," Marlowe muttered. Her bottom lip pushed

into a pout before she caught herself, teeth catching the soft skin like she could chew the reaction back. "Why do you have to leave already?"

Orion ruffled her hair. "I'll be back soon."

"You always say that." She crossed her arms.

Orion's smile faltered but just for a moment. I caught the faintest flicker of something heavy in his eyes before he looked away.

We said our goodbyes, one by one. Avene was the last for me. "Remember what I said," she whispered.

"I will." That was true. Her words would probably cycle around my head for far too long. The heaviness would deepen, and a slew of more anxious thoughts would follow.

We stepped out into the morning light. Every time I thought I'd seen the Autumn Court at its most beautiful, it proved me wrong.

Hades rested a hand at the small of my back and guided me toward the clearing. *Did you miss me?* Hess' voice filled my mind.

I groaned as I leaned forward, my hands brushing over her scales. She purred beneath my touch. I rolled my eyes. *You know what? I did.*

Hades handed me a pair of goggles, then pulled on his own. I hooked mine over my arm. I didn't want to block my peripheral vision yet. Hess didn't respond in words, but her satisfaction was clear, her golden eyes gleaming. I smiled and climbed onto the saddle atop her back. Orion, Gabriel, and Hades mounted their own dragons.

I turned in my saddle and waved to Orion's family standing in the distance. Even though it had only been a day, I would miss them. The goggles went on next, the straps tugging at my braided hair.

Hess moved beneath me, her wings stretching wide. Then, with a single, powerful beat, she launched into the sky. The ground dropped away, a grin breaking across my face.

We soared for about an hour, the crisp air growing colder as we moved closer to the Winter Court. A strange prickling washed over my skin, like static under every layer of clothing. It was faint at first, but then it intensified, seeping deeper until it coiled in my ribs and refused to be ignored.

I leaned forward in my saddle, my fingers tightening around the handle. A shiver raced through me that had nothing to do with the temperature. I looked over at Hades, his profile illuminated by the sun as he gazed at the horizon.

"What's going on?" I asked, my voice no louder than a breath. *Hades*, I said through the bond.

His attention snapped toward me, his eyes wide. *It's happening. Remember your dagger. I love you.*

What? Panic flowed freely through the bond—*my* panic. It twisted in my chest, clawed at my thoughts. *What's happening?*

Your first trial.

The edges of my vision blurred, tiny, shifting shadows swirling no matter where I looked. The world tilted beneath me. "Hess!" I screamed as everything spun. I clawed at her scales, desperate to stay on her back. She let out a sharp roar.

I reached for her, but she was already gone. The magic yanked me away, tearing me from her like smoke slipping through my grasp.

Darkness surrounded me. I ran my fingers across the flat, gritty surface I sat on. Dirt, maybe? Small pebbles rolled under my touch. I flinched as a sharp one pricked my thumb. I stretched farther, feeling nothing else but the rough surface.

Blinding light poured in. I squinted, raising a hand to shield my eyes. I gave myself a moment to adjust before opening them and peeking through a few spread fingers. I lowered my arm.

I was in a glass box near the edge of a cliff. I cupped my hand and brushed some of the dirt away, revealing the smooth surface beneath me. I stood up. The sky was white. There was no sun, no clouds.

The box hovered close enough to the cliff's edge that I could peer at the depth below. Across the chasm, another cliff jutted out, its edges jagged like a serrated bread knife. I looked down. The cliff face stretched in broken layers of rusty orange. I brushed a bead of sweat off my forehead with the back of my wrist. The box was warm under the strange white sky, the air heavy. The weight of the cloak made it worse. I yanked it off, pushed my goggles up, and tossed them aside.

The box shuddered. I spread my arms, bracing against the glass walls. "Persephone Koralis. Welcome to your first trial," a booming voice said.

I glanced around. I couldn't tell where it had come from, but I suppose it didn't matter.

The glass box dissolved in a burst of light, leaving me on solid rock at the edge, dirt and pebbles scattered under my boots. A cool gust slapped against my face, catching the strands of hair left out by my ears. Shimmering platforms appeared, hovering between the two cliffs. The platforms only looked a few inches thick, pulsing white before turning a blinding silver. "I'm supposed to cross those?" I asked.

There was no answer.

Of course there wasn't.

I reached for the mating bond, desperate to feel Hades. It was barely there, like a flame running out of oxygen. A lump formed in my throat. I tried to swallow it away, but it didn't disappear. I was on my own for this.

The first platform hovered only three feet away from the edge of the orange rock. It was close enough to jump, but I didn't trust it. I whispered a prayer to the Fates, hoping it might cancel out the years I'd spent praying for death. "Please let me survive this.

"It's just three feet," I told myself, but the words didn't make my legs any less shaky or slow my heart. I bent my knees and braced myself for the jump. "I can do this."

I leaped.

The platform was solid under my boots for half a second before a sickening groan echoed beneath me. The other platforms ahead shifted, floating erratically, darting closer and then farther away in yawning gaps, tilting at impossible angles. One platform dipped so low that it nearly vanished before snapping back up seconds later. I couldn't afford to just stand here. I had to do this.

The next platform drifted closer, then jerked to the left. I timed the movement and jumped again.

Mid-air, the platform shifted.

My boots missed the surface entirely. I slammed into the hard edge, my ribs taking the blow. My hands scrambled for anything to grip, barely catching hold before the chasm could claim me. Chunks of the unstable material tumbled into the depths below. I clawed at the crumbling platform with my aching fingers. "Don't look down," I whispered. But following my own advice was never my strength.

The rocks waited for me like hungry teeth hundreds of feet below.

I hauled myself upward, the platform digging into my chest below my collarbones. "Don't look down. Don't look down. Don't look down." I squeezed my eyes shut and kept pulling until I had enough leverage to swing one leg onto the surface and heave the rest of my body up.

The gale funneled straight into my ears. It burrowed deep, filling my head with a hollow roar that made it difficult to think. The platform jerked beneath me. I rose slowly, my arms burning and stretched wide for balance.

I sprang to the next one. *Don't crumble, please.* The surface held beneath my boots, but the relief barely had time to settle before my gaze snapped to the next platform. It surged upward, then sank down.

Quickly.

My legs trembled as the wind slammed into my side. The platform I stood on swayed, tilting like it wanted to toss me off to my death, but I counted.

One.

Two.

Three.

Four.

It took four seconds to lower before snapping up in two seconds. I shook my head and hurled myself forward.

For a long, sickening moment, there was nothing beneath me but air.

My boots struck the edge of the rising platform, sending a sharp vibration through my limbs. I fell forward, barely holding on before the platform plunged again.

A low growl threaded through the air. I froze, glancing back at the cliff where I'd started. I squinted, the up-and-down movement dizzying me. A massive wolf paced along the edge, its black fur rippling. Foam dripped from its jaws. It crouched, muscles coiling like springs, then launched.

"No," I whispered. "No, no, no."

It landed on the first platform, unnaturally balanced even as the surface rocked beneath it. The wolf didn't falter. Its gaze was locked on *me*. Another growl tore from its throat as it leaped to the next platform.

Then the one after that.

The wolf moved with quick, terrifying precision, closing the gap between us. I forced my legs to obey, my muscles screaming as I pushed off a platform and hurled myself toward the next.

I didn't look down. I didn't dare. The wolf at my back was *very* motivating. Terror gave me speed.

Platform after platform, each shuddering landing sent my heart into a frenzy. I prayed that they wouldn't give way underneath me. I'd cleared several platforms, but it was gaining—only three away.

The growl was louder, closer.

A platform crumbled the second I pushed off, shards falling into the depths below. My foot barely found a spot on the next. It slipped and I let out a strangled cry as my arms circled for balance.

Another snarl. Only two platforms behind me. I threw myself toward the cliff.

I tumbled onto hard rock. My chin hit the stone, sending a vibration through my jaw, teeth, and up my face. I scrambled to my feet. The wolf closed in, vaulting across the gap with terrifying ease. It landed only a few feet away.

"Hello, puppy." I forced a trembling smile as I held up my hands. "I don't taste very good."

White foam sprayed from its mouth as it crouched, preparing to attack. Its lips curled back, revealing a set of yellow, razor-sharp teeth.

It charged at me. I dove to the side, but it was fast. Its massive paw scraped my thigh, slicing through my pants. The sting was instant as its claws caught under my skin. I stumbled, falling to the ground. Its teeth snapped so close to my shoulder that hot, rancid breath washed over my skin, crawling up my neck and smothering my lower face. My fingers found the hilt at my thigh, and I ripped the dagger free, driving it toward the beast.

The blade sliced across its slime-slicked snout. It was a shallow cut but enough to make the wolf reel back with a loud growl. Dark blood dripped down its black fur, visible only by its glossy surface.

I couldn't wait. I forced myself up and launched at it, swinging my dagger, desperate for contact. But the wolf was smart. It knocked my arm away with a swipe of its paw. My wrist screamed, but adrenaline drowned it out. Not my first break—I recognized that hollow snap.

But a broken wrist was better than death. I didn't let go of the blade, ignoring the fire streaking up my arm. I couldn't.

The wolf lunged at me again. I dropped low and rolled to the side. My boots scraped the edge of the cliff. The brittle rock crumbled beneath my weight, sending terracotta fragments into the chasm.

I dragged myself upright. Saliva ran in thick, ropey strands from its jaws. I didn't think, only reacted. The wolf barreled toward me. I didn't have anywhere to go but forward. "Fuck this," I muttered, raising the dagger as I charged at it.

I plunged the blade into the beast's eye with a sickening squelch. Jelly-like fluid burst over my hand, but I didn't stop. I shoved the weapon deeper into the socket.

It howled, blood spraying across my face. The thick, hot splatter streaked down my forehead and cheeks. It slid into my left eye. I squeezed it shut, then blinked hard until it cleared. I wiped my lips on my forearm, trying to ignore the metallic tang creeping into my mouth.

The wolf thrashed wildly, slamming its body into mine. The force knocked the air from my lungs. I cried out, fighting for balance and twisting so I didn't have my back to the cliff's edge. With all the strength I could muster, I shoved it with both hands—one clutching my dagger, the other flat against fur and muscle. A raw grunt tore from my throat.

Its claws raked against the crumbling edge, but it was too late. The weight of its massive body tipped backward and plunged into the chasm. I dropped to my knees, gasping. The wolf's howls faded as it fell into the depths, and a moment later, a distant, sickening crack echoed from below.

Silence.

I cringed. *It was it or me,* I reminded myself.

Blood dripped from my blade. My thigh throbbed where its claws had dug into my skin. I switched the dagger into my good hand and chewed on my lip.

I didn't have the luxury of falling apart.

Not now.

Not here.

"Hello?" I called out as I stood. "Almighty voice? Am I done? Did I pass?"

Nothing.

"Great." I dragged my trembling hand across my face, smearing the fluid. "Just great."

A low rumble shook the ground. My stomach clenched as vibrations flowed from the soles of my feet all the way up my spine. Walls erupted upward, creating a vast open-air arena sculpted from the orange rock. The sides curved with precise symmetry.

I stepped forward through the entrance, my boots crunching on loose gravel. My fingers tightened around the hilt of my dagger, palm slick.

Tiered rows of empty seats climbed the arena's walls, forming a ring around the center. Dust hung in the air, stirred by the quake.

Another tremor rolled through the ground, and I flung my hands out to steady myself. Greenery burst skyward, hedges rising and unfurling in the arena's center. In mere seconds, a sprawling hedge maze stretched out before me. "Gods damn it."

There was no way around it. I had to go in. I swallowed the lump in my throat and stepped up to the maze's shadowed entrance.

As I crossed the threshold, the atmosphere shifted. It was heavier and cooler. The air carried a tinge of rain-soaked decay. A shiver ran down my spine.

The hedges closed in behind me with a soft hiss. They towered high above me, their foliage choking out most of the white sky.

I broke into a jog. I wanted to get this over with as quickly as possible. My boots pounded against the dirt path. The maze twisted, some turns narrow enough to brush my shoulders, and others several feet wide.

Left or right? I hesitated, then veered left. The sound of my footsteps bounced between the hedges. The maze stretched on, and I scanned ahead. Silence pressed in, broken only by the occasional whisper of leaves shifting where no wind blew.

A hand shot out from the hedge to my left, skeletal and clawed. Its bony fingers curled around my boot. I screamed, thrashing to get myself free. Its grip was strong as it yanked at my leg, pulling me into the hedge. Vines burst from my palms, lashing wildly at the hand. They coiled around the bones, tightening, but did nothing. The fingers only dug deeper into my boot, dragging harder.

Focus. Gabriel's voice echoed in my head. I shifted tactics, drew my vines back, and redirected the magic into a blast, turning the hand into a heap of ash.

I stumbled forward, and another one grabbed me. "Get off me," I screamed. My voice echoed back at me. *Get off me. Get off me. Get off me.*

Power surged, coalescing inside me. I sent another blast of magic at the new hand. The force of it knocked me off balance, driving me back.

More hands erupted from the hedge, skeletal fingers tearing at my limbs. I slashed at them with my dagger, the blade moving in quick, desperate slashes. Another blast of magic shot from my palm. I didn't stop until all the hands disappeared. "I hate this," I muttered.

I forced myself to keep moving, ignoring the burning in my thigh, wrist, and the ache in every other part of my body. My steps quickened into a full sprint as I went down different paths. The air grew colder, fog gathering at my feet. I tipped my head back. "Thank you for this," I screamed at the booming voice. I hoped he knew I was being sarcastic.

Behind me, a low snarl cut through the silence. I whipped around, dread moving through my stomach like a serpent. I had to stop myself from heaving up my breakfast.

A figure emerged from one of the hedges, staggering into the path. Its gray, decayed skin hung in loose folds over its skeleton. Empty black eyes pulsed red as they locked onto me.

An undead.

I'd read stories about these, but I'd thought them only that, *stories*. Its head was positioned at an unnatural angle, and its lips peeled back to reveal a mouthful of sharp black teeth.

It came for me.

I threw myself into one of the hedges, branches scratching at my arms as the creature's claws clutched the air where I'd just been. I brought up my dagger and sliced some of its skin. It didn't slow. The weapon was heavy in my hand, but I raised it, swinging it toward the undead's face.

It didn't even flinch.

I reached for my magic, vines bursting from my palms and wrapping around the undead. They pulled it back just enough to give me space. I stepped forward and drove the dagger straight into the soft hollow beneath its jaw, putting everything I had behind the blow. Rotten, sour blood spilled from the wound.

It screeched and went still before crumpling into a heap at my feet, limbs folding awkwardly as the vines released.

All the muscles in my stomach clenched, heat surged up my throat, and I doubled over, gagging. I wiped my mouth with one of my trembling hands, swallowing the rest down. My vision blurred before sharpening.

I had to keep moving.

The maze split into two directions. I glanced between the two options. I chose left again, but a low groan echoed from that way. *Nope.* I retreated a step and ran toward the right.

The ground collapsed into a gaping sinkhole. I skidded to a stop, my boots teetering on the unstable edge. Darkness yawned below, with no bottom, no end.

There was no time to waste.

I backed up a few paces, sprinted forward, and jumped.

For a heartbeat, I was weightless. Then the world tilted down. My hands shot out, fingers catching an outcropping just below the lip of the sinkhole.

My shoulder screamed as it took on my weight. I kicked my legs, searching for a foothold that didn't exist. If I slipped, I was dead.

Would Hades be notified if I died like this? Would he feel it? Would I feel it? Would I wake up in the Underworld? Would the court laugh because I let a hole win?

A bead of sweat stung my eye. I blinked it away and hauled myself upward, inch by inch. When I had enough leverage on the edge, I swung my leg over.

Cracks split beneath me. I shifted fast, scrambling onto solid ground before it could give out and take me with it.

Behind me, the edge gave way, crumbling into the hole. One second slower and I would have gone with it.

No time to breathe.

Another undead emerged from a hedge. It moved with speed that shouldn't be possible for something so decayed.

I screamed as its claws raked across my shoulder. It barreled forward, sending me sprawling to the ground. It loomed above, its eyes locked on mine. I scrambled back on my hands.

It lowered. Its teeth snapped inches away from my face. I thrashed, thrusting my blade into the spot that had worked to kill the last one.

Black blood spilled from the wound, coating my hands before the creature collapsed on top of me. Its weight crushed the air from my chest, pinning me with flesh and bone. The stink of rot filled my mouth and nose. I wrestled its corpse aside and staggered upright, the ghost of its body still pressing into me.

I kept running. Every turn was a gamble. My legs dragged. But stopping meant death, and I wasn't ready for that.

The path before me widened, and light crept into the maze. I pushed myself harder. The finish line was close. I could feel it.

A small voice called out from behind me. "Help me," it cried. "Please help me."

I turned.

It was her. *It's me.*

It was the young version of myself I'd seen in the Styx when I first came to the Underworld, maybe five or six, untouched by the shadows of Olympus. Pink flowers still crowned her umber waves, the lazy grin now gone, leaving only quivering lips. Her small frame trembled. "Help me."

I glanced between her and the finish line. It was right there, so close. I could taste the freedom. But how could I leave her here? How could I leave *me* here? I wouldn't abandon her.

I couldn't.

A growl echoed behind us, farther down the path. "It's okay. I'm here," I said as I scooped her up. "I've got you."

She clung to me as I ran, her tiny hands clutching my torn-up clothes.

The finish line was in sight, marked with a glowing white ribbon. "Persephone," the child said.

I glanced down at her. Her face was so familiar and innocent. It was like I had stepped back in time.

But her smile twisted.

I stopped.

The child's face sharpened into something cruel, her teeth elongating into points. Her eyes rolled back, turning solid white. Her little fingers turned into talons that dug into my shoulder. "How easy you are to fool," she hissed, her voice no longer soft and sweet.

Her claws raked over my already torn skin. I screamed, reeling backward as I struggled to fight her off. Her small frame contorted, limbs jerking as she attacked me.

"Stop!" I yelled.

She didn't listen.

She tore into my arm. I threw her with everything I had, and she went flying—just far enough to give me a breath. I avoided my dagger. I couldn't bring myself to use it, even if she was just some beast wearing my face.

But she was quick. She swiped at me again and I stumbled, barely keeping my balance. I couldn't kill her. I used my magic to pull her back with my vines. They coiled around her arms and legs, wrapping tight around her thrashing body. She clawed at them, talons raking through the green, but the bindings held. "I'm sorry," I whispered.

She let out a guttural cry, but this time I didn't wait. I turned. She wasn't real, and I knew that. But the guilt was. I sprinted to the finish, every step another battle.

At last, I crossed it.

And then everything disappeared. The maze, the girl, the arena. My knees met the orange rock as I collapsed. I clutched the dagger, my hand trembling.

My right forearm burned. I glanced down at it. It was no longer covered in fabric, torn off somewhere in the maze. Seven glowing circles appeared. The first one filled in, pulsing a faint white, before all the marks faded into my skin.

"Trial one of seven complete," the booming voice said.

I had survived. I couldn't even manage a grin. Darkness folded over me.

2 7

HADES

e had landed and set up camp as soon as the court's magic pulled Persephone into her first trial—hours ago. One moment, the space was empty, and the next, Persephone appeared, crumpled on the ground.

A searing wave of pain slammed through the bond, buckling my knees.

I pulled her limp, clammy body into my arms. The sharp stench of blood and decay filled the tent, curling in my nose and throat. My hands shook as I cradled her to my chest. "Gabriel," I yelled, my voice cracking. "Orion. She's here, but she's not—"

Awake.

My words faltered as they burst into the tent. Persephone's eyes fluttered. Her breathing grew shallower. I set her on the bedroll.

Orion reached into the aid kit, fumbling with vials his father had given him. He pulled out six and read the labels on them aloud, shoving one into my hand. "This should help," he said, looking at Gabriel. "Right?"

Gabriel scanned the vial and gave a tight nod. "Yeah."

I glanced down at Persephone. Dark blotches marred her face and body, her split lip still bleeding. I was certain the damage didn't stop there.

But she was here. She was alive.

"She made it," I whispered.

"Orion," Gabriel said. "We're going to have to hold her down for this."

I pried her cracked lips open, and Orion and Gabriel moved in, holding her shoulders steady. My fingers trembled as I uncorked the vial and tipped it, the thick liquid spilling onto her tongue.

Her body arched off the ground, convulsing so hard that it took both Orion and Gabriel to keep her from thrashing into further injuries. Foam spilled from her mouth as a raw sound clawed its way from her throat.

She sputtered, choking. "Turn her to her side," Gabriel barked. Together, they shifted her, and the tension bled out of her body. The spasms eased and finally stopped, leaving her limp, frighteningly still.

"She just needs to rest now," Orion said.

I slumped back and nodded, unable to speak.

Rest. Right. She's alive. That's what matters. "She can't stay in these clothes," I said to myself. Torn, filthy, stiff with blood—nothing worth saving. Orion and Gabriel stepped out of the tent without a word. My world was narrowed to the goddess lying in front of me.

Orion returned a moment later and handed me a bucket of warm water and a clean rag. "Thanks," I muttered as he left.

I cut her torn clothes away layer by layer with steel scissors. I dipped the rag into the water and wrung it out. Gently, I wiped away the grime and blood clinging to her skin, then cleaned and dressed her open wounds.

I froze at the sight of her wrist, bent at an unnatural angle, swollen, and discolored. My jaw clenched.

One.

Two.

Three.

Four.

Five.

I braced myself, focusing on the warmth of the rag still in my hand. Slowly, I set it aside. I wrapped my fingers around her injured wrist, tracing the warped line of bone beneath her skin. Swallowing hard, I guided it into place. My stomach turned. I was glad she wasn't awake to feel—or hear—the cracking of it.

Once the joint was aligned, I wrapped her wrist in cloth and braced it with slats of wood from the aid kit. Still blessed with her Divine healing, she would mend—just not fast enough for my liking.

I dressed her in fresh, warm clothes, choosing pieces soft and loose enough not to aggravate her injuries. We weren't quite in the Winter Court yet, but the last thing I wanted was for her to be cold. I pulled the blanket up around her shoulders, careful of her wrist and the worst of the bruises. Settling beside her, I let my fingers drift down her arm. "I won't let you go," I whispered.

PERSEPHONE

I woke with a groan, a symphony of aches and sharp pains coursing through me. Every muscle protested as I shifted on the soft surface beneath me. I lifted my hand to rub my face, but my wrist was covered in a wrapped splint.

I blinked hard, trying to clear the fog from my mind as the tent around me came into focus. Layered blankets and furs pressed in close, trapping heat against my battered body.

"You're awake," Hades said from beside me. I turned my head too fast. A sharp crack echoed through my neck. Hades already sat up with his eyes locked on me. I tried to gather my frayed thoughts.

"Yeah," I croaked, the word coming out more like a cough. My mouth was dry. "Water, please," I rasped.

Hades reached for a metal bottle beside the bedroll, uncapped it, and brought it toward my lips. I hesitated, then lifted my good hand and took it from him. My grip was shaky, but I managed, chugging half the contents. The water was cool and exactly what I needed. "Thank you," I whispered.

"You were in bad shape yesterday." He leaned back, his weight resting against the stretched canvas tent wall. "We gave you one of Orion's father's potions. It seems to be helping your injuries, but full healing will take some time."

His words triggered a surge of memories. The floating platforms. The wolf. The blood. The undead. The creature masquerading as my younger self that had attacked me. Fear pounded through my body as if I was still in the thick of it. I hadn't realized my hand was trembling around the metal bottle until Hades leaned forward, steadying me with a firm grip.

Hades didn't ask me what was wrong. For that, I was grateful.

"It's the trials." I handed him back the bottle but didn't pay attention to where he set it down.

He nodded slowly.

Tears burned at the corners of my eyes and slid down my cheeks. I didn't bother stopping them. "I should've listened," I said, my voice trembling.

Hades let his hand rest on the blanket just above my shoulder, hesitant, as if the nearness alone might hurt me. "There's no point in wishing things were different. What matters is that you focus on healing so you're ready for the next trial. Just the next one. Survive one at a time."

His words didn't coddle, but they weren't unkind. I nodded, unsure of what to say. I tried to sit up, gritting my teeth at the movement. A groan escaped before I could stop it. "Geez."

"You don't need to push yourself," Hades said, his expression softening as he stood. "Stay here. I'll bring you something to eat."

A few minutes later, he returned with a sandwich in hand. It was plain, the same as the others we'd been eating, but right now, I didn't care. My stomach growled as I took it with my good hand and tore into it.

When I finished, I rolled the foil into a ball and set it aside. My muscles and injuries screamed, but I moved. "What are you doing?" Hades asked.

"I'm getting up so we can keep traveling." I pushed off the blanket, the coolness of the air striking me and sending me into a shiver.

"No," he said as he reached out. "We're taking the day off so you can rest."

I moved away from him. "Not happening. Stop trying to decide everything for me," I snapped, pushing to my feet with a grunt. I'd already slept plenty, delaying us. My knees almost buckled, but I caught myself before he could rush to help. I grabbed a fur-lined cloak from the edge of the bedroll, the movement of bending down harder than I'd expected. I shrugged it over my shoulders.

"Persephone," Hades said, his voice dropping an octave.

"Hades." I squared my shoulders and met his eyes. "We're traveling. End of discussion."

Before he could argue further, I stepped out of the tent. The cloak dulled the worst of the chill, but it still lashed around my neck and ears, sharp as knives, as I walked toward the fire where Gabriel and Orion sat. They glanced up as I approached.

"You're awake," Gabriel said. "You slept through the night and all day today."

"Yeah." I moved closer to the fire.

"You didn't look too pretty yesterday," Orion said with a chuckle.

"Thanks." I stared into the flames. The embers crackled and danced. The longer I watched, the more spots bloomed at the edges of my vision. "Let's pack up the camp and travel."

Gabriel raised his brows. "You should probably rest more."

"I'm tired of people telling me what to do," I said, heat rising in my voice. "We're going."

"I—" Hades began, but my raised hand and daggered glare silenced him.

Gabriel glanced at Orion, who gave a half-hearted shrug. "I don't think this is the best idea," he ventured. "But you can just let us know if you need to stop."

"I will." My focus shifted back to the fire.

"Absolutely not. We're not leaving," Hades said.

"Yes, we are." I turned to face him, trying to hide my wince. "If it had been you, Gabriel, or Orion in that trial..." I trailed off. "If you were in my condition, what would you do?" My voice rose with each word.

Hades' jaw tightened, but he didn't respond immediately. My gaze flicked between the three of them. "Tell me," I pressed. "Would you keep going? Would you push through it?"

They exchanged glances, but the silence stretched, only broken by the sounds of the forest and the cracking fire.

I threw my hands up. "We still have a stone to collect! Let me remind you of why we're even here in the first place." Hades' magic was already stretched thin trying to hold Tartarus shut. We didn't have time to wait around for me to feel better. No one spoke. "Tell me. What would you do?" My voice shook, but I didn't stop. "Anyone. Somebody answer me."

"Damn," Orion muttered.

Hades exhaled. "We would likely keep going, but—"

"Exactly, so let's go," I said before he could continue.

I did what I could to help them break down the camp, though it was difficult. My hands trembled, but I forced them to move as I rolled the blankets. Then, before stowing my toiletries, I brushed my teeth and took a swig of water from the metal bottle.

As we finished packing, I crossed camp toward the clearing where the dragons were waiting for us. Hess' piercing gaze landed on me, and she angled her snout. *Wow, you don't look too good.*

"Not in the mood," I mumbled.

Her sour expression softened, just slightly. *I was really scared when you got pulled into the trial.*

You were scared for me?

Of course I was, she huffed. *I've seen how weak you've been.*

I arched a brow.

That's not how I meant it. I'm just glad you survived. You have grown stronger. She hesitated. *I don't like watching people I care about disappear.*

Her words hit me harder than I'd expected them to. *Me neither.*

Hades strode up behind me. He raised a hand to Hess and stroked her scales. A deep, contented purr rumbled from her like an oversized cat. *Pretty man is rubbing me,* she said, her eyes half-closing.

Hades turned his attention to me. "If you insist on traveling, you're riding with me."

I opened my mouth to argue, but Gabriel appeared behind us. "I'm afraid I agree. You're already pushing yourself."

Two against one wasn't worth the effort—and once Orion joined, it'd be three. A groan escaped me before I could stop it. I shuffled toward Falon, and Hess snickered as I passed her.

Don't worry, goddess. I'll keep you safe, Falon said.

I gave him a soft smile, and Hades helped me up into the saddle. A hiss slipped from between my teeth as I settled into it. He followed, wrapping his arms around my waist. Hades slipped a pair of goggles over my head. "Thankfully, we grabbed a few extra pairs at Orion's house."

Right. I had left mine in the trial.

Hess launched into the air, Seph following close after, and we went up, with Rys behind us.

The chill of the wind and altitude bit at my skin, despite the fur around my shoulders. Hades' body at my back was the only thing keeping me from freezing entirely.

We flew for hours. The rhythmic beating of the dragons' wings normally would've lulled me into a calm state, but my mind refused to settle. It raced instead, replaying the trial in vivid flashes. I couldn't stop thinking about just how close I had come to dying. And the terrifying truth was that it could happen again—at any moment, without warning.

I prayed to the Fates for time to heal, time to gather my strength before going into the next trial. Hades shifted behind me, his arms tightening as if he could sense my tumultuous thoughts. *You're quiet,* he spoke into my mind.

The horizon blurred as I stared into it. *I almost died yesterday, Hades. I almost didn't make it.*

His hold on me didn't loosen. If anything, it deepened. For a moment, I expected him to brush off my words, to tell me that near-death experiences were a part of the journey or that I needed to stay strong, but he didn't. *It's natural to feel shaken. You went through a lot yesterday. No one expects you to bounce back immediately.*

A sharp, bitter laugh slipped from my lips, lost to the wind. *I do.*

You shouldn't.

I have to. What's the alternative? Fall apart? Quit? I can't afford any of those.

No one can go through what you did yesterday and not feel it. Surviving doesn't mean you have to act like nothing happened.

I twisted, a stab of pain forcing me to slow as I stole a glance at him. *Do you think I'm weak for being afraid?*

No. Fear keeps you sharp. It's what will get you out alive.

I hate knowing it's not over, that it could happen again at any moment. I don't know if I'll be strong enough next time.

You'll be ready. And if you're not, you'll find a way. I believe in you.

I swallowed hard and pulled the cloak tighter around me, leaning back into him. Hopefully, his faith in me was enough to make up for what I lacked. For now, all I could do was hold onto the fragile hope that, maybe—just maybe—I would find a way.

PERSEPHONE

The packed snow was firm beneath my boots. I shifted my stance as I faced Orion, my wrist tucked in close to my body. Hades had insisted I take time to let my injuries heal. Gabriel had agreed, saying training was reckless in my condition. I didn't care, and I'd brushed them off. Resting wasn't an option. Orion was the only one who hadn't tried to talk me out of it.

My wrist pulsed. I ignored it.

Orion tipped his head. "Yes, you need to protect your wrist, but the moment your opponent notices, that's exactly where they'll strike."

I nodded, trying not to shift my weight too transparently.

He narrowed his eyes. "Too obvious."

I tried to make my stance more natural, but Orion shook his head. "How am I supposed to hide that I'm hurt?" I asked.

Orion circled around me. "You make sure they don't think it's the weak spot."

I frowned. "How?"

He used my moment of distraction. His arm shot out. I jumped back, barely dodging the blow. "Pain makes you predictable. You're favoring your strong side." Orion lunged at me again, and I used my good arm to block him.

"Balance your tells. Stop protecting your wrist so obviously. Shift your weight. Give me more distractions. Make me think that something else is the weak spot."

I shook out one of my ankles. His gaze flickered down. I shifted my weight, forcing a misstep.

Orion dropped and his leg swept out toward mine. I launched upward, leaving just enough room for his boot-covered foot to slide through empty space.

A jolt tore through my spine as I twisted, muscles tightening with the motion. He stood, but before he could fully recover, I brought my fist around, slamming into his shoulder.

His body jerked back, and I struck again. I *knew* just one blow wouldn't be enough. I used my good arm to strike below his ribs.

"Better," he murmured with a grunt.

I stepped back, cold air burning my lungs.

"Again. Switch it up. I'm done going easy on you," he said.

~

The wind howled around us. The gloves did little to stop the chill—my fingers had gone numb hours ago. Hades hadn't liked the idea of me flying solo, and we'd argued, but in the end, I made the call. He'd backed off, though not without a scowl and a muttered reminder to let him know if I needed anything.

I take back everything I ever said about the Summer Court, I grumbled. *This is so much worse.* I leaned forward, tucking myself closer to Hess to try to avoid the gale.

You complain so much.

I do not.

When you're not complaining, you're busy being anxious. Think warm thoughts, goddess, and try not to be cold.

I glared at the back of her head. *You're so helpful.*

Her laughter hummed through the bond.

Aren't you cold?

No. I'm built for survival. My body regulates temperature better than yours.

My breath curled into the air, the gust sweeping it away before I could see it fade. *The least you could do is distract me.*

With what?

I thought for a few seconds. *Do you have a mate? You never told me.*

Hess snorted. *I don't want to talk about that.*

That means there's something to talk about.

There isn't. Hess huffed. *It just means you're annoying.*

Who are they?

She snorted. *First off, I don't have one. Second of all, I hope I never do.*

You hope you never do?

I don't need another male around to underestimate me. I'm strong. My parents always wanted a male, and I spent much of my life proving myself to them. The last thing I need is some arrogant fool thinking he's entitled to me just because the Fates think it's a good idea.

My jaw tightened. I didn't know how to respond. *You're not open to it?*

Why should I be open? To appease someone else?

Why were you giving me a hard time about Hades then?

Hess banked, her wings slicing through the cold air. *That's different.*

It's not.

It is because your male is the opposite of all the things I mentioned. He cares about you. Dragons aren't like that. Females are good for breeding and nesting, but I don't want to do either of those things. I want to fly, fight, and explore, Hess told me. *I'm living my dream right now.*

Warmth prickled in my chest. My dream used to be simple—freedom. I'd only wanted a life beyond the estate, beyond Olympus.

But now?

After I'd ignited the trials, I flew through open skies with chains no one could see. Maybe that was the trick of it all. Cages didn't always come with bars. Sometimes they came in the form of thoughts and deadly trials. *Well, I'm glad I could be a part of it.*

She didn't respond right away. The air rushed past, but for a moment, it felt quieter. *Me too,* she finally said with a gentleness I hadn't expected.

PERSEPHONE

We reached the edge of the Winter Court just as the deep blue of twilight swallowed the pale remains of daylight. The temperature plummeted, and the wind clawed at the tender skin where my goggles had been. Snowflakes drifted down, disappearing into the white as they touched the ground.

We'd already set up the tents and lit the fire, its orange glow painting the snow-covered forest. Even wrapped in my cloak, the cold still gnawed through the layers. I pulled the hood tighter around my face.

One truth I'd learned through this journey was that I was not built for the cold. Or the heat. I did well at one temperature: lukewarm.

"Do you want to hit the tavern for dinner before or after we plan?" Gabriel asked.

"Definitely after," Orion said with a bitter laugh, pushing his gloved hands into his pockets. "I'm getting drunk tonight."

Gabriel glared at him. "Orion," he said sharply.

"What?" Orion grinned, flashing his white teeth. "We're about to do something dangerous. Let me have a few drinks."

Gabriel exhaled. He didn't bother arguing, just gestured for us to move closer. "Fine."

We all gathered on the same side of the fire, settling onto the log. Gabriel dragged a satchel into his lap. It creaked as he opened it, the worn leather flap folding back to reveal a stack of curled maps. I leaned in. The fire warmed one side of my face; the other stayed numb.

"We're here," Gabriel said, pointing to a smudge of ink near the border of the Winter Court. "And the drake is here," he added, tapping another mark in the Spirit Court with his gloved finger. Snowflakes landed on the map, leaving dark wet spots behind, but none of us dared move away from the fire.

"We're close. Too close," Orion said.

I squinted at the map, tracing the distance in my head. It was unsettlingly short. "How long do you think it'll take us to get there?"

"Thirty minutes on foot," Orion said, brushing some snow off his pants. "Maybe forty."

"Much faster if we take the dragons," Hades added.

The thought of being that close to the drake, that soon, made my stomach churn. I stared into the shadows of the forest, flinching at the snap of a distant branch.

"So," I said, my voice shaking, "what's the plan?"

Gabriel's green eyes caught the firelight as he glanced between Hades and me. "You can't use your magic until you're out of this realm, but Orion and I can," he reminded us. "We'll lead, with you two following. We can go when the sun is at its peak."

"Why peak?" I asked. Wouldn't night be better?

Gabriel's expression was distant as he rummaged through the stack of papers again. "From the notes that Aurelia and

Cassius gathered from their surviving men…" His voice trailed.

My fingers tensed around the edge of my sleeve at the way he said *surviving*.

"They think the drake is nocturnal. If we strike while it's sleeping, we'll have the best chance of avoiding a full fight."

I fumbled with the edge of my sleeve. "How do we kill it?"

Orion leaned back, grinning and staring up. "We have no idea," he said cheerfully. I followed his gaze, drawn to the moon suspended in the dark sky. I wished it could stay like this, but the sun would rise again. And with it would come our chance to get the stone piece.

I glared at him, but Gabriel spoke before I could. "I have a theory."

We waited for him to continue. Hades' enchanted blond hair caught the glow of the fire. "Care to share?"

"We don't know a lot, but we think the drake's blood is poisonous, and it regenerates. Maybe fire would stop the regeneration? Cauterize it?" He shook his head, glancing down. "Maybe it's stupid."

"No, that's a good theory." Hades shrugged. "But I suppose we won't know until we're there."

"We need to avoid fighting it then, just grab the stone and leave. We shouldn't risk it bleeding," I murmured.

"That would be ideal. So the plan is to go in and see if we can do anything. If we can't, we leave, regroup, and return," Gabriel said.

I blinked. *That* was the plan? I'd expected something more… strategic. "And if we can get the stone piece?" I asked.

Gabriel exhaled sharply, his breath turning into a wisp of steam in front of him. "We stay alive." He ran his gloved hands across the map. "You need to be focused tomorrow. You'll be able to feel the stone's energy. You can guide us to it."

"You'll be like our divine compass," Orion said with a grin and a light chuckle.

I didn't laugh. My stomach flipped. The thought of directing us toward a creature we barely understood made the cold feel sharper. One wrong step, and it wouldn't be just me who paid the price. "All right," I muttered, though the words ran hollow.

Hades patted my back. "We've got this."

The fire popped, embers scattering and fading into the night. I wanted to believe him, but I couldn't shake the sinking feeling in my gut.

Orion clasped his hands together. "Let's get to that tavern."

I gestured to the woods around us. "How do you even know there's a tavern out there?" I asked, my words dampened as I buried my chin deeper in my cloak.

"I've been to this one before. I made sure we landed close enough to both it and the drake. I figured it would be nice to have a hot meal."

"And a cold drink," Orion added.

My mind flickered back to the last time I was in a tavern. It had been in the Spring Court, where I'd felt so out of place.

"It's just a short walk away," Gabriel said.

Hades offered me a hand, helping me up to my feet. I flinched at the pull in my side, muscles still tender from healing, but I didn't complain. I shoved my gloved hands into my pockets and fell into step behind Gabriel and Orion.

The snow crunched beneath our boots, the trees closing in around us, branches sagging from the weight of ice. I was grateful that the men didn't hover or offer unnecessary help, but they walked slowly enough that I didn't fall behind.

Don't forget to shield your mind. We're close to the Spirit Court. It's possible we could encounter a spirit fae, Hades said through the bond.

I nodded and flicked a glance behind me at Hades. *Okay.*

I trailed behind the two fae, keeping my eyes on the ground, careful with every step.

After nearly ten minutes, red brick walls emerged, stark against the pale sweep of moonlit snow. A weathered wooden sign hung above the door, reading *The Hungry Moonstone Tavern.* Snow capped the roof, smoke twisting from the twin chimneys into the night sky. Amber light glowed through the windows, spilling onto the frozen ground. I could already feel the promise of heat, even as the wind made my eyes sting.

Gabriel didn't hesitate, moving quickly to the wooden door. He pushed it open wide, and a blast of heat washed over us as we stepped inside. The sting of thawing skin made me wince—but it was worth it.

This tavern was quieter than the one in the Spring Court. There was no press of bodies, no roar of music or laughter. Instead, a murmur of voices drifted through the space, underscored by the clink of glasses, a low violin, and the crackle of the fireplace. A long counter stretched along one wall, while the rest of the room was dotted with tables.

I followed Orion inside. The lighting was low, casting shadows across the dark walls and worn floors, scuffed by years of foot traffic. A large fireplace dominated the wall beside the counter. Orion chose a table near the fire, dropping onto the matching bench with a satisfied groan. "Finally. Drinks."

Gabriel sighed and motioned to the bar. "Go ahead. Just keep it under control. We have a lot to do tomorrow."

Orion didn't bother responding, already halfway to the bar. I took a seat next to Hades and Gabriel. "Order some food while you're at it," Hades called after him.

He lifted a thumbs-up and grinned. It was only a few

minutes before he returned with a tray of tall glass mugs filled with frothy, tan, sloshing liquid. "Food's on its way."

I took a cautious sip. The bitterness made my face scrunch. Hades popped his lips. Gabriel immediately set the mug back down. Orion puckered but said, "This will do."

"This is much worse than I remember it," Gabriel said.

The murmur of voices and the low roar of the fire filled the lull that followed until the barkeep, wiping his hands on his black apron, shouted, "Order up!"

Orion took another sip of his horrid drink and got up to collect the food.

He came back with four bowls, grinning. "Stew."

I took a tentative spoonful. Warmth spread through me, sliding down my throat, and settling deep in my belly. I groaned at the taste. It was hearty, with chunks of meat and vegetables swimming in a thick broth.

"So," Orion said, "anyone else considering just staying here instead of facing a giant death snake?"

Gabriel glared at him. "No."

"We could take up residence here, open a little shop. Sell some mittens or something."

"We'll be fine," Hades said. "It won't be awake, and we'll be in and out before it knows we're there."

Orion snorted. "Says the one who can't die." His voice was low, careful.

Hades shrugged, too casually. "I can still feel pain."

I took a long sip of the drink, letting its sour taste linger on my tongue. Had I not signed up for the trials, I would've been included in that Divine immortality statement. I focused on the burn in my throat instead.

As our meal wound down, Orion's drinking sped up. By the time the rest of us had finished our bowls of stew, he was halfway through his third glass.

"Is he going to be okay for tomorrow?" I whispered to

Hades. My fingers drifted over the table, absently doodling invisible shapes on the worn wood.

"He'll be fine. It'll wear off."

I wasn't convinced. Orion stood and wove his way toward the man playing the violin in the corner of the room. The musician, an older man with wiry red hair and a scowl carved into his face, paused mid-bow strike, eyes narrowing on Orion.

"Something less depressing, please," Orion said.

"Oh no," I muttered, thinking the man might beat him with the bow.

But then Orion fished a few gold coins from his pocket and dropped them into the violin case at the man's feet. The scowl on the musician's face didn't vanish, but it eased as he gave a nod, raised his bow, and launched into a lively tune.

Orion turned on his heel and tugged on the nearest girl's hand, spinning her into an exaggerated waltz. Her braided white hair spun as they moved, her light purple eyes widening.

Gabriel set his mug down. The thud made me flinch. "Maybe we shouldn't have brought him." His jaw was set in a tight line.

The girl laughed at Orion, her cheeks flushing. "You're terrible at this."

"Terrible?" Orion mocked being offended. "I am magnificent."

"You're drunk," she said through a laugh as he twirled her again.

Gabriel pinched the bridge of his nose, muttering something that sounded like a curse. "I can't watch this." He placed a palm on the table. "Let's go. We need to be ready."

"Party is over," Hades said as he stood. He clapped Orion on the back.

"Time to head back," Gabriel added, draining the rest of Orion's drink before he could reach it.

Orion leaned against Gabriel as we led him toward the door. "Walking to our deaths," he grumbled. "What a glorious adventure."

"Be positive," Gabriel snapped, shoving the door open and stepping outside into the freezing night. The bite of the air hit me like a snap, stealing the breath from my lungs.

The walk back to the camp was slow and uneventful. The only sounds were the crunch of snow under our feet, the howl of wind, and distant calls of creatures hidden in the night. I hoped we wouldn't come across whatever had made them.

Orion and Gabriel disappeared into their own tent as Hades and I entered ours. Hades reached back and fastened the flap shut, but a draft still slipped through the seam.

I pulled my cloak tighter and sank down onto the bedroll, curling into myself to conserve body heat. "It's freezing."

Hades glanced over at me. "Take off your clothes."

My mouth hung open. "Off? Clothes? Are you out of your mind? I'm freezing!"

His hands went to the buttons of his cloak. Once it was off, he reached for the collar of his sweater and pulled it over his head. The lantern light highlighted every ridge of muscle and caught on the sharp lines of his collarbones, the curve of his shoulders. "Skin to skin."

Before I could say anything, his hands were on my cloak. His fingers brushed the frozen skin at the nape of my neck, and I shivered—not just from the cold. He was careful, helping me peel off the heavy layers one by one until the last barrier between us was gone.

I swallowed hard as he settled behind me, pressing his chest to my back. His arms wrapped around me, and the heat from his skin was instant. A tremble slipped through me as he took my hands into his and rubbed, coaxing life back into them.

The chill still lingered in the air but not between us. He pulled the furs and blankets up, tucking them around our bodies.

"Gods, you're warm," I said.

He smirked against my hair. "What's on your mind?"

"That you're warm."

"Besides that."

I hesitated, appreciating that he was behind me. I stared at the shadows the lantern cast on the canvas wall of the tent. "I'm really scared," I said, my voice just above a whisper.

He squeezed me. "We'll be okay."

"I wish I had your confidence." My laugh was humorless. "How can you be so sure?"

"Because we've made it this far."

Silence stretched for several minutes before I dared to speak. "Ever since the trial, it's like a part of me is still there, just waiting for everything to end."

He ran a hand from my shoulder down my arm. "You survived. That's what matters."

"But I shouldn't have." My voice broke. "I brought it all on myself. I was so foolish signing up for the trials, like I thought I was invincible." I closed my eyes as the weight of it pressed down on me. "Now I'm just waiting for everything to fall apart."

"You—"

I didn't let him finish. "Why aren't you angry? Why don't you call me what I am? A fool. Reckless. Selfish."

Hades turned me in his arms, but I couldn't meet his gaze. "Do you think I see you that way?"

"Why wouldn't you? I made a mess of everything. I put myself in danger. I put *us* in danger. I've made getting the stone piece harder. And for what? Some twisted sense of power? For pride? To be free of my mother?" The word wobbled on my tongue—*mother*. It was the first time I'd called her that in a while. "Unless it's not obvious, I'm still not free. All the trials did was shove me into a different kind of cage and ruin everything I'd worked so hard to rebuild in myself."

"I—"

I cut him off again. "I hate it." My voice shook. "I hate that you're not angry."

"I could never be angry at you." He placed a hand under my chin and gently lifted until our eyes met. "You think I should condemn you."

I nodded. Tears burned my dry eyes. "You should. I deserve it. I deserve every cruel word you're not saying, every ounce of anger. I ruined everything."

"Persephone, I will give you everything you ask for. But not that. I will not condemn you. You didn't ruin anything."

"I did."

"No. You're not selfish or foolish. You're brave and resilient. And maybe you made a mistake, but who hasn't?"

I shook my head, a fresh wave of shame washing over me. "It wasn't just a mistake, Hades. It was so much more than that. I should've known better. I should've—"

"You should've what? Been perfect?" His words were sharp but not cruel. "I have made plenty of mistakes. You wanted something more. That's not a crime."

"But it cost us—"

"It cost *you*, and that's what I hate. Not you. Never you. I hate that you're hurting."

Hot tears slid down my cheeks, and I didn't fight them. His hand cupped my jaw. "I'm scared," I whispered. Why couldn't I be brave? All my life, why did I have to be so fucking scared? "Of losing everything. Of losing you."

"You won't lose me," he said.

He'd said I wouldn't lose him. He didn't say I wouldn't lose everything else, that I hadn't set the pieces in motion for something irreversible.

I didn't want to think about it, not now at least. I'd find some other inconvenient time for that. So I pushed it down, buried it beneath his touch and the steady rise and fall of his chest. I leaned up and kissed him.

It was soft at first, barely more than a brush of the lips.

He stilled, then responded, his hand coming up to cradle my face, thumb tracing the dampness left by my tears. "You're everything to me."

I pulled back and shook my head. "Don't say that," I whispered.

"Why? Because you don't believe it? Because you think you don't deserve it?"

All I could do was stare at him. His fingers traced the curve of my jaw, his eyes lingering on my lips. "I see you," he whispered against my lips. "Every part of you. And I wouldn't change a thing."

I tried to look away, tears stinging my eyes, but his hand held me in place. "You shouldn't always have to pick up the pieces of everything I ruin," I said. "I'm not—I'm not worth it."

"You're worth everything," he growled. "If I have to tell you a thousand, a million times, I will."

"Hades—"

"Let me speak." His hand squeezed my jaw. "Let me tell you how much you matter, how much I need you."

I opened my mouth, but he shook his head and continued. "You are strong because you're still here, still fighting, even when you think you've already lost."

Emotion swelled in my chest, but I stayed quiet.

"I will continue to fight you on this. I'll beg you to believe you're worthy of the good this universe can offer."

"Gods don't beg," I whispered.

"For you, I would. I'd drop to my knees if that's what it took." He let out a huff of laughter that held no humor. "You underestimate the lengths I would go."

"Hades," I whispered.

His eyes fluttered shut, like he was trying to memorize the sound of his name on my lips. "Say my name again."

"Hades."

"Again."

"Hades."

He kissed me hard, like he hadn't eaten in weeks or years even. Like I was the only thing keeping him alive. His hands gripped my waist, pulling me even closer as if he couldn't bear the smallest gap between us.

I tangled my hands in his hair. His body pressed into mine, the heat of him searing me. "Feel that, little goddess?" he growled.

I gasped as his hips pressed against mine, his length pressing into me. I stared at him.

"Use your words."

"Y-yes," I said. He pressed into me further. "I feel your cock."

He smirked. "Your mind likes to play tricks on you. You don't believe me when I tell you that I want—need you. Seeing is believing, right?" He kissed my neck, my head falling back as he moved lower, his teeth grazing just enough to make me gasp. I squirmed, but he steadied me by gripping my hips. His lips curved into a smile against my neck. "Do you need to proof, little goddess? Does my mate need to see what she does to me?"

A jolt went through me.

"Words, Persephone. I see how your body is reacting." His mouth trailed lower, nipping at my skin with his teeth. I gasped and arched into him, and a sound rumbled from his chest. "But I want to hear your words," he said, his lips brushing my skin. "Do you need to see?"

I nodded. He bit my skin. "Yes," I managed, the word catching in my throat.

"See? That wasn't very difficult."

He didn't move the blanket, just pulled back enough for me to look. He reached down and wrapped a hand around his length and pumped. His eyes stayed locked on mine. "You see what you do to me?"

I swallowed hard, unable to look away. My hand gripped the blanket, my body humming as my core throbbed. I squeezed my eyes shut. The bond flared with pleasure as he pumped his cock. He grunted but didn't say anything.

"Wha—"

He stopped.

"Remember the river?" I asked.

"How could I forget your little pussy clenching around my fingers?"

I sucked on the inside of my cheek. "Do you remember everything?"

He stroked his cock, giving it a squeeze. My eyes darted back and forth between his length and his eyes. "Of course I do."

"Remember when you said you were going to wait until I begged you?"

Hades chuckled. "Mm-hmm."

"And?"

"Don't worry. I won't fuck you tonight until you do."

I narrowed my eyes. "How are you so sure I'll beg you?"

A slow smirk pulled at his lips. "Because I know you." His gaze dipped to my lips. "I can hear how much you want this in the way you breathe. Your body is reacting, little goddess."

"You're making assumptions."

His eyes flashed in the reflection of the lantern light. "Am I?"

He pumped his cock. "My little mate likes to pretend she's not desperate. But your body gives you away." He nodded, gesturing for me to look down, tugging the blanket aside.

I was certain my cheeks were beyond red. Sure enough, the evidence of my arousal between my thighs gleamed in the lantern light. I rubbed my legs together and tried to ignore the tinge of pleasure it brought.

"Hmm, you're a little quiet." He pulled the covers back over us.

"Um—"

He pressed another kiss to my neck. His warm hand landed on my hip. I shivered under his touch. He drew it down along the curve of my leg, skimming from the outside in. "Feel free to tell me to stop."

His hand slipped between my thighs, then lifted. "Look," he said.

The lantern light wasn't kind—it illuminated everything, the wet sheen on his fingers flickering like it wanted to humiliate me. Hades brought his fingers to his mouth and sucked slowly.

Then his hand drifted back down, fingers parting me with practiced ease. One slipped inside. I swallowed a moan as he moved, leaving me empty. With that same hand, slick from me, his fingers wrapped around his cock and stroked.

His gaze burned into mine, eyes hooded with need as his hand moved. "Fuck," he muttered. "You're so beautiful." He leaned in and pressed a kiss to my lips.

As he kissed me, he took my good hand and brought it down to his cock. My fingers curled around him, and he let out a groan, lips grazing mine as he pulled away. With a gentle push, he eased me onto my back.

Hades ran his fingers over my breasts, avoiding my hardened nipples. The cold air kissed my skin, sending a shiver through me. He pinched one. "Ah." I gasped, the sound raw.

His featherlight touch continued downward, gliding over the curve of my ribs and the dip of my waist. I shifted, my thighs pressing together and my eyes closing. Each of his movements was slow. Just when I was sure he'd finally give me what I craved, his hand slipped away. My eyes snapped open. "Why did you stop?"

Hades smirked.

"Forget I said anything." I turned on my side, away from him. He came up behind me, his length pressing into my back. Hades' lips brushed over my shoulder for a few torturous moments. I shivered as he placed an open-mouthed kiss at the base of my neck.

A light flutter rose in my chest. The rough drag of his stubble brushed my skin as he moved his mouth upward, one kiss at a time. He paused as he reached behind my ear. Hades' teeth scraped my skin, followed by the soft stroke of his tongue. He put an arm around my waist and tugged me close. "You're trembling."

I didn't respond, but my body betrayed me, still shaking.

A deep growl rumbled from his chest, and his grip on my waist tightened. His hand shifted from my side. He dragged his fingers over my stomach and then down between my legs. I gasped as his thumb stroked my clit. He slipped his middle finger into my slick core. "Mine," he murmured against the shell of my ear.

I chewed on my lip. Hades curled his finger inside me. "Hades," I whispered.

He groaned and continued to finger me. I rolled my hips, aching for him deeper. "More, Hades," I said.

"Do you want me to fuck you, little mate?" he growled.

A desperate sound escaped me.

He slipped in another finger, and I gasped. "Words, mate."

"Yes."

He stopped pumping and took his hand away. I shut my eyes, but I could hear the pop of his lips around his fingers. Hades placed a hand on my hip and pinned me on my back. He moved between my legs. His cock pressed into my stomach.

A cruel grin covered his face. Hades wrapped a hand around his cock and pumped. He traced slow, deliberate circles over my clit with the head of his cock. I needed more. *More*, I said through the bond.

He lowered his length to my entrance and slipped just the tip in. My body arched up. *More*. I placed my palms on his muscled torso.

He gave me another inch, then pulled back, just to push in again—shallow, maddening.

Beg, he said.

"No," I moaned. He inched deeper with each tease.

He pulled out, making me writhe beneath him. My nails dragged across his back, but he didn't move. Didn't give me more. "Just a few words," he whispered into my ear. "Give me that, and I'll give you everything."

"I—" My voice cracked.

He pressed his forehead to mine. "Say it."

"Hades, please."

"You want my cock?" Hades slid in an inch.

"Yes," I whispered.

"More," he said. "Beg like the desperate little goddess you are." His voice dropped. "Your body is already pleading for me. I want the words."

I threaded my fingers through his hair, pulled him close, and kissed him. *Please, Hades. I need you. All of you.*

He stiffened, then let out a low sound, like I'd torn something loose inside him.

The bond flared between us, and I stopped holding it tight. I opened it wide, shoving every ounce of raw hunger and broken need through. I let him *feel* it. The ache, the heat, the way I was unraveling under him. *I'm begging. Not because you told me to. Because I can't take it anymore. Lose control. Fuck me like I belong to you. Because I do.*

His tongue slid against mine, the kiss deepening.

I want to feel your cock inside me, stretching me, owning me. I want every ounce of you until I can't think, can't breathe, can't move without you, I continued. *I need you.*

With one hard thrust, he buried himself in my center. *Fuck, that's what I needed,* he said. Hades pulled back, his lips brushing against mine. He growled and thrust harder. I clenched around his cock. His grip on my waist tightened. "You have no idea what you do to me," he said as his mouth traced my jaw. "You ruin me."

"Then we're even." I kissed the corner of his mouth. Maybe that was a lie. Maybe love wasn't ever really even. Maybe it was a fragile thing that could vanish the moment I pushed too far. But he was here, still wanting me like I wanted him, and for now that was enough, and I could let myself enjoy it, even if some part of me feared he'd still leave when the balance tipped.

"That feels so good," I moaned. Pleasure surged through me. I raised my hips to meet his brutal thrusts. Heat burned low in my core. My fingers clutched at his shoulders, pulling him tight against me. "Persephone," he whispered. I was inching closer to my orgasm. I teetered on the edge, seconds away from shattering. He leaned down, his lips brushing the shell of my ear. "I feel it. Let go."

I trembled as the wave crashed over me. His name spilled from my lips. "Hades."

"Fuck," he groaned as he finished inside me. We remained like that for a few minutes, catching our breaths. He pulled out and lay next to me, tugging me close. "Are you still cold?"

I huffed a laugh. "No. You're quite good at warming me up."

PERSEPHONE

I slept better than I thought I would. Hades must've gotten up shortly before me, his heat lingering on the empty side of the bedroll. I peeled off the splint, flexed my wrist, and slipped on gloves. The injury still made me cringe, but it was much better. I dressed for the day, layering a few sweaters under my fur-lined cloak. I stretched carefully, rolling my shoulders and bending at the waist, testing my mobility.

When I stepped outside, the crisp morning air bit at my cheeks, and I tugged my hood tighter. I moved toward the crackling fire where Gabriel, Orion, and Hades already sat.

Orion's tension was visible, even through the thick fur cloak wrapped around him. Gabriel paced, his boots cracking the frozen shell over the snow-covered ground. Hades lounged on a log, seeming unaffected, watching Orion and Gabriel.

The drake. The name hissed in the back of my mind. No one could kill it. No one even knew how. My throat tightened, fingers twitching and curling into fists at my sides. Every sound was muffled—the crackle of the fire, Gabriel's steps, the birds chirping in the distance. A bitter truth was louder.

I could die.

I used to pray for death—desperately, so obsessively. It had never come then. But now it stalked me like prey. My first trial had almost taken me out, and the phantom pain of claws raking at my skin still itched beneath my layers of clothing. I'd survived that, but who was to say this beast wouldn't be the one to finish the job?

The fire snapped, and Hades pressed a kiss to my temple. The scent of him, rich amber and leather, made me close my eyes. I extended my hands toward the heat, my gloved fingers trembling as it seeped through to my skin.

"I'm not made for winter," I muttered.

Orion snorted. "Told you. Autumn Court is superior." His words tried to lighten the mood, but his eyes betrayed him—too wide.

Hades handed me a sandwich. I peeled the foil open. "How soon are we leaving?"

Gabriel tossed another log into the fire, his brows furrowed. "After you finish eating. If everyone is ready?"

I wasn't, but I said nothing. Orion, usually the first to crack some morbid joke, stayed silent. His jaw was set tight. I glanced at him, half-wishing he'd say something wildly inappropriate just to cut through the suffocating weight of my thoughts. Instead, his gaze shifted to the trees.

Hades stood behind me and squeezed my shoulders. "We'll leave the camp up."

I nodded, fingers clamped around the sandwich, leeching whatever residual heat I could from it. We sat for a few more minutes before Gabriel extinguished the fire.

We didn't speak as we trudged through the snow to the clearing. The dragons waited for us there. Hess' scales shimmered under the sunlight, each one catching it like a fragment of broken glass. As I approached her, she dipped her head, the heat of her breath spiraled around me like a warm breeze. I trailed my gloved fingers along her neck, her purr vibrating through my body.

Be careful today, she murmured in my mind. *We're dropping you off a mile out. Too close, and the creature could wake.*

Thank you. I nodded, my throat tight as I climbed onto her back.

We'll be close if you need us.

I pulled my goggles on, the strap digging into my hair and scalp as I adjusted it. The frigid rubber rims sucked at the skin beneath my eyes. Hess launched into the sky, following Seph and Rys. Falon lifted off last. The wind knifed at me, tearing at my cloak as we climbed higher. I hunched forward, angling myself toward her neck. I gripped the leather handle, sure that my knuckles were white beneath my gloves.

Below us, the forest stretched out, a sea of white snow blanketing the earth, broken up only by the dark, skeletal trees. Gleams of silver peeked through the black and white, sunlight flashing across sheets of ice and crusted snow.

I forced myself to focus, letting the sting of the cold carve clarity into my thoughts. A roaring rush filled my ears, drowning everything out.

Be strong. I repeated the mantra again and again. I snorted at the absurdity, as if words alone could stitch strength into my bones.

Ahead, the trees thinned as a mountain swelled into view, its white slopes catching the sunlight. Its peaks pierced the sky like teeth. The wind picked up as we neared it.

Hess banked, flying lower. *Welcome to the Spirit Court*, she said. *It's not very different from the Winter Court, unfortunately.* We landed with a heavy thud, her claws sinking into the snow and sending a tremor rippling through the frozen earth. The other dragons landed beside us, their weight creating a plume of snow that glimmered in the air.

"We're only about a mile away. We'll walk, and we should hit an opening," Gabriel said as he slid off Rys. His hand lingered on the dragon's side for a moment as the rest of us dismounted.

I adjusted my cloak and followed Gabriel and Orion, with Hades behind me.

We walked through the clearing nestled in the shadow of the mountains. A whistle threaded through the gaps between them. The ground sloped unevenly as we moved, the snow thinning where jagged rocks jutted through slick sheets of ice.

I slipped once, but Hades was there like always to steady me with a hand on my arm.

A scattering of trees emerged ahead. The blackened trunks were stark against the white snow, their twisted, ice-covered limbs clawing at the steel sky. I shivered and pulled my cloak tighter. "This isn't creepy at all," I muttered.

Hades pressed a hand to my back as we continued walking. My breath escaped my lips in a pale puff. The faint crack of a branch somewhere made my pulse spike. *It's only the wind,* I told myself.

We pressed on until Gabriel came to an abrupt stop. I was so focused on watching my boots crunch through the snow, being careful not to slip again, that I nearly collided with him. My hands flailed out for balance just in time.

The cave mouth loomed ahead, hidden by the shadows of two sharp ridges. I wouldn't have noticed it if Gabriel hadn't stopped. He moved first. We followed, and the air stilled the moment we stepped inside. The silence was deafening. It was as if we'd passed through an invisible veil. I could no longer hear the whistle outside, the snapping of branches, or the distant animals. The only noise was the faint scuff of our boots against the stone.

I placed a hand on the wall, its cold seeping through my gloves. Gabriel pulled a small lantern from his bag and lit it, casting long, moving shapes across the stone.

The cave smelled of earth and faintly of snow. Ahead, darkness stretched endlessly.

No one spoke. We didn't need to. We only continued on. The farther we walked, the more irregular slabs of rock jutted from the walls, forcing us to weave between them. Smaller boulders littered the ground.

My pulse hammered in my ears. I couldn't slow it. The air grew harsher with every step we took. I couldn't stop the way my hands shook or how a knot cinched in my throat every time the shadow from the lantern moved.

Don't think about what is ahead, I told myself.

But it was impossible not to. My legs weren't just tired, they were trembling, knees threatening to buckle. *Turn back,* said a voice in my head—my own. I kept walking.

Steady, Hades said.

The word did nothing to soothe the terror running through my body. We reached a fork in the path, the cave splitting into two equally unwelcoming tunnels. The lantern light only reached a few feet into each before the darkness devoured it whole. Gabriel stopped and turned.

To me.

"Which way, Persephone?" he asked.

The weight of the question landed hard. I was the *compass.*

"Which pulls you?"

I blinked at him. "Pulls me?"

He nodded.

I stared at both dark paths. "I don't feel anything," I whispered.

"Nothing?" Gabriel asked, almost hesitant.

Hades stepped closer to me, his breath warm on the shell of my ear. "Think about the time you touched the piece of the stone," he murmured. "You are made of it. What calls to you?"

I squeezed my eyes shut, reaching for the feeling I'd buried. With it came the thoughts I was trying to push away. How I nearly died in the last trial. How I could die now. How if I chose wrong, I wouldn't just doom myself... I'd doom them, too. *What if I lead them straight to death?*

My mouth opened. Closed. *Say something,* I screamed at myself. My breaths were shallow and uneven. There was nothing—until I felt it. A subtle pull. My eyes snapped open.

What if I was wrong?

Gabriel. Orion. Hades. They were trusting me.

I didn't want to be the one to choose. I didn't want this to be mine. But it was. "Left," I whispered.

Gabriel nodded once, turning to the left without hesitation. Orion followed. Hades took my gloved hand in his. "Good," he said.

There were no questions, no second-guessing. Just belief.

I forced my legs to move.

After only a few minutes, a low vibration hummed through the walls. I glanced at the others, but no one spoke. The rumble grew deeper and louder with every step we took. My stomach churned, the sound sinking into my bones.

Something else prickled at the edges of my awareness—a sensation I knew but wished I didn't. I stopped dead in my tracks. *Hades,* I said through the bond.

Hades' head snapped toward me, his eyes wide. His hand curled around my arm, like he could keep the magic from taking me away. "It's happening again now, isn't it?"

I nodded, swallowing against the growing tightness in my throat. Hades stepped in, one hand cradling the nape of my neck, the other against my lower back. His forehead met mine. Then he kissed me—slow, despite the fact we didn't have much time before I'd be gone.

I broke the kiss first. "I'm scared," I whispered.

"I know."

I clung to him as the pull grew stronger.

"It's going to be okay," he murmured.

I leaned into him, but the air around me shifted. The warmth of his touch vanished.

And I was gone.

PERSEPHONE

The darkness was absolute. I steadied my breathing. *Inhale.*

Exhale.

Inhale.

Exhale.

Where am I? My head swam. Groggy, like when Demeter's pills began to loosen their grip after hours of numbness. I needed to focus on what I could control. But my thoughts rebelled, spiraling into worst-case possibilities that I couldn't shut out.

A voice snaked through the darkness, curling around me and slithering into my ear. "Persephone."

Am I hearing things? Breath tangled in my chest. I would know that deep, rich voice anywhere. A shiver ran down my spine. "Hades," I called.

"Little goddess," he whispered, his voice closer this time.

I peeled off my gloves and pressed my palms onto the cold, smooth floor beneath me. The chill seeped in. Slowly, I pushed myself up, reaching out into the black void. My fingers met nothing but empty space.

I stretched my arms out farther, searching for the boundaries of this place. Eventually, my hand brushed a wall. I moved left and found another, about eight feet away.

A box.

"Hades," I said, the word sluggish.

Silence.

The walls shuddered with a metallic groan. A door I hadn't known was there yawned open, spilling blinding light into the room. I recoiled, squinting against the glare.

My vision swayed at the edges, but the silhouette standing in the threshold was tall, broad, and unmistakable.

Hades.

I took a slow step forward, my heart pounding. "What are you doing here?" I whispered.

He didn't answer. A harsh white light flickered on above. The sterile glow made everything feel clinical and empty.

Hades' glamour was gone, replaced by his messy black hair and gray eyes. I moved closer, aching to reach for him.

A trial, I reminded myself. And yet… the sound of his voice, the way it wrapped around me, was too precise. *Little goddess*. That was ours. The Divine wouldn't know that. I didn't care how he was here, just that he was. Maybe the Divine weren't *entirely* cruel. Maybe I didn't have to face this alone.

The bond hummed in my chest. I parted my lips, ready to say his name again.

He snarled. Low, sharp. It hooked something deep in me. I flinched and stepped back, widening the space between us.

Cold flushed through my veins. The same chill as the day Demeter slammed the door, her smile gone, her eyes hollow. One moment, I was her lily. The next, I was cursed—a mistake to punish. Unlovable. It was the same blade, only this time, Hades held it. "Hades—" I said.

He didn't answer or move.

"Okay..." I let out a laugh, trying to shake it off. "This isn't funny."

His gray eyes dragged over me with a look that made my stomach twist. It wasn't concern, not anger. It wasn't even indifference.

It was disgust, like he could barely tolerate the sight of me. I wanted to speak, to ask what I'd done wrong, but the words caught somewhere between my lungs and my lips. "Say something," I whispered.

He didn't. Hades flicked his hand, a sliver of his black magic wrapping around my mouth. The gag sealed tight.

I tried to scream, to speak, anything. But nothing passed through his binding, not even the sharp breath I tried to take. My knees shook, a cold sweat breaking out across my spine as the bond tightened. I staggered back until I hit the wall. Pain radiated through my elbows and the base of my skull, but I paid them no mind.

Another flick of his hand and slivers of his writhing magic curled around my wrists and ankles, yanking my limbs together. "What are you doing?" I tried once more, but again there was no sound. I collapsed to the floor with a bone-rattling thud.

Tears spilled from my eyes, hot and sharp against my cheeks, but Hades was unmoved. He didn't care. There had to be an explanation. Hades wouldn't treat me like this.

But the face I loved stared back at me, cold.

He stepped farther into the room. I bucked, aching to free myself, and the black tendrils bit deeper. The more I struggled, the tighter they squeezed. Hades' boots echoed against the floor as he took another few steps, standing only a foot away from me. "You're such a fool. As if you could ever think I would like you—let alone love you," he continued.

My stomach dropped further. I shook my head. *No.* But

he just stood there, expression unchanged. I searched his face for hesitation, regret, remorse. *Something.*

"I thought—" I tried to say, but the gag held firm, not even a strangled whimper escaping. The silence stretched between us, and a thought crept forward.

A truth that hurt more than broken bones or bruises.

It wouldn't matter if I could speak. The truth would not change.

Deep down, I knew he was right. My heart hammered against my ribs. How could anyone ever choose me? Over and over, I had cried and begged and hoped that the Fates would be kind, that someone would want me.

Anyone.

"You're a liability." His voice sliced through me. "I can't stand to be around you anymore. Look at all the chaos you've caused me." His words crushed me more than his magic ever could.

My throat seized. Not that crying out would've helped— the gag held still. Tears leaked around it, trailing down my neck and soaking the fabric at my collar. I trembled beneath his gaze.

Hades sneered down at me. "You'll never be more than a warm body I wanted to fuck." His voice snaked around me like a living thing. "Actually," he said and barked a laugh, "soon you'll be a cold body because you're going to die in these trials. Everyone knows that."

I shook my head. *No. No, this isn't real. This isn't real. This isn't real.* I tried to recall all the times he'd held me. The way he'd brushed my hair behind my ear and whispered sweet words. The way his voice had always softened when old fears pulled me under and I panicked. How he'd called me his goddess, his mate.

He'd said I was strong. That I mattered, that I wasn't broken. But I'd heard beautiful words before, seen them backed by tender actions and soft smiles. Until the mother who cherished me turned cold overnight. Until the hands that once held me with love struck me instead.

But Hades turned and walked away. The door slammed shut, cutting off the blinding light and leaving only the harsh glow overhead.

I was alone again.

Perhaps he was the next person who got tired of pretending I was worth loving. It was only a matter of time because love always spoiled. Demeter had nicknamed me after a flower, but maybe I was never the bloom at all. I was the rot at the roots, the quiet ruin that ensured it would wither.

My body shook until the tremors burned themselves out. I could barely breathe through my nose with all the snot dripping from it. I pressed my forehead to the floor. A soundless scream tore through me, but it never left my chest. I didn't have the air. Or the strength.

I counted.

One.

Two.

Three.

Four...

I meant to keep going, but the numbers slipped, scattering like beads off a broken string. His words kept replaying. His face had been so vivid, the disgust on it...

~

What felt like hours passed. I had tried counting the time—seconds folding into minutes, minutes into hours—but somewhere along the way, the numbers blurred and disappeared altogether. My limbs felt distant, heavy and unresponsive when I begged them to move. Hades came back. I lay motionless on the floor, staring at his boots as he walked in.

The terror was back, his power injected into me. "I don't love you and I never did."

My breath hitched as I looked up at him. The words landed like a crack to my ribs. I flinched, even though he was across the room.

He was lying. He had to be.

My thoughts tripped over themselves, desperate to make sense of it all. The world tilted, a haze pressing in at the edges of my vision. I had to find some loophole in his voice, some trace of the softness I knew. This couldn't be him.

Unless it was.

Maybe I had imagined it all—every single look, every touch, every time he told me he loved me. Maybe I'd fallen too fast, rushed into this relationship because I wanted it so badly to be real. Because I needed it to be.

I reached for the bond. *Please, Hades.* I shoved everything I had at it: fear, love, need.

"I only need you to help me get the stone piece we lost because of you." His magic poured out faster. I'd felt fear before, but Hades' was different. With nothing more than a flick of his wrist and some intention, he could plunge me into a storm.

And I was drowning in it.

I couldn't stop it. I sucked in a ragged inhale through my clogged nose. Pressure built with no release, no escape. Sweat beaded on my forehead. Every muscle in my body trembled under the weight of his power. Why was he doing this to me?

I didn't understand. I probed at our bond, trying to pull at the tether between us. *You don't mean this*, I sent the words across. *Tell me you don't mean this.*

He smirked at me. *I mean every bit of it.* "I curse the Fates for giving me a mate like you."

Shame dragged my eyes to the floor. His disgust was suffocating. His face, the words, the wall, they all bled together. *This isn't real. This isn't real. This isn't real.*

But his voice cut through my thoughts. "It's very real, Persephone."

I don't want it to be real. I won't let it be real. Panic squeezed my chest. My wrists burned. I waited for him to crack a smile, to laugh, to tell me this was some cruel joke. My eyes raked from his head to his toes. I stilled.

His boots.

They were tied wrong at the top.

Hades always double knotted his laces. He tied them loop over loop and pulled until they were *exactly* the same length. I had teased him about it, called him obsessive and dramatic, told him it was just a pair of shoes. He never got mad. He just smiled.

One night, I'd watched him redo the same knot three times. "Are you okay?" I'd asked.

He hadn't looked up, just kept working the laces. They weren't perfect yet. "Some days, my mind runs too loud," he'd told me. "Things like this make me feel in control. It helps," he'd said as he tugged the final knot into place. He had stood up and walked over to me, then pulled me close and pressed a kiss to my lips. It had felt so steady. So safe.

Nothing like the Hades standing before me.

A single knot on his left boot was loose. Sloppy.

This wasn't Hades.

It couldn't be.

I blinked a few times, staring at the uneven knot, trying to process what I was seeing. No matter how real this felt, the detail didn't change. The loop was off.

I was torn between relief and grief. Because even if it wasn't him, the pain was still there.

It looked like him, sounded like him. But the knot... Gods, the knot. He would've *never* missed that.

I reached for my magic, and to my surprise, it responded.

It roared within me, volatile, fueled by my fear. *Burn through his hold*, I commanded it.

"You're so weak."

I gritted my teeth and kept pushing, forcing the power outward, trying to break through his bindings.

The first bind snapped. The gag around my mouth disappeared. A ragged cry tore free, raw and desperate.

Hades laughed, his tendrils tightening and swirling around me, sending another wave of unnatural horror crashing through my body. Every instinct urged me to run, to hide, but there was nowhere to go. His magic made sure of that.

And through it all, he just stood there, watching.

I won't stop. I won't stop. I won't stop.

My magic burned hotter. It wasn't a flicker but a roar. It surged up from my chest, racing along every limb, searing past his hold, burning away the terror, the *illusion*.

Another scream tore from my throat. The sound cracked through the air as a blinding white burst erupted from within me, flooding the small room and swallowing everything whole.

Everything was white.

There were no walls, no floor, no ceiling.

No Hades. No fear.

Nothing.

A sharp burn covered my forearm. I flinched and shoved up my sleeve.

The seven glowing circles appeared again, the first two

filled in. They flared bright against my bruised skin, then vanished.

"Trial two of seven complete," said the same loud, booming voice from the last trial.

I didn't move.

The light drained into black. I sat there, not victorious or relieved.

Just empty.

I shook, unable to tell if it was from the magic or exhaustion—or both. I curled my arm back against my chest. If that was trial two, what would be left of me by trial seven? My eyes burned as Hades' voice echoed again inside my skull. *You'll never be more than a warm body I wanted to fuck.*

I *knew* it wasn't him.

I knew it.

But the words lived inside me like parasites, chewing through the soft places that hadn't turned hard yet. What if some part of that did come from the real Hades?

HADES

Persephone appeared, her body materializing on the bedroll before me. She'd been gone for hours, but daylight still filtered in through the seam between the tent flaps. Her chest heaved, skin damp with sweat.

I couldn't move. I went still, air locked in my throat. She sucked in a breath that sounded more like a sob, then shot upright.

"Persephone." My voice was lower than I'd intended.

She turned her head. Our eyes met.

I knew fear well. I'd seen fear in every form. I'd crafted it, fed on it.

But never like this.

Not from my mate.

Wide, unblinking eyes held mine, frozen in a silent kind of horror that didn't need words. Her trembling lips parted.

And it was all directed toward me, as if I were something birthed from a nightmare. Persephone scrambled backward, frantic, like a wounded animal trying to escape a predator. She didn't stop until she collided with the back of the canvas tent. I moved closer, reaching out.

"Stop," she said.

I froze.

She recoiled before I even moved. Her body curled in on itself. "Stop. Stop. Stop," she muttered the words over and over again, her hands pressed against her temples.

She'd never flinched from me like that before. Not when I first met her, not even when she saw the full weight of my power. "Perseph—"

"Get out," she croaked. Her eyes locked on my boots.

I took one step back, then another. My hand twitched at my side. Every muscle screamed at me to go to her, to pull her into my arms, to fix whatever had happened between us.

Turning away took everything, but I forced my legs to move.

When I slipped outside, the Winter Court's cold slammed into me. The wind clawed at the edges of my cloak, sneaking beneath it. The air burned my lungs, but I didn't care. I welcomed it. I needed something to hold onto before I lost control. I closed my eyes, tapping my gloved fingers on my pants.

One.

Two.

Three.

Four.

Five.

Stay in control. I inhaled and exhaled. The counting always helped when nothing else did. It was a thread to hold onto as everything unraveled. Back in the Underworld, I could whisk to the mortal realm and cut a few threads—sever ones that deserved it. That act brought clarity, control. But here, I couldn't do that. Whisking would use my magic. Without that release, the darkness was hard to push down.

"Clearly, she's back," Gabriel said from the fire.

I nodded. "I don't want to talk about it. I'm going for a

walk." I couldn't put it into words, not yet. Gabriel gave me a pitying smile, but I left before he could say anything else.

I moved through the trees, the snow giving way under my boots. I'd inflicted fear on countless souls, but never had I seen someone look at me the way Persephone did.

This was not a stranger, not an enemy. This was my *mate.* Fuck.

What had she seen? What had she gone through to make her look at me like that? Like I was the thing that had broken her.

I walked for hours. Snow fell in a light, lazy rhythm, like the realm was at peace. I couldn't feel the cold anymore. I didn't feel the air slicing my skin, or the ice crusting my gloves. Nothing. Just the dull throb of her words in my chest.

My magic thrummed through my veins, but I pushed it back. I couldn't undo all our hard work here in Faerie. We didn't have the stone piece yet.

When the sun finally dipped in the sky, I made my way back toward the camp. A thin ribbon of smoke rose above the trees, and my pace faltered. I hesitated before stepping through Gabriel's ward.

Gabriel and Orion sat beside the fire, their faces covered in its flickering light. "I tried to offer her some warm water and some dried berries, but she told me to leave them by the entrance of the tent," Gabriel said.

They didn't ask me what was wrong with Persephone. They were smart for that. The question was clear in Gabriel's eyes.

I almost wanted to tell them. The words rose to the back of my throat, just a sentence. *She looked at me like I was a monster.*

But I couldn't.

Saying it would make it real.

I stared into the flames, refusing to look back at the tent behind me. I wanted to barrel in there and demand answers, but the memory of her eyes—wide with fear, her body shrinking away from me—rooted me to the spot I stood.

PERSEPHONE

I sat in the tent, knees drawn to my chest, staring at the wall like it might give me answers. The lantern's glow danced, but every flicker made my heart lurch. I tightened the blanket around myself, clutching it as if it could shield me from the thoughts swirling in my mind.

I knew it had been a trial. I *knew* that. But my body hadn't caught up. My hands still shook, and his voice still echoed in my ears.

It wasn't real. None of it had been real.

And still, it clung to me like it was. I hated how deeply—how easily—the court's magic had gotten under my skin.

A soft knock on the stretched canvas snapped me out of my haze. I tensed, rubbing the blanket between my index finger and thumb. Gabriel had been here earlier, dropping off some water and snacks.

"It's me." Gabriel's voice filtered through the fabric.

I let out a quiet sigh.

"Can I come in?"

I hesitated. *No* hovered on my tongue, but loneliness pressed harder. I swallowed past the lump in my throat.

"Yes," I croaked. The tent flap pulled back, opening just enough for him to step through. A flash of firelight seared the dark before the canvas closed again.

Gabriel crouched near me. "We're going to the tavern for warmth and a hot meal. Would you like to come?"

The thought of being around people—of smiling, or worse, seeing pity in their eyes— made my stomach twist. I shook my head.

He frowned. "Are you sure?"

My gaze dropped. Wool socks hugged my toes; the blanket pressed against my shins, its weight pinning me in place. "I don't think I'm up for it." My voice was just above a whisper.

Gabriel's brows knitted together. "Are you hurt? Do you need anything?"

"You already asked me that earlier."

"Yeah, because this isn't like you," he said.

I exhaled slowly. Maybe this was exactly like me—the *real* me. Now they'd see it too. "I just want to be alone right now."

Silence stretched between us. "All right," he said finally, pushing himself up. "If you're not coming, Hades will stay here with you."

Pressure built in my throat. "I—" I bit down on the inside of my cheek. "I don't want him in the tent." The moment I said it, I hated how small my voice sounded. I stared at the rug. The fibers were coarse, woven in haphazard rows of brown that reminded me of little twigs. A few strands stuck up where the weave had loosened. I traced all the imperfections with my eyes. I didn't want to look up. Didn't want to see whatever could be in his gaze—confusion, judgment, understanding. None of it.

"Okay." He stepped outside, the flap closing behind him.

∼

A faint rustling outside the tent drew my attention. I shifted under the blankets, my body stiff from sitting too long in one position. With a sigh, I pushed myself upright and stretched my legs before slipping to the entrance to peek out. I'd said I didn't want Hades to come in. But now, wrapped in silence, I wasn't sure I meant it.

Hades stood with his back to me, his broad shoulders outlined by the flickering fire. He didn't turn or acknowledge me. My heart stuttered. I chewed on my lip, debating whether I should say something. But what would I even say? What could make up for the way I'd recoiled? The words died before they could form. I shook my head and retreated.

Time dragged forward, quiet and heavy.

A knock rattled the canvas. "We're back," Gabriel said. "Can I come in? I have something for you."

I gave a small nod before remembering he couldn't see me. "Yes."

I sat up as he stepped inside, carrying a small paper bowl with a lid, a metal spoon resting on top. "I brought some soup for you."

Gabriel crouched down and set the bowl beside me. "What happened in the trial?"

I tensed. "I don't want to talk about it."

He exhaled. "What does it have to do with him?"

"It's just… in the trial, Hades—" The words detonated inside me, a white-hot bloom in my chest. I gasped, clawing at the ache as magic strangled the rest of my voice.

Gabriel's expression hardened. "Shit. I forgot you were bound."

I managed a shaky breath. "It's okay."

His jaw ticked, but he said nothing. He stripped the lid from the bowl and set it in my hands. "Will you be okay in here on your own?"

I nodded.

"Call for us if you need anything."

I brought a spoonful of broth to my lips and sipped, letting the warmth spread through me. It was barely luke-warm, but it was something. I took another mouthful. My stomach had been so tight with stress, I hadn't realized how hungry I was.

Once I had eaten enough, I set the bowl aside. I lay back, pulling the blankets higher, cocooning myself in their weight. Maybe if I closed my eyes, I'd stop seeing the way Hades had looked at me in the trial.

I closed them. He was there again. Not the real him—the other one, the one who had made me bleed with his words. I kept my eyes open after that.

Hades had seen me recoil from him when I returned from the trial. I'd hurt him. I knew it. He hadn't deserved that. I shifted on the bedroll, trying to sink deeper into the fabric, wishing it would swallow me whole. I should have known sooner. *What kind of mate believes the worst of the one they love?* He shouldn't have to hold someone who couldn't tell the difference between a truth and a lie.

If this was only the second trial... How many pieces would be left of me by the end?

I used to think love meant safety, that if someone looked at you like you were worth something, you'd finally be protected and whole. But maybe love just gave you more to lose.

35

HADES

I lay on the rug, tracking each slow rise and fall of her chest. Sleep hadn't come. It probably wouldn't, not with her just a few feet away.

I'd given her hours before coming in. By then, she was quiet, her breaths steady in sleep. Space was the only thing I could really offer her now.

Her breathing hitched, turning shallower. She rolled in her sleep and faced me. Her fingers flexed against the furs. I sat up. Her shoulders tensed, like she was bracing for a blow. She let out a soft, broken sound that didn't belong to the Persephone I knew.

"Persephone." Her name fell from my lips before I could stop it. She writhed, her face contorting in pain, fear. She flinched hard, and I was on my feet, moving without thought.

I hovered at the edge of the bedroll, staring down at her. Her brow furrowed, and a whimper shaped a word I hadn't expected.

My name.

I didn't think. I didn't plan. I lifted the edge of the blankets and furs and slipped beneath them, careful not to wake her. "I'm here, little goddess," I whispered.

She shifted again, but she didn't stir.

I inched closer and eased an arm around her. Even in sleep, she curled into my side. A tear slipped from the corner of her eye and down her cheek. I brushed it away with my thumb, letting my hand linger a few seconds longer than I needed to.

I stayed with her until the tension melted from her brow and her whimpering stopped. Then I eased out from beneath the warmth of the covers, tucked them around her, and I settled back onto the rug.

36

PERSEPHONE

I lay on my side, hands tucked beneath my cheek. I stared at the fur-covered lump on the ground.

Hades.

He was sprawled on the rug, wrapped in a single fur, one arm hooked behind his head, his whole body at ease. My chest ached. I bit down on my lip. Guilt gnawed at the edges of my thoughts, even as the memory of the trial rolled through my mind. I squeezed my eyes shut, but his face appeared again, etched with disgust for me.

My eyes snapped open. I didn't have time for this.

Emotions were dangerous right now. The stone piece was all that mattered. I had to stay focused or I'd crack open again. Still, they clung to me. If there was a silver lining, it was that the mess of them left me too distracted to think about fighting the drake today.

I pushed off the blanket and furs and started dressing, my fingers working through muscle memory while my mind dragged itself back to reality.

Movement caught my eye. Hades stirred, his eyelids

twitching. I moved, shoving my boots on and slipping outside before he could sit up.

The cold air bit at my skin, needling every strip of flesh my cloak left uncovered. Goose bumps prickled beneath my clothes. My breath spilled out in wisps that vanished into the chill. Gabriel was already up, crouched by the fire and chewing on a sandwich. He looked up, green eyes settling on me. "How are you holding up?"

I cringed. "I could be better."

He huffed out a humorless laugh. "Well, you need to get better soon. We don't have time for you to wallow."

I nodded, swallowing down the words threatening to spill from my lips. He was right. We didn't have time for my emotions. All they did was make things worse.

Gabriel handed me a sandwich. I peeled back the foil, and it warmed my fingers. The fire crackled and popped. I let myself sink into its heat, pretending that it could thaw the cold that had taken root inside me.

Eventually, we moved. No one said much.

Now we stood at the mouth of the cave.

I'd avoided Hades all morning. Hess had noticed first. Her gaze had lingered on me longer than usual. *You're keeping something from me*, she had said.

Falon had picked up on it too, asking if I was all right. Of course I'd just nodded.

A shiver ran through me, born of nerves, not the temperature. "We're really doing this," I murmured, my voice barely audible over the snowy wind's howl.

We stepped inside, the cold roar muffled behind us. I pushed up my goggles, feeling the tingling imprint of the rims and straps on my skin. I'd kept them on even after dismounting Hess. They shielded my eyes from the dry air and from seeing Hades hovering in my peripheral vision.

Gabriel's jaw tightened. Silently, he lit the lantern. A warm glow bloomed.

Our footsteps echoed as we moved, cautious and quiet. When we reached the familiar fork, I pointed to the left, the path I'd marked last time. My pulse quickened, and I forced myself to breathe evenly.

Step by step, the ground tilted steeper beneath us. The light jolted with every movement, throwing restless shadows across the stone. No one spoke. Words would've been a waste, a distraction.

We came to another fork.

The men all watched me, waiting. I swallowed hard and closed my eyes, shutting out the dim, flickering light.

Inhale in.

Exhale out.

My eyes snapped open. "Right," I whispered. Gabriel nodded once and led the way, Orion following behind him. Hades' gaze lingered, heavy on my back. But the ghost of his illusion still clung to me, whispering all the things I feared were true. My shoulders tensed, but I kept my focus forward.

We walked.

And walked.

The tunnel stretched endlessly before us, a single path taking us deeper. Some boulders forced us to weave around them. I cleared my throat. "Are you sure this is going to lead us there?" My voice was low but still loud in the quiet of the cave.

"Let's just keep walking," Orion said.

The tunnel continued its descent, the air growing even colder. The walls opened, the space expanding both high and wide. The lantern's light barely reached the ceiling, just revealing jagged formations that looked like fangs. Ahead, the narrow path extended forward, a strip of stone ground between two pools of still, murky water.

I glanced down. The dark water reflected my face. "Gross," I said, louder than I meant to. Gabriel shot me a sharp look and pressed a finger to his lips. I bit the inside of my cheek to keep from apologizing aloud.

A low, deep tremor rolled through the cave, rattling my ribs. The ground beneath us shook, small stones tumbling from the walls. My eyes went upward. I sent a quick prayer to the Fates that those serrated rocks wouldn't fall on us.

Orion grinned—the kind of smile that made my stomach turn. "I think we found it," he whispered, so low that I almost didn't hear him.

This was it.

I didn't return his grin. My lips parted as my face tightened. I couldn't even pretend to be brave. Instead, I gave him a look surely full of pure horror. Dread gripped my chest.

Gabriel turned to me and leaned in close. "Your main objective is to get the stone piece. Don't worry about us."

I nodded slowly. I understood, but I didn't like what he was saying.

"If you have an opportunity, you take it and leave. Don't wait for us. Hess will give you instructions from Rys."

I couldn't imagine leaving without them. They had become a part of my life, and the thought of letting go made my chest ache. I tried to bury the panic rising within me. If it came down to it, I wasn't so sure I'd be able to obey.

"We'll all be okay," Hades added.

I nodded again, not because I agreed but because I didn't trust myself to speak. We moved deeper into the tunnel at the end of the path, stepping into another stretch of darkness.

The ground shook again. The vibration rolled through my feet and up my body, rattling my teeth. A hand gripped my arm and I shuddered.

Hades.

"Close your eyes," he said. "Feel for the stone. I'll guide you. Just focus. I won't let you run into anything."

I nodded. *Breathe, Persephone*, I told myself. I shut my eyes and reached for the part of me that remembered the stone that had sealed Tartarus shut.

It hummed through the darkness. *I feel it*, I said to Hades through the bond.

"Out of the way!" Gabriel shouted.

Hades' grip on me tightened as he threw us backward. I barely registered Gabriel's words before my back struck the stone. The impact punched all the breath from my lungs in a violent gasp. I tried to inhale, but it caught, producing only a wheeze.

My head spun. My eyes snapped open, but all I saw were scales.

Massive, glistening, gold scales.

The creature slithered through the tunnel with a sickening hiss, scraping against the stone. Its body was endless, spilling into the tunnel, every ripple of muscle announcing its raw strength. I couldn't believe the sheer size of it.

I pressed myself harder against the cold rock, wishing I could melt into it. Beside me, Hades, Orion, and Gabriel did the same. The massive serpent filled the corridor, a living wall.

It slithered forward, moving into the wide space with the water. We all shared a glance. *Go*, Hades said as he gripped my wrist. Gabriel handed Hades the lantern.

Hades and I silently sprinted forward, while Gabriel and Orion drew their weapons and waited in the tunnel, watching the drake move through the first cavern space.

I swallowed my fear, as much as I could of it. We stepped out of the tight corridor and into another cavern, this one bigger than the last. The air turned thick and wet, clinging to the exposed skin on my face. The stench hit next.

Rot.

Decay.

My stomach churned as I took in the sight of layers and layers of skin. Thick, pale, discarded serpent husks littered the cavern in heaps, curled and shriveled. Some were shredded into brittle ribbons, some ground into the chalky powder beneath our feet, while others—fresher—were still intact.

The dried crunch of skin beneath my boot echoed in the cavern. I tensed, and the sensation shot up my leg. I dared a glance down, and it crumbled further under my weight. A sour taste crept up my throat, and I retched back the urge to vomit. I shut my eyes and swallowed hard. I had to move before that snake came back.

I tried to block out the sickening feel of the skins catching on my cloak. They were dry and fragile but disturbingly soft in some places. The farther I moved, the deeper I sank into them. *What if I fail?* I shook my head. I didn't have time for doubt.

They reached my shoulders. I nearly swam in them. *This is disgusting*, I thought. I pushed forward, forcing myself to focus on the pull—the steady thrumming pulse guiding me. It was here. I knew it. I felt it.

I dropped to my knees, holding my breath, and clawed through layers of old, crumbling skins. Hades lowered beside me and helped move them. The pulse grew stronger.

I froze.

Eggs.

Massive, ivory shells clustered together, their surfaces dappled with tiny black spots. Oh gods. A cold realization slammed into me. *Hades, tell me the drake can miraculously lay eggs on its own...*

Hades' lips pressed into a thin line. *I don't know, but I think there would have to be another involved.* We gave each other a glance. *We have to do this quickly,* he said.

I nodded.

Carefully, Hades and I moved forward, lifting one. A deafening screech roared through the cavern. My stomach lurched. *Faster,* I said. My ears rang, but there wasn't time to slow. We moved to the next egg.

Then the next.

I crouched, fingers digging and clawing through what felt like fertilizer but smelled much worse. Gods, *so* much worse.

I gagged but pushed through.

There.

I shoved my hands deeper, clawing past the layers until my gloved fingers brushed something solid, warm. The stone. It thrummed like a living thing, the vibration crawling from my fingers, up my arm, and to my chest like a second heartbeat. I recognized its power. I yanked it up.

Hades caught my gaze, and a grin spread across his face. "Let's go."

"Incoming!" Orion shouted.

A gust of hot, rancid wind slammed into me. Hades dropped the lantern and lunged, locking his arms around me before hefting me over his shoulder and bolting through the sea of molted husks. The sudden movement sent my head spinning. *Put me down.* I pushed against his back. *I can handle myself.*

He let out a quick, annoyed sound but lowered me, grabbing my wrist and dragging me into a crevice in the cavern wall.

The drake burst into the space. Its gold scales caught the half-smothered lantern light as it filtered through the debris. Its long body curled around its eggs, protective and seething. It reared back, throat swelling, and it roared.

The sound hit like a shockwave. Stone vibrated beneath

our feet. My ears rang from the pitch of it, the loud whine swallowing every other sound, and lodging itself deep in my skull.

Move, Hades said.

I didn't hesitate. I sprinted. Hades ran beside me, but the drake moved faster than I expected, quicker than anything that big should've been able to. A gold blur surged past my peripheral vision, its tail swinging straight toward me.

Hades yelled my name as he shoved me hard. I stumbled, momentum pitching me forward, but I caught myself.

The crack of impact split the air as the tail slammed into him instead.

"Hades!"

His body struck the stone hard, limbs folding wrong, head whipping sideways. He groaned and rolled to his side. One hand pressed to his temple. The abandoned lantern's distorted light revealed the blood running down the side of his face in dark, relentless streams. Not a smear, but a torrent.

I skidded to a stop. That blow had been meant for me. If he hadn't moved—

My instincts screamed to run, but my feet didn't move. My jaw tightened. The echo of his illusion's voice twisted in my mind. *You're a liability.*

I hated how much of it still lived inside me.

I hated that wounded part of me that believed it for embarrassingly long.

Hades tried to stand, blood continuing to pour down from the wound. His eyes met mine. They didn't hold any disgust or anger.

That illusion wasn't him.

This was. I turned and ran toward him as the drake surged closer, jaws widening for another strike.

"Go!" he shouted, his voice hoarse. "I told you to go. I'll be fine."

I skidded across loose stones and husks, dropping hard beside him. The drake hissed, so loud it drowned my pulse. "When have I ever listened to you? You're bleeding."

He grunted, steadying himself. "Doesn't matter."

"It does to me." The words tore from my chest. The serpent reared, its massive body rising so high its scales scraped the ceiling, sending rock splintering down around us. One piece struck close enough to send a spray of shards across my cloak. "*You* matter to me."

A ghost of a smile touched his lips, and even now, it made my stomach flip. My fingers curled around his arm and I pulled with everything I had. "Come on," I said.

The drake's shadow swallowed us whole as it closed in, each thunderous breath rattling the walls and the ground as we sprinted.

Across the cavern, near the tunnel we'd come in through, Orion pulled a large, dark bottle from his pack. A slow grin spread across his face. "Let's play with some oil and fire." He uncorked the bottle. When we reached them, Gabriel and Orion fell into step behind us, the bottle spilling its thick, dark liquid in their wake.

The drake roared. It closed in—too fast, too close. Gabriel turned, his sword striking back through the drake's eye. The beast screeched, a wet spray bursting from the wound. Fluid splattered the ground, narrowly missing us as the drake thrashed and reared back. Its tail smashed against the stone with a deafening crack, spraying fragments of rock everywhere.

"This is our opening," Orion yelled.

We ran.

I didn't look back. I couldn't.

We burst from the cavern and back into the main tunnel of the cave. "I'm putting up a ward," Gabriel yelled, already turning. The drake surged into view, its massive shape shrinking the distance between us.

Gabriel planted his feet and raised both hands. Orion tossed the empty bottle and struck a match, the tiny flame flaring to life. He dropped it on the trail of oil. Gabriel's power flowed from his fingertips, forming the ward.

The fire caught instantly.

Flame raced down the tunnel, eager, hungry, before it erupted into the cavern with a deafening *whoosh*. A wall of flame surged behind Gabriel's magic, a tidal wave of orange and gold. The creature vanished behind it, lost to the blaze. The drake's shriek pierced the sound of the fire's fury. Its ancient spite reverberated through the stone.

Gabriel clenched his jaw. "I can only hold this for so long. We need to get to higher ground. The drake is strong, and I don't know if the fire will be enough to stop it."

We didn't argue.

We ran.

Piercing cries chased us through the tunnels. Plumes of black smoke curled from the fire once Gabriel's ward dropped. It stung my eyes and clawed at my throat.

Faster.

My legs burned, but we couldn't stop.

We ran until only smoke and silence followed us. Our steps slowed. Gabriel huffed out a cough. "This only worked because of the men Aurelia and Cassius sent. Many of them died for our information. The maps, the timing. We owe this to them."

I swallowed hard.

"They went in with nothing so we wouldn't have to," Hades said.

"We survived because they didn't," I whispered.

No one spoke. The weight of it pressed in on us. We weren't just carrying the stone. We were carrying the cost of the lives we'd never met, names I didn't know.

PERSEPHONE

The stone pulsed through my gloves, its jagged edges biting through the leather. Its power slipped past the barrier and into me. I clenched it tighter anyway. Gabriel had said we'd put it into a small, protective sack once we got it, but in the chaos, we couldn't find it now. I had no choice but to hold onto it myself.

Gabriel raised a hand, pressing a finger to his lips. "Shh."

I stilled. *Someone is here*, Hades spoke through the bond as he tugged on my hand, gesturing for Gabriel and Orion to follow. This section of the cave was choked with jutting slabs and scattered rock. I'd been dreading this area, but now I sent a silent prayer of thanks to the Fates.

We pressed against the stone wall, flattening ourselves behind a large rock wide enough to shield the four of us. Hades' hand settled on my shoulder, firm and protective. Footsteps pattered closer.

"She's going to kill us if we don't get it," a voice hissed from the darkness.

"Where is all this smoke coming from?" another asked.

A sick feeling coiled low in my stomach. Carefully, I slipped the stone down through the layers of my clothing, pushing it into my bra. It cut into the sensitive skin between my breasts.

Let it. Better me than anyone else. The Underworld depended on it.

I glanced at Orion, Gabriel, and Hades. Since we'd abandoned the lantern, my eyes had already adjusted to the darkness. They stood motionless, their weapons drawn but steady. My toes curled inside my wool socks, grounding me.

A dim glow came closer. The footsteps grew louder—more than just one set. I swallowed hard, pressing myself flatter against the rock.

"You owe me big for getting me wrapped into this," a new voice grumbled.

"Oh, shut up, Rillon," another replied. "We're going to be paid so well. Demeter is rich."

At the mention of her name, I sucked in a sharp breath. Demeter had sent men for the stone? Hades moved quickly, clamping his hand over my mouth to stifle any sound that might escape. His index finger brushed just under my nose.

Oh no.

The tickle hit a second too late. My nostrils flared.

And then—

I sneezed.

The sound wasn't loud, but in the stillness between footsteps and voices, it cracked through the air like lightning. My eyes widened. The footsteps stopped, then moved faster, closer.

"What the fuck was that?" one of the voices asked.

I squeezed my eyes shut, cursing at myself. I didn't move. My spine pressed so tight against the wall that it hurt. Every muscle tensed in preparation for what I knew would inevitably happen.

"Hello?" one of the voices asked. "Is anyone there?"

The four of us didn't move.

"If you are, you're not coming out alive," the man said, his voice dropping into a cold growl.

Their lantern's glow flared brighter as it neared. The movement of the light sent shadows twisting and stretching, distorting the shapes around us. "Rillon, check behind that big-ass rock," a voice barked.

Gabriel tapped Orion. I glanced up at Hades, who met my gaze with a quick nod before shifting his attention back to Gabriel. Rillon rounded the rock, and the smug smirk on his face faltered, his entire body stiffening.

Gabriel moved. A sharp burst of magic exploded from his palm, slamming into Rillon's chest. The force knocked him backward. He hit the ground hard, cloak smoking where the magic had struck. Around us, the other men scrambled, shouts and curses filling the cave as blades were drawn. Hades launched forward, shoving me behind him.

The moment they charged, I moved. I dropped low, slipping behind a narrow column of stone just beyond the rock we'd hidden behind. I drew my dagger from its sheath, keeping it hidden beneath my cloak. The others—Hades, Gabriel, Orion—met the fight head-on.

I hated hiding while they fought. It scraped against the little pride I had left. I wanted to stand beside them, but I couldn't risk it. I needed to protect the stone. So I stayed low and peered beyond my hiding spot, just enough to see the fight unfolding.

Hades caught the wrist of the man closest to us mid-swing, twisted hard, and didn't stop until bones popped and the weapon clattered to the ground.

Orion held two daggers, his hands moving so quickly that they blurred in the dim light.

A blast of magic shot toward Hades from one of the

attackers. Hades moved out of the way with ease. From the side, Rillon staggered to his feet, catching my gaze. He swayed slightly, jaw tight, but his sneer didn't fade.

My fingers clenched around the hilt of my dagger, a question flashing hot in my mind: *should I strike him?* But one wrong move, one slip of steel, and the Underworld would bear my mistake. Faces of the souls rose behind my eyes, pressing in. They were counting on me. No one ever had before. My hand trembled on the weapon, but I did nothing. I held back.

Rillon took a small step toward me. His lips curled back, and his dismissive eyes lingered for a beat. "This is no place for a woman." He turned away, back toward the men he came with.

I pushed my hood up, the fabric brushing my cheek, and let myself sink farther into the shadows. Let them ignore me. Let them think I was harmless. The fools didn't realize the stone they hunted was pressed against my skin, beating with every breath I took. They were too focused on fighting Gabriel, Orion, and Hades to notice something as *insignificant* as a woman. I swallowed my rage, banking the fire, letting it smolder beneath my ribs.

Hades twisted to block a strike aimed at Orion. Gabriel called out a warning, but his voice was swallowed by the chaos.

In a flash of movement, Rillon lunged. Fast, desperate, and quiet.

Rillon restrained Hades, his magic wrapping around him as he pressed a dagger to his throat. He had no idea how close he stood to dying. The cold meant they wore gloves and cloaks, keeping Hades' skin from contacting his. If Hades could use his touch or his magic, the man would've been long dead.

I had let this happen. One strike—one breath of courage

—and I could have stopped Rillon. The weight of my choice dug into me. Something in me snapped. Immortal or not, no one touched what was mine. I rose, my silhouette folding into the dim cave walls. I supposed being a woman was just as good as being invisible to these men.

Big mistake.

I was ten steps away.

Six.

Three.

One.

I maneuvered behind Rillon, my steps silent, weaving between a few large stones. The man focused solely on keeping the magic locked onto Hades, unaware of the danger creeping up behind him.

Gabriel and Orion fought off the others, their opponents collapsing one by one. The clash of steel and magic dulled, leaving only the man restraining Hades. I stepped up onto a large rock at Rillon's back, evening the height difference between us.

This was the last man left.

His shoulders heaved with ragged breath, his head whipping around as he searched for backup that wasn't coming. "I swear to the Fates, I'll kill this piece of Faerie trash," he spat, his voice shaking. "I have a mission. I'm not leaving without the stone."

Hades chuckled in his grip but didn't tell him that his little knife or magic couldn't kill him. "Give it up."

"No. I'll kill you!"

"I'd like to see you try," Hades said.

The weight of the stone pressed against my chest, nestled between my skin and my clothes. Its power surged through me, syncing with my heartbeat. Energy thrummed through my bones, humming like an untamed beast. I *liked* it.

Rillon stilled as I pressed my blade against his throat. A

tremor ran through him, shoulders twitching beneath my grip as he tried to twist away without losing leverage. I pressed in harder. "Release him," I whispered, my voice slipping into a low purr. "If you don't drop that dagger, I will slit your throat, and my *mate* will punish you in the Underworld."

His knife still pressed against Hades' throat. The stone buzzed, its energy licking at me. I leaned in closer, my lips brushing the shell of the attacker's ear. "Don't mess with me or my mate."

Hades let out a laugh. "You've made her very angry. What a mistake."

Rillon jerked his head to the side, straining against me. "I should've killed you when I had the chance. Fuckin' woman. You won't do it," he said.

That was the wrong thing to say.

The stone throbbed—wild, alive, hungry. The dagger pressed deeper, beads of blood welling beneath the blade.

"I'm not leaving this place without the stone piece," he said, his voice trembling.

My lips shifted into something between a smirk and a snarl. "Then you're not leaving."

I didn't hesitate. The dagger sliced clean across his throat, the sharp metal parting flesh and muscle. A wet, gurgling sound followed as blood spilled down the front of his cloak. His grip on Hades fell away. Clawing at the wound, he staggered forward before collapsing.

Silence settled once more. I exhaled slowly. The dead man lay near my feet, blood pooling beneath him. The stone's presence pressed warm against my chest, steady now. Satisfied.

I wiped the blade clean on my sleeve as if I were cleaning off dirt, not death. My heart should've been racing. My hands should've been shaking. But there was nothing. I placed my dagger in its sheath.

"How deliciously ruthless," Hades said. *Watching you kill for me?* Hades' voice slipped into my mind, thick with heat. *I'll be thinking about that for a long, long time.* I shot him a sharp glare, but he only smirked.

I rolled my shoulders back, trying to shake off the lingering magic from the stone. "Are we going back to the camp?"

Hades shook his bloody head. "We were successful. We'll give Cassius and Aurelia the coordinates and have them take care of it."

Orion coughed, and then again, bracing his hand on his thigh. "I'm not feeling too good…" he said quietly. Orion's shoulder hit the cave wall with a loud thud before he crumpled to the ground.

"Orion!" Gabriel lurched toward him, nearly tripping over a chunk of rock in his rush. He caught himself with a hand on the stone, then dropped to his knees beside him, fingers scrambling across Orion's torso, searching. "Shit, shit. They got you here."

"Pois—" Orion grunted.

"Poisoned weapon," Gabriel finished, ripping his gloves off and tossing them aside. He slashed Orion's cloak open with his blood-covered weapon, the fabric parting in jagged strips. The sweater beneath followed, cut away with frantic strokes. Blood slicked Gabriel's palms as the torn fabric peeled back, revealing a deep gash across Orion's abdomen. It was as though the blade had torn more than cut.

Hades and I moved in closer, stepping over Rillon's dead body. Our attackers' lanterns lay toppled on the ground, their lights still alive.

The wound was ugly. Black edging spread outward, the

flesh around it mottling gray-green as if rotting while he still breathed. Veins spiderwebbed in inky lines, racing across his muscled torso beneath the skin. "Fuck," Gabriel hissed, grabbing his pack. He yanked it open, rummaging frantically as vials spilled from his shaking grip.

"How can we help?" I asked, forcing my voice to stay steady.

Gabriel's eyes stayed locked on Orion like we weren't even there, like if he blinked, Orion might disappear. "Hold him up."

I nodded and slid behind Orion, hooking my arms under his armpits to lift his upper body. He was heavier than I expected—pure muscle. Heat radiated off him in waves. My shoulders strained under his weight, arms trembling slightly as I tried to keep my expression calm. I didn't want Hades to think he needed to help me. Assisting Gabriel with the wound was up to him.

"Hades, find the other one of this," Gabriel said, holding up a vial with blue liquid. "There are two of them, and by the looks of this"—he gestured to the wound on Orion's abdomen—"he'll need both."

"I'd complain about the manhandling," Orion said, his voice weak, "but, Persephone, you're not a man... and I enjoy being manhandled. Isn't that right, Gabe?"

My fingers twitched. I froze, the stone still pulsing against my chest.

"Stop talking," Gabriel said.

"Gabe," Orion wheezed. "You're acting like this is the first time I've been stabbed."

"It's poisoned, and I don't know with what," Gabriel snapped.

"Here it is," Hades said, handing Gabriel the other blue vial.

Gabriel opened both and poured the contents onto the wound.

Steam hissed. Orion arched up, letting out a hoarse scream that made me flinch. "Okay, *that's* new," Orion said between pants. "Shit."

"Shut up," Gabriel said. "If you pass out, I'm going to kill you."

"Aw, I love you too." Orion managed a weak grin, eyes fluttering half-shut.

Gabriel paused. Just for a breath, and then he moved faster. He pulled the stopper from another vial, this one holding a dark emerald green liquid. Gabriel placed a thumb on Orion's bottom lip and pulled down, then tipped the vial at his mouth. "Drink."

Orion clamped his lips shut, breath hissing through his nose. "Admit it to me or I'm not drinking it."

Gabriel growled. "If you don't drink it, you'll die. Your veins are darkening."

Orion coughed, grinning weakly. "Exactly. Tell me what you know I want to hear." Orion twitched, convulsing with another wave of pain. His grip on my arm tightened.

"Fuck you, you stubborn, arrogant, idiot ass." Gabriel pried his lips apart and shoved the vial forward, the liquid spilling into Orion's mouth. "I love you too," he said, quieter.

I glanced up at Hades and back at Gabriel's trembling hand. I'd been so caught up in my own mess that I hadn't seen what was unfolding between them right before my eyes.

They've always been complicated, Hades said through the bond.

You knew?

Yes. Hades paused. *Though they never fully admitted it to themselves. Not until now, I suppose.*

At first, nothing happened. But then Orion stopped

convulsing in my arms. His body sagged, boneless and damp with sweat, but he was still breathing.

Gabriel leaned down, his forehead resting against Orion's. "You're going to be okay," Gabriel whispered. He sat back on his knees, pulling gauze and supplies from his pack. Blood smeared across the fabric, but he didn't stop to wipe his hands. He just worked quicker and pressed the covering into place, like if he could patch the wound fast enough, he could undo the fear of the last few minutes.

Orion coughed—a low, deep, wet sound—and broke into laughter.

Gabriel scowled. "Stop laughing. You're moving too much."

"No way," Orion said between ragged chuckles. "If all it took was a poisoned blade for you to admit your feelings for me, I would've stabbed myself decades ago."

"Enough. Let me fix you," Gabriel snapped. He exhaled, the sound rough, like something he'd been holding in too long.

"You love me." Orion tilted his head back. His eyes searched mine. "You heard that, right? I'm not dreaming?"

I swallowed the lump in my throat, smiled, and nodded. "He said it."

Gabriel's lips quirked up into a half-smile. He shifted his weight and leaned in, pressing directly onto the edge of the wound.

Orion yelped. "Okay, okay."

Gabriel chuckled, a low, resonating sound.

Orion groaned and flopped his head back against my shoulder. "Is this what love feels like? Because it's kind of painful?" Orion's gaze flicked from Gabriel to the wound.

"Don't make me regret saving you." Gabriel's voice softened.

Orion tried to sit up but let out another pained sound and slumped into me again. "You said you love me."

Gabriel snorted. "Don't make it weird."

"Oh no." Orion let his head loll back dramatically. "Too late. I'm dying with joy."

Gabriel opened his mouth, then closed it. He adjusted the dressing, his jaw clenched.

Orion ran his tongue across his bloody teeth as he smiled. "I mean, for a confession, it was kind of underwhelming. No epic kiss. You're lucky I'm injured, or I'd have higher standards."

"You're lucky I like you just enough not to stuff a gag in your mouth."

"Like, huh?" Orion raised a brow. "I'm getting downgraded already?"

Gabriel didn't respond, only hooked a bloody finger under Orion's chin and grinned.

"You're lucky I'm into emotionally constipated assholes, Gabe."

"You have terrible taste," Gabriel muttered, then moved, his fingers brushing over Orion's temple, then his cheek. He cleared his throat and looked at Hades. "You and Persephone should get out of here."

"What about the two of you?" I asked.

Gabriel's attention stayed locked on Orion. "We'll be fine. I'll take Orion back to the camp, and we'll meet you in the Underworld soon. You need to get that stone back in Tartarus."

"He's right," Hades said, patting Orion's shoulder and nodding at Gabriel. "Take care of yourselves."

Gabriel cracked his knuckles. "Aurelia and Cassius have everything set up for you. Have Falon or Hess ask Rys for directions. He already knows where to go."

I wrapped my hands around Orion in a careful hug,

mindful of the wound, and eased him against the wall. He smelled of blood and still managed to wink at me. I rose and turned to Gabriel. His face was tight, like he'd shoved all his emotion somewhere deep down. I hugged him anyway. His arms came around me after a second, strong but brief.

Hades and I turned to leave.

We walked in silence for a few minutes, Orion's laughter growing quieter with each step. "I still don't know why you're upset with me," Hades said as we neared the mouth of the cave.

I swallowed, closing my eyes, hesitating. "The last trial… it messed with my head."

He let out a frustrated sound. "Involving me?"

I nodded.

He sighed. "Whatever it was, it's still haunting you."

I wanted to explain. To tell him what I had experienced—*him*, hating me without warning. But the blood bond silenced me. "I hate that I can't explain. It was just so real to me."

His grip on me loosened. "You know I would never hurt you."

"That didn't stop it from feeling real. I-I need time to sort through it all," I said, my voice cracking.

Hades held my gaze for a moment longer, but then nodded.

We emerged from the cave, the cold air hitting us. Hades scanned for threats. I let my fingers drift to my chest, pressing against the stone hidden beneath my layers.

A prickling feeling I recognized too well washed over me. "It's happening again," I muttered.

Hades pulled me close in a rush, like he couldn't risk another second of space between us. His arm locked around my waist, the other cupped the back of my neck, and his mouth crashed into mine.

I kissed him back before I could think better of it.

Because this was the first time my mind had gone quiet since the last trial. No second-guessing. No anxiety.

Just him. Just this.

The kiss wasn't soft. It was desperate and rough and alive. He pulled back, cradling my face, thumbs brushing my cheekbones like he was memorizing every inch.

"You can be upset with me later if you must. I won't apologize for kissing you while I still can." He stared into my eyes until everything went black.

PERSEPHONE

I pushed upright, my hands sinking into a pile of treasures. Goblets and cups, gold and silver trinkets, diamonds and rubies, porcelain tableware and crystal spilled out in all directions. I stood, the uneven hoard shifting underfoot, crunching and clashing with every movement. The room was stuffy, the air thick and still. I pulled off my cloak and gloves, slid the goggles off my head, and set them all aside. I pressed a hand to my chest, feeling the steady warm pulse of the stone tucked against me.

No windows broke the gray stone walls, only an open doorway through each. Beyond them, stairwells climbed upward, but darkness swallowed them after the first few steps.

The same booming voice from the previous trials echoed through the small room, vibrating my bones—and everything else. "Find the object and place it on the pedestal."

"What?" I asked. The object? What object? Thousands surrounded me. My fingers curled into fists at my sides. I closed my eyes and inhaled deeply. *Focus on what you can control.*

My heartbeat slowed, just enough so I could think. I needed to start looking. I dropped to my knees and dug through the glittering chaos. I lifted a little gold necklace with a sapphire pendant. I felt nothing. I dropped it and kept digging.

A tarnished silver goblet, etched with a fancy crest. A pristine gold teapot. A chipped porcelain plate rimmed in gold leaf.

Still nothing.

"What am I even looking for?" I groaned. There had to be something different here, something that didn't belong.

All I had to do was find it. I huffed a laugh.

A thunderous boom made me jump, sending trinkets flying. One of the four exits disappeared. The wall turned smooth and seamless as if the passage had never been. No handle, no latch, no cracks, and nothing to pry open.

Panic constricted my ribs.

I continued digging frantically, tossing things aside without care, some of the porcelain shattering. The objects seemed endless, multiplying and swallowing the space around me. I dug deeper.

The second boom hit harder, the treasure mound rippling like a living thing beneath my boots. Another door had shut. Only two remained. *Think, Persephone.* I squeezed my eyes closed. I pressed my trembling hands flat on my leather-covered thighs, forcing myself to still. I thought back to just earlier, leading the group toward the stone.

I took one breath, then another. Faint, but I felt a pulse of magic.

The third door slammed shut. My eyes flew open. One door left. I crawled through the mountain of multiplying items, keeping my focus locked on that pulsing energy. My fingers scraped across metal, porcelain, stone, but none of them had the magic I was looking for. "Come on," I whispered.

I followed the pull. It was close. I glanced up at the remaining door. I dug faster. My fingers closed around something smooth that hummed under my fingertips. A golden teacup.

It looked just like the one Demeter had never let me touch.

I lifted it. Nothing about it seemed particularly special, nothing to prove it was the right object, but magic thrummed through it.

No time remained to second-guess myself. A boom shook the ground. The final opening slid into motion.

No. No! Adrenaline surged through my veins. *I'm not going to make it.* I launched myself, slipping on the shifting treasures. I pushed harder, leaping over the items.

I threw myself through the closing gap and sent a quick prayer to the Fates that I wouldn't be squashed today.

The force of the stone door slamming shut blew a gust of air against my back. I stumbled, and my fingers tightened around the golden teacup.

Sconces flickered to life along the walls, their flames casting uneven dancing shadows. I swallowed hard. "Only one way to go."

Up.

My legs were still trembling from the dash to the door, but I climbed the steps. Each rise sent fire spiraling up through my calves and into my thighs, but I didn't stop.

Tick. Tick. Tick.

The sound boomed in my ears. I wasn't sure if it was my pulse or something else. I pressed a hand against the cold wall, and a vibration shivered through me. I pushed my legs to move. When was this going to end?

The thought had less than a second to settle before my

foot landed on… nothing. I lurched forward. A scream tore from my throat as I threw my arms out, gripping the cup in one hand while I struggled to regain my balance. Pebbles tumbled off the step and into a dark abyss below. The moonlight above cast just enough illumination to see the depth, but not enough to see the bottom.

The silver light caught on something, and I squinted down at it. A rope.

It stretched horizontally from where I stood to the opposite cliff, a white platform glowing at its edge. My stomach clenched. I already knew what this meant. There wasn't a bridge. There weren't any more stairs. I'd have to cross using the rope.

"I hate this." My words were carried away by the whistling wind. But I couldn't complain. I had done this to myself, and now I just had to survive. My fingers shook as I reached for the necklace Hades had purchased for me at the market. I unclasped it and threaded it through the handle of the golden teacup, then fastened it and let it fall against my chest.

There was no way I could walk across the rope. That would be an instant death for me, especially with the wind lashing at my clothes and hair. I dropped to my knees and gripped the rope with both hands.

I let myself fall, dropping off the edge. My stomach lurched. For a few—terrifying—seconds, I was weightless.

But my arms held me. I clutched the rope above my head, the rough fibers rubbing into my palms. My muscles were already screaming, but I didn't let go.

I swung my lower body upward, hooking my ankles around the rope, squeezing tight.

Forcing away as much of the terror as I could, I put one hand in front of the other. *Move*, I told myself. *Don't look down. Don't think about it. Just move.* I pushed on, gripping the rope, inching my hands and legs along its length.

"I will not let fear win. I will not let fear win. I will not let fear win," I chanted. Not again, not after all the times it had paralyzed me, stolen my freedom of choice. Not this time.

I kept moving.

Tick. Tick. Tick. The sound returned, faster this time. A sick feeling coiled in my gut. When I glanced back, I resisted the urge to heave into a vomit. The rope was on fire.

The flames ate hungrily at the fibers behind me, burning through them quickly, and I still had half the distance to go. I couldn't look down. My throat closed. My chest rose and fell too quickly. I pressed my tongue to the roof of my mouth and focused on the rope. I needed to move.

I gritted my teeth and shoved one hand in front of the other, ignoring the strain in my arms and the skin rubbed raw on my palms. My legs helped drive me onward. Faster. I had to move faster.

I risked one more glance back. The flames were getting closer, only a few feet away.

The rope snapped.

A scream clawed its way from my throat as the tension holding me up vanished, my body plummeting into open air. I clutched the rope. The world tilted.

Then, impact.

I slammed against the cliff face, driving the air from my lungs. My vision splintered into millions of tiny fragments of light. Agony shot through my side and radiated outward, splintering across my ribs, down my spine, and setting every nerve alight. My fingers were locked around what was left of the rope, my limp body pressed against the stone.

Maybe I should let go.

The ache in my limbs and the burn in my lungs would

stop if I simply opened my hands and gave myself to the abyss.

I used to pray for an opportunity like this... to be *done*.

Copper flooded my mouth—or maybe it was in the air, seeping into every breath. I couldn't tell if I was tasting it or smelling it.

I heaved as tears fell down my face, rolling off my chin and plummeting into the darkness below. Maybe this was my punishment for always failing. For giving into fear. For just having some unearthly ability to make people hate me. Would Hades still love me if I were a soul?

I turned my face into my shoulder and rubbed my nose against the fabric, sucking in a shaky breath.

A soft whisper curled in the back of my mind. *Don't let fear win.*

With a shudder, I tightened my grip on the rope and climbed. My shoulders screamed, and every inch up was worse than the last, but I kept going. One pull at a time.

Against my better judgment, I looked down.

The fire had spread to the end of the rope, just feet below me. Heat rose in waves, warming the bottoms of my boots.

I pulled. Faster. Faster. Faster.

Tick. Tick. Tick. It returned, louder.

My hands found the cliff's edge. I swung my leg over and pulled myself up. My vision swam, but I couldn't stop. With trembling hands, I reached for the necklace and took it off. The teacup dangled for a moment before I slid it off the chain and placed it on the pedestal. I shoved the piece of jewelry into my pocket.

The moment it touched the surface, the ticking stopped. Heat flared on my shaking forearm. I pushed up my sleeve. The seven glowing circles emerged. The first three went solid and flashed white before disappearing.

I was still afraid.
But I hadn't let fear win—this time.
"Trial three of seven complete," the booming voice said.

PERSEPHONE

My chest heaved, my eyes wide and searching. They landed on the familiar fabric of the tent overhead. The scent of fresh snow and firewood filled my nostrils. My trembling hand flew to my chest. For one agonizing heartbeat, I felt nothing. Then a faint hum pulsed beneath my clothes.

The stone. Thank the Fates I hadn't lost it.

"We didn't know how long you'd be gone, so we came back here," Hades said. His head was no longer bloody. I blinked, focusing on him leaning against a stack of leather bags across from me. The violet gaze of his glamoured eyes pinned me in place. Hades moved, kneeling beside me, his face twisting from relief to concern.

"Do you need anything? Water?"

I shook my head. Thankfully, my black sweater hid the blood from the trial, though I could still smell it on myself.

"She's back," Hades called, and only a minute passed before two figures stepped in. Gabriel was first, holding the flap as his other arm wrapped around Orion's shoulders. Orion's steps were uneven, his weight leaning into Gabriel.

"Orion—" Gabriel said.

"Don't say anything. I'm fine."

"He's not. I gave him stitches while we waited for you. I already had to redo them once because he tore them open," Gabriel muttered. "But he insisted on seeing you. I told him to rest, but—" He adjusted his grip, lowering Orion carefully near the bags. "You know how he is."

Orion grinned at Gabriel.

I swallowed hard, working to settle the shake in my hands. "How long was I gone?"

"Only about two hours this time," Gabriel said.

My fingers dragged across my face. I pressed my hands into my eyes and groaned.

Hades made a soft, disapproving noise. "You're hurt."

I shook my head and focused on the buzzing against my chest. "It doesn't matter. I just want to get out of this realm. Let's go."

Orion let out a dry chuckle, empty of amusement. "Usually, I'd take offense to someone wanting to leave my home so damn badly, but right now, I want to leave this place too."

Hades' mouth pulled tight. "Do you still have the stone?"

I tapped my chest, feeling its power thrum beneath my touch. "I kept it safe."

I pushed myself to my feet, wincing at the pain that sliced up my side. I bit down a gasp, my vision blurring at the edges. I forced one leg to step forward, then the other. I schooled my face before turning to the men. "Do we have another cloak I can use? I left mine in the trial."

Hades nodded and pulled off the heavy fur cloak he wore. "You can have this one."

I stared at him. "And let you freeze?"

He shrugged. "I'll be fine."

I chewed on my lip. "No."

Hades studied me, moving closer with the cloak. "You're shivering."

"You'll be cold," I murmured.

Hades didn't argue. He stepped in front of me and lifted the cloak over me. His fingers brushed the edges of my collarbone as he fastened it. The fabric still carried his body heat, wrapping me like a cocoon. I exhaled, the warmth seeping into my frozen skin as he adjusted it.

His hands lingered at my throat before he pulled away, and my breath caught. I shifted beneath the weight of the too-big fabric, swallowed by the scent of him—amber, smoke, leather, and something that was just... Hades.

"Hades—"

He placed a hand on my cheek. "You'll keep it."

"But you—"

"I'm fine," he cut me off. I reached for the clasp, and his hand settled on mine. "Keep it on, Persephone."

"Fine," I said.

"I have something Hades can wear," Orion said.

Gabriel pulled gloves and goggles from his pocket. "You can wear mine. I have an extra set."

I sighed, grateful, and took them from his hands. "Thank you."

"Let's get moving," Gabriel said.

I glanced back at the tent one last time before we stepped outside. The cold whipped against my exposed skin, and we moved toward the dragons. Hess watched me as I approached, her golden eyes steady on me.

As I climbed onto her back, my jaw locked as pain lanced through my ribs. I swallowed it down. I couldn't let the others see. Hess let out a soft purr, her voice slipping into my mind like a silk thread. *You keep getting sucked into these trials.*

Behind me, Gabriel and Orion climbed onto Rys

together. Hades mounted Falon. I tightened my grip on the leather handle. *Yes.*

What are they like?

I can't tell you.

Or you won't *tell me?*

I shook my head, my hands running over her scales. *No. I can't. The magic binds me. I'll try, though—*A searing spike shot through my skull, cutting my words off. I blinked against the dizziness that followed. *I can't. It hurts.*

A long pause stretched between us. *Oh, goddess.*

I'm going to miss you.

And I, you.

I hadn't let myself think about this, not fully. This was goodbye.

You'll have to visit me, Hess said.

How will I know where you are?

She hummed. *I'll be with the others.* Her head turned, gesturing to the other dragons. *They are my... friends now.*

I pulled Gabriel's goggles into place over my eyes and slipped on his gloves. *Friends?*

Something like that.

Hess shot into the air, following Rys.

What will you do when I'm gone? I asked.

Explore.

You're not going back to the dragon field? Finding a new rider?

She huffed, clearly offended. *That's not how it works. Once a dragon chooses a rider, they are bonded until the rider's death.*

Well, hopefully I don't die anytime soon.

Hopefully.

A lump formed in my throat. *Will I still be able to speak to you?*

Hess hesitated. *I don't think so. When the others leave Faerie, they lose access to the connection with their dragons. It will likely be the same for us.*

My chest tightened. *Then I guess I have a reason to return.*
Hopefully under different circumstances.

A laugh slipped from my lips, too hollow to mean anything. The wind slapped against my face, biting into my skin, but I didn't care. I relished the sensation. This would be the last time I'd feel it. I wanted to come back to Faerie another time—not for a stone, or duty, but for myself, to explore and visit Hess on my own terms.

But for now, all I wanted was to leave.

Hades' voice slipped through the bond. *We're about twenty minutes from the location.*

Where exactly are we going?

We're heading to the Winter Court's capital, but we're going to a specific location Aurelia and Cassius gave us. We're going to sneak in without drawing attention.

I frowned. *We're sneaking in?*

Aurelia's mother, Queen Morrissa Frost, runs strict security in the capital. If we fly in like this, it'll raise too many questions. We need to blend in.

The flight was silent after that. The Winter Court sprawled below us, a sea of white, black, and silver. Twenty minutes passed in a blur of cold before we landed with a heavy thud on the snow-covered ground.

Hess' voice rumbled in my mind. *Well, I guess this is it, goddess.*

Leaving home hadn't been hard. Nothing tied me there— no love, no warmth, few good memories. This was different.

I swung my leg over the saddle, slid off her back, and nearly collapsed. Everything inside me locked up. My boots hit the snow, but my knees buckled. I forced myself upright and masked the grimace that pulled at my face. I didn't want the men to slow down because of me.

I caught sight of Gabriel getting off Rys and helping Orion down.

"Easy," Gabriel said, his arm bracing under Orion. Orion didn't complain. His gaze shifted to Seph, who had landed nearby, waiting silently. "You sure?" Gabriel asked.

Orion nodded, pulling away from Gabriel just enough to move stiffly toward the creature. "Yeah. I just need a minute."

Hades stood beside Falon, his gloved hand resting on his thick scales, saying his own quiet goodbye.

Hess shifted beside me, her eyes narrowing. She didn't speak. She didn't have to.

"I promise to come back soon," I whispered.

Hess lowered her massive head, her snout brushing my gloved palm. I raised my hand to my mouth and bit down on the edge of the glove. It slipped free with a soft tug. I reached out, needing to feel her scales beneath my bare fingertips. Her eye, glowing like molten gold, was nearly the size of my hand.

Be strong, Persephone. Her voice was soft, almost hesitant. *I know I made fun of you for being weak, but I was only teasing. You have strength. I chose you because of it.*

My throat tightened. *I'll try.*

None of that 'I'll try' nonsense. You will be strong. You will survive the trials. She paused. *Because I'm a little attached to you, and I don't want a new rider. Got it?*

A shaky laugh bubbled up from my chest. *Got it.* A single tear slipped down my cheek. For someone who had craved so many endings in life, I never thought I'd wish one wouldn't come. Leaving Hess wasn't the kind of ending that freed. It hollowed.

She huffed at me. *Don't cry, goddess. You'll see me again.*

I nodded, but deep down, something inside me twisted. Yes, I had survived three trials, but I still had four more to go. I wasn't naive enough to believe that victory was guaranteed.

Hess' voice slipped through my spiraling thoughts. *I can feel you gnawing at your mind. Enough of that.*

It's hard. I can't help it.

You can and you will.

I'm going to miss you. My fingers traced the ridges of her snout, her breath warm on my cold skin.

I know. She nudged me. *Do what you came here to do. Put that damn stone in Tartarus and ease the load on your mind... and your mate.*

I nodded once before stepping back, forcing my feet to move away from her warmth. I cleared my throat. "Where are we going?" I gestured all around us. "There aren't any doors or buildings, just trees and snow."

Hades exhaled. "We need to find a tree with a knot in it."

I arched my brow. "They all have knots."

"This one will be different," Gabriel added.

I didn't know exactly what I was searching for, but I stepped forward anyway, dragging my gaze over the gnarled trunks and the snow-laden branches. I slipped my bare hand back into the glove. I moved from tree to tree, tracing every knot I could reach.

Eight trees in, I felt it.

My fingers brushed a rough surface, an X carved deep into the wood. It was nearly invisible, hidden beneath a layer of ice. "I found it."

"Good work, Persephone," Gabriel said, dropping to his knees in front of the tree. His gloved fingers plunged into the snow, scooping and clawing it aside until the ground beneath peeked through. "It should be right here," he murmured. After a few minutes of digging, Gabriel rapped the ground, filling the air with a hollow sound. Hades crouched beside him, then helped scoop snow aside.

With a soft groan, Gabriel lifted the heavy lid. A dark hole gaped before us, its edges lined with frost. A ladder clung to one side, vanishing down into nothingness. The scent of earth drifted up from the shaft.

Gabriel gripped the sides of the ladder. "Orion and I will go first. We'll get that out of the way."

Orion let out a low hum, the corner of his mouth quirking into a half-smile. "I can climb down myself, Gabe. My arms and legs still work."

"You're going to reopen your wound if you're not careful."

"I'll be careful."

Gabriel nodded, his expression making it clear he knew it would be a waste of effort to argue. Without another word, he swung his legs down onto the first rung and descended, his boots clanking as he disappeared into the shadows.

Orion glanced back at Seph and jerked his chin at the entry. "Can you cover this when we're down? Make it look undisturbed?"

The dragon released a huff before nodding. *Of course.*

"Good. Thank you," Orion said.

"You're next, Orion." Gabriel's voice drifted up, followed by the sharp ring of metal. Hades helped lower Orion into the opening.

Orion gripped the ladder and raised a hand to his forehead, saluting us before climbing down.

"Easy. Take it slow," Gabriel said to him.

"Yeah, yeah, yeah," Orion muttered.

My wounds throbbed beneath my clothes, but the stone's magic had kept the worst of the pain at bay. I knew the moment it was gone, that fragile protection would shatter, but I didn't say anything. Orion, Hades, and Gabriel would overreact, and we didn't have time for that.

I sent Hess a sad smile. I gripped the ladder, the cold seeping through my gloves, and climbed down.

When my feet hit solid ground, Gabriel tapped the ladder twice, the sharp noise echoing through the space. Hades got onto the ladder last and pulled the latch closed, sealing us in. The darkness was absolute.

He climbed down, the sound of his feet scraping against the metal the only thing telling me he was getting closer.

Gabriel riffled through his pack. A soft flicker of light in his lantern illuminated the space. The tunnel around us was narrow and carved into a dark brown stone, the walls rough and frosted in places. The ceiling was just high enough for the men to pass without ducking.

"How far are we?" I asked. "I don't like tight spaces."

"A couple of miles," Hades replied, his voice low, but it reverberated off the stone walls.

Our footsteps resonated in the close space as we moved forward. "Gotta love the scenic route." Orion braced against Gabriel for support.

"Better than having Queen Morrissa question us," Hades said. "If she even suspects something's off, she'll detain us and demand answers we don't have time to give."

"I don't know how Cassius and Aurelia came from her," Orion said.

We kept moving, the tunnel stretching on. At some point, it widened, nearly doubling from four feet to eight feet.

After what felt like forever, we reached a dead-end. Hades ran his hand along the rough stone. "There should be a latch here somewhere…"

"And there should be a box. Aurelia said there would be clothes for us," Gabriel added.

Orion nudged something with his boot. "Found it." He crouched down, then hissed a curse as he pried open a wooden crate, its hinges creaking in protest.

"Damn it, Orion," Gabriel snapped. "Tell me you didn't rip the stitches again."

Orion scowled but pulled out four bundles. Gabriel took one from him and handed it to me. "I'd assume the woman's outfit is for you."

I took it from him, and the bag was heavier than I'd

expected. I pulled out a heap of fabric—a thick, elegant dress. I couldn't tell its exact color. The lantern's dim glow cast flickering shadows, shifting it between blue, green, and lavender. I stared at it for a long second before my cheeks flushed. The realization sank in like a stone in my gut. I'd have to change in front of them. They'd see the bruises, the gashes on my skin, the evidence of the last trial. I swallowed hard. "Can you guys turn around?"

Gabriel nodded immediately. "Of course."

Orion didn't say anything but turned.

"You too, Hades," I added.

Hades sighed, the ghost of a smile playing on his lips. Without a word, he turned to face the tunnel wall. I slipped off my clothes, trying to ignore the way my wounds throbbed.

I kept my bra on, the stone still nestled securely between my breasts. I stepped into the dress, then pulled it up and over my shoulders. The heavy fabric fell in folds around my legs. My shoulders loosened as the tension in my chest unraveled. Thank gods Aurelia had chosen something with long sleeves and a high back, concealing my injuries.

I twisted, biting my lip from the pain as I reached to fasten the laces—

My fingers slipped.

I tried again, slower this time. I couldn't reach the loops.

I didn't want Hades to see, but time was running out. I hesitated. "Hades, can you help me?"

Silence. Then his boots shuffled closer.

"Of course," he murmured.

I flinched at the sound. I held still as his fingers brushed over one of the fresh bruises.

Oh, little goddess. The ache was unmistakable in his words.

Just lace it up, please. I'm fine.

One by one, Hades pulled the laces carefully, securing the

dress to my form. Every time his fingers grazed over my skin, the mating bond between us pulsed. He paused when he reached a deep gash along my upper ribs. It must've come from when I crashed into the cliff face, hitting a jagged piece. It had all hurt too much in the moment to really notice anything but the suffocating coppery smell of my blood. His fingers stilled.

I didn't move. I didn't breathe.

For a moment, the tunnel disappeared and the mission faded. All that existed was the warmth of his hands and the way my heart beat too quickly in my chest.

He tightened the last lace. "There."

I exhaled before turning to face him. "Thank you."

His eyes lingered on mine, unreadable in the dim light. Orion and Gabriel had finished dressing already. Hades pulled off his clothes. *Should I ask you to turn around?*

If you want some privacy.

Oh, little goddess, I wish for anything but privacy from you. His voice lilted, but his face remained still—serious.

My cheeks heated. I tried to look away, but I couldn't. His body was chiseled, every inch sculpted muscle. My chest tightened as I lingered on the spot where his mating bond mark should've been, where it had been glamoured away. He was my mate, but the memory of the trial rattled around my mind, squeezing. It wasn't real. I knew that. But my heart didn't.

It had given me a glimpse of a world where he had left me... hated me. A tremor rippled through me, my tired muscles locking tight. I resisted the urge to shut down, to retreat into myself the way I always had.

I turned my head, looking into the void of the tunnel. Hades' expression from the trial waited in the black shadows. I looked back to him.

Like what you see? he asked.

I snapped my gaze away again. A beat passed and I glanced back.

Can't keep your eyes off me?

I huffed.

You look beautiful, by the way.

I cleared my throat. "Let's get this over with."

Everyone was dressed and ready. The men wore fitted dark button-ups and matching pants.

Gabriel stepped forward, and his hand rested on the latch. But before he pulled it open, I said, "Wait."

The men all turned to me.

"What are we supposed to do?" I asked.

"Act natural. Act like you belong," Gabriel said.

I nodded, and Gabriel pulled the door open.

Light spilled over us. I braced for guards or people to see us, but the small room was empty, no furniture or anything on the dull gray walls. I looked down. My dress was lavender. Gabriel stepped forward, leading the way. We navigated through a series of small rooms and a few long, bare corridors.

We climbed a short staircase, stepping into a hallway that was no longer utilitarian. Our footsteps tapped against the marble floors. As we moved, I straightened my shoulders and lifted my chin, repeating *I belong.*

I didn't feel it, but it didn't matter. A few maids passed us along the way, their gazes barely flickering in our direction. The corridors were striking. Tall ceilings arched above us, the molding intricate and adorned with silver filigrees every few feet. The walls were covered in patterned wallpaper, a cool pale blue.

We ascended another staircase, this one spiraling. My muscles burned with each step, the weight of the dress pulling at my limbs, but I forced myself to keep up. We reached a row of windows. My feet stilled. The view hit me like a spell. I'd seen the Winter Court from Hess, but we hadn't been close to the capital. It was beautiful, the shimmering lights reflected on the snow and ice.

"Wow," I murmured.

Gabriel cleared his throat, disguising his words in a cough. "Belong."

A few winter fae passed us in the corridor. I snapped out of my daze, forced a smile, and stepped forward. We fell in behind Gabriel, Orion trailing close after him, his stride careful, the faint hitches in his steps masked as best he could. Gabriel led us with quiet confidence, navigating the winding halls as if he'd walked them a hundred times.

Before we could enter the next corridor, two guards shifted, blocking our path. They were tall, both with hair pulled into tight knots at the napes of their necks—one with blond hair, the other with glossy black braids. The silver buttons on their crisp navy uniforms gleamed. Swords rested on their hips.

"This hallway is restricted," the dark-haired guard said, narrowing his brown eyes. He placed a hand on the hilt of his sword.

"Princess Aurelia is expecting us," Gabriel said.

"No one gets through without the approval of Queen Morrissa," the other guard said.

"Check with the princess," Gabriel said evenly.

The blond guard pressed on a small violet crystal attached to his ear and spoke. A pause, then a sharp nod. "You may pass."

They stepped aside, and we walked down the corridor in silence. The space opened to a vast room with high, painted ceilings and polished white floors that reflected the chandelier's light. Guards stood at each of the ornate columns that lined the walls, and thick velvet curtains framed the tall, arched windows.

Aurelia stood at the far end of the room, wearing a navy blue dress covered with embroidered silver constellations. A shimmering silver crown rested on her head. Her gaze lingered on us for a moment before she gestured to the large, engraved stone set into the wall beside her.

Gabriel bowed. "Thank you, your majesty, for allowing us entry."

"Of course," she replied, her lips curving into a smirk. "I wish you safe travels."

Orion held back a huff of laughter. "Yes, your majesty. Thank you."

The guards watched us closely but said nothing. Hades moved to the wall and pressed a flat hand to it. A ripple of magic spread through the stone. It responded, parting to reveal the gateway.

Travelers walked along the corridor, their gazes fixed ahead. *I've never seen anyone here before,* I said to Hades through the bond.

Travelers are only allowed to move between realms once a month, for a few hours. Most never leave their realms. It's a luxury to travel. As Divine, we don't abide by those rules.

Can Gabriel and Orion get in trouble?

I wouldn't let that happen. They travel often.

I sent Aurelia a small smile before we walked down the corridor toward the last portal. Hades took my hand, and we stepped through the obsidian shimmer.

40

PERSEPHONE

he familiar magic of the Underworld rippled across my skin, a dark energy that felt like home. I blinked hard against the grit in my eyes. The tan, dusty, barren expanse of the Underworld lay before us. I'd never been so grateful for its eerie stillness. A shaky sound slipped through my cracked lips. I tipped my head back and let the light of the twin suns bathe over me.

My knees nearly buckled. The stone between my breasts grounded me as its power buzzed, sending tingling through my chest, my arms, and into my bones.

I couldn't believe we had it. After everything, we'd actually gotten it.

"Come on. Let's go," Hades said. He squeezed my arm and we whisked, leaving Gabriel and Orion behind.

Darkness folded over us and sucked the air out of my lungs. We stood on the slick floor of Tartarus. My lip twitched, but it didn't curl at the sour mildew smell that clung to this layer. I was too giddy to care.

I didn't even mind the squelching under my boots or the droplets of moisture clinging to my skin.

We moved toward the gate, the towering ancient iron wrought in intricate designs. "Undo the laces of my dress," I said.

Hades obliged, his fingers brushing against my skin. I let the dress fall from my chest and pulled out the stone. My hand trembled as I held it out for him.

"Here," I said. I needed this to be over.

But Hades didn't move. He didn't even acknowledge me, his gaze fixed on the wrought iron.

"What?" I muttered, thrusting the stone closer to him. "Hades," I said louder. "Take it."

Still nothing. His jaw tightened, his shoulders rigid. "We —" His voice broke. "We're too late."

"What do you mean?" My heart seized, my grip on the stone faltering.

"Damn it." He raked a hand through his dark hair, no longer glamoured. He stepped forward and took the stone from my outstretched palm. Pain flared through my body as the stone left my touch, but I clenched my jaw and endured it. I thought he would place it in the gate, seal it.

But he hesitated.

"No." I yanked the stone out of his hand. If he wouldn't do it, I would. I shoved the white iridescent piece between the gates. It buzzed underneath my fingers. The gates groaned as the dark iron pulsed a bright white.

"The stone is in the gate now. Tell me what's wrong," I snapped, studying Hades' profile in the darkness. I probed the bond, half-expecting the strain on him I was used to—the pull of him stretched too thin, the ache he never let me feel in full.

But this time, I found strength.

His magic was no longer bleeding out into the gates, no longer clawing itself apart just to keep them closed. The stone was doing the work.

"We were too late," he said again, his voice a flat, brittle echo of itself. "How didn't I feel it? Where is Thanatos?"

"Late for what?" I asked.

"The Titans. They're free."

A cold, heavy weight settled in my chest and moved to my ribs. I stepped back.

The Titans.

Released.

The Titans had been locked away for a reason. Power like theirs didn't just destroy. It ended *realms*. The Divine had fought a war to put them away.

And now they were free.

One thought screamed through the chaos in my head: *What could be worse than this?*

END BOOK 2

LEAVE A REVIEW

Thank you for joining me on this journey. I sincerely hope you enjoyed the story as much as I enjoyed writing it.

If you have a moment, I would greatly appreciate it if you could leave a review. Your feedback is incredibly valuable—it helps other readers discover the book.

Thank you for your time and support!

Amazon: https://www.amazon.com/author/lenajcastle

Goodreads: https://www.goodreads.com/book/show/ 232928252-a-serpent-of-stone-and-spite

ACKNOWLEDGMENTS

There are so many incredible people I have to thank.

To my friends and family,

Thank you. Your support throughout this journey has meant the world to me. Writing this book was an extremely challenging experience. I faced a slew of obstacles. It was stressful, exhausting, and at times, overwhelming. But every word of encouragement, every moment of kindness, and every bit of patience helped carry me through. I'm endlessly grateful.

To all my amazing readers,

Thank you for all the kind DMs and emails! Every time someone shared that they resonated with Persephone, I was reminded of why I wrote this story in the first place. Your words inspired me more than you know.

To my editors,

Thank you for your help. It's such a gift to have sharp, thoughtful people step in, catch the blind spots, and assist with wrangling my messy grammar.

Ana,

A special thank you to you—one of the editors on this project, and honestly, a superstar. You stepped in on a tight timeline and helped shape my writing with clarity and care. I'm not sure this book would be in readers' hands without you. I'm so excited to continue working together.

To my wonderful beta readers,

Thank you! Your early feedback, honesty, and enthusiasm helped this story grow in ways I couldn't have done alone.

And finally, to **you**,

Thank you for picking up this book, for spending time with these characters, and for being part of this journey. Your support means everything. I can't wait for you to read the next one!

ABOUT THE AUTHOR

Lena J. Castle is a fantasy romance author. When she's not busy building imaginary worlds, you'll find her cozied up with a good book, spoiling her very fluffy cat, or experimenting in the kitchen.

For more about her books, visit www.lenajcastle.com and join her newsletter (https://www.lenajcastle.com/pages/ newsletter) to stay up to date with new releases, deals, and giveaways.

amazon.com/author/lenajcastle
tiktok.com/@lenajcastle
instagram.com/lenajcastle
threads.com/lenajcastle

www.ingramcontent.com/pod-product-compliance
Lightning Source LLC
Chambersburg PA
CBHW020231010826
48973CB00006B/1460